PRAISE FOR *THE HOME*

'Good characters, clever story, plenty of scares. A great read. Admit yourself to *The Home* right now'
John Ajvide Lindqvist, author of [illegible] *One In*

'Mats Strandberg is a literary cult waiting to happen'
Elizabeth Hand, author of *Generation Loss* and *Hard Light*

'Mats Strandberg knows how to write horror!'
Åsa Larsson, bestselling author of
The Second Deadly Sin and *Until thy Wrath Be Past*

'With *The Home* Mats Strandberg nails his position as one of the best Swedish horror writers'
Skånska Dagbladet

'With a never-failing humanism and a deep understanding of the genre, *The Home* is the true proof that Sweden has a new horror king'
City/SWE

'Mats Strandberg is marvellous when he lets us feel the approaching catastrophe: we feel an ice-cold chill . . . Psychology, guilt and painful secrets'
Tara

'*The Home* gives me goosebumps . . . there is no need for armies of aliens, zombies or blood-sucking foxes. A different voice is just enough'
Expressen

'What a storyteller! The characters' failures, love stories, everyday matters, insights and shortcomings shimmer in his hands: the very ordinary life becomes a little bit more beautiful . . . the horrifying becomes much more horrifying'
Dagens Nyheter

'Very cinematic, and with characters wh[illegible]
Mats Strandberg scares his readers in a[illegible]
SVT

Also by Mats Strandberg

Blood Cruise

THE HOME

MATS STRANDBERG

Translated by Agnes Broome

First published in Great Britain in 2020 by Jo Fletcher Books
This paperback edition published in 2021 by

Jo Fletcher Books
an imprint of
Quercus Editions Ltd
Carmelite House
50 Victoria Embankment
London EC4Y 0DZ

An Hachette UK company

A CIP catalogue record for this book is available
from the British Library

PB ISBN 978 1 52940 215 5

10 9 8 7 6 5 4 3 2 1

Typeset by Jouve (UK), Milton Keynes

Printed and bound in Great Britain by Clays Ltd, Elcograf S.p.A.

Papers used by Jo Fletcher Books are from well-managed forests and
other responsible sources.

THE HOME

Joel

He strains his ears. Scared to even breathe.

Sunlight is seeping into the room round the edges of the blind. Joel lifts his head up and squints at the digits on his old stereo. It is not even half past five in the morning.

His mouth is dry and his sheets are soaked with sweat. He stares at the closed door and slowly lets the air out of his lungs. He must have imagined the scream: the remnants of a dream that faded as he woke and can no longer be recalled.

He puts his head back down and tries to close his eyes, but his eyelids keep popping open. His body is tired – he just wants to sleep – but his brain is wide awake, inundated with thoughts of what he needs to get done today.

He gives up and traces the cord of the bedside lamp until he finds the switch. The light is so bright his face contracts into a grimace. Brett Anderson and Debbie Harry watch him from the posters pinned to the slanted wall of the sleeping alcove. Kathleen Hanna stares urgently at him from a torn-out newspaper page at the foot of the bed.

Get up. Get up. You might as well get going. Get out of bed. Shower before Mum wakes up. Get up now. You're not going back to sleep anyway.

But he doesn't move. Standing up seems to require strength

he simply doesn't have. The bed is a damp cloth tomb. If he doesn't get a full night's sleep soon, he is going to lose his mind.

He stares out into the room, where nothing has changed since he left home. He is the only thing that is not the same.

When he was eighteen, everything seemed possible. The world was waiting for him. Outside this house. Far away from this village. And now he's back, twenty years later, and he can't even make himself get out of bed.

Downstairs, the door between the kitchen and the hallway opens. Joel holds his breath again.

'Hello? Where is everybody? Is there anyone here?'

The voice is shrill. Frightened. It cuts Joel like a knife and makes his stomach contract into a knot.

And then he hears a heavy thud from below.

Mum.

Joel throws his duvet aside and dashes across the yellowed pine floor into the upstairs hallway. The June sky outside the window is pale blue. This early, the garden is still in shadow, but the rising sun has set the trees on the mountain ablaze. The stairs are brightly illuminated, as is the pattern of butterflies dancing across the lemon-yellow wallpaper.

'I'm coming!' he calls out, racing down the stairs.

The hallway is empty. Nothing but his mother's fleece jackets and her windbreaker, hung neatly on their hooks next to Joel's tattered leather jacket.

'Mum?'

Silence. Joel tries the front door. It's locked. Thank God. His mother's still in the house then.

The bathroom door is open, so he walks over and is greeted by a sweet, musty smell. A pair of knickers, yellow in the crotch, lie discarded on the floor. Dried-in droplets of urine surround the toilet. The shower hose is coiled like a sleeping snake in the tub.

She could have fallen over trying to wash herself. Broken something. Cracked her skull. Called for help. I may not have woken up.

Wouldn't it be typical for that to happen on their last day together in the house? The last day he's responsible for her?

He walks into the kitchen. The long rag rug is askew. The memory of the thud reverberates through him like an echo.

'Mum? Where are you?'

He picks up the wine box sitting on the counter where he left it last night.

Almost empty.

'Joel? Joel!'

Joel hurries into the living room and finds his mother staring at him from the spot where the small dining set used to be. Her pale eyes are childishly fearful in a face that has aged rapidly over the past few months. Her hair has several inches of grey roots; she looks almost bald. He will have a go at dyeing it before they leave.

Poor Mummy.

She's so badly stooped over, the old T-shirt she's wearing is hanging halfway down her thighs. Her knees are just bony protrusions on her emaciated legs.

'Call the police,' she says. 'We've been burgled.'

Joel tries to smile soothingly, but he recognises the look in his mother's eyes. Wherever she is now, she can't be reached.

So far, she has always come back for short periods, allowing glimpses of who she once was. But those periods are becoming fewer and further between.

'It'll be okay,' Joel says.

'Be okay?' his mum snorts. 'Can't you see they've stolen the furniture your grandpa made! And the armchair your dad loves so much!' She totters towards the open bedroom door. 'And the dresser! Would you believe they managed to steal the dresser even though I was asleep right next to it? They've even taken the photographs!'

She points accusingly at the wall. The faded wallpaper is darker where the framed portraits used to hang. Joel walks over to stand next to his mother in the doorway and puts an arm around her shoulder.

'What could they want with our photographs?' she says, shaking her head.

The bedroom looks naked. Exposed. The edge of the vinyl floor is curling where the chest of drawers used to be, while the old textured wallpaper is fraying in the corners and the greasy spot next to the headboard that Joel has tried to scrub clean several times has reappeared yet again. One of the closets is open. Empty hangers dangle abandoned on the railing inside. The clothes that are going with her have been folded and packed in a suitcase underneath her bed.

'We haven't been burgled,' Joel says. 'The movers came to pick up your things yesterday. Remember?'

He realises his mistake the moment the words leave his lips.

Never remind Mum about how forgetful she is. It only makes her more anxious.

'What are you talking about?' she snaps.

'The movers. You're moving today. Isn't that exciting?'

Hearing the feigned levity in his voice makes him want to crawl out of his skin.

Things can't go on like this, Mum. I'm doing this for you.

'Look,' he continues, and pulls out the suitcase. 'Yesterday you helped me pick out the clothes you wanted to bring, didn't you?'

'Stop it, Joel,' his mum says sternly. 'I don't like these jokes of yours.'

'Mum . . .'

'Just where am I moving to then, according to you?'

Joel hesitates. Can't bring himself to say Pineshade. The name of the nursing home has been a symbol for so long. A joke to mask the fear. Every time his mother misplaced her reading glasses or couldn't find the word she was looking for: *I guess I'll end up at Pineshade soon.*

'You're going to live with other people your age,' Joel says instead. 'Down in Skredsby. It's going to be great. There will always be people there to look after you.'

His mum's eyes widen. She seems to recognise that Joel is serious, even though what he's saying must sound insane to her.

'But . . . we're happy here, aren't we?'

'You'll be happy there, too. You'll see. I've been down there to sort out your room – you're going to . . .'

'I don't know what you're trying to do, but that's quite enough now. What do you think Dad would say if he came home and I had moved out?'

Not this, too. Not today. When he says nothing, his mum shuffles into the kitchen. The water starts running. Something topples over and shatters against the floor. Joel sighs.

Pineshade

Pineshade is located in Skredsby, a small town on the west coast of Sweden invariably overlooked by the hordes of summer tourists headed for the popular nearby resort of Marstrand. The one-storey brick building is nestled behind blocks of flats, past the football field, at the foot of the wooded slopes of the mountain. It's a square, compact building. No superfluous ornamentation. Wide steps, flanked by wheelchair ramps, lead up to the front doors. During office hours, the doors slide open automatically when you approach. The vinyl flooring in the lobby is green, stippled to prevent stains and scuffs from showing too clearly.

It's not a large care facility. Just four corridors surrounding an atrium referred to as the common room. The shared spaces also include a number of smaller lounges for the residents. The wallpaper, though contemporary, imitates old-fashioned motifs. There are plastic covers on the sofas and armchairs.

The vinyl flooring in the corridors is so shiny it reflects the fluorescent ceiling lights. There are railings along the walls, painted a shade of pastel green that is intended to be soothing, but which in reality only lends a sickly pallor to everyone's skin. Each corridor is its own ward with a total of eight suites, which are small and can accommodate only so many furniture configurations. They have bathrooms but not kitchens; no hobs to accidentally leave on. The windows can only be opened a crack. You can lock the doors from the inside if you want, but the staff have keys so they can always get in. The suites of wards B and C, which overlook the forest, have balconies, but they are encased in chicken wire to block that route of escape. And if you're in the habit of getting up at night, or you have a history of falling out of bed, motion sensors and guard rails on your bed will be installed to prevent it from happening again.

The new owners want the staff to call the residents clients, even though almost none of them are there voluntarily. When the home was built in the seventies, the residents were younger and healthier. These days, you have to be significantly frail to secure a spot at Pineshade. This is supposedly in the best interests of the elderly; it is said they benefit from staying in their home environment for as long as possible. When a tenancy is offered at Pineshade, the client's relatives have, at most, a week to decide. To avoid under-occupation, which is a drain on profits, things need to move along at a brisk pace. If you don't want it, someone else will.

The most recent Pineshade resident to pass away was Britt-Marie in D6. She stopped eating and drinking. Started sleeping more often and for longer. Let herself slowly fade away. It's not uncommon behaviour among older people who become depressed. Their death certificates give anorexia as the cause of death.

At Pineshade, death is always present. This is the end of the line. What everyone knows, but no one talks about, is that any form of life support is rare here.

A new set of furniture has been waiting in D6 since yesterday. A small dining arrangement. A dresser. An armchair. Photographs on the walls. A new home at the home. The bed is the only item of furniture provided by Pineshade. It has been disinfected since Britt-Marie died in it and made up with fresh linens.

In the D Ward staffroom, Johanna is scrolling through the feed on her phone, staring vacantly at the screen. She finds nothing new. This early in the morning, no one's posting anything. Every once in a while she glances through the windows into the common room where sunlight is pouring in through the skylight. Just a bit longer, then she can leave. She regrets applying for this summer job. She hates the night shifts; she hates when Petrus in D2 or Dagmar in D8 wake up and she has to take care of them by herself. But the worst thing about working nights is her fear that one of the old coots might croak when she's alone on the ward.

Johanna jumps when she hears a door opening further down the corridor. She gets to her feet and pops her head out the door. *Finally.* It's Nina, coming to relieve her. She's early as usual. Nina, who stays longer than she has to, who always picks up extra shifts, who bakes with the old people when she runs out of chores. Nina, who never talks about her life outside Pineshade. *Does she even have a life?* It's hard to imagine her in normal clothes, in anything other than the light-blue smock and baggy trousers. She's clean and proper, with trimmed nails and cropped hair. She smells of nothing.

'Has it been okay?' Nina asks, and Johanna shrugs, says 'The usual', and hands over the binder with her reports about the night before. 'I'm off, then,' she adds.

Nina watches Johanna leave, her ponytail swinging back and forth as she walks. Then she goes into the staffroom, turns the coffee machine on and wipes down the countertop and the table.

Sucdi, who's working the morning shift with Nina, bumps into her husband, Faisal, on the front steps. He has just come off the night shift in the B Ward. He's tired and stressed. Their oldest daughter looks after her younger siblings when their shifts overlap, and he wants to get home as quickly as possible. Sucdi gives him a quick peck on the cheek before heading into D Ward. She declines the coffee Nina offers her, but they go over the reports together while Nina drains her cup. Then they start the morning routine.

They go into each suite along D corridor, one after the other. There they gently stroke foreheads and change nappies. They wash the old bodies with cloths, soap and lukewarm water; apply cortisone cream; administer medications orally, anally and vaginally: sedatives and laxatives, painkillers and blood thinners. They help the old people get dressed and put their teeth in. Comb their hair.

In D1, Wiborg moans in her sleep when they enter. She's hugging a stuffed animal tightly, a dementia cat with built-in heating under its long polyester fur. When she wakes, she doesn't recognise either of them.

'Why isn't Mummy waking me up?' she says, eyeing Sucdi nervously. 'Did she buy you from Africa?'

Wiborg continues to stare at Sucdi while they remove her nappy. The iron supplements she takes have made her stool jet-black. They meticulously wash her clean before pulling mesh underwear up over a clean nappy.

'Where's Mummy?' Wiborg whimpers. 'I want to call Mummy.'

She reaches for the phone and manages to grab the receiver before they can persuade her to wait. The number Wiborg wants to call has long since been disconnected, and it never fails to upset her when no one picks up.

Sucdi helps Petrus in D2 to shave. She uses a trimmer instead of a razor so there's no risk of injury if he suddenly attacks her. Nina is careful to stay out of reach of his strong, quick hands when she empties his catheter bag. Then she checks his blood sugar.

In D3, Edit opens her eyes as soon as Nina and Sucdi enter.

'Good day,' she says drowsily. 'My name is Edit Andersson and I am Director Palm's secretary.'

They nod as usual. Edit blinks.

'Good day. My name is Edit Andersson and I am Director Palm's secretary.'

They pull on fresh gloves and help Edit, while she continues to inform them of who she is.

Bodil in D4 peers mischievously at them when they lift up her nightgown to change her nappy. 'Guess how old I am?'

And even though Nina knows the answer – Bodil is well past ninety – she says, 'Seventy, maybe?'

Bodil grins contentedly. 'That's what everyone says, no one can believe I'm as old as I am. I'm still so beautiful, they tell me.'

Nina and Sucdi assure her they agree.

It is Lillemor's turn to have a shower today. They help her into the bathroom in D5. Undress her. The mesh underwear Pine-shade has left a chequered imprint on her bulging stomach. The wellies and plastic aprons and gloves make it sweaty work, but at least Lillemor is biddable. They carefully lower her bottom onto the shower seat. Shower her gently once she has had a chance to approve the temperature. Nina lifts up Lillemor's heavy breasts to wash properly underneath.

Lillemor looks up at her and says, 'I long to return to the Lord but I've decided to live a while longer,' and Nina replies, 'That's good to hear, Lillemor.'

There are angel stickers on the tiles, smiling mildly at them.

They walk past the closed door to D6 and go in to Anna in D7.

'I think the apple has popped out,' Anna informs them as they enter.

Her bright red intestine is, indeed, poking out of her anus. It's a rectal prolapse surgery has been unable to correct. Anna happily prattles on about her plans for the day while they wipe her clean with washcloths, carefully push her bowels back in and pack her bum with cotton wool.

'I'm going to France – I've always wanted to,' she says.

When Nina asks her what she is planning to do there, Anna tells her she's going to see the Eiffel Tower and eat lots of patisseries.

'I hear it's lovely in the spring, so that's when I'll go. God willing, and if my shoes hold up.' She laughs happily and gazes dreamily out the window.

D8 is the only suite housing two residents. Dagmar is already awake when they enter. Sucdi wakes Vera, who is asleep in the other bed.

'Good morning, Dagmar,' Nina says. 'Did you sleep well?'

Dagmar stares at her with her red, watery eyes. The wall next to her bed is covered with watercolours and pencil sketches of the young woman Dagmar once was. She starts to grin expectantly when Nina approaches. A hand appears from under the cover, smeared with poo. Dagmar waves at them and laughs.

'Dagmar!' Vera scolds from her bed. Then she turns to Sucdi, her eyes wide with shame. 'Don't be angry with her. She doesn't mean anything by it.'

A little while later, in the kitchen, Nina makes porridge while Sucdi prepares sandwiches. They put coffee mugs and spouted drinking cups on trays, alongside wide-rimmed bowls and easy-grip spoons.

After breakfast, some of the old people head for the telly in the lounge. Nina grabs an old black and white film from the DVD shelf and pops it in the player. Dagmar is already nodding off in her wheelchair, but Petrus is studying the ditsy maid on the screen with intense interest. 'You fucking cunt!' he bellows. 'You fucking whore!'

Vera shushes him impatiently. Dagmar begins to snore.

Joel

Joel's mother is sitting stock still in one of the green plastic chairs in the front garden, chewing the sandwich Joel made for her. It's the only thing she wants to eat these days. She has no appetite and can't taste her food anymore. Joel, for his part, is utterly unable to eat at all today.

His mother's hair is damp and Joel has used clips on either side to pull it back. The grey roots are still there. His mother had been so furious at being made to shower that he didn't dare to try to use the dye, which would probably have gone in her face and on the walls and furniture – everywhere but her hair. And then, to top it off, he would have had to get her back into the shower to rinse the dye out. His mother's surprisingly strong when she is angry.

But right now, her shoulders are drooping. Her eyes are vacant.

Joel takes a sip of his instant coffee, leans the back of his head against the grey fibre cement wall and shuts his eyes. The day is already hot, but a faint breeze rustles through the overgrown bushes that his mum and dad planted to shelter the terrace from view. Hardly anyone ever drives past here now. Several of the houses further up the road are empty – the neighbours who lived around them when Joel was growing up have passed away, one after the other. Soon, this house will be abandoned too. There are four days until his meeting with the real estate agent.

Does anyone he knows still live in the area? Has he been spotted by old school friends at the supermarket in Ytterby or at the petrol station down in Skredsby? Are there rumours swirling about his return? *That Joel bloke, the one who was so full of himself.* He opens his eyes again and empties his cup. Puts it down on the rickety table. The chequered vinyl tablecloth is full of old coffee stains and rings.

His mother has stopped chewing and the remains of her sandwich sits on its plate, the cheese sweating in the sun.

'Not hungry?' he says.

His mum shakes her head.

Joel can't be bothered to wheedle with her. He points at the pills next to her plate.

'Get those down you,' he says.

'No. I don't know what you're giving me.'

'They're for your heart,' Joel says.

'There's nothing wrong with my heart,' his mother retorts and presses her lips shut.

Stubborn old bat. Just take the bloody pills. Can't you see I'm trying to help you?

But he can't say that. So he lights a cigarette and tries to ignore the tightening knot in his stomach.

Nina

Towards the end of the morning meeting, Elisabeth, the ward director, tells them a little about the new client moving into D6 today.

'Monika Edlund,' she says, consulting her binder. 'Seventy-two years old. From Lyckered.'

Nina looks up. The name sent a jolt of electricity through her, but no one around the table seems to have noticed.

'Fluctuating confusion after a heart attack,' Elisabeth reads. 'Collapsed in the Kungälv pharmacy, well, at least she chose a good place for it . . .'

Nina looks back down at the tabletop. She feels a droplet of sweat trickle out of her armpit and is suddenly very aware of the sun beating down through the glass ceiling in the Pineshade common room. It's like being in a greenhouse.

'Heart failure. She died, but was resuscitated in the ambulance . . .'

The droplet of sweat turns cold as it makes its way down Nina's side.

'Angiographic intervention using a stent . . . Following rehabilitation, she has lived at home for nearly six months with in-home care and visits by a registered nurse. The police have picked her up a few times when she's gone wandering about, so we're going to go straight to motion sensor. She has also fallen out of bed more than once, so I have already obtained a bed-guard permit.'

Elisabeth's sentences are succinct, effective. Devoid of inflection. Of emotion. And why wouldn't they be? Monika Edlund is just another name to her. After this meeting she won't even be that; she will simply be D6.

'Nothing out of the ordinary, in terms of medications,' Elisabeth continues. 'Aspirin, Lipitor, Metoprolol, Ramipril and Brilique. Haloperidol as needed and Zopiclone at night.'

Haloperidol. If Monika is on antipsychotics, she's in a bad way. It means her dementia is a dark place and she is scared. Possibly violent.

'Who's bringing her in?' Nina asks.

'Her son, Joel, who has been living with her recently.'

Joel. *He's back?*

More sweat escapes her armpit when Nina tries to imagine Joel today. She has scoured the internet for pictures a few times, but he's not on social media. She has only found a handful of photographs. Joel has dark hair in them and is too thin, his features too angular. He never smiles. The most recent picture is more than seven years old.

It's hard to imagine Joel as an adult. That he kept on existing, after that morning when he left Skredsby in the used car he'd just bought.

'Do you know when they'll be here?' Nina asks, managing to make her voice sound normal.

'After lunch,' Elisabeth says. 'Do you know the son? He must be roughly your age, no?'

Does she know Joel? How is she supposed to answer that? How would someone like Elisabeth ever understand? And who would believe that she, Nina, was once the person she was with Joel? She can't even believe it herself.

'We went to school together,' she replies.

Elisabeth has no further questions, having already lost interest and moved on. She closes her binder and stands up.

'All right then, that's it for today,' she says. 'And remember to make sure all our clients drink plenty of fluids. Apparently, this heatwave is here to stay.'

Chairs scrape softly against the vinyl when the others get to their feet. The four wards need to start setting up for lunch, which will soon be delivered from an institutional caterer in Kungälv. But Nina stays seated and looks over at the D corridor, where Wiborg is pacing around with her dementia cat pressed against her chest.

'Are you okay?' Sucdi asks.

Nina looks up.

'I'm just a bit tired,' she says, trying to smile.

She's not tired. Not in the least. Her whole body is crackling with nervous energy.

'Is that Joel bloke an old boyfriend or something?'

'No,' Nina replies. Her smile feels like a spasmodic twitch of the lips.

Sucdi walks off with their coffee cups; Nina watches her go, watches her open the dishwasher in the D Ward staffroom through the glass window, and then gets up herself.

Edit enters the common room, stooped over her rollator. Advanced osteoporosis has left her spine curved at a nearly ninety-degree angle.

'Good day,' she says. 'My name is Edit Andersson and I am Director Palm's secretary.'

Her milky eyes stare urgently at Nina.

'Hello,' Nina replies absently.

Edit shakes her head disapprovingly, possibly upset by Nina's failure to introduce herself. Then she blinks. Her perpetual mental loop resets.

'Good day. My name is Edit Andersson and I am Director Palm's secretary.'

'Good day to you, too,' Sucdi, who has come back from the staffroom, says. 'I think it's time to change you.'

The alarm goes off and Nina glances down the corridor. The light outside D2 is flashing. Petrus.

'I'll do it,' she says.

Sucdi gives her a surprised look.

'I'm sure Edit can wait.'

'Good day,' Edit says. 'My name—'

'Are you sure you're okay dealing with Petrus on your own?' Sucdi continues, loudly, to make herself heard.

'I'll be fine,' Nina replies.

Right now, she'd do anything to distract herself from thinking about Joel and Monika.

Joel

There's a scraping sound from the rain gutter above the terrace, followed by a faint whoosh of air when one of the swallows nesting under the eaves plummets towards the ground and then takes off skyward. His mother seems to rouse herself, blinking and looking straight at Joel. Her eyes are clear. Present. Intelligent.

She's his mum again.

'Nils was waiting for me,' she says. 'On the other side.'

Joel lights another cigarette and tries to hide his disappointment. He knows what's coming next and he doesn't want to hear it.

'He'd been waiting for me the whole time. I don't know if I was in heaven. I think so. But then they brought me back.'

Her pale eyes well up and Joel wishes he could believe what she believes. That the light at the end of the tunnel and the loved ones waiting with open arms are something more profound than the hallucinations of an oxygen-deprived brain.

'Nils came back with me but it's so hard for him to stay here on Earth. He's not supposed to be here. And neither am I.'

She looks at Joel like a small child seeking comfort. His mother, who never once allowed herself to show weakness. Joel reaches across the table and takes one of her hands. He strokes her knuckles as a sudden gust of wind soughs through the trees up on the mountain.

'I miss him so terribly when he's not here,' his mum says. 'He was so handsome, my Nils.'

She trails off, disappearing again; Joel wonders if she's lost in memories of his father. What does she see?

Joel has no idea who his father was. He has been looking at photographs of him all his life, but there's nothing outside the frames. He is pure hagiography, the love of his mother's life who died of cancer when Joel was a couple of years old.

Now Joel is almost forty, older than his dad ever was.

'They should have let me die, the doctors,' his mother says. 'Why did they bring me back? I was finished.'

She pulls her hand away and wipes her cheeks, seeming to reach a decision.

'Oh, listen to me go on,' she says. 'Just imagine if the children could hear me.'

Joel goes cold. He should be used to it by now, but it always comes as a shock.

'Mum . . .' he says. 'It's me.'

She looks at him. Her eyes are still alert but also genuinely puzzled.

'It's me. Joel. Your son.'

His mum snorts irritably.

'What kind of fool do you take me for?'

Joel takes a drag on his cigarette. The smoke mingles with the stale aftertaste of the coffee.

'Who do you think I am?' he says, even though he knows he shouldn't.

'Well, I . . . you're you! I know who you are. You'll have to forgive me for not remembering your name; there are so many of you always coming and going, looking after me. Though most are girls, I suppose.'

She eyes him nervously and wraps her arms around herself as though she's cold.

'But I am grateful. I am,' she adds. 'You all do such a terrific job.'

Not even dementia can erase the importance of not being ungrateful.

Joel's mother worked as a switchboard operator at Kungälv County Council when Joel and his brother were growing up. Their dad had left them a small pension so they never had trouble making ends meet. It was only after Joel moved to Stockholm that he realised middleclass there and middleclass back home were two different things. His friends in Stockholm have connections and never hesitate to use them. They make demands. They get angry when they don't get what they want. But his mum would never dare to complain, never ask for anything twice. That could bring prestige into the matter, and then you could be sure no one would give you any help whatsoever. Joel knows his mother hated her in-home carers, who never cleaned the house the right way; hated having strangers come by without warning. And now she thinks he's one of them.

'But it's me, Mum,' he says. 'I'm Joel. And Björn is grown up too. He has a family of his own now.'

'Don't be silly,' his mother retorts.

Joel takes another drag. Tries to stay calm.

'Take your pills now,' he says.

'You do go on about those pills. What's actually in them?'

He bends down to the paved ground and pulls the glass jar

filled with a sludgy mix of water and old cigarette butts closer. His cigarette goes out with a hiss when he drops it in. He might as well pack up the last of his mother's things and try the pills again later when she might be more compliant. He stands up and walks around the corner to the front door.

In the bathroom, he gets his mother's floral toiletry bag ready. Perfumes and lotions that were Christmas and birthday presents from Joel sit untouched on the top shelves in the medicine cabinet. His mother thought they were too fancy to use, and now they're past their expiration date.

He tries to will his pulse to slow; he closes the cabinet door and meets his own eyes in the mirror. They are the same shade of grey as his mother's and he wonders what will become of him when he grows old one day. With all the things he has done to his brain, could there already be holes in it? A slowly spreading rot? Eating away at his memories, at his self?

Or will it happen suddenly, like it did for his mother?

Anxiety seeps into him. He has no idea how he's going to get through this.

It's almost over. Soon. Just another hour or two. Then she's someone else's responsibility.

Pineshade is only a few miles away, on the other side of the mountain, but it's a completely different world. What's going to happen to his mother when she moves there? When she doesn't even have the garden and the house and all her familiar things around her? What will jog her memory then? Coax out those little glimpses of the person she once was?

But what choice do I have?

He can feel frosty pinpricks in his face, his fingertips.

He digs through the bag of his mother's medications that's

sitting on top of the washing machine and finds the packet of Haloperidol the nurse gave him. 1 TABLET AS NEEDED FOR ANXIETY, the label reads. They usually calm her down.

He hesitates. It has been six years and two months since he allowed himself the aid of chemicals, not counting alcohol. But this is, after all, the day he is putting his mother in a home. That has to count as an exceptional circumstance.

Joel grabs two pills, bends over the sink and drinks from the tap.

Nina

When Nina enters D2, Petrus has pulled off his duvet. His leg stumps are spread wide and he's tugging on his flaccid penis. Staring at her.

'You'd like a taste of this, wouldn't you?' he says.

She looks at his catheter.

'I'm mostly worried about chafing with you going at it like that,' she retorts.

Petrus laughs.

'Show us your cunt then,' he says. 'The cock goes in the cunt.'

It's not Petrus' fault. It's not Petrus doing these things, saying these things. It's his frontal lobe dementia. Sometimes she needs to remind herself of that fact, in order not to detest him. She moves closer to his bed.

'Yes, that's good,' he says. 'Come lie down next to me. Or on top, I like that.'

He's tugging harder and harder, but his penis remains limp, nothing but old skin and dry mucus membranes. Nina has not once seen it erect in all his years at Pineshade.

'Why don't we leave that alone now,' she says, and pulls his duvet up.

Petrus' hand shoots out, quick as lightning. His strong fingers close around her wrist. He was a sailor before diabetes took first one of his legs, then the other. His grip is still like a vice. She can't break free.

'Let's fuck,' he says, pulling her to him so hard she almost loses her balance.

Nina fumbles for the emergency alarm Petrus wears around his neck, but she can't reach it. She turns towards the door to call for help and spots Petrus' wife hurrying over to them from the hallway.

'Petrus!' she yells, running up to the bed. 'Petrus, stop it right now!'

He looks at her without recognition, but he is sufficiently distracted for Nina to pry his fingers off and back away. She glances at her wrist, marked with angry red welts from his grip.

Petrus laughs raucously. His wife stares fixedly at a spot on the floor a few inches in front of Nina's feet, mortified.

'I'm so sorry,' she says.

'Don't worry about it.'

'The real Petrus would rather be dead than act like this,' his wife says, still without looking at Nina. 'It makes me so ashamed to think what you must see.'

'Whatever he gets up to, we've seen worse,' Nina says. 'I promise. We're used to it. Really, don't worry about it.'

Petrus' wife smiles weakly and nods. Nina puts a hand on her shoulder and leaves the suite. Before the door closes behind her, she hears Petrus starting up again inside.

The corridor is quiet. Wiborg's granddaughter is waddling towards her with her big belly hanging out over the waistband of her skirt. This heatwave must be a nightmare for a pregnant woman. She's flushed and sweaty, and her face looks like a shiny, red apple. But she waves happily before opening the door to D1.

Nina lingers outside D2 for a moment, then looks at the closed door to D6. She feels it pulling her like a magnet.

It's only just over a week since she sat vigil in there for Britt-Marie. Sometimes it can feel like the dead linger for weeks after they pass. But she hasn't sensed the faintest trace of Britt-Marie. And why would she stay? She had wanted to leave.

The ghosts Nina is afraid of meeting in D6 are of a completely different nature.

She opens the door and steps inside. Contemplates the coats already hanging on the hooks under the hat rack, then moves further into the room. The curtains are drawn, the suite dim. She instantly recognises the furniture. It's odd seeing it here, jammed into this too-small space. Joel must have brought it yesterday, when she was off work. The dining set Joel's grandfather made. The cornflower-blue plush armchair. Monika's bedside table next to the Pineshade bed. Her dresser has been wedged into the corner by the window.

Nina walks over to it, opens the window a crack to let some fresh air in and takes a deep breath. She can hear children shouting out on the football field. A distant car. She moves over to the bed, studying the pictures that have been hung up on the wall. The largest is a wedding photo; a twenty-year-old Monika looks out from the oval frame made of black plastic. Her dark hair is cropped in a short sixties style, her lips are dark and full, her eyes bright as though lit from within. Her husband's blond and broad-shouldered. Handsome like a film star. Nina shifts her focus to a photograph of Björn outside Lycke Church. Joel's brother has the same blond hair as their father. In the picture he is wearing a beige jacket with enormous shoulder pads, and there are confirmation presents in his arms. Next to him is a photo of two pre-teen boys. They must be Björn's sons. They're smiling broadly at the camera from an unbelievably turquoise swimming pool. Their teeth look big in their little faces.

And then there's Joel. Nina feels a sharp twinge when she spots the photograph from their last year of secondary school. His bleached hair is parted to one side and he looks relatively proper.

Joel had been everything to her. She'd loved Joel; she'd loved who she was with him. Someone else. Someone braver. But it had never been her. That photograph had been taken only months before she decided to betray him.

She had betrayed Monika, too; never even gave her an explanation for what happened.

Nina has seen Monika in the supermarket from time to time, or in her car, passing in the street. But she has always avoided her; pretended not to see her. She has never told her how important she was to her. And now it might be too late – given that Monika's moving into Pineshade, she may not even remember Nina.

'He's on his way now.'

The voice is so close it nearly makes Nina jump out of her skin. She turns around and meets Bodil's eyes.

'Who?' Nina says.

'The man who's moving in here, of course.'

Bodil looks at Nina expectantly. She's wearing sheepskin slippers; Nina marvels at how preoccupied she must have been not to have heard Bodil approaching.

'The person moving in is a woman,' Nina says. 'Her name is Monika.'

'Don't be silly. He's a man,' Bodil says, studying the room excitedly. 'And he's handsome, too. I saw him walking around here last night.'

Joel

It is stiflingly hot in his mother's old Nissan, even though it has been parked in the barn. Joel turns on the air conditioning. Dry, chilly air floods the car, cooling his damp forehead as he reverses out into the yard. His mother is sitting quietly in the passenger seat, clutching her handbag. She closes her eyes when they roll down the drive. She hasn't grasped that she's leaving the house she has lived in her entire adult life, forever.

The house recedes in the rear-view mirror and finally disappears behind the trees once they've gone around the sharp bend and continue down the hill towards what his mother used to call 'the big road'. In reality, it's so narrow that passing cars have to use the verge.

Joel's sunglasses keep slipping down the sweaty bridge of his nose. He wipes his forehead and stops to wait for a motorhome to pass before taking a deep breath and turning onto the main road, past the graffiti-covered corrugated metal bus shelter where he used to wait for the school bus. He continues towards Skredsby. Fields and pastures stretch out towards the mountains on their left; on their right, beech trees climb steep slopes. Sunlight reaches through the foliage in harsh, blinding stabs. His mum has shut her eyes tight and is muttering something inaudible.

Joel wipes the sweat from his face again and realises he's

grinding his jaw. Clenching it in a way he's all too familiar with. The world outside the car is too full of impressions; he can't process them. Every leaf on every beech tree, every blade of grass along the side of the road fill his brain. He keeps glancing at the speedometer; everything seems to be moving too fast, but he's only doing thirty. A dragonfly swoops past the windscreen and his heart races as though he saw a deer step into the road.

He's high from those pills and it's getting worse with every heartbeat, pumping that shit out into his body. He rolls his window down to let fresh air into the car.

They reach the roundabout, go past the petrol station and continue into Skredsby town centre. It doesn't amount to much more than a carpark flanked by a pizzeria, a recycling station, the hairdresser that never seems to be open and the florist that shuts all summer. There's also a supermarket that is unable to compete with the massive superstores in Ytterby and Kungälv. A few teenage boys have congregated around their mopeds, play-fighting and bleating at each other in breaking adolescent voices, oblivious to the fact that they're painfully clichéd.

Joel grabs his chin to keep his jaw from moving. He passes the football field and pulls into the carpark in front of Pineshade, then removes the key from the ignition.

It feels like the car continues to rock as he stares out the windscreen. The trees from which Pineshade derives its name are swaying dreamily. The building seems to grow and shrink.

He manages to get his phone out and wipes his damp fingertips on his denim shorts so he can use the screen. He googles Haloperidol and learns that it's not just a sedative, it's an antipsychotic. A new wave of perspiration makes his tank top cling to his body as he reads. The list of side effects is long. Very long. He tries to estimate how many hours might have passed since his final glass of wine last night.

What have you done, Joel? What have you gone and done now?

His mother opens her eyes and straightens up in the passenger seat, looking around.

'What are we doing here?'

Joel clears his throat.

Happy. Have to sound happy.

'This is where you're going to live now, Mum.'

He clears his throat again. Wonders if it's his mind playing tricks or if his tongue actually is going numb. If only he could have a drink of water it might be easier to speak.

'But . . . what do you mean I'm going to live here?' his mother says.

'Yes, you are,' Joel replies, and squeezes the steering wheel hard. 'Your furniture's already here.'

Must keep it light. Nothing to worry about here.

'It's going to be great,' he continues, pushing his sunglasses back up yet again. 'You know how difficult it's been for you to get by on your own—'

His mum opens her mouth to lodge another protest, but Joel ignores her, forcing his tongue to keep contorting inside his mouth.

'—and Björn and I are both worried about you.'

'There's no need,' she counters quickly.

She almost sounds slightly defensive. Does she suspect something might be wrong with her after all?

'It's because we care about you, you know,' Joel says.

He just wants this to be over now. He wants his life back. But his mother purses her lips and isn't having any of this. Joel is suddenly furious. With her. With Björn, who's not here. With the pills. With his entire fucking turd of a life.

'I just wish I knew what this is about,' his mother says.

Yeah, that would actually be great for me, too.

'Come on,' Joel says, and gets out of the car.

The sun is beating down on the carpark, blinding him. The air is so humid and heavy it's almost like there's resistance in it and the ground tilts slowly back and forth. He clenches his teeth against the lurking nausea, then fetches his mum's suitcase from the boot before opening the passenger door.

'Come on.'

'I want to go home,' his mother says. 'I have to be home when your father gets back.'

Goddamn it, you old bat, I'm doing this for you, don't you get that, no, you don't, because you don't get anything anymore, you can't look after yourself, you'd burn down the house or trip and die, or disappear into the night again and get run over or lost in the woods, I can't take care of you I can't do it I can't do it anymore I'm sorry you always took care of us but I can't.

'You're going to like it here, I promise,' he says.

'But I can't just move away from Nils! What would he say?'

He wouldn't say shit because he's DEAD.

'Can't you at least give it a go? Just for one night?'

Apparently, he's willing to say anything.

'Come on,' he says again, and holds his arm out to support her.

Surprisingly, his mother takes it and climbs out of the car. She studies the square brick box and nervously pushes a strand of hair behind her ear.

As they walk up the steps, the wide doors open with a sigh. The lobby is cooler, but the floor sways underneath Joel, and for a moment, he's unsure whether his mother is leaning on him or it's the other way around. The vinyl floor looks like it's under water, its dotted pattern rippling on the surface.

There are two doors. Straight ahead is the A Ward. The D Ward is to the left. He pulls his mother towards the latter and rings the doorbell, peering through the window into the green corridor beyond. It seems to be revolving slowly around its own axis. Gorge rises in his throat.

Joel wants to run away, wants to dump his mother here like a foundling, but now the ward director is approaching on the other side of the glass. She walks with brisk steps, crocs on her feet, elbows moving energetically by her sides. She waves at them and Joel waves back, pretending to scratch his chin to make sure it's still.

The door opens and the director beams at them.

'Welcome, welcome,' she says in a voice like a children's TV presenter. 'It's so good to meet you, Monika. My name is Elisabeth and I'm the ward director and head nurse here.'

Joel says nothing, afraid he might slur his words. He carefully ushers his mother into the corridor. The door shuts and locks behind them. There's a strong smell of cleaning products and vinyl flooring and stuffy air, and underneath it all are faint but noticeable whiffs of old urine. Joel gets the feeling it's a smell that never fully fades. He reluctantly removes his sunglasses and hangs them from his collar, wondering if his pupils will give away that he is high. An alarm goes off somewhere and the sound bores its way into Joel's cerebral cortex.

Elisabeth is telling his mother about the home, but Joel's not paying attention. He has already been given the tour and has his hands full trying not to come off as deranged. He nods in what he hopes are appropriate places.

'And here's the lounge,' Elisabeth says.

His mum stares vacantly into the room; Joel follows her gaze. He takes in the plastic-covered sofas. The TV. The bouquets of dried flowers on top of a cabinet full of DVDs and books. The framed reproductions of Marcus Larson paintings on one wall: ships on stormy seas, frothy waves crashing against rocks, flaming skies. They seem much too dramatic, unsettling.

'Shall we continue?' Elisabeth asks, and he realises he has stared for too long.

They walk down the corridor. An old lady bent over a rollator watches them curiously with milky eyes. She's so badly stooped her spine seems to have snapped in half. Her hair is tufty, showing her pink scalp. There is dried saliva in the corners of her mouth.

'Good day,' she says, in a clear voice that sounds surprisingly young. 'My name is Edit Andersson and I am Director Palm's secretary.'

Joel's mother stops and gives her a tight smile.

'Monika,' she says. 'It's nice to meet you.'

'Good day,' the other lady replies. 'My name is Edit Andersson and I am Director Palm's secretary.'

'Yes, of course you are,' Elisabeth says. A note of impatience mars her otherwise light-hearted tone. 'But you know, Edit, dear, we're giving Monika a tour.'

His mum shoots him a helpless look. A look that says *See? And you're leaving me here? With people like her?*

A woman in a beige hijab and light-blue work clothes comes over.

'Welcome to Pineshade,' she says, holding out her hand to shake. 'My name is Sucdi and I'm one of the carers on this ward. I take it you're our latest addition?'

There is none of Elisabeth's forced cheerfulness in her voice.

Joel's mum glances uncertainly at him before taking Sucdi's hand. When it's his turn to introduce himself, he manages to squeeze out his name.

'Good day,' Edit says. 'My name is Edit Andersson and I am Director Palm's secretary.'

Sucdi puts a hand on the woman's curved back.

'Are you out walking again?' she says. 'I thought you were going to have a little lie-down?'

Edit looks at her. Blinks.

'Good day. My name is Edit Andersson and I am Director Palm's secretary.'

'All right then, let's move on,' Elisabeth says, and leads Joel and his mother further down the corridor. 'This is our lovely common room, where all our clients take their meals together. But if you prefer to eat in your own suite, Monika, that's of course completely up to you.'

Joel follows them into the atrium and looks up at the glass ceiling; the world lurches precariously and he quickly lowers his eyes. He notices openings leading to other corridors flanking each side of the room. A smell of meat and fried onion hangs in the air, but lunch is over – only a couple of old ladies linger at one of the pine tables. One of them is staring straight ahead, her face twisted into an angry grimace. Something that might be fruit yogurt is dripping down her chin. The lady sitting next to her seems to have just given up her attempts at feeding her. She looks up at them curiously.

'This is Vera and Dagmar,' Elisabeth says. 'They're sisters and live together in suite D8.'

His mother says hello, but Joel notices that she tries to avoid looking at the sister with food on her face. The other sister has knitting on her lap. She seems to have forgotten the pattern half-way through. Little headless Santa Clauses are frolicking through a snowfall.

'We have a lot of activities,' Elisabeth continues. 'There are sing-alongs, and chair exercise sessions . . .'

Joel nods. Smiles. It feels as though his lips have stretched far beyond the confines of his face. Elisabeth gives him an odd look.

She must think I'm drunk. Or high. Maybe I should explain that I needed . . .

Needed to steal drugs from your own mother? Bloody hell, Joel, you're the one who should be committed.

They leave the common room and head back into D corridor. They pass suite doors with laminated, colourful sheets of A4 posted on them. Names like Wiborg, Petrus and Bodil are written in crayon. Wiborg's name is surrounded by childishly drawn horses and cats and ladybirds. A yellow sun in the left-hand corner is spreading greasy crayon rays.

'Have you written a letter to the staff about Monika?' Elisabeth asks.

'No,' Joel replies. 'I forgot.'

'That's fine, but try to remember next time,' Elisabeth says. 'It doesn't have to be long. Just something about who Monika is and what her interests are and if she has any particular likes and dislikes.'

They stop in front of D6. The only door without a name sign.

'And this is your suite, Monika,' Elisabeth says, opening the door.

Joel's mum looks at him and shakes her head.

'Come on, Mum,' he says quietly. 'Let's go inside and see what it's like.'

She sighs and takes a step across the threshold, looking at the little sink with a soap dispenser and hand sanitiser just inside the door, and the hat rack with hooks that is part of the standard equipment.

'That's my coat. And my shoes.' They move further into the room together. 'And the dresser Father made. There it is.'

There's too much furniture in here. The walls seem to be closing in on Joel.

What has he forced his mother into? An entire house has been replaced with just over two hundred square feet. A large garden exchanged for locked doors, windows that only open an inch or two.

What if the move traumatises her? What if she doesn't survive it?

Joel is well aware of why this suite became available. Someone died. Most likely in that very bed.

No one makes it out of a place like Pineshade alive.

Nina

Nina folds and sorts clothes in the laundry room in the basement at Pineshade: baggy T-shirts that are easy to pull on and off; trousers and skirts with elastic waistbands; fabrics worn soft and smooth after countless high-temperature washes. Nina's movements are precise and efficient. She almost always knows to whom each item belongs, without checking the nametags their relatives have been asked to put in them. She wonders if Joel has remembered to tag Monika's clothes and has a hard time imagining it.

Work has always been a place where she feels safe, where she knows what people need from her and how to give it to them. Everything is scheduled. The rules are clear. Dotted lines need to be signed; boxes checked. There are rotation logs for those at risk of bed sores. Food logs. Medication lists. Stool records.

Nina knows who she is here. She's in control.

Except now she's hiding in the basement.

This is obviously not a long-term solution. She's going to have to see Joel sooner or later. She's just not ready yet. And she tries to tell herself it's for Joel's sake as well. This day must be traumatic enough for him without having to deal with seeing her for the first time in almost twenty years.

Water rushes through the pipes in the ceiling. The clothes are folded and sorted. She throws an armful of wet sheets in the dryer and meticulously wipes the detergent spatter from around the door. Just as she's rinsing out the rag, a shadow flits past at the edge of her vision. She turns towards the dark rectangle of the doorway but there's no one there.

'Hello?'

She looks out into the basement corridor, where the fluorescent lights have gone out. The light from the narrow windows up by the ceiling barely makes it down to floor level. The shadow must have been someone walking by outside.

She walks into the storage room and does inventory. Counts boxes of latex gloves and gauze. There was a nappy delivery this morning, so she tears open the plastic wrapping and starts stacking the individual packs on the shelves.

Nina hears the door to the stairwell open in the corridor and the fluorescent lights tinkle when they're switched on. This is followed by quick steps that she immediately recognises as Elisabeth's. She sends up a silent prayer she won't be asked to help out in D6.

'Glad I found you,' Elisabeth says as she appears in the doorway. 'I was almost starting to wonder if you'd left early.'

Her tone is accusatory. As if Nina has ever left early. Red blotches are spreading from the neckline of Elisabeth's smock, climbing up her neck in patches. She's stressed about something.

'I thought I'd try to get things a bit organised down here,' Nina says.

'Right. Well, I just spoke to Johanna on the phone. She has come down with a *stomach bug*.'

Elisabeth looks at her significantly.

'I see,' Nina replies.

They both know that, in reality, Johanna just doesn't feel like coming in to work today. Nina hopes she'll quit soon. Not only is she unreliable, but she's also unable to hide her revulsion at dealing with the old people.

On the other hand, if Johanna really is ill, unlikely as that may be, she should stay home. When a stomach bug manages to invade the ward, it's a nightmare for the staff and life-threatening for the residents.

'She was supposed to do the night shift,' Elisabeth adds. 'And I have no one else I can ask.'

They both know Nina is going to acquiesce. She always does. It's a waste of both their time to drag it out. But Nina can't help herself. Elisabeth looks at her impatiently.

'You know I would have asked one of the casual employees if I could,' she says. 'Sucdi and Faisal can't be at work at the same time and Gorana refused. We can't really afford your overtime, so this isn't fun for me either. But you need the money, don't you?'

Nina makes no reply.

'And someone needs to be here to take care of our clients, right?' Elisabeth adds.

'Yes, of course.'

'I can find someone to take your morning shift. So you won't have to work a triple shift.'

Nina nods. That's more than she had expected.

A day off. Another day when she won't run the risk of bumping into Joel.

'Fine,' she says.

'Good.'

Elisabeth disappears from the doorway, but then pops her head back in.

'By the way, shouldn't you head up and meet the new client?' she says. 'I thought you knew her son.'

'I figured I would straighten up in here.' Nina hesitates. 'But how does he seem?'

Elisabeth leans further into the storage room, as though there were someone out in the corridor who might overhear. There's a sudden glint in her eye. And Nina knows. It's bad.

'Well, I shouldn't be saying this,' Elisabeth says, 'but I thought he might be *drunk* or something.'

Nina nods and is filled with a shameful sense of righteousness.

She had to do what she did. Had to break free of Joel, just like she broke free of her mother.

Joel

The sound of quick steps as someone enters the room. Joel looks up and catches Elisabeth putting her smile back on.

'And how are we getting on here?' she asks jauntily.

Joel nods, wishing she would leave. He sits down on the bed and puts an arm around his mother. Closes his eyes.

She smells good. Like shampoo and fabric conditioner. He forces himself to open his eyes again. Part of him just wants to lie down on the bed. He has no idea how he's supposed to drive in this state.

'I have to get going now,' Joel slurs quietly to his mother.

'You're really leaving me here?' his mother says. Her chin scrunches up. Her lower lip trembles.

'I'll be back tomorrow,' Joel says.

His mother's thin fingers fiddle anxiously with her skirt. Joel kisses her on the forehead. Her skin feels cool against his lips.

'I wish I knew what I'd done wrong,' his mother says. 'If you'd just tell me I could make it right.'

'You haven't done anything wrong. Of course you haven't.'

'Then take me home with you. I don't want to be here. Nils won't be able to find me if I—'

'I assure you that you'll be very happy here,' Elisabeth cuts in.

Joel's mother gives her a brave smile.

'I'm sure it's a lovely place,' she says. 'I just don't think it's for me.'

'A lot of people feel that way at first, but they always change their minds!'

Really? Always?

But Joel can hardly accuse her of lying to his mother when he's doing the exact same thing himself.

'I feel horrible saying this, when you've gone to so much trouble,' his mum says, seemingly weighing her words carefully. 'But I really would like to go home now.'

There's a knock on the door and Sucdi enters the suite. With her is a plump old lady with a buzzcut. Her arms swell out of her short-sleeved dress like so much overproved dough. She peers interestedly at Mum through thick spectacles.

'Hi,' Sucdi says. 'I wanted to introduce you to Lillemor.'

Lillemor gives Mum a beaming smile.

'I think we're going to be neighbours,' she says, and nods to one of the walls, her double chins jiggling. 'I live right next door.'

Mum politely returns the smile. Lillemor looks around curiously.

'What a lovely dresser,' she says.

Mum's smile becomes genuine. She starts telling them about her father, who did carpentry in his spare time. That some of his furniture can even be found at Tofta Manor. It turns out Lillemor has heard of him.

'Lillemor,' Sucdi says. 'Maybe you could give Monika a tour?'

'Of course!' Lillemor exclaims. 'You have to see my room first. Do you like angels?'

'Sure,' Joel's mother replies with a chuckle. 'I suppose they can be nice.'

Joel shoots Sucdi a grateful glance; she nods back at him almost imperceptibly.

'Well, that sounds wonderful,' Elisabeth says. 'I have to be on my way, but I'm *so* happy to have you here, Monika.'

Mum barely has time to say goodbye before she's distracted once more. Lillemor says something and then laughs hard at her own joke as she pulls Mum out into the corridor. A door opens and then Lillemor's laughter can be heard through the wall.

'I really love old people,' Elisabeth says. 'They're so delightful, aren't they?'

It seems an absurd thing to say. Sucdi shifts uncomfortably, and Joel gets the feeling she doesn't think much of the ward director either. It makes him like Sucdi even more.

'Stop by my office later, so you can sign for your swipe card,' Elisabeth says to him and exits.

He and Sucdi go into the suite next door, and Joel stops mid-step.

There are angels everywhere. Chubby cherubs with their heads thoughtfully in their hands in a framed poster above the bed. Lillemor is taking figurines and dolls off a shelf, showing them to Joel's mother, who nods politely at the mild plastic smiles, shimmering porcelain wings and swelling wool bodies.

Joel stares at them; it feels as though the angels are staring back at him, accusingly.

The walls are covered in framed, mass-produced banalities in cursive fonts:

WE ARE NEVER SO LOST THE ANGELS CAN'T SEE US.

HOWEVER YOU'RE FEELING AND WHATEVER YOU'RE DOING, YOUR GUARDIAN ANGEL IS WATCHING OVER YOU.

THE DUST BUNNIES UNDER YOUR BED ARE ACTUALLY ANGELS' SLIPPERS.

But there are no dust bunnies under the neatly made bed. The room is clean and tidy, though there is still the persistent smell of urine, old bodies and perspiration.

Lillemor is telling Mum about the photographs lined up on the windowsill.

'This is me and my husband,' she says, pointing to a wedding photo. 'And these are my children. And that one there, she was my primary school teacher. She was so kind I cried when the school year ended.'

Lillemor chuckles and prattles on. Eventually, she circles back to the wedding photo.

'Those are my parents,' she says. 'And that's me and my siblings. And that one there, she was my best friend.'

Joel needs to get out of here. Away from the smells. Away from the staring angels. He's going lose his mind if he stays any longer.

'Mum,' Joel says. 'I have to get going now.'

His mother opens her mouth to say something, but Joel anticipates her.

'I'll be back tomorrow.'

She pushes a strand of hair behind her ear.

'Tomorrow,' she says. 'That's fine.'

'Great. Tomorrow it is.'

His mother nods; Joel wonders what she is feeling. If she's resigned to the fact that this is going to be her home now. If she even understands it.

He gives her a quick hug and steps out into the corridor.

Sucdi catches up to him and says something about Elisabeth's office and the swipe card, but he shakes his head. He's starting to stagger; every time he puts his foot down it's as though the vinyl flooring's further away or closer than he'd anticipated.

The corridor stretches out before him, growing longer and longer.

A heavily pregnant woman is pouring tea at a serving cart. She waves to him and he responds with a quick nod. He can't talk to any more people just now.

'It'll get easier,' Sucdi says. 'She just needs to get used to it.'

'Me too, I think,' he manages.

'You have to give it a few weeks. It's like when children start preschool.'

Joel nods as though he knows all about that.

They've finally reached the end of the corridor. On the other side of the glass door is the lobby. The exit.

'Try not to worry tonight,' Sucdi says. 'You need a good rest.'

He wonders if that last sentence is a dig at him. He pushes the handle down, but the door's locked.

'The code's up there,' Sucdi says, pointing to a tiny note taped to the doorjamb. 'To keep the old people safe.'

He likes that she doesn't call them clients.

Sucdi punches in the code and opens the door. Joel mumbles a thank you and focuses on crossing the lobby without wobbling, then breathes in the warm air from outside when the automatic doors open.

When he reaches the parking lot, he wonders if his mother's watching him from Lillemor's window. He doesn't turn around, just walks up to the car and fumbles with the keys in the lock. After finally sitting down in the driver's seat and closing the door, he screams at the top of his lungs.

Nina

There's half an hour left of Nina's shift and she can't hide in the basement any longer. She'll be back here in eight hours anyway, and she and Sucdi need to write today's reports for Gorana and Rita, who will be taking over soon.

She reluctantly heads up to the lobby and peers into D corridor through the window in the door, fully aware of how pathetic she is. She can't see Joel or Monika. Only Anna, who has put on her spring jacket and beret to go on one of her daily walks.

Nina swipes her card and steps into the ward. Anna lights up when she spots her.

'Hullo there!' she hollers. 'What lovely weather we're having today!'

'Isn't it, though?' Nina replies.

Anna believes she's outside when she walks around under the glass ceiling in the common room. In reality, she hasn't been outside for weeks. Maybe months.

'A new family has moved in down the street,' Anna says, and points to D6. 'I reckon she's bit of a nervous Nellie. But he is very happy to be here.'

Nina follows her finger. The door to Monika's suite is closed. She wonders if Joel's in there now.

'I don't think he's her husband,' Anna says.

'No, that's her son, Joel.'

It feels strange to say his name again.

'Not the son,' Anna says. 'I mean the one who's going to be living with her.'

Nina nods absentmindedly and continues towards the staff-room to write those reports.

They work quickly and efficiently. Sucdi's eager to get home to her family; Nina just wants to leave.

'And then, there's Monika,' Sucdi says as they reach the report for D6. 'She was anxious and tried to persuade the son to bring her back home again. But it got better after he left.'

Nina stifles a sigh of relief. Joel's not here anymore.

'I had Lillemor distract her with her angels,' Sucdi goes on. 'She's asleep now.'

'Good,' Nina says, managing to keep her voice steady.

Rita arrives while they're writing up the last of the reports. She sits down at the table and the smoker's wrinkles around her mouth deepen as she purses her lips contemptuously.

'I assume Gorana hasn't deigned to show up yet.' She looks around as though Gorana might be hiding somewhere.

'Things have been quiet today,' Sucdi says. 'Maybe we could do the handover without her?'

Rita sighs theatrically, but for once she makes no objection.

Afterwards, Nina and Sucdi head downstairs to change. Nina's glad Sucdi doesn't ask what she was doing down here the greater part of the afternoon.

Gorana is smoking on the front steps when they come out, with no outward sign of being in a hurry.

'Good day at the Hotel Incontinental?' she asks, her sharp, heavily made-up little face breaking into a grin.

Nina tries not to show that it riles her. Gorana loves to push her buttons, and Nina makes it far too easy.

'Things are pretty quiet,' Nina says. 'But I'll see you later. I'll be covering Johanna's night shift. Since you didn't want to.'

Gorana shows no sign of having noticed the swipe.

'She really doesn't have much of an immune system, that girl,' is all she says, raising one of the jet-black lines she passes off as eyebrows.

'I have to be going,' Sucdi says, jangling her car keys. 'See you.'

Gorana nods goodbye and puts her cigarette out in the wall-mounted ashtray.

'Would you mind smoking out back instead?' Nina says. 'It doesn't look very pleasant with the staff puffing away out here.'

Gorana gives her an amused look.

'See you tonight,' she says, and goes inside.

Nina sighs, wishing she'd kept her mouth shut.

She gets into her car and sets her course for Tofta. She drives down this narrow road hundreds, maybe thousands of times every year. Now, for the first time in forever, the turn-off to Lyckered makes it hard to breathe.

Is Joel at the house now?

Nina turns her head when she goes past the derelict bus shelter. The first time she got off the bus here, the steep slope hadn't been paved yet, and it had been lined with high snowbanks.

Nina wishes she could muster some pity for the teenage girl she'd been back then. She knows she should. It wouldn't be difficult if it were someone else. But now a wave of the old, familiar shame crashes over her: Nina, the daughter of an alcoholic from the ugly estate in Ytterby. A priggish goody-goody. She was a teacher's pet, desperate to be liked by the grown-ups, the safe people. It was in seventh grade, when they all changed schools and were mixed in with students from Skredsby and other minor towns, that the bullying began in earnest. Nina tried to tell herself that her new classmates were just having a laugh. That she was being too sensitive. She tried to laugh with them and to think of ways to make them like her. It's the shame of all those failed attempts that almost make her physically duck down behind the steering wheel.

Joel was the first person to advise her not to give a shit. He didn't fit in either, but he was proud of it. He was the first person to tell her she was beautiful. Sometimes, she almost dared to believe him.

Joel had been like a brother to her – she'd even thought of him as a kindred spirit. And Monika had felt more like her mother than her actual mother. Nina wanted to be perfect for Monika, but that became harder as they got older and she'd had to hide more and more secrets about Joel from her.

Nina can breathe more easily now the turn-off can no longer be seen in the rear-view mirror. She drives on until Lycke Church appears, and then takes a left towards Tofta Manor, past barns and gardens, grazing sheep and horses. She continues up the tree-lined road to the manor and turns right. The smell of animals fills the car when she passes the stable and heads up the hill. At the top, two riders halt on the verge to let her pass, and she waves to them before rolling down the other side of the hill and continuing along the meandering strip of asphalt. Cows graze by the side of the road and the bay glitters beyond the meadow. The masts of the sailboats are dazzlingly white against the cliffs. On the other side of the road there's a string of houses with trampolines in the gardens and children's bicycles leaning against garage walls.

Nina turns into the driveway of the yellow two-storey villa at the end of the road.

The lawn still hasn't been mowed.

She climbs out of the car, drinking in the salty air. She must calm down before going inside; mustn't be angry or unfair.

It's impossible for him to understand how important these things are to me since they're not actually important. I know that. It's Joel and Monika making me crazier than usual.

The air in the hallway is warm and fusty, so Nina leaves the front door open. She hangs her purse on its hook and the keys in the key cabinet. Places her shoes neatly on the shoe rack.

The kitchen is bathed in sunlight and the marble countertops are spotless. She opens the fridge, studying the satisfyingly well-stocked shelves. But for how much longer? What happens if Markus can't find a job soon?

Nina pushes down the thought spiral that starts with mortgage interest rates and ends with visions of herself as homeless. She realises she's not hungry, so she drinks a glass of water instead, standing by the sink.

She loves this kitchen, this house, the sparkling sea outside its windows. But now Joel's intruding. Her perspective shifts. She sees everything through disapproving eyes.

Everything can be picked apart. The neat little life Nina has scraped together for herself becomes paltry, trite.

Go to hell, Joel. Leave me alone.

'Hello?' she calls, and checks the living room.

Markus is lying on the sofa with his laptop balanced on his thighs. He pulls off his headphones and looks at her drowsily.

'Is it already that late?' he says.

Nina doesn't reply. She goes into the bathroom and notices the wet laundry from this morning still sitting in the washing machine.

Rage fills her, almost intoxicating. It's harder to hold back now.

It's not Markus' fault. We both have our foibles, I'm a pain in the neck, too.

They're different. He doesn't know what it was like to grow up the way she did; to always have to keep the chaos at bay. The tiniest loose end could unravel the whole world. The tiniest crack could grow into a chasm. It was never like that for Markus. He trusts that everything will work out, sooner or later.

Fine, he might not get it. But he knows it's important to you and he still doesn't give a shit. He doesn't give a shit about you. He doesn't give a shit that we're going to have to move unless he finds a new job soon.

Nina pulls out a handful of wet socks and sniffs them. They're okay. She pulls the rest out and shoves everything in the dryer.

God, it's just a load of bloody laundry. It's not the end of the world. This is about Joel being back. And about Monika.

She collects herself. Turns the dryer on and walks into the living room.

'Up late last night?' she says.

An unintentionally sharp edge to her voice.

'I couldn't fall asleep,' he says.

'Maybe you should try not sleeping all day.'

Markus gives her a hurt look. She sighs and forces out a smile.

'I'm sorry, I'm in a bad mood. I'm going to have to work tonight.'

Blaming work is so convenient.

'I think there's still coffee in the thermos in the kitchen,' he says.

She wonders if he has to try as hard to sound polite as she does. The politeness is the worst part of this. It's like a straitjacket she can't get out of.

'I should probably stay off the coffee,' she says. 'I'm going to try to catch some sleep now so I can get through the night. Have you heard anything from Daniel?'

'No. Was he supposed to call?'

'It would be nice to at least know he's alive.'

'I'm sure he'll be in touch when he needs more money,' Markus replies with a smile.

He moves to put his headphones back on.

'Joel's back,' she says.

Markus looks up at her. His eyes are suddenly much more alert.

'Blimey,' is all he says.

'Monika has been admitted to Pineshade.'

'Did you see him?'

Nina hesitates.

'No. But Elisabeth said he seemed drunk or something.'

'Right,' Markus says with a sneer. 'Well, that's not exactly a surprise. He's probably still dreaming of becoming some kind of fucking rock star.'

He sounds smug, which reminds Nina of her own forbidden feelings.

'I feel sorry for him,' she says.

'He has no one but himself to blame,' Markus declares, and puts his headphones back on.

Joel

The phone wakes him. He looks around in bewilderment before realising he must have fallen asleep on the sofa in the living room. All the lights in the house are off and there's the same kind of blueish twilight inside as outside. Not day, not night, neither light nor dark. It feels as though he himself is blurring at the edges, dissolving into nothingness.

He picks his phone up off the coffee table and sees his brother's face on the screen. The picture was taken here, in this house, on their mother's sixty-fifth birthday. Björn had lost weight and kept going on and on about the fad diet all the tabloids were pushing that year.

Joel hesitates long enough for the call to go to voicemail. There's a long list of missed calls from his brother on the screen; he must have slept through them. And there's a call from the restaurant where he sometimes works, but he doesn't even contemplate calling them back. Even if he did, he has no idea when he can go back to work.

The fridge is humming softly in the kitchen. Other than that, the house is calm and quiet. Joel catches himself listening for sounds of his mother.

But she isn't here.

They haven't called from Pineshade. That must mean everything is okay over there. Otherwise they would have been in touch, wouldn't they?

Joel rubs his face. His back's so numb he can't even feel the cushions underneath him. He sits up and looks out the window – wishes a car would go by, or a neighbour out on a walk. Even a fucking deer would do. But everything's as still as a painted back-drop. He gropes about between the cushions until he finds the remote, then turns the TV on. The room fills with voices from a current affairs programme. He gets up, turns on the main light, walks out into the kitchen and turns on all the lights in there too. He washes a handful of cherry tomatoes and eats them standing up, one by one. Their smooth surfaces against his tongue, the crunch when he bites down, the explosion of innards make his feeling of unreality recede a little.

Mum.

It's unfathomable that she no longer lives here. That no one lives here. This is no longer a home. Just a house.

He could go through the storage spaces tonight if he wanted. Decide what to sell, bin, donate, save. He could throw away all the expired food. There are mealworm beetles in the pantry and the chest freezer in the basement has meat in it that should have been eaten several years ago.

He could write that bloody letter about his mother to the staff at Pineshade.

The phone rings again and this time he picks up.

'Hey,' Björn says. 'You're hard to reach.'

He sounds slightly winded, like he is out walking.

'I was in the shower.'

'For several hours?'

'What do you want?' Joel asks wearily.

'How did it go with Mum today?'

'It was okay. She was sad when I left.'

'She'll get used to it.'

'I guess. She doesn't have much of a choice.'

A pause. More heavy breathing. The sound of cars in the background. The loud ticking of a pedestrian crossing.

Hustle and bustle. Björn's life carries on exactly as before.

'Are you coming down this weekend?' Joel says.

'Actually, that's why I'm calling.'

Joel reaches for his cigarettes and tries to stay calm. Not even Björn can bail on this, but if they get into an argument now, he might.

'I'm not going to make it. I have so many things to get done before we go to Spain.'

Joel lights his cigarette. Inhales deeply.

'You're smoking inside?'

'Yep. The fuck do you care anyway, if you're not coming?'

'Come on. I would do anything to be there. I just can't right now, what with—'

'Whatever,' Joel cuts in. 'So you're leaving me here to deal with all of this?'

'What do you want me to do? Cancel our trip? You do understand I can't do that to the kids, right?'

'But you can leave me here with this shit?'

'How was I supposed to know this was the week there would be an opening at Pineshade?' Björn counters.

'Yeah, it really sucks they didn't take your schedule into account.'

'I get that it's hard—' Björn says.

'No, you don't get it!' Joel shouts. It makes no difference now.

'You haven't been here, worrying every goddamn second about her falling down or wandering off in the middle of the night again, and you haven't had to try to make her eat her food and take her meds or wiped up piss—'

He breaks off to suck hard on his cigarette.

'But haven't there been, what do you call them, assistants there?' Björn puts in, but Joel pretends not to hear.

'—and you haven't had to force her into Pineshade even though she's begging to go home, and you don't have a selfish fucking brother who doesn't give a flying fuck about her or you!'

There's silence on the other end now.

'And the carers weren't here around the clock,' Joel adds. He takes another drag, pulling so hard his cigarette crackles. 'Hello?' he says.

'I was just waiting for you to calm down. There's no point talking to you when you're hysterical.'

'You have to come, don't you get it? I can't do this by myself.'

'I actually need this holiday too. This hasn't been easy for me either.'

Joel bursts out laughing. It sounds jarring and shrill. *Hysterical.* 'Woe is you, I guess,' he says.

'You'd understand if you had a family of your own. I have an obligation to them as well.'

Joel flicks the cigarette butt into the sink. Realises he's shaking with rage. 'Just because I don't have children doesn't mean I don't have a life.'

Björn makes no reply, but it feels like an *Oh, really?* echoes between them.

'I can't afford to put everything on hold because you're going to Spain!' Joel exclaims. 'I have to get back to work or I'll lose my flat.'

'Don't you have some money put aside?'

Dear God, he hates his brother. Björn has forgotten what it's like not to have money. He thinks anyone can make plenty of it if they just set their minds to it. Like he has.

'You really do have to come,' Joel says. 'Please. I need your help.' The begging is disgusting. But what he says is true, nonetheless. 'Mum needs you,' he adds.

'I doubt Mum knows the difference.' Björn falls silent. Seems to be bracing himself. 'Maybe it's only fair that you deal with this, considering how much you've made her worry over the years. It's time for you to grow up and take some responsibility.'

Joel lowers the phone and glares at Björn's smiling face on the screen – then ends the call.

He wishes he could cry. Maybe that would help him shake the sense of unreality, of everything being a cheap imitation of life.

Well done, Joel. I almost believe you. Is that why you're popping Mum's pills and drinking anything you can get your hands on? Because you want to feel closer to reality?

Face the facts: you've never wanted that.

Maybe Björn's right. Maybe he never did grow up. Joel has seen that happen to other people who did drugs for too long. Their development is arrested. And he was barely sixteen when he started.

He thinks about the teenage boys in the town square in Skredsby. Was he really ever that young? He grew up with the strident anti-drug propaganda of the eighties. The news stories. The public health campaigns. The young adult TV shows where priggish main characters became alcoholics after getting drunk once. Desperate junkies after their first joint, line, pill. Since those lies had been so easy to see through, he'd figured everything he was told was a lie. He'd thought he was unique. Impervious. He'd been wrong.

But at least you quit. Six years and two months ago.

He coaxes the bag out of the cardboard box that's still sitting on the counter, squeezes the last of the wine into a glass and takes a sip before going into his mother's bedroom and turning the light on. He looks at the bed his mother will never sleep in again. Joel's grandfather built the frame, carved the amateurish flower intarsia on the headboard. It must have been a labour of love. But who will want it now?

He sits down at the head of the bed. Dust and a few of his mother's hairs have stuck to the stain on the wall. At first, he figured his mother must have been rubbing her head against the wall in her sleep, but that's not it. It's too greasy and comes back too quickly.

At least it hasn't grown since this morning.

Joel leans closer to the stain and sniffs it; it's completely odourless.

Could there be something leaking inside the wall?

He fetches a sponge, finding a bottle of all-purpose cleaner under the sink. When he comes back, he sprays the stain until foam covers it, and rubs hard with the scouring side of the sponge, refusing to stop until both the stain and the wallpaper patterns are gone.

He goes back into the kitchen and bins the sponge, washes his hands twice to get rid of the feeling that his fingertips are still coated with grease, and then checks his phone. It's too late to call his mother's direct line – he doesn't want to risk waking her and making her anxious again – but maybe he could call the ward?

Is it weird to call this late? Is it weirder not to call at all?

He finds the number and dials. The phone rings.

'Pineshade, D Ward.'

The woman on the other end has the same broad dialect he had when he still lived here. Joel wonders if she has already been told about the stoned son who dropped off poor Monika.

What if they call Björn to inform him?

'Yes, hello. My name's Joel and my mother Monika was admitted today, or moved in, I guess, and I just wanted to check how she's doing.'

A brief hesitation on the other end.

'Everything has gone well, as far as I know,' the woman says. 'She's asleep now; it's probably best not to wake her.'

'No, sure.'

An alarm can be heard in the background over at Pineshade.

'I have to go,' the woman says.

Something about her voice feels familiar.

'Of course,' Joel says. 'Thank you.'

But the woman has already hung up.

Nina

Nina opens the door to D1, reaches for the button in the hallway and turns the alarm off. She hears a rumbling snore from inside the suite and enters. The bedside light is on. Nina catches her own reflection in the window, ghostly translucent against the closed blinds. Wiborg is asleep with her mouth wide open and her chin resting against her chest. Her scrawny neck is wrinkled like an accordion.

Wiborg's dementia cat has fallen out of bed and triggered the motion sensor. Nina picks up the stuffed animal and strokes its flameproof fur. She wedges it in between Wiborg's body and the wall, then quietly walks back out and closes the door carefully behind her.

The atmosphere at Pineshade is different at night. A couple of hours from now she's going to wake the old people to change their nappies and administer nutrition drinks. They haven't eaten since dinner was served around five, and preferably shouldn't fast until breakfast. Some of them will be angry. Others anxious. It's always the same. Wiborg will want to call the number that's no longer in use to talk to people long since dead. Petrus will try to pull her into bed again, calling her a cunt and a whore. Edit will launch into her never-ending loop about being Director Palm's secretary. But on this particular night, Nina will have to speak to Monika.

Still, she would happily do all of it to avoid listening to the echo of Joel's voice. How could she have forgotten what it sounds like?

Husky. Deep. In those days, he'd sounded much older than he was. Now he sounds much younger than he is. His voice hurled her back in time, as though the past twenty years never happened. *Come with me tonight. It's no fun without you.*

Nina walks over to the cleaning cupboard and fetches some rags, wiping down rollators and wheelchairs to pass the time.

How had she found the courage to show Joel her poems that first time? She has no idea, but that was the day they started dreaming together. He taught her how to play guitar and encouraged her to write lyrics to his music. He helped her be braver, go further, dig deeper. She never felt better than when she was writing. Her lyrics became her safety valve. There she could be angry, sad, make demands. She could make herself understood, at least to herself. She could give voice to what was going on inside her, even if Joel was the one who ultimately sang them.

They got good. Really good. And that's when Joel started to go off the rails in earnest.

Nina tends to the plants in the lounge, then moves on to the staffroom and unloads the dishwasher. When she closes the last cupboard door, she hears someone laughing, loudly and excitedly.

She steps out into the corridor and hears the laughter again. Old and girlish at the same time. It's coming from D4. The door to Bodil's suite is closed, but in the silence, it carries. Nina knocks before opening the door and hears Bodil giggle.

'You scoundrel,' she coos. 'You're a proper rogue, you are.'

Heavy breathing in the dark.

Nina walks into the room and turns on the overhead light. Bodil is sitting up in bed. Her washed-out flannel nightgown is taut across her heavy bosom.

'What are you doing up so late?' Nina asks.

But Bodil doesn't reply; she's staring fixedly at the window. When Nina puts a hand on her shoulder, Bodil starts and turns to her.

'There's a lecherous man outside my window,' Bodil informs her elatedly.

'Oh dear,' Nina says, looking at the closed blinds.

'He's hoping to see me naked, I dare say, but he won't,' Bodil declares and turns back to the window. 'Shoo, away with you. Ghastly man.'

Her delight is so contagious Nina can't help but smile. There are no pictures of Bodil as a young woman, but Nina reckons she was beautiful. She wonders if Bodil always loved men this much. If she has had many or a select few. Either way, Nina can sympathise with Bodil's current frustration. Pineshade is a realm of women. Most of the staff is female. Most of the residents are widows who have outlived their husbands, and most of the visitors are daughters, girlfriends, sisters.

'Maybe we had better draw the curtains as well,' Nina says.

Bodil gives her a sidelong glance.

'Let him have his fun. I'm sure he'll give up soon.'

'All right then,' Nina says. 'I'll be around in a bit with your nutrition drink.'

'If you say so,' Bodil replies, waving her hand impatiently.

She clearly wants to be left alone with her admirer. Nina walks back out into the corridor and has barely closed the door behind her when the alarm goes off again.

The light is flashing outside D6. Monika's suite.

She doesn't want to go in, and yet she is relieved. Now she won't have to wonder when it is going to happen.

This is when they are going to meet.

Joel

> Mum grew up on a farm in Lycke. She married my dad at twenty and moved to Lyckered on the other side of the main road. That was her life's adventure.

Joel stares at the blinking cursor line in the Word document, then deletes the last sentence. The ice cubes in his glass clink when he takes a sip. He unearthed a bottle of fortified mulled wine in the pantry earlier and is now trying to pretend it's a sugary cocktail, rather than the result of a desperate search.

He has opened the window to air out the kitchen, but there is not a trace of wind tonight. Mosquitoes and moths bounce against the mesh screens, drawn to the light. He's sweating; he'll need to buy a fan tomorrow.

> Mum was married to my father Nils for fifteen years before he died of cancer. As far as I know she never met anyone else.

He takes another sip. Deletes the last sentence. His mother was always so careful to keep her private life private; she would hate that he's writing this letter, that strangers are going to read it. There are many aspects of her current life she would hate if she knew about them.

> They struggled to conceive for a long time, but had a happy marriage nonetheless. My brother was born when my mother was twenty-eight. I (Joel), arrived when she was thirty-two. Ironically, Dad died a couple of years later after a long illness. Which is to say that they didn't have very long to enjoy the parenthood they had dreamed of for so long.

What does he really know about his parents' marriage? In the family chronicle his mother has created, his father is a saint. If there was anything that didn't fit into that image, she would never have let on. Why talk about things that are difficult? Why dwell? Why pay it any mind at all?

But she must have loved him. She never got over his death. And there was never any doubt that Björn was the one who took after him. Both blond, blue-eyed. Family men with honest employment. What's more, Björn had been old enough when their father died to remember him, to share their mother's memories.

> I was never like them. I was strange and listened to strange music. I dyed my hair and wore black clothes. I know she hoped I would get together with my best friend, Nina. No one would have been happier than me if things had worked out that way. Mum and I never talked about it, naturally. We never talked about anything. She has never actually told me she loves me, and I don't know how I would have reacted if she had.

He stares at the paragraph. What is he doing? He deletes it and lights a cigarette. The smoke seems to cling to his sweaty face. The cursor line blinks. The ice clinks.

Björn lives in Jönköping now and is married to Sofia. They have two children, Wiggo and

Joel's fingers hang suspended over his laptop's worn keyboard. He can't remember what Björn's other son is called. He backs up, deleting Wiggo's name as well. Maybe it's not relevant anyway. He has no idea what the staff at Pineshade might want to know about his mother, what might help them help her.

After the heart attack that triggered Mum's dementia, she often talks about a near-death experience and seeing Dad waiting for her on the 'other side'. Sometimes she says he came back with her but has difficulty communicating. Sometimes she even seems to forget that Dad is dead.

A scraping noise makes him look up from his screen. He hears it again and realises it's the swallows under the eaves, but even so, a childish fear of the dark suddenly wells up inside him.

What if his mother has been right all along? What if his father's ghost is present in the house and is looking for her?

Joel shakes his head at himself. Takes a sip of mulled wine.

We visited Mum at the hospital after her heart surgery. It was shocking to see how poorly she was, but we figured rehab would help her recover. Björn was here when she moved back home, and everything seemed to be working out with her in-home care. When Mum disappeared in the middle of the night and a motorist found her half-dead from exposure, we realised how bad things really were. I came back home and quickly understood I had no choice but to stay until she could move into a residential facility like Pineshade.

The reek of urine-soaked pants drying on the radiators. Drawers full of letters his mother had failed to open.

He became her legal guardian and fought to secure a place for her in a nursing home. Phone calls and meetings with care assessors, doctor's appointments during which his mother invariably seemed to become more alert, soaking up the attention. She always answered no when they asked if she wanted to move. Naturally. She was terrified of change, given that even the familiar had become incomprehensible and frightening. And Joel never understood why they asked his mother at all – she was no longer capable of running her own life, that was the whole problem.

But none of that belongs in this letter. And in any case, it does nothing to describe his mother.

Joel tries to corral his thoughts but can't find anything to hold onto. They just slide around on the surface. He refills his glass. The ice has melted and the lukewarm mulled wine is so sweet it burns his throat when he swallows.

The cursor line keeps blinking. What else can he say about his mother? What does she actually like? What are her interests? She has no close friends. A lot of them had drifted away when his father was taken ill. She didn't stay in touch with her colleagues after she retired. Their old neighbours are gone. She has no family in the area. What did she do all day, alone in this house? Did she just wander about, thinking about her husband? Waiting for her sons to call?

She must have been so alone. At least that's one thing they have in common.

Joel sighs loudly. Self-pity is a sure sign he's getting too drunk.

Ash from his cigarette falls onto his keyboard. He blows it away and stubs his cigarette out. He recalls that Elisabeth said something about favourite foods, but he doesn't even know that.

He should have called more often. He should have been more patient when he did call. He should have asked more questions and listened to her answers.

Joel closes the document and moves it to the recycle bin, then shuts his laptop.

Nina

Monika must have climbed over the guard rails on her bed. She's standing in the middle of the room and has managed to pull her coat on over her nightgown. She stares, terrified, at Nina when she enters.

Nina has seen the glazed look of dementia countless times over the years. The vacant eyes. But she has never seen it in anyone as close to her as Monika and it's not at all the same. It's almost unbearable.

She looks over at the bed and reminds herself that she has to report this to Elisabeth. Old people who can climb over guard rails risk getting caught in them, or falling from a more dangerous height than they would have done without them.

'Please, can you help me get home?' Monika says. 'I have to get home.'

Nina takes a step closer and catches the unmistakeable smell of wet nappy. She's going to have to change Monika. Handle her naked body, her exposed genitals.

Proud Monika who never wanted to show any weakness, who never asked for help.

'Come here,' Nina says. 'Let's sit down and have a chat, you and me.'

'I don't want to sit down,' Monika says. 'Why won't anyone listen to me? I just want to go home, how hard is that to understand?'

Nina puts her arm around her, but Monika shies away.

'Someone has to come pick me up. I can't find my car keys.'

'It would be better if you went to sleep, Monika.'

'I don't want to sleep! I want to go home!'

Her bottom lip begins to tremble.

'I'm not supposed to be here,' she sobs.

'You'll feel better in the morning, I promise.'

Something suddenly shifts in Monika's eyes, a faint glimmer; Nina holds her breath.

Does she recognise me?

But the glimmer fades.

'You don't understand,' Monika says. 'No one understands. Everything's so strange all the time and no one listens to me.'

'I'm listening,' Nina says. 'Let's sit down, you can tell me everything.'

Monika heaves a deep sigh but allows Nina to usher her back to bed without further protest. She doesn't seem to notice when Nina removes her coat and puts it down on a chair.

'My husband . . . his name was Nils,' Monika says, and points tremblingly at the wedding photograph.

Nina nods and folds down the guard rail.

'He won't be able to find me here,' Monika continues and sits down heavily on the edge of the bed. 'And now I'm so afraid he'll think I want nothing to do with him.'

Monika shakes her head.

'I need to go home.'

Nina strokes her back and has to choke back her tears. Not react. Not worry her.

'It'll be all right, I promise,' she says. 'I'll look after you.'

Like you looked after me.

Joel

He has given up on falling asleep and has instead decided to attack the fridge, armed with a black bin bag. He fills it with jars of pickled herring he's afraid to open, mould-covered olives, plastic containers full of unidentifiable things. There are puddles of dried-in gunk on the greasy shelve – he should have taken care of this much sooner. He sprays everything with kitchen cleaner, scrubs and rubs, then moves on to the pantry, binning syrup bottles with trickles of stickiness running down their sides, jars of baking powder with no lids, flaked almonds from a bygone decade. He climbs up on a chair to reach the back of the top shelves. As he gropes around he suddenly comes across familiar rounded plastic corners.

Desiccated coconut and breadcrumbs rain down on him when he pulls out his old Walkman.

Joel realises there's no point trying to comprehend why his mum has hidden it in the pantry. He wipes it on his T-shirt and smiles when he feels the familiar weight of it in his hand. He'd bought it on mail-order because it had a built-in microphone and had never gone anywhere without it; always carried spare tapes in his pocket so he could record ideas for songs.

He opens it and pulls out the cassette to study the BASF logo, his teenage handwriting on a strip of masking tape: NINA AND JOEL MIX AUTUMN -94.

Joel sits down on a chair. Wipes the sweat from his eyes and lights a cigarette. He normally studiously avoids listening to music from that era. It reminds him too much of the life he never had, the life that had once been within reach.

This time, curiosity wins. He puts the tape back in and presses play, but nothing happens. Either the batteries are dead or the Walkman no longer works. He takes the tape out again and slaps it against the palm of his hand. That it was recorded in the autumn of 1994 is not much of a clue, really. Nina and he had just got to know Katja, who owned the record shop in Kungälv. They hadn't been able to afford to buy more than a couple of albums a month, but she let them borrow from her private collection – taught them more about the music they loved and what had come before it. After a while, they were invited to her house in the woods outside Gullbringa. She had a rudimentary studio in her basement where they could record demos and she helped them find inexpensive guitars. A natural gloss, second-hand Ibanez for Nina, a cherry-red Stratocaster knockoff for Joel.

She sold him other things in her house in the woods, too. Taught him other things. Like how speed could make him indefatigable and cocaine could make him brave.

Joel throws his cigarette into the sink and stands up. He brings the bottle of mulled wine up to his room and kneels down in front of the stereo, before opening one of the cassette decks and sliding the tape in. He considers rewinding it but pushes play instead.

The picked chords streaming out of the speakers are soft, dreamlike, almost eerie. Joel recognises them instantly. It's the start of 'Song to the Siren'. Elizabeth Fraser's voice comes in, fills the room, fills him. He closes his eyes as goose bumps spread up and down his arms and neck. A memory surfaces of Nina, sitting on the floor in front of these speakers with pen and paper, struggling to make out the words and understand what they *mean*. What their *meaning* is. But Joel didn't have to analyse. Everything was there in her voice. Everything that hurt turned into something beautiful, so beautiful it hurt.

He opens his eyes when the song ends. Jesus and Mary Chain take over. 'Just Like Honey'. He smokes cigarette after cigarette and keeps listening. Sonic Youth. Hole. Echo and the Bunnymen. Skunk Anansie and Smashing Pumpkins. The tape reverses in the middle of Björk's 'Play Dead'.

He has run out of mulled wine. The sky has grown pale and the first light of the rising sun is already touching the treetops up on the mountain. Joel moves over to the window. He used to sneak out this way at night. He'd walk across the little roof above the front door and climb down to the lawn. If Nina wasn't with him already, she would be waiting down by the bus shelter.

He wonders where Nina is now. Who she is. If she ever thinks about him.

Together, they were going to leave all of this behind, the claustrophobically small lives this place offered. *Us against the world*. But Nina stayed. Chose all the things she'd said she despised over Joel.

If only he had someone to call. Someone who could drown out the thoughts jostling and slithering inside his skull. But he has no one.

The realisation hits him like a blow: he's all alone.

Nina's no longer in his life. And when he got clean, his only friends in Stockholm disappeared. Drugs were the only thing they'd had in common.

There's no one left who knows him, really knows him. Only superficial acquaintances, one-night stands, temporary colleagues. Ever since that morning he quit, he has wandered around like a ghost, as though he were the one who died that night.

Six years and two months.

What happened that night changed everything. It had scared him so badly the memory of it has kept him strong through every temptation. But right now, he would swallow or snort anything without hesitation, just to get away from himself.

Pineshade

Nina is in the D Ward staffroom, writing reports about the night. She's humming 'Song to the Siren' but stops abruptly when she catches herself. The pen stops moving. She's astonished she still knows the words.

The morning staff will be in soon to start the morning routine, but for now, the ward is quiet. Almost all the residents are asleep. Vera has crawled into Dagmar's bed and is holding her close under the duvet. Wiborg is hugging her cat in her sleep, letting it warm her rattling chest. Petrus is running through his dreams on young, strong legs. Bodil fought sleep for as long as she could, her eyes fixed on the window, but now she's sleeping deeply.

Only Monika's awake. She's lying in her bed, staring out into the room with a happy smile on her face. Tears are trickling down her temples, disappearing into her hair. The wire filament in her bedside lamp crackles and the light flickers, reflecting in a greasy stain on the wall next to the bed. Monika sniffles and pushes a strand of hair behind her ear. *If only I were prettier to look at*, she says. She laughs when she hears the answer. The light flickers again; she listens intently. The shadows grow and shrink. *I promise*, she says, wiping the tears from her cheeks. *I can't believe you found me. I can't believe we're going to be together again.*

Joel

It's midday and the sun lies like a heavy weight over the Pineshade carpark. It follows him on his way to the entrance. He only woke up an hour ago and he feels worse than hungover – he feels poisoned. But he has showered, shaved and combed his hair neatly. He's even brought magazines. Anything to show that the person ringing the doorbell of D Ward is respectable and caring. A normal, sober person.

Sucdi lets him in this time.

'Hi,' she says, and steps aside. 'Come on in.'

'Thank you.'

He glances furtively at her as they walk down the corridor together.

'I must have seemed odd yesterday,' he says tentatively. 'Bringing Mum here was so bloody tough I actually took a sedative . . . but it was stronger than I thought. I just want all of you who work here to know I'm not normally like that.'

Not anymore.

'I know it must be hard,' Sucdi replies. 'But you did the right thing bringing her here.'

Joel nods, wishing he could bring himself to believe her.

An older woman in the blue Pineshade uniform comes up to him and introduces herself as Rita. She has a slate-grey bob and the characteristic west-coast tan. Must be close to retirement. He wonders what it's like, working with senile people not much older than her. After they shake hands, she disappears into the lounge where she gives one of the old ladies a beaker.

'How did Mum do last night?' Joel asks, turning back to Sucdi. 'Do you know?'

'I read in the report that she was a bit anxious, but that's to be expected. And she was happy this morning.'

He lets that sink in.

Happy?

Mum was happy?

Only when the relief washes over him does he realise he was bracing for yet another disaster, and how depleted his own reserves are by now.

An old lady steps into the corridor from the common room. She's wearing brown trousers with pleats, a sparkling brooch on her jumper. A red beret sits atop her head at a jaunty angle.

'Excuse me, where's my room again?' she asks.

'Hi, Anna,' Sucdi replies and points down the corridor. 'You live that way. In D7. I'll take you there.'

'They're always changing things around,' Anna declares and shakes her head good-humouredly. 'It's not easy finding your way back home after they've been at it.'

'I would think not,' Sucdi agrees.

No conspiratorial wink at Joel. No suppressed mirth in her voice.

'It's cold outside,' Anna says.

'Is it?' Sucdi replies. 'I haven't been out since this morning.'

Joel watches them. At Pineshade, his mum's going to be surrounded by people who understand everything that is so incomprehensible to him. They have knowledge. Routines. To them, his mum is just another day at work.

Joel notices Anna eyeing him curiously.

'Aren't you a strapping young man?' she says. 'You'd better watch out for Bodil.'

'Don't scare him away,' Sucdi says warmly.

Joel smiles, wondering who Bodil might be and why he should watch out for her.

'Do you have a piano at home?' Anna says before he can ask. 'It's important to treat yourself sometimes.'

'No,' Joel replies. 'But I'll consider it.'

'What's to consider?' Anna retorts. 'Just start playing.'

They walk towards the suites together while Anna rambles on.

The pregnant woman comes out of D1. This time, he makes sure to meet her eyes and say hello. She smiles back and presses a hand against the small of her back. A few lumps of mascara cling to her cheek.

Joel stops outside D6. He contemplates knocking, but doesn't want to wake his mother if she's asleep.

'This is it, Anna,' Sucdi announces when they reach D7. 'Do you want me to come in with you?'

'Yes, I think you'd better,' Anna says. 'I think the apple has popped out again. But I can't make you coffee; I'm all out.'

'That's all right,' Sucdi assures her.

Joel waves to them and opens the door to his mother's suite. A draught from the window makes the curtains flutter. His mum is sitting at the table and she smiles broadly at him when he enters.

He gets the feeling his entrance interrupted something. A conversation that just broke off. Words seem to be lingering in the air.

'Joel!' his mum exclaims. 'Finally! I have so much to tell you!'

Her eyes are bright, her smile eager. Seeing her like this, it would be easy to think there's nothing wrong with her. That it was all a misunderstanding, something temporary that has passed now.

She can move home again and I can go back to Stockholm, but this time I've learnt my lesson and I'm going to keep in touch and—

Joel reminds himself that's the wishful thinking of a child. He takes off his shoes and sits down across from her. He puts the magazines on the table, but his mother doesn't so much as glance at them.

'Nils has found his way here.'

'Is that right?' is the only thing he can think of to say.

His mother nods eagerly. Her smile grows even wider. Reaches a tipping point and becomes manic.

'You didn't see him when you came in?' she says.

Joel has to look away. He gazes out the window, sees her car in the carpark and tries to decide what this means. Should he be happy for her? Is this a good thing? Should he play along with this fantasy of hers or try to snap her out of it? All he knows is that he doesn't want to say the wrong thing, to break the spell and make her sad, angry or afraid again.

She laughs and nods at something behind his back.

'Yes,' she says. 'Now you can finally get to know each other. He's very proud of you, Daddy is, let me tell you, Joel.'

Joel smiles, but feels exhausted. His father was a manual labourer, in all likeliness a man of his time. Joel sincerely doubts he would have been proud of him.

His mother frowns. She looks over at the door and then back at Joel. Her eyes bore into him.

'Nils says you don't believe me.'

The curtains flutter. Joel hesitates.

'You do believe me, don't you?' his mother says. 'You can see him, too, can't you? He's standing right behind you.'

The hope shining in her eyes is so strong Joel can barely breathe.

'Look at him at least,' she says.

Joel turns around. For a split second, he thinks he can see a shadow, but it's just his mother's coat hanging on a hook by the door.

No one there. Of course not.

And yet, it feels like someone's looking back at him. A gust from the window caresses the back of his neck.

I'm going as crazy as she is. They're going to have to put a cot next to her bed for me.

Joel turns back to his mother, to her anxious expectation.

If she thinks her husband has come back to her, it must be considered a blessing. It would be cruel to take it away from her.

'Yes,' he says. 'Of course I believe you.'

Nina

Nina climbs out of her car in the nearly deserted carpark in Skredsby. A gang of teenagers on mopeds eye her as she walks towards the supermarket. She quickens her step, knowing they're trying to think of something to holler at her, something to break up the tedium for a few seconds. Teenagers in groups still make her nervous. When her son reached that age, she would come home to piles of their stinky trainers in her hallway, their adolescent voices filling the house, and she'd have an overwhelming urge to turn and run.

She can breathe more easily after stepping into the coolness of the shop. She grabs a trolley and walks up and down the aisles, filling it with familiar things. Catches herself looking for Joel at every turn. She called Sucdi with a made-up story about a lost wallet and found out Joel had been back to visit Monika.

Maybe I should take a few weeks' sick leave. Only until Joel's gone.

No. She can't afford to. But she can't exactly spend her workdays in the basement, either.

Rage seizes Nina as she pays at the till. She's not going to be afraid of Joel. She has nothing to be ashamed of. She's in charge of her own life now. Waiting is the hardest part and she can do something about that.

Suddenly, Nina's in a hurry. She throws the food into carrier bags and walks back out to the carpark, glaring at the teenagers while she opens the boot, forcing herself to see how young they really are.

Nina drives too fast, aware that she's taking unnecessary risks. Realising she has a choice has made her high, but she's fully aware the bubble can burst at any moment.

She barely slows down at the Lyckered turn-off, heading up the hill for the first time since Joel moved away. Some of the houses along the road have new additions or have been painted different colours, but for the most part, everything's uncannily unchanged. She drives around the last bend and the grey fibre cement house comes into view.

It looks exactly like it did back then. Just a little bit smaller, as though it shrank. But of course, it's her – she's bigger now.

There's no car in the driveway or the barn, but that doesn't necessarily mean Joel's out. The gravel crunches under her tyres when Nina drives up to the house. She pulls the key out of the ignition and resolutely climbs out of the car. Looking up at Joel's window, she sees nothing except the blue sky reflected in the glass.

Nina marches up the front steps before she has a chance to change her mind. She rings the doorbell; the familiar discordant jar from inside is an echo of the hundreds of times she has stood here breathlessly before. Nothing moves on the other side of the warped, green glass of the front door.

There's chirping from the lawn, wind soughing softly through the evergreens up on the mountain. But not a sound from the house.

Joel

A silver Volvo that can't be more than a couple of years old is parked in the driveway. Joel catches a glimpse of short, blonde hair and a somewhat stout figure waiting on his front steps.

What is Nina's mother doing here?

But she's dead. His mum told him about the obituary in the local paper just a few years after he moved away. Presumably the alcohol did her in. Joel had only met her a handful of times. Nina made sure it almost never happened.

He parks next to the unfamiliar car and climbs out. He's already caught on, and yet it's a shock to see her.

Nina.

She stands up and brushes off her backside.

'I'm sorry to turn up unannounced like this,' she says, and Joel gets the feeling she's been rehearsing a little speech while she waited. 'I figured I might as well come out here so we could meet in private. Since we were bound to run into each other sooner or later.'

In private? Joel's heart is racing. He's glad he's wearing sunglasses – his eyes would give him away.

'I work at Pineshade now,' Nina explains.

'Right,' Joel manages. It takes him half a second to make the connection. 'Was that you on the phone last night?'

'Yes.'

'I didn't recognise your voice. Did you know it was me? I guess you must have, actually, since I introduced myself.'

'Yes. I know I should have said something, but I didn't know . . .' Nina trails off. 'This is an odd situation.'

Joel lets out a chuckle.

'Yes,' he says. 'It is.'

Nina eyes him uncertainly. There's still a hint of teenage Nina in this older face. Maybe her prepared script didn't extend beyond this point.

'Can I offer you a cup of coffee or something?' Joel says.

He almost laughs again. It's such a grown-up question. So polite.

'I'm good, thanks,' Nina replies.

'A glass of water, perhaps?'

She shakes her head.

'And I don't suppose you still smoke?' Joel says, pulling his cigarettes out of his denim shorts pocket.

'No,' Nina says. 'Not since . . .'

She trails off, but Joel understands.

Not since I got pregnant.

He lights a cigarette. Walks over to the garden furniture and sits down in one of the chairs. There's no wind here. The air he breathes feel as warm as the cigarette smoke.

'When I started at Pineshade, I worked as a care assistant,' Nina says. 'But I finished my nursing degree a few years ago.'

'Did Mum recognise you?' he asks.

Nina shakes her head and looks genuinely sad. Joel feels a pang of sympathy. His mum meant a lot to Nina. As a grown-up, he's had an easier time understanding her need for a role model.

'Some days are better than others,' Joel tells her. 'Maybe next time.'

'Maybe,' Nina replies. 'How are you?'

Joel takes a deep drag. The question is immense. The possible answers innumerable. He chooses to limit the conversation to things concerning his mother and Pineshade.

'I'm all right. It's hard to see her so confused. Though I assume that, as far as she's concerned, it's the rest of us who are acting weird.'

Nina smiles wanly.

'But she was in a great mood today,' Joel says.

'Good,' Nina says. 'And don't worry if there are ups and downs at first. You have to give her some time to settle in.'

'Yeah, that's what people keep telling me.'

She looks down and brushes a few lingering breadcrumbs off the vinyl tablecloth.

'And what about you?' Joel asks. 'What do you get up to when you're not at Pineshade?'

'Markus and I live in Tofta,' Nina says. 'Out on the isthmus behind the manor.'

Joel pushes up his sunglasses, which have been sliding down his nose.

'Huh,' he says.

That's a posh area. Expensive, as far as these parts go.

He doesn't know what he pictured Nina doing these days, but he'd never have guessed she would have stayed with Markus. Dull, insipid Markus who had his dull, insipid future planned out for him at his father's hardware shop in Kungälv. How did she bear it?

'We love it,' Nina says. 'We have a view of the bay.'

'And the child?' Joel says. 'Though I guess he's not a child anymore.'

Nina smiles.

'Daniel's nineteen now.'

It seems impossible. But the maths checks out.

When did we get so bloody old, Nina? How can you have raised someone who's all grown up when I don't even feel like a grown-up myself yet?

'He's starting Chalmers in the autumn,' Nina adds. There's a pleased glint in her eye. Her smile grows wider.

She has changed. Or maybe it's that he can see her more clearly now. Maybe it's not hard at all for Nina to endure her life. Maybe this is exactly what she aspired to all along. Nina always wanted to be a good girl, obsessed with neatness and not ending up like her mother. It was only with him she'd been able to pretend to be someone else sometimes. Their dreams about the future, the music, their friendship: maybe it was all pretend.

The old anger rears up in Joel, surprisingly powerful. As though the past twenty years never happened. Nina hasn't understood a thing. If she had, she wouldn't be smiling like that.

'And you?' she says. 'What are you up to these days?'

Joel leans forwards and grinds the cigarette into the glass jar, then settles back into his chair.

'I work in a bar,' he says.

Nina seems to be waiting for more, but Joel has nothing to add. He has no intention of telling her about the soulless tourist trap in Stockholm's Old Town, or his most recent sublet, which he has no idea how long he'll be able to keep.

He wants another cigarette already, but Nina knows he always chain-smoked when he was nervous or upset.

'Okay,' Nina says. 'So are you still doing the music thing?'

She seems to regret her words the moment they leave her

mouth. They're closing in on the big unspoken undertows lurking behind the pleasantries. Nina's probably hoping Joel will spare them both from going there.

But he doesn't want to, can't. His anger is a freight train careening through him on clattering wheels.

'No,' he says calmly. 'I'm not *doing the music thing*.'

One of the swallows under the eaves scrapes its claws against the gutter.

'Look—' Nina says apprehensively.

'I tried, but it was *us* they wanted. They were counting on *us*. *Our* songs.'

'We don't know it would have amounted to anything regardless,' Nina says.

Joel laughs. A mean, harsh laugh that makes Nina blink. 'That's what you're telling yourself, is it?' he says. 'We had a record deal. But you ruined it, and you know it.'

Nina shakes her head. 'How did it happen, anyway? I didn't even know you and Markus were going out.'

'I don't want to talk about that. It's a long time ago. It doesn't matter now.'

'Maybe not to you. You have your lovely fucking life with *Markus* and your view of the bay.'

Nina's quiet for a long time.

Joel wonders if she's thinking about the morning when he turned up at the block of flats where she lived with her mum. He'd bought a used car with the small inheritance from his dad he'd received when he turned eighteen. His bags were in the back. He'd made a mix-tape that would last them all the way to Stockholm. A room was waiting for the two of them there, lodging with an old lady in a posh flat on Östermalm. But when Nina came out, her eyes red from crying and her clothes rumpled from having been slept in, he *knew.*

'You promised,' Joel says. 'Plans were made. You must have known long before ... and you never even gave me an explanation.'

'I was pregnant! What was I supposed to do?'

Joel studies her from behind his sunglasses. His unspoken reply makes Nina get out of her chair.

'I think you meant to get pregnant,' Joel says. 'You chickened out, but you didn't know how to tell me. So you set yourself up with the best excuse you could find for staying.'

Nina looks like she's fighting back tears and Joel instantly regrets his words. Wants to take them back.

'You can't blame me for your life not turning out the way you wanted,' she says.

'You know nothing about my life.'

'I know you were drunk, or high on something when you brought Monika to Pineshade.'

He feels like he's falling. But he's sitting dead-still. His face expressionless. He has turned it into a stiff mask of flesh and blood.

'What else is there to know?' Nina continues. 'Think what you will of Markus. Tell yourself I betrayed you for him. But that's not what happened. He saved me from you.'

Joel forces air into his lungs. 'Go fuck yourself,' he says.

And Nina leaves without another word.

Joel still hasn't moved a muscle when he hears the gravel crunch under her tyres.

Nina

Nina slows down after passing the manor's stable. Her whole body's shaking.

She can't go home yet. If Markus is on the sofa with his laptop as usual, she's going to see him through Joel's eyes. The way he said *Markus* is still echoing in her brain. She needs to get it together. Become herself again.

She turns down the narrow gravel road by the granary. The theatre group that puts on plays there every summer is having lunch on the lawn outside. Their conversations stop when she approaches, but they quickly lose interest when they realise she's not there for them. She drives on into the woods. Dust rises like a cloud behind her and the car jounces over potholes. She passes the far end of the golf course, continuing on past the meadows with their dramatically twisted trees. She barely notices them. Keeps picturing Joel: too skinny, but with sinewy strength; broad-shouldered, but with that same terrible posture. He looks the same. As though the drugs preserved rather than destroyed him.

Thankfully, there are only a couple of other cars in the nature reserve carpark. It's windy as usual down here. The breeze snatches at Nina's hair the moment she climbs out of the car, and it picks up as she walks out onto the cliffs. She gazes out at the beach, the meadow and the grazing horses. The sun is low in the sky, warming her back despite the wind. She hears snatches of distant voices and catches a glimpse of a yellow windbreaker disappearing below the cliff she's standing on, but no one can see her.

Meant to get pregnant.

The best excuse you could find for staying.

She hadn't planned to get knocked up. Don't all teenage girls forget to take their pills sometimes?

And she'd wanted Daniel. She'd been scared, absolutely. But she'd wanted him. Nina had always wanted to be a mum. Maybe not right then, not like that.

Not with Markus.

But she'd wanted to keep the child. She's happy she did.

Nina walks aimlessly back and forth across the cliffs. Joel was right about one thing: the child *had been* a way out. Without Daniel, Nina would never have been able to stand up to Joel.

She'd loved Joel. She'd wanted to get out, too. But there had been a moment that changed everything, that divided the story of her and Joel into a before and an after. It's not what he thinks. It wasn't the morning when he came to pick her up. It wasn't when she found out she was pregnant.

It happened before that.

She was on a train back to Gothenburg, staring at the empty seat next to her. It was Christmas break and out of the corner of her eye, she could see the snow-covered landscape rush by outside.

They'd been up to Stockholm; their demo had landed them a gig at a club called The Studio. She'd been so nervous she'd thrown up several times backstage – Joel had done nothing to calm her down. He was deathly pale himself and snorted rail after rail. He was on fire on stage, but he collapsed the moment they got off. When she tried to get him to go back to their hostel, he called her a *fucking prig* and went to an afterparty with some people they didn't know. Nina lay awake all night, but he didn't come back. He might have been dead for all she knew. They had no mobile phones. And sitting on the train back home, staring at his empty seat, she knew she couldn't go. She couldn't go with Joel after they graduated. Their twenty-four hours in Stockholm was just a tiny taste of what it would be like, and she promised herself never to put herself through that kind of anxiety again.

Joel had apologised when he got back. He'd probably meant it. But when the spring term began, he was high even at school. That was probably why he didn't notice her and Markus making eyes at each other. And she hadn't wanted to tell him – she knew exactly what he thought of the philistines from the seaside villas, with their boat shoes and turtleneck/blazer combos.

She couldn't go with Joel. But she'd been unable to tell him. Because she hadn't wanted to hurt him, she'd overcompensated for her sore conscience by acting more enthusiastic than ever. Carefully hiding how much she hated going to Katja's, hated all the junkies hanging around there, the smoke enshrouding the ground floor. Hated being left alone there while Joel fucked one of the countless long-fringed pop boys Katja surrounded herself with. She hated the drugs that took over more and more.

So, yes. Joel's right. Getting knocked up solved everything.

And Markus was there for her. The awkward teenager who took her to a fancy restaurant and held out an engagement ring in his sweaty hand, asking her to stay. To keep the baby.

Everything had seemed black and white when she was eighteen. It had still been easy to change her stripes, to trade one life for another, to throw herself into all the new things.

But, then, Nina had been trained to do just that from a young age. It might be the only thing her mum ever taught her: how to move on and never look back.

Markus was safe. He loved her. And he loathed Joel. With him, she wouldn't be one of those children of alcoholics who end up like their parents. She didn't have to worry about him, didn't have to fix him. She wasn't going to mistake obsession for love. Wasn't going to try to find safety in chaos, just because it was what she was familiar with.

She already had Joel for all that. And she was determined to break the vicious circle.

Nina stands motionless on the cliff.

She'd done the right thing. She has no regrets.

Leave, Joel. Just get out of here. Let me live my life. I can take care of Monika. You never appreciated her anyway.

She walks back to the car. When she drives by the granary, the theatre people are gone.

'How long were you at the shops for?' Markus says, looking up from his phone when she enters the kitchen.

She doesn't have it in her to tell him about Joel. Doesn't have it in her to even think about him.

'I need a hug,' she says.

Markus looks so surprised it hurts her. When did they stop touching each other?

He puts his arms around her and she leans her head against his chest, breathing in his scent. After a few more exhales, she relaxes in his embrace.

It's going to be okay. They belong together. They do. All relationships have their ups and downs, right?

But he lets go of her much too quickly.

'Did something happen?' he asks.

Nina straightens up to kiss him. Opens his mouth with her tongue. Is that resistance, hesitation, she senses?

'I've missed you,' she says.

'We see each other every day.'

'You know what I mean.' She presses herself against him. 'I'm just going to tidy up. Maybe you could get in the shower first?'

She strokes his jeans tentatively. Pulls her hand away in disappointment when she realises he's not hard.

'Do we always have to shower before we . . .' he says.

'Please,' she whispers. 'I know it's silly.'

Markus sighs and Nina kisses him again before he has a chance to object.

She loads the dishwasher and hears the water running in the bathroom. When it's her turn, she quickly rinses off after soaping up her entire body. She's still damp when she lies down next to Markus in bed. The wind blowing through the open window is balmy, even though night is falling.

He has a hard time getting going, but she's patient and focused; she knows how to keep him from feeling stressed. When he finally enters her, she manages to block out the world for a while. Afterwards, she falls asleep first.

She wakes up around midnight. The bed is empty and she can hear Markus downstairs.

A thought refuses to leave her alone:

You, who wanted to control everything, did you really just forget to take your pill?

She lies awake for a long time staring up at the ceiling. She suddenly remembers that the food she bought is still in the car. Given how hot the afternoon was, it's bound to be ruined now.

Joel's back and the cracks are already appearing. The chaos he always brings in his wake threatens to start pouring in.

Pineshade

It's night and Johanna's in the D Ward staff bathroom when the alarm goes off. *I don't even get to piss in peace.* She tears off a piece of loo roll and fervently prays the alarm isn't coming from Petrus' suite. She wipes quickly, washes her hands and steps out into the corridor, noting that the alarm is coming from D8. Not Petrus, but not that much better. She hates Dagmar and Vera and the eerie way they seem to read each other's minds. Sweat stains emerge on the back of her smock as Johanna walks towards the room at the end of the stuffy hallway.

Wiborg hears Johanna pass her door, but barely registers it. She's sitting up in her bed in D1 listening intently to the voice on the other end of the line: *The number you've called is not in service. The number you've called is not in service. The number you've called is not in service.* Wiborg shakes her head.

'Why won't you help me?' she says. 'Stop talking, woman, and help me instead!'

Johanna reluctantly picks up the pace when she hears noise from D8. She unlocks the door and turns off the alarm. Vera is standing naked in the middle of the room, screaming. Johanna walks up to her and, even though she would prefer not to touch the aged body, she puts a hand on Vera's shoulder.

'What are you doing?' she asks.

Dagmar is laughing excitedly in her bed. Vera continues to scream without even drawing breath and points towards the bathroom. Johanna tries to soothe her, but she's unreachable. Eventually, Johanna gives up and walks over to the bathroom door. It's open a crack. The light is on in there. She tries to tell herself not even a crazy knife murderer would have any interest in breaking into a care home for dementia patients.

But maybe one of the old people wandered in here and died on the toilet or on the floor, contorted into some horrible position with staring eyes and gaping mouth . . .

Johanna's never going to let her boyfriend talk her into watching horror films again. Vera's scream cuts off abruptly behind her. Dagmar's laugh subsides into a low chuckle. Phlegm rattles in her throat with each guffaw. Johanna opens the bathroom door and—

no one there

—exhales. Nothing looks out of the ordinary. When she turns around, Vera is standing right behind her. Peering into the bathroom with frightened eyes.

'There was someone there,' she says. 'Someone was standing there staring at me when I went in.'

Johanna heaves a sigh and leads her back to bed.

'It was just your reflection, okay? Don't be scared.'

Revolted, she leaps away when she hears a wet hiss, a splashing against the floor. Vera doesn't seem to notice that she's peeing as she staggers across the room towards her bed. *This is so not okay,* Johanna thinks to herself. *So very not okay.*

Dagmar laughs again.

In D5, Lillemor is dreaming that an angel is hovering above her bed. Its gown shimmers like mother-of-pearl, billowing as though it were under water. Its golden hair is curled around a pale, androgynous face wearing a faint smile. It extends its hand. Lillemor, still asleep, sits up in the dark to take it. A greasy spot, no bigger than a coin, glistens on the wall above her bed.

Johanna walks down the corridor towards the cleaning cupboard. She has swabbed the floor in D8 and the dirty water sloshes against the inside of the bucket. The weight of it has made her sweaty again. *There must be something wrong with the ventilation. God damn it, I hate this place.* When the fluorescent lights above her go out with a whirr, she freezes mid-step. The contents of the bucket spill over the edge, splattering the floor and Johanna's shoes. She lets out a disgusted yelp. The alarm goes off in the hallway. The light above the door next to her is flashing. The new lady in D6 is groaning loudly in there. Johanna considers simply walking away.

But if something has happened, they can probably sue me for neglect or something, plus, I have to go in anyway to shut off the bloody alarm.

She puts the bucket down next to the door, leans the mop handle against the wall and enters D6, fumbling around until she finds the alarm button and the beeping stops. She turns on the hallway light. There's whimpering from inside the suite – it sounds like a wounded animal. Johanna quickly washes her hands and sanitises them, trying to ignore that one of her trouser legs is clinging to her calf, that the water she spilled is full of Vera's urine. *So not okay.*

Johanna forces herself to go in and turn on the overhead light. She screams when Monika's eyes stare straight into hers. She's sitting up in bed and her old face has contracted into a grimace. Her mouth is wide open. The tendons on either side of her neck are pulled taut. She's clutching the guard rails and there's a faint, metallic rattling; Johanna realises the whole bed is shaking. *Un-fucking-believable.*

She moves in closer and it feels like the air grows thicker, pressing against her skin.

'Hello,' she says. 'Hello, can you hear me?'

Her heart is pounding in her chest. She reaches out, but quickly pulls back again when Monika lets out a drawn-out moan from deep inside her chest.

I have to get help. I hope Adrian's working.

When Johanna turns to leave, the low note turns into slurred words, hard to make out at first, then increasingly clear:

'I know what you did. I know what you did and he's going to find out, too.'

Johanna doesn't turn around until she's almost at the door. She knows what the old bat is referring to, but it's impossible. *She can't know. No one knows.*

The face in the bed smiles.

'Oh yes,' it says. *'I know. But now I'm going to tell you something.'*

Nina

The thunder rolled in at dawn, and with it, driving rain. Nina is soaked after the short dash from her car to Pineshade.

When she gets down to the changing room, Adrian from B Ward is standing next to one of the lockers, bare-chested. Keys rattle in his jeans pockets when he pulls them off, too. He turns around when the door clicks shut behind Nina. Smiles sleepily, apparently completely unconcerned about her seeing him in nothing but his underwear.

'Hiya,' he says, pushing a strand of his blond Kurt Cobain hair behind his ear.

Was he even alive when Kurt Cobain died? Either way, he's only a few years older than her son. She picks a locker as far away from him as possible. She would prefer to wait until he leaves to get changed, but what would she do in the meantime? Stand around and stare?

'How's things?' he says, pulling on his smock.

'Good,' she replies. 'And you?'

'I don't know,' he says with a grin. 'Ask me when I've woken up.'

She smiles and nods while Adrian tells her about a gig in Gothenburg. A venue she's never heard of. His band opened for a group with the unlikely name Arse Sweat.

'They're from Tranås,' Adrian says, as though that explains everything.

Nina hides behind her locker door as best she can while she pulls off her denim jacket and T-shirt and hurriedly pulls on her smock. Not that she thinks Adrian cares or is trying to sneak a peek.

What would he say if she told him she used to be in a band, too?

She changes into her work trousers and indoor shoes, then slams the locker door shut.

'Bloody hell, I just want to go home and sleep,' Adrian says, shutting his locker, too.

'Yes, and the weather doesn't exactly help, either.'

There. Middle-aged. So bloody predictable. Halfway to a suite at Pineshade.

They exit into the basement corridor together.

'You're playing today, right?' she says, turning on the overhead lights.

'Yeah,' Adrian replies. 'Good thing I have such a loyal fanbase here at Pineshade. Just not a lot of groupies.'

'I wouldn't say that. There's always Bodil.'

His laugh echoes up and down the stairwell as they walk up to the ground floor.

They part ways in the lobby; Nina heads down D corridor. It's quiet and deserted and the air feels stuffy and electric. Down by the suite doors, she spots a bucket and a mop propped against the wall.

She looks into the dark lounge as she passes. Rain is pattering against the windows. The furniture is just vague shapes in the gloom; squares of pale morning light are reflected in the black TV screen.

Nina is halfway to the staffroom when she hears a metallic

scraping from the ceiling. She stops and waits until she hears the sound again, then manages to trace it to one of the air vents. She pushes up on tiptoe and reaches out to the cover, tapping it gingerly. Black flakes rain down like ash from the pipe inside. She hears the scraping sound again, further down the corridor. It sounds like claws against metal. Could a bird have accidentally got into the ventilation system? Is that why the air is so stuffy?

She continues into the staffroom. It's empty. Normally, Johanna's virtually jumping up and down with impatience when the morning staff come to relieve her. There's a dirty plate on the table, alongside an open celebrity magazine and a half-filled coffee cup in which the milk has curdled. Nina peers into the common room through the glass. No one in there, either. She pulls out the binder with the reports, but there are no notes from last night. She steps out into the corridor again.

'Johanna?'

No answer. She continues down the corridor, past the common room where the rain thrums against the glass ceiling.

The bucket is outside Monika's room. Nina's just about to go in to look for Johanna when she hears crying from D8.

The smell of cleaning product and urine greets her when she enters the sisters' suite. Vera's sitting up in bed, looking unhappy.

'Hi,' Nina says. 'Are you okay?'

When she approaches the bed, her shoes stick to the floor. Johanna didn't do a very good job mopping.

'What if he comes back?' Vera whispers.

'Who?'

'The one who was in the bathroom.'

'It was probably just Johanna,' Nina says. 'The girl who works here.'

'No. She didn't see him either.'

Vera is shaking so badly she might need an Oxazepam. Nina wonders how long she's been this frightened.

And where the fuck is Johanna?

'He's mean,' Vera says. 'Really mean. He shouldn't be here.'

'It's okay,' Nina says, glancing over at the bathroom.

There's no one in it.

'But he wants to kidnap Dagmar!' Vera whispers, peering over at the bed where her sister's still asleep.

A creeping feeling of unease spreads through Nina. The old people can be so convincing sometimes. Vera's obviously imagining this intruder, but her fear is real.

'He'll have to go through me,' Nina says, as gently as she can. 'Now try to rest and I'll bring your breakfast in in a minute.'

When she turns to leave, Dagmar is sitting up in bed, too. Her eyes gleam in the gloom and watch her silently as she exits the room.

Nina thinks she can hear rattling laughter as she shuts the door. She walks back up the hallway and calls out for Johanna. No reply. She stops outside D6, where the mop is still leaning against the wall, then opens the door as quietly as she can, in case Monika's asleep.

But Monika's lying in bed with the lights on. There's a crossword puzzle on her thighs. She turns to Nina when she enters.

'Hello, sweetheart,' she says.

Nina takes a seat in the armchair and studies her. Tries not to get her hopes up.

'Hi,' she says. 'Do you remember me?'

Monika chuckles and puts her pen down, closes the magazine.

'Of course I do. You're little Nina, though I suppose you're all grown up now.'

Nina nods. Tears burn in the corners of her eyes.

'I suppose I am,' she says.

Monika tilts her head to the side and smiles warmly.

She's Monika again.

It's not going to last. It never does for people sick enough to end up at Pineshade. But right now, she's here.

'I'm so happy to see you,' Monika says. 'It's been so long since you came to visit.'

'Yes,' Nina says.

'Come closer so I can have a look at you.'

Nina stands up and Monika fumbles around for her hand; Nina takes it. Squeezes it gently.

Her touch sends the tears trickling down Nina's cheeks; she wipes them with her free hand.

'Oh, sweetheart, don't cry,' Monika says.

'I'm sorry I've not been in touch all these years,' Nina says.

'You were busy with your own family,' Monika says. 'I understand.'

'But I . . .'

'You've done more than enough for us. You were always so kind and capable. And so good for Joel. I always felt safe when he was with you.'

Nina tries to smile, but new tears well up instead.

'Sweetheart,' Monika says, looking on the verge of tears herself. 'Why are you so sad? Did something happen?'

Nina shakes her head.

'I just didn't realise how much I've missed you,' she says.

The shame is almost unbearable when she thinks about all the times she has seen Monika at a distance and avoided her.

'I'm sorry,' she says again.

'You have nothing to apologise for,' Monika says firmly. 'You did what you had to do.'

She pats Nina's hand and lets go of it.

'I was going to get up and make breakfast,' Monika says. 'What would you like?'

She makes as if to get out of bed then stops and stares bewildered at the guard rail.

'You stay here,' Nina says. 'I'll see to it.'

'You're a good girl,' Monika says. She leans back against her pillows and closes her eyes. 'I'm actually feeling a bit tired.'

'I'll be right back,' Nina says.

Monika doesn't reply. She has already drifted off.

Nina watches her for a minute, then carefully dries her eyes and composes herself until she feels ready to leave the suite. Something shiny catches her eye as she turns around to leave.

A greasy spot on the wall next to the head of the bed. A few droplets have trickled down the wall, leaving faint grimy tracks in their wake.

She exits the suite, carries the bucket back to the cleaning cupboard and fetches a rag and all-purpose cleaner. She's on her way back to D6 when she hears someone in the staffroom.

'Johanna?' she says, and walks over.

But it's Sucdi, who spots Nina in the middle of a yawn. She covers her mouth and gives her a quick smile.

'Morning,' she says. 'I'm sorry I'm a bit late.'

The coffee machine slurps and hisses.

'Don't worry about it,' Nina says. 'Have you seen Johanna?'

'No, but I just talked to Faisal. He said Johanna left here around four.'

Nina stares at her. Sucdi nods.

'Johanna asked him to keep an eye on our ward, too. Then she just took off.'

Anger swells in Nina. Elisabeth shouldn't let all these young, inexperienced girls work here. They definitely shouldn't be left alone with the old people at night. They have no idea of the responsibility involved. They can't fathom it. But clearly they're also the only ones who apply for the jobs and who are willing to accept the paltry pay.

'What was her excuse this time?'

'She didn't give one,' Sucdi says.

'Well, that's new, I guess. I suppose she realised there *was* no excuse.'

'Faisal said she looked shaken. She didn't even change before leaving.'

Nina snorts derisively. She knows the home can feel creepy at night, but leaving the old people—

leaving Monika

—like this is simply unforgiveable.

'It's Petrus' turn to shower today,' Sucdi says turning to the coffee machine. 'Did you bring your ear plugs?'

Joel

The rain beats against the roof of the car while Joel reads the email from his brother on his phone. Björn has sent a list of all the things he wants from the house. The crystal glasses their parents had been given as a wedding present. The East India china they collected over the years. The silver jugs from Joel's great-grandparents.

These are things that were still in use when Dad was alive, so they have emotional significance for me. And you don't have twelve guests over for dinner a lot, do you?

He's right; Joel doesn't give a toss about the china or the glasses or the rest of it, but he's not blind to the fact that Björn only seems to see emotional significance in the few items that are worth any money.

Joel shoves the phone back into his pocket, opens the car door and dashes across the Pineshade carpark. The smell of wet asphalt is warm and heavy. His jeans become stippled with rain in seconds and big drops trickle down his back. He jumps over a big puddle at the bottom of the front steps and heaves himself into the lobby the moment the doors slide open, then rings the bell for the D Ward.

'We'll set you up with a swipe card so you don't have to keep ringing the bell,' Elisabeth says as soon as she opens the door.

An almost imperceptible hint of tension mars her cheerful smile. *So you don't have to keep ringing the bell, disturbing us.*

He hears music from somewhere. An acoustic guitar. A chaotic chorus of elderly voices.

The wet soles of his Converses squeak against the vinyl floor. Joel pulls off his sweatshirt as he follows Elisabeth to the office where he first met her. Low bookshelves groan under the weight of binders. The visitors' chairs are upholstered in a green, itchy fabric. A framed Mickey Mouse poster by Lasse Åberg is the only decoration.

Joel's handed a white plastic card and Elisabeth puts a form in front of him, pointing to the line where she wants a signature.

'Thank you,' Joel says. 'I should have come by to sort this out on the first day. It's just been . . . a lot.'

'Of course,' Elisabeth says. 'Did you write that letter about your mother?'

'No, I'm sorry.'

Elisabeth's displeasure is palpable now. He thanks her again and goes back to the D Ward corridor. The singing grows increasingly loud as he approaches the common room.

Joel peeks in and sees a man sitting on a stool in the atrium. Messy blond hair hides his face when he looks down at the strings. His fingers are long and thin, his forearms tanned. The room is virtually packed; a sea of white heads. It must be residents from all four units. Joel notices Lillemor's ecstatic smile. She's rocking back and forth with her hands folded at her chest.

Joel's eyes scan the crowd for his mother. From time to time, they linger on the bloke with the guitar, on his hands with those long, thin fingers.

It has been so long since someone touched him.

He spots his mother at one of the tables. She's laughing with Nina, their heads close together. Joel feels something that's not quite jealousy and not quite sadness. It's a feeling he's familiar with – Nina was always able to talk to his mum in a way he wasn't. As though they shared a native tongue, while he and his mother had to communicate in a language neither one of them mastered fully.

Nina's eyes are the same shade of blue as the Pineshade uniforms. She looks younger than she did yesterday; the tension is gone from her face and body language.

Joel considers heading down to his mother's suite and waiting for her there, but that would be too pathetic. He pushes his way into the common room, where he watches toothless mouths singing and bodies swaying back and forth in wheelchairs. Several of the old people are clapping along. The bloke with the guitar has moved on to a new song without Joel noticing. Joel gets the feeling the old people have waited a long time to hear this one. Only one of them looks unhappy. She's the tiniest woman he's ever seen, fragile and birdlike. She's clutching a raggedy stuffed animal to her chest and seems to be talking to it under her breath.

Nina looks up when Joel reaches the table. Her eyes are cold and hard like sledgehammers. He's shocked to realise how much she hates him.

He always figured she'd be ashamed if they ever met again. That she'd ask him for forgiveness. But in her narrative, he's the villain.

He saved me from you.

'Joel!' his mum exclaims happily.

'I can come back later if you're busy,' he says, glancing furtively at Nina.

'Don't be silly,' his mum replies. 'Let's go to my room, it's very loud here.'

Nina's face is expressionless. His mother pats her cheek and stands up. Joel walks out of the common room ahead of her, wondering if Nina is watching him go.

The chorus starts again. The bloke looks up from his guitar and smiles at his enthusiastic audience. He's a lot younger than Joel thought. Far too young.

He's relieved to step out into the hallway.

'Do you want me to close the door?' Joel says as they enter his mum's suite.

'Oh no. I don't mind hearing it.'

Joel sits down on the sofa and tries to think of something to say.

'Did you sleep okay last night?'

'I think so. I don't remember, so I suppose I must have.'

She smiles. The sound of the opening chords of a new song he can't place drift in from the corridor.

'I'm sleeping so much better now I know Nils is back,' his mum says.

Joel looks over at the door.

'Is Dad here now?' he says.

'No. Can't you tell?'

Joel nods. His mum doesn't seem offended. Her face is mild and dreamy. Contented.

'Where is he?' Joel says. 'When he's not here, I mean?'

His mum seems to ponder that.

'He's sleeping,' she says. 'He's still weak. He needs to build up his strength.'

Joel wonders what the next step is if she's going to insist on keeping Dad as her imaginary friend. Are they going to have tea parties? Put out a little plate of biscuits for him?

He stifles a nervous giggle. Focuses on the song echoing down the corridor. He remembers it now. An old pop song from his youth. *Like fever in my heart, your love has got me burning. I'm dying when we're apart, on fever clouds of yearning.* The old people sing along, but less enthusiastically now.

Joel studies the intarsia on the back of the sofa, identical to the one on Mum's bed back at the house. He thinks about his grandfather, whom he never knew either. Mum lost both her dad and her husband in the space of a couple of years, and was left alone with two young children.

He suddenly understands how hard that must have been for her. Intellectually speaking, he's always known, of course. But now, for the first time, he *feels* it.

His mum watches his eyes trace the pattern in the wood.

'It wasn't easy for Father to keep up the carpentry towards the end,' she says. 'You should have seen his fingers.'

She curls her own fingers to demonstrate.

'I was always worried the two of you would inherit his bad joints,' she goes on thoughtfully. 'I suppose it's different nowadays. There are drugs for everything. Do you know what they did to him when he was still living up north? Back then, he lugged timber. Sick leave was unheard of. He had to ride his bike all the way from Hocksjön to the hospital in Östersund, where they'd break his joints back into place.'

Joel has never heard this story. A wave of nausea washes over him as he imagines the cracking sounds.

'And then he had to ride his bike all the way back again,' his mum concludes with a sigh.

'Is that true?' Joel hears himself ask.

His mum shoots him an impatient look.

'Are you implying I'm lying to you? He was a few years past

thirty then, my father was. It was after that he and Mother decided to go south.'

She shakes her head.

'They had nothing to live off up there, such poverty. Imagine. When they got down here, they'd never seen running water indoors. Isn't that incredible?'

They're back on well-trodden paths now. His grandparents' poverty has always been part of Joel's life, the constant backdrop for his mother's admonitions not to waste food, not to complain, not to forget how lucky he was.

Suddenly, his mum gives a start and looks over at the door. A smile spreads across her face.

'I will,' she says eagerly, looking back at Joel. 'Your dad's here now.'

Joel waits. Hears the singing stop in the common room. The rain is still pattering against the window.

'Nils wants to thank you,' his mum says.

Joel looks at her uncertainly.

'For what?'

'Nils is so happy we moved here,' his mum says. 'He feels the house was too lonely.'

Joel feels a flicker of hope in his chest. He realises his mum's really talking about herself, even if she's unaware of it. Her imaginary husband's like a mirror she's holding up to herself. 'Nils' tells her what she's feeling.

'Is that right?' Joel says.

His mum nods firmly.

'He likes being able to visit the other residents. He's already made new friends.'

Joel looks at the door and smiles at the coats hanging next to it.

'That's great,' he says. 'I'm so happy for him.'

Nina

'You have to help me call Mummy and Daddy. They have to come get me. I'm calling and calling, but they're not picking up.'

Wiborg strokes her dementia cat harder and harder. She's holding it in front of her mouth and is speaking so softly Nina has to bend down to hear her over the music. Adrian has started singing 'Änglahund', which is usually his grand finale.

Nina glances over at D corridor. She's still shaken from seeing Joel again.

'I'm so lonely. Everyone's having fun except me.'

The muffled voice trembles.

'You're not alone, Wiborg. You have a granddaughter. Her name's Fredrika. She comes to see you almost every day.'

Wiborg shoots Nina an incredulous look.

'She does?'

'She does.'

Wiborg's hand stops stroking, resting on the raggedy fur.

'I have a granddaughter?'

'You do. She said she would come by today, too.'

'Then I have to have something for her to eat,' Wiborg says, panic-stricken. 'How would it look if I don't?'

'It'll be okay,' Nina says. 'Fredrika usually brings something. She's so sweet to you. I can tell you mean a lot to her.'

Wiborg looks reassured for the moment. Nina pats her shoulder and glances over the D corridor again. No sign of Joel.

The song ends and Adrian stands up from his stool.

'That's all folks,' he says with a deep bow.

Bodil coos and flutters her eyelashes in her wheelchair, fiddling with the alarm button hanging around her throat on a lanyard as though it were a precious piece of jewellery.

'Isn't he dashing?' she says to Lillemor. 'I think he's handsomer than Elvis.'

Adrian puts the guitar down and helps one of the old ladies from B Ward back to her corridor. Bodil gazes after him longingly. Above them, the rain picks up against the glass ceiling. The shadows of the droplets form patterns on the walls.

Nina's surrounded by happy faces. The sing-along is the highlight of the week for many of the residents. Memories of who they used to be resurface and the effect can last for hours afterward. It's usually one of the week's highlights for Nina, too. But Joel has ruined it.

She can't bear the thought of having to bump into him all the time. Of never knowing when he's going to pop up next. She just can't. And she realises there's a solution. Johanna might have done her a favour after all.

Nina leaves the common room and glances over at the open door to D6 before going the other way.

Anna hurries after her in her red beret, waving eagerly.

'It's pretty chilly out today,' she pants, and tugs at Nina's arm.

'You think so?' Nina replies automatically.

'Yes, indeed, but I had to try to catch a glimpse of the Queen since she's come to visit. She's not as stuck up as I would have thought.'

'I'm glad to hear it.'

'Yes, the Queen was very pleased to see that so many had come.'

Nina looks down the hallway impatiently.

'But she left when she found out this place is haunted,' Anna says. 'I tried to tell her it's no wonder we have ghosts, considering how many people die here. But the new one who just moved in is different. He doesn't belong here.'

'Is that right,' Nina says.

'Haven't you noticed?'

There's a scraping of chairs in the common room. Nina has to be quick so Sucdi isn't left alone with the elderly for too long.

'I'm sure it'll be fine,' she says.

Anna nods, looking thoughtful.

'I've always said it's important to marry someone with a sense of humour. I hope she and the king have a good time together. It's vital, don't you think?'

Nina pushes down a sudden thought of Markus. When did they last laugh together? When did she last laugh at all?

The way I used to laugh with Joel.

'I have to go,' she says.

'Yes, busy times,' Anna says, and waves. 'Take care.'

Nina promises she will. She hurries down the hallway and turns left, then knocks on the ward director's door before opening it.

Elisabeth looks up and nods, though she turns her attention back to the pile of documents in front of her, quickly signing the bottom corners of the pages. Nina takes a seat in one of the visitors' chairs and waits until Elisabeth puts her pen down and fastidiously gathers all the papers into a neat pile before looking up again.

'What can I do for you?'

'I heard Johanna just took off last night,' Nina says. 'I know it's difficult to find staff, but we can't have an employee who—'

She cuts off when Elisabeth waves her hand dismissively.

'Johanna won't be coming back.'

'No?' Nina says.

Ridiculously, she's disappointed. She'd gone in ready to fight for her cause.

'That's good,' she continues. 'Faisal can't look after two units by himself; Johanna really dropped him in it. Anything could have happened.'

She sounds far too ardent.

'Well, either way, no need to dwell,' Elisabeth replies. 'Johanna texted me early this morning, saying she can't work here anymore.'

So it had been Johanna's decision.

'Now I just need to find a replacement,' Elisabeth says.

'That's what I wanted to talk to you about. I can take the night shifts. That would make it easier for you to figure out the day schedule.'

Elisabeth shakes her head.

'I can't justify paying a trained nurse that much extra,' she says. 'I was going to ask Sucdi if she wouldn't mind working nights until we can find someone . . .'

'She and Faisal have the children. It would mean losing someone who can work nights in B instead.'

Elisabeth frowns. She's not convinced.

'You were right before,' Nina says, though it pains her. 'We need the money now that Markus is unemployed. It won't make that much of a difference to your budget; it's only until you find someone new. But it will make a big difference to us. We can't even afford to go on holiday.'

Elisabeth's face softens. She loves feeling like a good Samaritan.

'It's hard to find people willing to work nights in the summer,' she says. 'And it's almost the midsummer weekend, too.'

Nina waits obediently.

'Can you start tonight?' Elisabeth asks.

Joel

Yet another sleepless night. But for once, Joel's okay with it. His mum's progress at Pineshade has given him a burst of energy. He has started to clear out the basement and the car is full of rubbish he's disposing of tomorrow. Now, he's standing in front of the slant-top desk in the living room. Back when Mum was still with it, the desk was the only place where chaos was allowed to reign. It was where she put anything she didn't know what to do with. Joel pulls out the drawers one by one, filling a bin bag with rulers, rubber bands, dried-up glue sticks, stray paper clips, long-expired coupons, charity Easter and Christmas cards that will never be sent.

Joel squats down to open the bottom drawer and spots a lumpy manila envelope with his name on it.

He opens it and pulls out the contents. The first thing he sees is a yellowed evening paper clipping he instantly recognises. His and Nina's gig at The Studio is number two on the Hot or Not list. They'd heard she'd be in the audience, and he was so nervous he'd snorted the entire stash he'd bought from Katja. The rest of the night is a blank. It was his fifteen minutes of fame and he doesn't even remember it. Joel stares at the brief paragraph. Nina and he had screamed when they opened the paper.

Had Nina been as ecstatic as he, or had she been playacting?

And when they called from the record label?

He hadn't sensed any hesitation in her when they talked about the future. Quite the opposite. And in hindsight, he wonders if that should have been a red flag. Nina always worried about everything.

Joel puts the clipping down and picks up other ones from various music magazines that mention their demo. More neatly folded pages about their song 'Grand Guignol'.

And underneath that, their demo. Recorded on a portable in Katja's tiny home studio. Joel used the double cassette deck in his stereo to make copies. He cut and pasted a cover that Nina then secretly copied in the school office. BABYDUST sprawled across the front in large letters. Him and Nina, looking solemn in a picture taken with a timer in the middle of the night on Skräddar Island. The flash makes their faces look washed out. All that's left are lined eyes, nostrils, the shadows of cheekbones. Both are bleach blonde. Nina's Courtney Love, she's Patricia Arquette in *True Romance*. An old-fashioned film star who has ended up in the gutter. He has a cigarette between his lips and is squinting against the smoke. His clothes are black, as ever, so his face seems to hover, unattached, in the dark.

Joel takes the cassette out, looks at the back of the cover. He cut the letters from different papers to make the song titles look like a blackmail note. 'I Will Take You Home'. 'Watershed'. 'At the Foot of His Bed'. 'Grand Guignol'.

He puts the cassette back in its case and doesn't even consider listening to it. He threw away his own copies a long time ago. He keeps going through the stack and comes across their interview in the local paper, the one that made everyone at school talk even more behind their backs. Joel looks into his own teenage eyes in the picture. There's a glowing cigarette in his hands and his pupils are so large his eyes look black. Nina's looking at him, laughing. She'd hated that picture. But, then, Nina invariably hated any picture of herself.

Joel finds more loose sheets of paper, torn from various fanzines they sent their demo to. Flyers for their gig at The Studio. When he finally reaches the bottom of the pile, he stays on the floor, dazed.

His mum never commented on the clippings he gave her. Never said a word about their music. And yet she has saved all these things.

Nina

There's half an hour left of the night shift and Nina has just finished the last inspection round. She's writing reports for the morning staff. Flags that Anna has a cough and Petrus is developing a bed sore on his right buttock. Nina's scalp still smarts at the temple when she gingerly touches it with her fingertips. Petrus grabbed her hair and tried to pull her into bed with him when she put a pillow under his hip.

She lowers her hand and continues to write. Vera has a new fungal infection, and is still scared to enter the bathroom in D8 because she's sure someone's hiding in it. Dagmar refused to drink her nutrition drink; Nina suspects her dementia is so far gone she has difficulty swallowing.

The pen stops moving when Nina hears a scraping sound from the hallway. She looks up and listens intently, but all she hears is the rain against the glass ceiling in the common room. She resumes writing. Lillemor has been having trouble sleeping; she's all atwitter about a guardian angel having come to Pineshade. Monika slept through the night. Bodil tried to open the window so her admirer could get in so Nina gave her Oxazepam.

Another scraping sound. This time, Nina's sure. A shadow flits past the doorway as she looks up.

'Hello?'

No answer.

She stands up resolutely and walks out into the corridor only to realise the fluorescent lights are flickering, making it look like shadows are sidling along the walls.

The storm is wreaking havoc with the power again. Nina stares at the flickering lights until her head begins to hurt. She walks over to the common room. The light from the fluorescents in B Ward on the other side of it is steady. She spots Faisal, but he doesn't notice her waving.

Nina's just about to go back to the staffroom when she hears sobbing from D1. Wiborg is curled up at the head of her bed, clutching the receiver of her phone.

'How are you feeling, Wiborg?'

Wiborg turns to her. The lower half of her face looks deflated, as though it's been punctured. Her dentures are sitting in a glass of water on her bedside table.

'I call and call, but Mum and Dad aren't picking up,' she says, her mouth sounding sticky and dehydrated. 'And I'm so scared . . .'

Nina hands her a beaker with watered down lingonberry squash and tries to coax her to drink. Wiborg shakes her head, staring at the phone in her hands.

'How old am I?' she asks.

Nina strokes her shoulder.

'You're almost ninety-five.'

Wiborg looks unhappy.

'It's your birthday soon,' Nina says, hoping that might distract her. 'It's on Midsummer's Eve this year, so we're going to have an extra big party.'

'Ninety-five. Am I really that old? But that means Mum and Dad are . . .' Wiborg starts counting on her fingers. 'No. That's impossible. They're gone, aren't they? They're dead? Is that why they're not picking up?'

Nina nods gently. Wiborg's face contorts and she starts wailing inconsolably.

'Why didn't anyone tell me?'

A string of saliva trickles out of her toothless mouth.

Tomorrow, Wiborg will have forgotten this. But she will remember again. And each time, it's like she's receiving the news for the first time.

'But Fredrika stops by almost every day,' Nina says. 'Your granddaughter.'

'I have a granddaughter?'

'Yes. And she's pregnant. Her belly's really big now,' Nina says, hoping it might trigger a memory. 'You're going to be a great-grandmother.'

Wiborg shakes her head.

'Why doesn't anyone ever tell me anything in this place?'

Nina fetches tissues and helps Wiborg blow her nose.

'You should go to sleep now. Fredrika said she'll come by tomorrow. You don't want to be tired when she's here, do you?'

She pries the receiver out of Wiborg's hands and manages to make her take the beaker. While Wiborg drinks, Nina fluffs up her pillows.

'I could have baked something if I'd known I had guests coming,' Wiborg mutters and lies down. 'Will you stay until I fall asleep?'

Nina promises, grateful it's a quiet night.

She sits by Wiborg's bed for so long she starts to nod off herself. When Wiborg's chin drops onto her chest, Nina goes back out into the hallway. The overhead lights have stopped flickering. She checks her watch. The morning staff will be here any minute.

She has almost reached the staffroom when she realises it is dark inside.

The lights in the staffroom are never off. She reaches for the switch she has never used before and flicks it tentatively. Her heart skips a beat when the lights turn on and she looks into a pair of staring eyes.

Monika is sitting at the table. The binder with the reports is still open, seemingly untouched.

Nina's heart is racing, as if to make up for the skipped beat. One corner of Monika's mouth curls up into a crooked smile that looks strange on her face.

'Well, well, if it isn't little Nina?' she says.

The alarm. Why didn't the motion sensor go off when she got out of bed?

'Come on,' Nina says, and holds out a hand. 'We'd better get you back home.'

The power. It must be the power messing with the alarms. Must remember to put that in the report.

Monika glances at her outstretched hand. There's a flash of amusement in her eyes.

'Back home?' she says. 'I remember when you preferred my home to yours. You clung to me like nothing I've ever seen before. Not even my own children.'

Nina lets her hand fall. Monika's voice sounds different. It's darker, and seems to be coming from somewhere deep inside her, as though she is hollow.

'You were so anxious for me to like you,' Monika presses on, laughing hoarsely. 'You were like a puppy, wagging your tail, almost drooling whenever I let you help out . . . We barely had time to finish our food before you started washing up . . .' Her voice grows darker still as she goes on. 'You were a real pain,' she says. 'A cuckoo trying to force its way into our nest.'

Nina's face turns cold.

It's not her. It's the dementia. She doesn't know what she's saying.

Monika cocks one eyebrow, as though she can hear her thoughts.

'No wonder your own mother had to drink to put up with you,' she says. 'I know all about it now. I've talked to her. In here.' Monika taps her temple. 'She's not happy with you, let me tell you.'

Nina's mother died a long time ago. She was cremated and buried in a cemetery in Lycke. Every year, Nina puts flowers on her grave on Christmas, her birthday, Mother's Day and All Saints' Day. Lights a candle and says the Lord's Prayer, even though she doesn't think anyone's listening.

Monika never knew her mother. And they definitely haven't been talking now.

'Come on, let's go back to bed,' Nina manages.

Monika blinks, as if she has just woken up from a dream. She looks at the corridor behind Nina.

'Good morning,' Rita says as she enters. 'Are you two having a little chat?'

Nina can only nod, afraid her voice will fail her if she tries to speak.

Monika watches them with empty eyes. Present and not present.

'Is everything okay?' Rita asks, looking inquiringly at Nina.

Nina smiles wanly. Clears her throat. 'Maybe you could help Monika back to her room?'

Rita checks the clock on the wall. The morning shift started a few minutes ago. It's her job now, not Nina's.

'Sure. Though I wouldn't have minded a cup of coffee first,' she sighs, and walks over to Monika, who obediently gets up from the table.

Nina watches her.

It's the dementia. Nothing more to it than that.

She knows how she would console a loved one: what a person with dementia says doesn't necessarily correspond to what they actually feel. It's a myth that dementia makes a person's true self come out unvarnished.

But it's harder to tell herself that. *A cuckoo.* Is that what Monika thought of her all that time? Or did Joel plant that thought in Monika's head? Have they been talking about her, laughing at her?

Monika turns in the doorway and stares at Nina with that strange smile before she and Rita disappear down the corridor.

Joel

A beggar jingles the coins in his paper cup outside the liquor store. Joel digs through his pockets but finds no cash, and makes an apologetic gesture without looking the beggar in the eyes.

He continues to avoid meeting anyone's gaze as he walks up and down the aisles, wanting to minimise the risk of having to talk to someone he knows. Someone from school, or some old acquaintance of his mother's. *How is she these days? Pineshade? Oh dear.* Joel doesn't need to look around for the boxed wine. He's been here often enough to know exactly where he's going.

He's reaching for a box of Riesling when someone sidles up to him. He can smell smoke and damp hair, hear the creaking of a leather jacket. A hand with chipped, blood-red nail polish touches his elbow.

'So, you're back in town?'

He reluctantly turns to her and studies the upturned face. Katja barely reaches his chest.

'Looks that way,' he says. 'How are you?'

'Can't complain.'

She's older now. Her lipstick has seeped into the smoker's wrinkles above her top lip, like red spikes along her cupid's bow. Other than that, she looks the same. Still Katja.

'I didn't think I'd ever see you around again,' she says.

‘I’m here to sell the house. Mum’s moved into Pineshade.’

‘That’s rough.’

‘Yeah. The real estate agent’s coming by this afternoon.’

They say nothing for a while.

‘I had a mate who ended up at Pineshade when he was just fifty,’ she says. ‘It was the booze. They call it Cossack’s disease, I think.’

Joel doesn’t bother to correct her. Doesn’t want to get into a discussion that will inevitably remind him of the details of Korsakoff Syndrome. Especially not while buying alcohol. *A particular form of dementia almost always caused by chronic alcohol abuse.* Joel stumbled across a link to the Wikipedia entry when he was trying to understand what dementia really is.

‘Well, it’s good to see you,’ he says, and takes the box off the shelf.

‘You look better than when I last saw you,’ Katja says.

At first, he thinks she’s making fun of him. But the last time they met was when he was back for his mother’s sixty-fifth birthday. His hair was shaved and he had a full-body rash. He’d weighed even less than in high school. His mum cried when she saw him. Joel had promised himself to stay clean while he was back home, but he’d been knocking on Katja’s door before his mum’s birthday party was even over.

‘Have you stopped partying?’ she says.

And he knows exactly what she means by *partying*.

‘Yes,’ he replies, and starts walking towards the tills.

‘Shame,’ she says, and follows him, picking up a couple of bottles of gin on the way.

They both light cigarettes the moment they step out onto the street. Katja sticks her hand into the pocket of her jeans and pulls out a rumpled note that she gives to the beggar. Then she points towards the side street where her record shop used to be.

'There's a fucking raw food café there now. Just what the world needs more of, am I right?' Katja puffs angrily on her cigarette. 'But then again, considering what they play on the radio these days, I'm happy I don't have to peddle the shit.'

Joel has to smile. 'You hated everything they played on the radio back in the nineties, too,' he says.

'It's worse now,' Katja sneers.

'Worse than Ace of Base?'

She grins. Flicks the filter with her thumbnail so the ash falls onto the pavement. 'Even worse than that fucking "I Will Always Love You",' she says.

Joel finds himself laughing. But Katja is suddenly serious.

'At least there were alternatives back then. The kinds of things you and Nina listened to. What alternatives do the kids have now?'

She grimaces. Joel has no doubt the world is full of amazing new music, but he knows nothing about it. He signed up for a streaming service and was so overwhelmed by the infinite number of options he didn't know where to begin.

They stand in silence for a minute. Joel drops his half-finished cigarette on the ground and grinds it under his heel, shifting the wine to his other hand.

'It was good seeing you. I have to go now.'

'Give me your phone. I'll give you my new number.'

Joel can't say no. He'll just have to erase it later. Katja snatches the phone out of his hand and snaps a selfie while blowing smoke rings at the camera. Then she grins and carefully types in her number.

'There,' she says, handing it back. 'In case you change your mind.'

Joel watches her walk down the hill with her clinking bag.

His thumb hovers over DELETE CONTACT. But he locks the screen instead and slips the phone back into his pocket.

In case you change your mind.

Pineshade

Lunch is almost over at Pineshade. The common room is emptying. Wiborg is still eating. Spearing teeny, tiny bites with her fork. Chewing with only her front teeth. Rita glares at her in silent fury. *Come on*, she thinks. *Hurry up so I can go have a smoke.* Wiborg painstakingly pulls a tiny sliver of potato out of the gloopy salad and cuts it in two. Rita wants to strangle her.

Vera is struggling to make Dagmar eat. She holds a spoon up to her firmly shut mouth. Dagmar grunts angrily.

'Yes, I know,' Vera tells her. 'They're always on about how dangerous salt is these days, but must they make the food so bland? Try this now.'

Monika and Anna are sitting at the other end of the long table with a box of crayons between them. Anna is drawing a princess with long, yellow hair, waving from a tower. Monika's pink paper is still blank. She's supposed to make a sign for her door. She's clutching a blue crayon and her hand's trembling. Anna looks up at her from time to time, smiling encouragingly.

Lillemor breaks into song in her suite. The door is open and her shrill voice echoes down D corridor. *Joy to the world, the Lord is come.* She's walking among her angels. Touching their full cheeks. The colour has worn off in places from countless previous caresses. Lillemor thinks about the angel that has come to the home to watch over them all. Her prayers and praise have drawn him here. *Let Earth receive her King.*

Out in the common room, Rita listens to her singing. She vaguely recognises it from when her sons attended playtime at the church in Lycke. The melody brings back the smell of candles and wooden pews.

Petrus is waking up in his wheelchair in front of the TV in the lounge. Looks around angrily, but there's no one around.

'Shut up!' he bellows. 'Shut up, you fucking whore!'

Monika puts the crayon to her paper. The letters come out big, uneven. Her hand moves faster and faster. She's in a hurry. Anna watches her, looking at the paper and trying to understand what it says.

'You're doing it wrong,' she says. 'You're supposed to write your name.'

In her room, Lillemor closes her eyes, and lets the Lord's light fill her, turning her vocal cords into a golden trumpet. *Let every heart, prepare him room.*

Dagmar suddenly smiles. Her mouth opens and she closes her wrinkled lips around the spoon, chewing loudly.

'Good, Dagmar,' Vera says. 'You have to eat.'

Dagmar laughs silently and spits the food back out. It dribbles into the pocket of her bib. Wiborg averts her eyes and puts her cutlery down.

'I'm sorry, Miss, but I don't think I can eat any more,' she says in a tiny voice.

Rita stands up abruptly and picks up her plate. She's going outside for a fag now. Dagmar's laugh turns into a coughing fit. She's too weak to cough properly; it's more like a series of loud moans.

They can hear Lillemor start the hymn over from the top. Even louder now. Petrus is just about to shout again when the TV flickers. The picture warps and turns into a black-and-white grid. He reckons he can make out a naked woman, smiling at him. He forgets about the singing and leans forwards in his wheelchair as far as his seatbelt allows, squinting.

Monika hurls the crayon across the room, slaps her hand down on the paper and crumples it up. The bang makes Anna jump and her princess's smiling mouth ends up outside her face. Monika tears off a piece of her paper with her teeth. She chews quickly, swallows and tears off another piece. Pink pulp, soggy with saliva, fills her mouth until she has swallowed all of it, with great difficulty. The rest of the paper disappears into her mouth. Her cheeks balloon. She struggles to breathe through her nose while her jaw works.

The sound of Lillemor's singing trails off.

Sucdi enters the common room and realises Monika is choking. She runs over and takes a beating from Monika's flailing fists as she digs around the chewing mouth, while Anna watches them anxiously.

'He's angry now,' she says.

Sucdi manages to pull out the last lump of paper. Monika glares at her, then relaxes. Her eyes become vacant and expressionless; her mouth goes slack. It happens so quickly it reminds Sucdi of when the batteries run out in one of her children's toys.

Dagmar is rocking back and forth in her wheelchair, and Monika moves like a sleepwalker when Sucdi leads her back to D6; she doesn't react when Lillemor's head pops out when they approach her door.

'The angel's here again,' she says. 'My song drew him. Can you feel it? He likes it here.'

Sucdi nods. 'I can see why he would,' she says.

Monika turns to her with eyes that seem alive once more. 'But it's not good enough for your father,' she says. 'He'd rather go back than end up here.'

'How do you know that?' Sucdi blurts out before she can stop herself, staring at her.

Monika just grins. It's a smile that makes Sucdi want to let go of her thin arm and back away, to put some distance between Monika's face and her own.

Back in the common room, Anna gets up from the table and tilts her head to look at the glass ceiling. It's going to be a lovely day, but she wants to go home. The ghost is back. She looks uncertainly at the corridors framing the common room. Paris is lovely, but there are so many backstreets around this square. They've moved everything around again. She picks a direction at random. It doesn't matter. She usually finds someone who can show her the way.

'You smell like wee again,' she cheerfully tells Wiborg as she passes her.

Wiborg starts to cry, silently.

* * *

Sucdi finds Rita in the staffroom and tells her she's taking a quick break. Rita nods, annoyed, because she knows what Sucdi's going to do on her break.

'Maybe I should become religious, too,' she mutters. 'I barely have time to step out for a cigarette.'

Sucdi looks at her. 'And what were you doing just now, when Monika almost choked?' she says. 'I thought you were supposed to be keeping an eye on them.'

She doesn't wait for a reply, just goes down to the changing room in the basement. She tries not to think about Rita, about what Monika said about her dad, about her hunger. It's Ramadan and she hasn't eaten since sunrise. She quickly rinses off and changes into her one-piece prayer outfit.

How did Monika know?

Sucdi tries to clear her mind while she rolls out her prayer rug on the floor, tries to let go of everything that happens at Pineshade, if only for a moment.

Nina

The rain has stopped, but the clouds act as a lid, keeping the humid air from escaping. She's sitting in the front garden, drinking her coffee. Markus still hasn't mowed the lawn; it smells warm and moist, like a living creature.

Nina slept so lightly after coming home from Pineshade after the night shift that the rain pattering against the windows became part of her dream.

Daniel was screaming from his room as though he was being torn to pieces. He was little again. He needed her. She tried to run up the stairs, but her legs wouldn't obey; they were numb, weak; she could barely lift her feet. And the screaming grew louder and louder. Somehow, she made it up to his room and the rain was hammering against the windows, but when she turned on the lights Daniel didn't react. His eyes were wide open but unseeing. He was waving his fists about, fighting for his life against something she couldn't see. His screams were growing intermittent. Punctuated by ragged inhalations. Nina held his arms pinned to his sides in an embrace. Whispered soothing words in his ear to calm him down. Kissed his damp, blond locks until she woke up.

The doctors tried to tell her it was nothing to worry about. They had a name for it. *Night terrors.* Far worse than nightmares and no one really knew what they were. Nina is just thankful

Daniel never remembered any details afterwards. She was the one who couldn't sleep at night because she'd lie in bed waiting for him to start screaming. His night terrors filled her nights with terror, too.

Nina's phone rings in her dressing gown pocket. She pulls it out and is disappointed to see Elisabeth's number. The ward director tells her she has found a new casual employee who might be able to start immediately after Midsummer. Nina can keep working nights until then.

They end the call. Nina closes her eyes and turns towards the sun. Midsummer's a week away. Hopefully, Joel will have left by then and everything will go back to normal.

She should be planning the dinner party she and Markus are throwing on Midsummer's Eve, making a to-do list. Put her mind to work at something useful instead.

Her phone rings again. Daniel's name on the screen. Finally.

'Hi, sweetheart!' she says, far too enthusiastically.

She can almost hear him rolling his eyes.

'Did something happen?' he asks. 'I had, like, a million missed calls.'

Nina contemplates telling him about her dream, but she would sound like an idiot.

'No, no, I just wanted to hear how you're doing. Are you okay?'

'I'm fine.'

'What are you up to?'

'I'm talking to you.'

She stifles an exasperated sigh. Why does he have to make things so difficult for both of them?

'You know what I mean,' she says, and clears her throat to rid her voice of that needy tone. 'How's the café?'

'It's fine. Not particularly busy. But I guess there are worse summer jobs.'

'Dad and I were thinking of stopping by sometime next week.'

'Okay.'

'How's the weather in Gothenburg?' she asks.

'It's hot.'

Judging by his tone, it requires a great deal of effort to deliver that terse reply.

He probably agrees with Monika. *A real pain.*

'Mmm,' she says. 'Here too. Though we did just have some rain.'

Nina tries to think of something that might interest him more than talking about the weather.

She remembers when Daniel screamed every night and sleep deprivation almost drove her insane. For the first time, she'd been afraid she'd made a terrible mistake having a child. How was she supposed to be a mother when she'd never learned how? Her own mother had been such a poor role model. Nina didn't know the rules, hadn't been given the manual everyone else had. The screaming little creature in her arms was more than a stranger, he was *alien*. In a way, he still is.

There were times she'd wanted to run away from it all.

'I have an acquaintance who has been admitted to Pineshade,' she says. 'Her son and I were best friends in high school.'

'Right.' Pause. 'So, how's Dad?'

'Fine, the usual.'

Her cheerful tone sounds so disingenuous. She would despise it, too.

A puppy that just wants to be loved.

You were practically drooling.

'No news about jobs or whatever?' Daniel says.

'No, not yet. But I'm sure it'll work out after the summer.'

'Okay. I have to go now.'

Her one consolation, and it's a shameful one, is that Daniel is as uninterested in Markus as he is in her. Maybe there's not something wrong with her.

'Thank you so much for calling.'

Far too needy.

'Sure,' Daniel replies.

He pauses, as if he's considering something.

'Hey, by the way,' he says.

'Yes?'

'Don't be offended or whatever, but I really prefer when you text me to when you leave messages on my voicemail. Listening to them just takes such a long time.'

Joel

'Can I get you some coffee? Water?' Joel offers, but the real estate agent declines with a fleeting smile, opens her briefcase and places a folder on the kitchen table.

Joel sits down across from her and realises he's already forgotten her name. He tries to visualise her email address, but draws a complete blank. She's in her fifties. Neatly dressed in a navy-blue suit, despite the heat. She doesn't look like someone who sweats.

The new table fan he bought in Kungälv is humming softly on the kitchen counter. Slowly turning back and forth, making the documents the real estate agent is spreading out on the table flutter intermittently.

She shows him similar properties she's sold in the area. He realises he's supposed to be impressed, but the truth is he's shocked.

'You can't even buy a studio flat in Stockholm for that,' he says, trying to strike a light-hearted note.

'I suppose not,' she replies, in a way that makes it clear she thinks he sounds arrogant.

'What I mean is, I know there are a lot of empty houses around here, but I figured . . . it's a sizeable plot, after all. Half an acre, that's not bad, right?'

'Well . . . At least it's well-maintained,' she says. 'If you're lucky, we can find someone who's interested in the land, even if they don't want to keep the house.'

It takes him a moment to understand what she's saying.

'You mean they'd tear it down?'

While he'd lived here, he wanted nothing more than to get away. And yet, the thought makes him sad.

'Would that be a problem for you?' the real estate agent says. 'Because, to be honest, I'm hoping to find a buyer who's looking to build a summer house. We're starting to see that kind of development around here. That's why this is a great time to sell. There's a lot of movement on the market.'

Joel shakes his head. 'I . . . no, that's fine.'

'Good, good,' she says.

He wonders whether he really had any say in the matter or if she's just relieved not to have to deal with hurt feelings.

She licks a finger and flips through her folder. 'I have the paperwork from the land registry,' she says, and hands Joel document after document.

Words like *title deed* and *lien* and *taxable value* flash by. He knows nothing about these things and should be asking questions, but instead he just sits there, nodding, as though he knows exactly what she's on about.

'And the barn is used for storage nowadays?' the real estate agent says.

'Yes.'

'Good, then the tax assessment should be correct . . .'

She slides him the business card of a property inspector, in case he wants to have an inspection carried out. A list of auctioneers in Gothenburg that could come out and appraise the estate. She opens the calendar on her phone and they decide that Monday after the Midsummer long weekend would be a good day for the photographer to come out and take pictures.

'But it's not like in Stockholm. Thankfully, if you ask me. We don't do home styling and things like that. Just tidy up a bit, like if you were having friends over.'

Joel nods again. 'And how does it work with Mum?' he asks. 'She can't stop the sale somehow?'

'Oh no. Since you're her guardian, you can sign the listing agreement and once we sell, all we need is the official go-ahead from the Office of the Public Guardian. That's never a problem.'

'And my brother, does he need to be involved somehow?'

'Not if you're her guardian.'

'He's much better at stuff like this,' Joel says. 'He should have been the one to sort this out.'

The agent gives him a bland smile. Joel glances down at the listing agreement, which she has placed at the top of the pile. She has already signed it, so at least now he can see what her name is. Lena Nordin. Next to her signature is the dotted line with his name and personal identity number. He wonders if he should have invited more real estate agents and compared what they had to say. But how big can the difference be when prices are so low? He doesn't want to waste any more time. Just wants all of this to be over. Wants his life back.

He signs on the dotted line.

'Okay then, I think that's all of it,' Lena Nordin says. 'Shall we have a look around?'

They take a tour of the house. Go through the rooms, which feel strangely dead. A body without a soul.

'My husband and I live on the other side of the manor now,' the agent says as they walk up the stairs. 'And our kids go to the Ytterby School. My goodness, when did we get so old . . .'

They reach his room and she looks around.

'Right, so this is where you grew up. Nice view of the mountain, that's good.'

She studies his posters. Scans the bookshelves still filled with eighties editions of Stephen King and Dean R Koontz.

'Mum hasn't changed anything in here, as I'm sure you've noticed,' Joel offers.

'It's actually fun to see it,' the real estate agent says. 'I was always curious about how other people in our class lived.'

'What do you mean?' Joel says.

Then he gets it. He takes a closer look and realises he has misjudged her age – she might actually not be older than him. But he doesn't recognise her. Not at all.

'I suppose I had a little real estate agent in me back then, too,' she says, turning to him.

And then she gets it, too.

'Well, I suppose it's no wonder you don't recognise me,' she says curtly. 'I guess I wasn't much of an attention-seeker.'

Unlike me?

He searches his memory. She said something about Ytterby. Secondary school. Joel decides to take a chance on that being the class they were in together.

'I'm sorry,' he says. 'I was barely ever at school and . . .'

She'd said something about her husband, so she's probably married.

'And your name wasn't Nordin back then, was it?'

'No, Jonsson. Lena Jonsson.'

She says her name like an accusation. At least now Joel knows who she is. Lena Jonsson. They were in the same class in upper secondary, too. A teen queen in bohemian dresses with white

T-shirts underneath, who was proud of her 'clean features' and was always going on about the modelling scout who discovered her on a street in Gothenburg. She loved Kevin Costner in *Dances with Wolves*. Her clique always moved through the hallways in a pack, or sat outside classrooms reading aloud from teen magazines, chewing gum loudly and rating each other's 'jeans bums'. Nina and he had used to make fun of them in this very room.

'I'm sorry,' he says. 'I don't remember much from those years.'

'I suppose not.'

Lena eyes him coldly, and now it seems incomprehensible that he didn't realise who she was straight away.

Nina

Anna's cough is worse since last night, but at least she doesn't have a temperature.

'Do you think you'll be able to fall asleep now?' Nina asks.

Anna coughs again. Nods weakly.

'I never get sick,' she says. 'I suppose I must have caught cold when I was out walking. It was terribly windy in Paris.'

'That's probably it. But you'll be up and about again tomorrow, fit as a fiddle, you'll see.'

'God willing,' Anna replies.

'Exactly.'

Nina puts an extra blanket over her and reaches out to turn off her bedside lamp.

'No, leave it on,' Anna says. 'He keeps his distance if there are lights on.'

Nina's hand freezes mid-air.

'Who?' she says.

'The new ghost. He's trying to scare me.'

Nina studies the wrinkled face on the pillow. Anna's almost always happy. But now a tear is trickling down her cheek.

'Anna? What's the matter? Do you want to talk about it?'

Anna looks around the room. Shakes her head. 'Don't tell anyone I'm in here bawling.'

'I promise.'

'No one likes women who cry, you know.'

Nina looks at her worriedly. 'Don't you want to tell me what happened?'

'I can't. He'd be cross. You should have seen how angry he was in Paris when she wrote that letter.'

'Okay,' Nina says. 'Then let's leave the light on.'

'If it's on, he'll think twice before coming for me,' Anna says, and closes her eyes.

'If he tries anything, you push your alarm button and I'll come running. It's around your neck, remember?'

Anna pats the alarm button resting on her chest.

'Good,' Nina says. 'Good night, Anna.'

Her only response is an ear-splitting snore.

Nina steps out into D corridor. Everything is calm and quiet. Monika was already asleep when she got to work. They haven't spoken since the early hours of the morning.

A real pain.

Cuckoo.

Nina glances over at D6. There's still no sign on the door. She read in Sucdi's report that Monika tried to eat the paper.

She's getting worse. What she said was just part of her disease.

Nina startles when she hears something shatter at the other end of the hallway and then bare feet against the vinyl.

The sounds are coming from the lounge.

Nina runs over. She sees Monika's silhouette against the window, surrounded by a faint, sulphurous glow from the streetlights on the other side of the carpark. The glass in one of the cabinet doors has been smashed and the dried flowers have been torn down, crumpled up and scattered across the floor.

How did she get here?

Monika turns to her. Her eyes look enormous; Nina is struck by how much weight she's lost in the past few days. Her mouth opens and shuts.

'How are you, Monika?' Nina says, her voice steadier than she had dared to hope. 'Can I help you with something?'

Her mouth opens and closes, opens and closes. Her jaw clicks and creaks.

'Do you need a glass of water?'

Monika shakes her head. The tendons of her neck strain under her skin.

'Home,' she says, and moves closer. 'I need to go home.'

'It's the middle of the night,' Nina tells her. 'Come on, let's go to bed.'

Monika's bony fingers seize Nina's shoulders. A guttural sound finds its way out of her throat.

'Help. Me,' she grunts. 'Help . . . me. Get out of here.'

Her dry lips continue to move, but her voice seems to have stopped working. Sounds emerge from deep in her throat.

'Are you having trouble breathing?' Nina says.

'No. I just need to *get out of here . . .*'

The muscles in Monika's face contract into an expression Nina has never seen before. It's almost as though there's another face underneath Monika's. Impatient. Malevolent. Monika's fingers dig deeper into Nina's arms.

'Monika,' Nina says. 'Monika, listen to me. I'm going to give you something to help you sleep. You're going to feel better tomorrow, I promise.'

Monika leans her forehead against Nina's collarbone. A sob racks her body.

'Help me.'

'I will. Come on, let's go to your room and tuck you in, and then . . .'

'You don't understand!' Monika screams, then she starts to sob uncontrollably.

Nina strokes her back; she can feel every rib through her nightgown.

'I can't go on like this,' Monika says.

The strength seems to drain out of the fingers that have been digging into Nina's arms. Monika totters and Nina takes a firmer hold of her.

'It's going to be all right,' she says.

She leads Monika down the hall and into her suite. She holds the older woman under the arms when she sits down heavily on her bed. The pits of her nightgown are soaked.

Monika is shaking from head to toe. She's on the verge of hyperventilating when Nina helps her to lie down.

A panic attack. It must be a panic attack.

'It's going to be all right. Everything's going to be all right,' Nina says, as much to herself as to Monika.

She feels Monika's damp forehead and takes her pulse. Her heart is beating fast, but not worryingly so. If it is a panic attack, that could be causing it. Nina fetches Oxazepam and lifts Monika's head to help her swallow the pill with water from a beaker.

But Monika doesn't want to.

'Leave me alone,' she says, and clenches her jaw shut.

'You'll feel better if you take this medicine,' Nina wheedles.

Monika seems not to hear her. Her eyes open wide but seem to be staring inward.

As though she's trying to look inside herself.

'You shouldn't be here,' she hisses.

'Monika,' Nina says. 'Look at me. You need to take your medicine.'

Monika suddenly raises her hand. Before Nina understands what's happening, Monika has scratched four angry red lines down her own cheek. Blood begins to well up in them.

'Get out,' Monika groans with a voice that is quickly tumbling down to the bottom of her register. 'Get out, get out, get out! Leave!'

Nina manages to grab her arm before she can scratch her face again. She inspects Monika's short nails—

have to file these down as soon as she's asleep

—and holds her hand in a gentle but firm grip. Strokes it softly. Looks back up at Monika's furious face.

'I'm not going anywhere until you're asleep,' she says. 'You can shout about it as much as you like.'

Joel

'I was just in Mum's room. She has scratches all over her face.'

'Yes,' Elisabeth says, folding her hands on her desk. 'She had an episode last night.' The children's TV presenter voice is back.

'An episode?' Joel asks.

'She had a panic attack and scratched her face. But the lacerations are superficial. It looks worse than it is.'

He stares at her. Shifts in the visitor's chair.

'She was given a sedative and this morning seemed to have forgotten the whole thing,' Elisabeth continues. 'I saw her myself at breakfast.'

She tilts her head. Her eyes are more sympathetic than ever, but she doesn't fool him for a second.

'I'm afraid this is what dementia is like,' she says. 'Things go from good to bad and back again in the blink of an eye.'

'But from a long-term perspective, she will get worse and worse, right?' Joel says. 'It's all downhill.'

'I'm sorry. But we're taking good care of your mother. She will be as comfortable as she can be.'

Joel remembers when he came here to sign the tenancy agreement. He was so relieved. Finally, his mother would be someone else's responsibility. It had seemed so simple.

'Has Mum had *episodes* before?' he says.

Elisabeth looks down at her desk. Taps her pen against a closed binder.

'Monika tried to eat paper the other day,' she says. 'But we stopped her.'

'Paper? What kind of paper?'

'A sheet of drawing paper. She was supposed to make a sign for her door. And last night, she smashed the glass in the breakfront in the lounge.'

Joel swallows.

His mother still needs him. He can't shirk his duty just because she's here.

'She looks thin to me,' he says. 'Is she eating okay? Anything other than paper, I mean?'

It's a lame attempt at a joke, but Elisabeth smiles politely.

'Don't worry. We keep track of everything going in and coming out. She receives sufficient nutrition.'

Everything going in and coming out. That's what his mum has been reduced to.

'I understand,' he says, noticing that his voice is dangerously close to breaking.

He thanks Elisabeth and steps out into the corridor. Edit is standing at the sharp bend that marks the beginning of D corridor, stooped over her rollator.

'Good day,' she says. 'My name is Edit Andersson and I am Director Palm's secretary.'

'Good day,' Joel replies. 'I think my mother's almost as batty as you.'

Edit's milky eyes narrow. Her tiny hands squeeze the handles of the rollator so hard her knuckles turn white. But in the next moment, the wrinkled face goes blank again.

'Good day. My name is Edit Andersson and I am Director Palm's secretary.'

Joel continues towards his mother's suite.

She's lying completely still in her bed and doesn't seem to have moved since he left for Elisabeth's office. Sunlight is pouring in through the windows, a hard, white light that makes all contrasts too sharp.

The scratches on her cheek are shiny; something's been smeared on them. Her eyes have sunk deep into her skull. They're surrounded by dark shadows. Her mouth is half open and her teeth look bigger in her gaunt face. He checks to make sure she's still breathing. Steps in closer and sees the pulse flickering at her throat. Every throb is an echo of her beating heart.

It stopped several times on the operating table after her heart attack. Now, it keeps pumping away like nothing's wrong.

Forty years ago, he was part of her body. They shared the same circulatory system. Her heart pumped for him, too.

Joel picks up a couple of magazines and a pen from the bedside table. Fetches a cup of coffee from the serving cart in the hallway and peeks into the empty lounge. He looks at the cabinet door where a pane of glass is missing. Hesitates for a moment before taking a seat at one of the tables and flicking past chicken recipes and ads for omega-3 capsules. An interview with a mother of nine. Ask-the-doctor columns and garishly illustrated short stories.

The crossword puzzles are printed on matte paper. His mother's upper-case letters fill the squares. Neat at first, then increasingly uneven, shaky. Tentative. He tries not to think about it and keeps turning the pages, looking for an unsolved puzzle. He comes across a page where his mum's letters no longer form words at all. Joel stares down at the grid.

Just . . . a jumble of letters.

He pictures his mother lying in bed with the magazine neatly propped against her pulled up thighs. Did she consider it before writing, thinking she'd solved the clues? Or were these just mechanical hand movements, unconnected to her mind?

'I'm sorry to bother you,' a voice says. 'I just wanted to ask how you're doing.'

Joel looks up. The heavily pregnant woman is standing in the doorway with a teacup in her hand. She's watching him with a concerned expression; he closes the magazine and pulls himself together.

'I'm fine,' he says. 'Thanks. It's just a bit too much for me today.'

'I know the feeling,' she says, and enters the room.

She sits down across from him. Joel casts about for an escape route, an excuse to leave. *I was just about to head back to my mother's room.* But then he meets her warm gaze and relaxes a little.

The woman wipes her forehead with the flimsy sleeve of her maternity dress, and stirs her tea.

'Looks like it's almost time,' he says, nodding towards her big belly.

'Yes, he'd better come out soon. I'm already a week overdue.'

Joel gets up and holds his hand out so she can reach it. She introduces herself as Fredrika.

'I don't get how you can bear to come here every day with that belly,' he says, and sits back down.

'Me neither. You know what the worst part is? I think you might be the only person here who hasn't come up and touched it. The old ladies throw themselves at it the moment they spot me. And the staff's not much better.'

'I promise to keep my hands to myself,' he says. 'Is it your first?'

'No. I have a five-year-old boy as well. But he thinks this place is creepy, and I don't want to force him to come.'

'I can't blame him.'

Fredrika sips her tea gingerly. 'I suppose it can get rather lively at times,' she says. 'Petrus scared him.'

'Petrus?'

'The one with the amputated legs,' she says, and makes a slicing gesture across her thighs. 'He was sitting in here, shouting about cunts and whores, the first time we came.'

Fredrika sips her tea again and shakes her head. 'He's a real charmer, that old geezer,' she says.

'I would have been terrified, too, if I were five,' Joel says.

'I'm terrified of him and I'm an adult. Nana lives next door to him and you can hear him loud and clear through the wall when he gets going.'

'My mum's next-door neighbour is Lillemor,' he says. 'The lady with the angels.'

'Congratulations. There's going to be a lot of hymns in your future.'

'It's been pretty quiet so far.'

'Just you wait.'

They both let out a chuckle at the same time. He drinks his coffee.

'Has your grandmother been here long?'

'Almost two years.'

'Does she like it?'

'I don't know. Being around people she doesn't know makes her anxious, but what other options are there?' Fredrika smiles again, but sadly this time. 'It was harder at first. Back then, she still had lucid moments when she knew what was happening to her. It must be a nightmare.'

Fredrika shakes herself. For the first time, Joel wonders in earnest if his mum has ever grasped that she has dementia. He realises how little he knows about what her illness looks like from the inside. He's only ever thought about it from the outside, how it affects him. That probably makes him selfish.

'When did you realise your mum was sick?' Fredrika says.

'The dementia came on after a heart attack. Her brain didn't get enough oxygen and . . . It was sort of . . . there wasn't really ever any doubt about it. But it took a while before we realised how bad it was. She says she had a near-death experience and . . . it's almost like a part of her actually did die on that operating table.'

He falls silent. Surprised at how much he has said. He lets his own words sink in.

'What about your grandmother?' he says. 'How did you realise she was sick?'

'It was small things at first. She got people's names mixed up. But then, she's always been like that. I am too, for that matter. After a while, though, I realised she didn't know who I was sometimes. She kept thinking someone had stolen things she'd lost. She wouldn't let her carer in and she reported me to the police several times – told them I'd taken her jewellery and money. Even a dog called Iago, which she had when she was a little girl.'

Joel nods. Remembers his mother's last morning in the house.

Call the police. We've been burgled.

'In the end, the police were fed up with her calling them and said I should disconnect her phone,' Fredrika continues. 'But I couldn't do that. I needed to be able to call her.' She shakes her head. Drains her teacup. 'People who haven't been through this don't understand.' She lowers her voice. 'Like that Elisabeth. My god, so bloody insincere. Have you noticed?'

'Yes.'

'*I loooove old people*,' Fredrika says in an affected voice.

The impression is spot on. They laugh.

'Having at least one loved one with dementia should be a prerequisite to running a place like this,' Fredrika says.

Joel's happy she sat down, happy he stayed.

He looks around the lounge and realises the dried flowers on top of the cabinet are gone. He studies the Marcus Larson reproductions.

'Aren't they awful?' Fredrika says. 'Having them on the walls here is frankly grotesque. I always think Nana's like one of those ships that's just drifting along in the storm without anyone to steer her.'

'They could have picked something cheerier,' he agrees.

They sit in silence for a while.

'Sometimes, I wish everyone here could have known Nana before she got sick,' Fredrika says. 'She was so funny. And she wasn't afraid of anything. The complete opposite of what she's like now.'

He nods. Pictures the little old lady with the stuffed animal.

'I wonder what someone like Lillemor looked like when she was young,' he says.

'Her husband visited quite a bit before he passed away. He said Lillemor wasn't religious in the slightest before she got sick. It came with the dementia.'

Joel shoots her a surprised look. Thinks about the angels crowding Lillemor's suite. The framed banalities.

'And the sisters, Vera and Dagmar?' Fredrika goes on, lighting up. 'Vera likes to knit. Dagmar's the one in the wheelchair who's always spitting out her food.'

He nods to indicate that he knows who she means.

'Dagmar was a *doctor*,' Fredrika says.

Joel tries to picture the angry, spitting creature in a white coat. He can't. All the knowledge her brain once contained is gone now. She must be able to see what he's thinking because Fredrika's face breaks into an amused smile.

'Yep. Vera's son brought them in. He said she was one of the first female doctors in the area. And Petrus was a sailor—' She breaks off abruptly. 'I'm sorry. Am I talking too much?'

'No,' he says. 'This is the first time I haven't felt completely alone in this.'

Pineshade

The heatwave doesn't break until the end of the week. The day before Midsummer, cooler winds finally blow in and the temperature drops. Anna's in her bed in D7. She has put on her beret and is clutching her handbag to her chest, but she's not sure if she wants to go for a walk today. She doesn't want to run into the new ghost, and he can pop up anywhere. He's cross with Anna because she won't do what he tells her.

I don't care what Lillemor says. He's no angel.

Anna saw what Monika wrote with her crayon, before he stopped her. *HELP ME*, it said. Again and again.

I need to talk to Monika. Anna repeats that silently so she won't forget. But it's dangerous. She knows that. He would be even crosser if he found out. *And he's always watching Monika.*

* * *

'Apparently, I'm the only one who cares,' Rita says in the staff meeting in the common room. 'But we really do have to do something about the ventilation in D.' She fixes her stare on Elisabeth challengingly.

'It's not easy getting someone to come out right now, everyone's on holiday,' the ward director replies. 'And thankfully, it's cooler out now.'

Rita snorts derisively. 'It's a miracle the old people haven't dropped like flies,' she says.

She's seen ward directors come and go. They all want to cut costs and think they can just ignore any problem that comes up. But Rita knows nothing solves itself. *You should never have been promoted to management*, she thinks, eyeing Elisabeth. *They should have asked me. But I suppose I'm too good at what I do. That's the thanks I get for doing my job properly: I get to be stuck where I am for life.*

Elisabeth concludes the morning meeting by informing the others she has found someone to replace Johanna. And this time it's an experienced woman who has worked in care her whole life.

'She's a godsend. She can start after the weekend.'

Rita laughs and empties her cup. 'Godsend,' she mutters and stands up. 'Well, we'll see. If she'd been a godsend, I reckon she'd have started before Midsummer, so I didn't have to work the holiday.'

Elisabeth closes her binder and glares at Rita's ramrod-straight back.

'I think it's kind of nice here on Midsummer,' Sucdi puts in.

Rita sneers at her. 'That's easy for you to say. You don't celebrate Midsummer anyway, do you?'

Sucdi stares back. Doesn't want this discussion, but can't stay quiet, either. 'I've lived here my whole life,' she says. 'And since when is Midsummer a religious holiday?'

Rita purses her lips.

Fucking bitch, Sucdi thinks, walking out into the corridor. She looks over at the door to D6 and makes a decision.

* * *

Anna stares up at the ceiling. A greasy spot has appeared up there. It's not particularly big, but it glistens when the sunlight hits it. She hears the door to Monika's suite open and close. *I was supposed to talk to her about something. Something about a letter in Paris. Something about the ghost.* She can't remember.

* * *

Sucdi walks up to the bed in D6, where Monika has just opened her eyes.

'I'm sorry if I woke you up,' Sucdi says, and sits down on one of the chairs. 'It's almost time for lunch.'

Monika smacks her dry mouth. Sucdi pours her a glass of water from the jug sitting on the table and watches Monika drink. The scratches on her cheek have faded. Monika is relatively young compared to the other residents at Pineshade. She still heals quickly.

'I just need to ask you something,' Sucdi says. 'Do you know my father?'

Monika blinks at her, confused.

'You said Pineshade wasn't good enough for him,' Sucdi presses. 'Remember that?'

Monika blinks. Her eyes clear. 'Your dad doesn't want to die here,' she says, and Sucdi asks her how she knows that.

'He will go back to Somalia so he never has to end up in a place like this,' Monika says.

Sucdi's stomach lurches, and Monika nods.

'He never asked you and your sister what you thought of it,' she goes on. 'Shouldn't he have if he cares about you?'

It feels like a punch in the gut.

'How do you know this?' Sucdi asks again, but Monika doesn't answer. Just licks her lips.

Sucdi hurriedly leaves the suite. Monika's heavy breathing seems to follow her into the corridor.

Joel

The rain is hammering against the windows in his room. The wind picked up during the evening and it's whipping around the house, making it sigh and creak as though it were Dorothy's house in the tornado. The world spins when Joel closes his eyes. His stomach is full of white wine; it's pressing against the bottom of his throat, cold and sharp. He wants to escape his body, slip into sleep, but his mind is still wide awake.

I just need some help falling asleep. A couple of nights would do the trick, get me back on track. A couple of times won't get me hooked. Sleep deprivation is more dangerous than popping a couple of pills.

His addict's brain never has to look very far for a rationalisation.

The cassette tape he found in his old Walkman is rolling in the stereo. Depeche Mode. The Cure. Sinéad O'Connor is singing about Troy and the lyrics seem to be about him and Nina.

Joel heaves himself out of bed, throws up in the upstairs toilet, then staggers back into the covers. The sweat-soaked patch on his sheet is an almost exact imprint of his body. He lies down by the wall where it's still dry, then turns his duvet over and tentatively closes his eyes. The world has stopped spinning. His body feels clean and hollow. He sinks through the mattress towards a vast, welcoming darkness. Somewhere far away, the cassette player clicks as the tape turns over. A gust of wind howls past the wall Joel is pressed against and the rain beats even harder against the window like the wet breaths of a giant. He focuses on the music. P J Harvey. Siouxsie and the Banshees. The Clash, which their classmates only knew from the Levi's commercial. He falls asleep to Nirvana's 'All Apologies' from the *Unplugged* album.

He has no idea how much time has passed when he wakes up, but his heart is pounding so hard the bed seems to quiver with each beat. He sits up. The rain has stopped. Everything is quiet except the sound of static from the speakers.

His mum's voice. He's sure he heard his mum's voice.

Joel climbs out of bed. The floor is cool under his feet. The speakers crackle, then the static is back, mesmerisingly monotonous. It's a sound he associates with old TV sets.

He pushes the door open.

'Hello?'

The butterflies on the wallpaper in the hallway seem to grow and shrink in the gloom. He peers out the window. The trees on the mountain are swaying wildly; enormous bodies moving as one. In his confused brain, the noise from the speakers morphs into the rushing of the wind through the heavy, evergreen limbs.

'Hello?' he calls out again.

The answer is instantaneous and coming from inside his room.

'Hello?' his mum whispers. 'Are you there?'

As Joel whips around in the doorway he has to grab hold of the doorpost to keep from losing his balance. But the room is empty.

'Hello?' his mum whispers again. 'Can you answer me?'

Her voice is pleading. Frightened.

It's coming from the speakers.

Joel swallows.

What if she's dead? If this is how she contacts me?

It's a pathetic thought, but it makes his skin crawl.

'Hello?' his mum says on the tape, a little louder this time. 'Are you here? Nils, say something if you're here.'

A wet sob in the speakers. There's a scraping sound and his mum mutters something. Seems unsure if she's pressed the right buttons. The static has changed. It's still just as monotonous. But it's grown denser. The aural equivalent of white dots bleeding into each other.

His heart pounds and pounds.

'Nils?' his mum pants. 'Say something. Otherwise, they won't believe me.'

Joel squats down in front of one of the speakers. Listens to the static and his mother's breathing.

Is there a whisper there?

A faint, faint 'k' from someone answering *Monika*?

Joel reaches out. Turns the volume up.

A crash roars out of the speakers and his heart almost stops. His mum lets out a curse and Joel deduces that she's dropped the Walkman on the floor. More scraping noises, a resigned sigh and then a click as his mother turns the tape off. The dreamlike intro to 'Song to the Siren' takes over.

Joel's hand is trembling when he pushes stop, then rewind. Play.

'Nils?' Pause. 'Say something. Otherwise, they won't believe me.'

He turns the volume up even more. This time, he hears no answer in the static.

Just his imagination.

He turns it off before his mother can drop the Walkman again.

Nina

It's 5 a.m. on Midsummer's Eve. Nina is writing reports in the staffroom at Pineshade. From time to time, she glances up at Wiborg, who's mixing cake batter. Her dementia cat is sitting on the chair next to Nina's, forgotten for the moment. Wiborg measures out flour, humming calmly and moving confidently. Her body still remembers.

When Nina found Wiborg crying in her bed, she let her get up early. Nina had planned to make her birthday cake at some point during the night shift anyway – had brought strawberries and candles the night before.

'You're very good at baking,' she says when Wiborg pours the batter into a tin Nina helped her grease and cover in breadcrumbs.

Wiborg shoots her a shy, toothless smile. Nina gets up from the table and opens the childproof oven door.

'What do you say we make some coffee while it bakes?' she says, and slides the tin in.

'I think we'd better, or we might be too tired to whip the cream later,' Wiborg says; Nina laughs.

'You're absolutely right.'

She turns on the coffee machine and looks through the window into the common room. The rain has stopped. The sky above the glass ceiling is light-blue and cloudless.

Nina glances at the reports she has just finished and hopes Anna will feel better soon. Last night, she barely recognised her. Anna was just staring at the ceiling. She didn't answer when spoken to and her hand was ice cold in Nina's.

A few days before death comes, old people often seem to turn inward, to prepare themselves for their departure. Sometimes they go cold, as though their bodies are preparing, too. Nina knows the signs. But she's surprised it's Anna. It has happened so quickly. Anna who has always been happy and cheerful. Whose dementia seems to have made her forget all her troubles and cares. She has been taking her 'walks outside' in the common room almost every day.

If the good weather holds, the residents will eat their Midsummer lunch out back. It would be a sad irony if Anna missed her first chance in a long time to go outside for real.

Nina swallows the lump in her throat. The coffee machine has begun to sputter so she gets two cups out and fills Wiborg's halfway to the top with cream before pouring in coffee. They drink in silence while the smell of warm sponge cake spreads through the kitchen. Wiborg seems at peace and she closes her eyes every time she takes a sip.

The frenzied ringtone of the staff phone makes them both jump.

'It might be for me,' Wiborg says.

'Only one way to find out,' Nina says, and fetches the phone from the kitchen counter.

Wiborg looks at her expectantly when she answers.

'I'm afraid I have bad news,' says a clearly still-drowsy Elisabeth on the other end. 'Rita has called in sick.'

Wiborg picks up her dementia cat and places it in her lap. 'Is it for me?' she says, and when Nina shakes her head, it's as though Wiborg completely deflates.

Nina sits down next to her, stroking her back consolingly. Elisabeth says she can't get hold of anyone else; Nina has to take the morning shift with Sucdi, and it goes without saying that she's very sorry, but there will be a lot of overtime pay on Midsummer and that's good news for Nina, if not the budget.

Elisabeth rambles on, but Nina's listening to her own thoughts now. Making lists in her head.

. . . home around two, I can get a couple of hours of sleep in before the guests arrive, goddamn it I don't want to, can we cancel, no, we can't, it's okay, it's going to work out, the food doesn't need cooking, it's just shellfish and bread and a few cold sauces and the cheese pie just needs reheating and Markus just has to vacuum and do the bathrooms and change the towels, that'll do, and Joel might not even come by today, it's Midsummer, after all, and he's probably celebrating it by passing out in some junkie flat . . .

'It's okay,' she says, just as the egg timer rings. 'I have to go now.'

She walks over to the oven and opens the door, then sticks a toothpick into the middle of the cake.

'Done,' she says, and puts on the oven mitts. 'Now it just needs to cool before we add the fillings.'

Wiborg looks at her tearily and says nothing.

Believe me, Nina thinks. *If it had been up to me, it would have been for you.*

Pineshade

The staff from all four wards have helped to set up foldable tables in the shade in the backyard. They have rolled out vinyl tablecloths, put out little vases with wildflowers, set out paper plates and plastic cups and Swedish flag napkins. Just over twenty out of thirty-three residents and a handful of relatives attend the lunch. They eat herring and potatoes. Spiced cheese on crispy bread. Some have been allowed a glass of beer and a shot of schnapps. The flavours jog the old people's memories. Even Dagmar smacks her lips contentedly when Vera feeds her, even though she spits most of the food out again.

Adrian pulls out his guitar. Edit turns to him.

'Good day,' she says. 'My name is Edit Andersson and I am Director Palm's secretary.'

Adrian nods warmly and looks out across the tables. 'What song do you want? The one about the frogs?'

'No!' Wiborg whispers and claps her hands over her ears. 'That one's scary.'

'"Frosty the Snowman",' Petrus says, and his wife laughs nervously.

'That's a Christmas song,' she tells him and pats his shoulder.

Petrus bangs his fist on the table, making the people around him jump. 'I want to hear about Frosty, you fucking whore!'

His wife retracts her hand, but Adrian smiles, unperturbed.

'All right! Then let's do "Frosty the Snowman"!'

Lillemor's piercing voice soars high above everyone else's. She turns her face skyward as though singing directly to her angels in heaven.

'Good day,' Edit says, staring intently at Petrus. 'My name is Edit Andersson and I am Director Palm's secretary.'

Nina mimes along. Singing is associated with that other period in her life. She looks over at Monika, who shoves a whole potato into her mouth and barely seems to chew before swallowing. Sucdi bends down to her.

'Take it easy – you don't want to make yourself sick, Monika.'

Monika makes no reply, just runs her tongue over her teeth and spears another potato.

Bodil is staring rapturously at Adrian. She has seen him in the crowd of men who are always trying to catch a glimpse of her naked. She winks at him. Relishes the thought that all her girlfriends are trying to draw him in, but it's outside her window he's standing. *If only they knew. The men are all crazy about me.*

'Good day. My name is Edit Andersson and I am Director Palm's secretary.' Edit waves a bony hand in Petrus' face.

'Shut up!' he screams. 'You're ruining everything, you fucking whore!'

Petrus' wife tries to shush him, but he glowers at Edit. She stares back, her eyes glazed. Blinks.

'Good day. My name is Edit Andersson and I am Director Palm's secretary.'

Petrus lunges at her, but the straps that bind him to his wheelchair pull taut, draw him up short. He roars with rage. His wife looks around nervously and waves away a wasp that has landed on one of his stumps.

Monika bursts out laughing.

'Good day,' Edit says. 'My name is Edit Andersson and I am Director Palm's secretary.'

Monika laughs even harder.

Vera stops feeding Dagmar. The spoon is left hanging in mid-air. She stares at Monika. *That's him, the one I saw in the mirror. He's here now. In broad daylight.*

Wiborg starts crying inconsolably. 'Can I go back to bed now?' she says, looking around for someone to help her.

Nina pats her shoulder. 'Maybe we should go inside and decorate your cake instead?'

Wiborg eyes her anxiously. Tries to figure out what she means.

'We started making a cake, you and me,' Nina says.

Wiborg doesn't remember. It's hard to keep it together when things are so loud and chaotic.

'Come on,' Nina says. 'We'll go prep while the others finish eating.'

Wiborg still doesn't understand, but she wants to leave. She seizes the opportunity and follows the friendly young woman. They walk towards a door and are just about to enter when a man steps through it. For a moment, Wiborg is worried it's the new, scary one who has suddenly appeared in this place. And the woman holding her hand stiffens, as though she's afraid of him, too. Wiborg watches them greet each other.

'Do you have a minute?' he says.

'Not now,' she replies and nods towards the tables. 'Monika's out there.'

They barely look at each other and Wiborg is relieved when she and the woman enter an empty corridor.

* * *

In D7, Anna hears them pass her door. She tries to call for help, but she can't breathe. The panic is almost more than her old heart can handle. Anna struggles to fill her lungs, but it's as though she's forgotten how to. She opens her mouth wide, but it doesn't help. She fumbles for the alarm button on her chest. Almost reaches it. But then her hands are pressed down into the mattress.

Her lips are turning blue. Anna stares up at the ceiling. Looks at him. She understands now. She and Lillemor were both wrong.

That's neither an angel nor a ghost. That's something else entirely.

Joel

It makes him feel ashamed that he keeps averting his eyes from the residents. The open mouths, the drool, the old tongues covered in cake cream and finely chopped strawberries. The thought of nappies and *everything going in and coming out.* Cleaning up his mum's accidents almost pushed him over the edge. It wasn't just the smears and the smell; it was the intimacy of it.

He glances furtively at Nina. How can she bear to work here, with all the smells and ailments and helplessness, all the confusion and fear and anger?

But then, he has no idea what she went through at home, with her alcoholic mother. Did she have to take care of her, too? How bleak was it? Not even when they were best friends had they been able to talk about it. She wouldn't or couldn't tell him. And he was far too young to know how to ask.

Now he knows what it's like to parent one's own mother. And he can barely handle it, even as an adult.

Nina is talking to Wiborg, Fredrika's grandmother. There's no sign of Fredrika herself. Wiborg is staring intently at the two candles, a nine and a five, still sitting in the cream. When Wiborg blew them out, a thin film of saliva blanketed the entire cake. He declined the piece he was offered.

Ninety-five years old. The birthday girl pets her stuffed animal and Joel tries to imagine what she was like as a teenager during the Second World War. The world has changed so incomprehensibly much during her lifetime. And yet, people don't seem to evolve at all.

He turns to his mother. Twenty-three years younger than Wiborg. It's so unfair. It's too early for her to be here.

'Mum,' he says.

She doesn't react. Just continues to shovel cake into her mouth and swallow greedily. He hopes it's a sign of health that her appetite is back. But the circles under her eyes have darkened. Her cheekbones look like they're coming out through her skin.

'You know how I'm cleaning out the house,' he continues. 'I found the old clippings I gave you a long time ago. Do you remember? The ones about me and Nina?'

She stops chewing.

'I didn't know you saved those,' he says. 'I haven't seen them in years.'

'Nina,' says his mother. 'I remember her. She spent a lot of time at our house.'

Joel notices Nina watching them and wonders if she can hear them.

'Yes,' he says. 'She works here now. She's sitting over there.'

His mum looks worried and puts her spoon down. 'Could you ask her to leave? Nils has told me she can be very mean.'

The bloke with the guitar starts playing a summer hymn and Lillemor gets to her feet, her whole body swaying as she sings along. Her eyes burn with zeal. Other voices join hers. Old, cracked. Someone sings something else entirely, seemingly making up a melody as they go along.

'She's not mean,' Joel says softly. 'She's one of the people helping to take care of you.'

'She killed her mother.'

'No,' Joel says. 'Her mother died because she was an alcoholic. That's why Nina spent so much time at our house.'

His mum shakes her head stubbornly. 'Nils wouldn't lie about that,' she says.

Joel steals another glance at Nina and hopes the singing drowns most of their conversation out.

'She's *very* mean,' his mum insists.

Joel tries to think of how to respond, but maybe it's best not to respond at all. Maybe it's better to redirect her before this latest delusion takes hold.

'Björn and Sofia wanted me to tell you Happy Midsummer,' he says, and pulls out his phone. He finds the email and holds the screen out for her to see.

'Is that Björn?' she says.

'Yes.'

'He wants to come visit so badly,' his mum says. 'But Joel won't let him.'

Joel looks at the picture that fills the screen. His brother and his family are posing in front of a beach bar in Torremolinos. They just landed and are still paler than the people in the background. His sons are wearing blue-and-yellow football jerseys. Sofia is in a crocheted bikini and straw hat. Björn's arm is wrapped around her waist. They look happy. Well-rested already.

'Yeah?' Joel replies. 'I'm sure they'd rather be here.'

His mum nods while Joel shows her more pictures. The children staring in awe at an ice-cream counter. Flavours of every colour of a synthetic rainbow. Police officers riding Segways along a paved beach promenade. Big platters of shellfish. Björn's nose red from the sun.

'My boys have never got along,' his mum says. 'I don't know what to do.'

Joel slides the phone back into his pocket.

One of the old ladies is staring at him. She puckers her lips and throws him a coquettish little kiss when their eyes meet, then fiddles with the plastic alarm button dangling around her neck.

'Good day,' puts in Edit, who's sitting on his other side, and tugs at his tank top. 'My name is Edit and I am Director Palm's secretary.'

He has to get out of here, but he doesn't want to go back to the empty house. He doesn't even want to go back to Stockholm anymore, because what does he really have waiting for him there? Unlike his mother, he can, in theory, go wherever he wants, and yet, he has nowhere to go.

He stands up, tells his mum he needs to go to the loo. She nods absently.

The silence in D corridor is a relief after the chaos outside. He passes his mother's door and notices there's a sign on it now – although it's in someone else's handwriting. He thinks about the jumble of letters in the squares of the crossword puzzles and wonders if she was trying to write her name and failed; wonders if that's why she decided to eat the paper, in frustration and shame at not being able to make the letters obey.

Being unable to even write one's own name.

Sucdi comes out of the staffroom with a coffee urn in each hand. She smiles warmly at him. 'Is everything okay out there?' she asks.

'It's not like any Midsummer party I've ever been to, I can tell you that,' he replies. 'Can I help you with those?'

'Thanks,' she says, and hands him one of the urns. 'Hey, can I ask you something? Do you think Monika knows my dad?'

'Your dad?'

'His name's Khalid and he's about her age. He worked at the biscuit factory.'

Joel shakes his head. 'I don't think so. She didn't socialise much in the last few years. At least not as far as I know.'

Sucdi looks like she's hesitating. 'It's just that . . . it sounded like she knew some things about him.'

'She just told me Nina killed her mother, so I'm not sure she's the most reliable,' Joel says with a laugh.

Sucdi smiles back.

'Is there a problem?' he asks.

'No. I was just wondering.'

Sucdi stops outside D7. The door next to his mother's. The lady with the beret. The name ANNA is on the door and something that might be a butterfly hovers above the letters.

'You know what?' Sucdi says, handing him the other urn. 'Would you mind taking this, too? I'm just going to look in on her.'

'Of course,' he says. 'See you out there.'

The door opens behind him. He just has time to hear Sucdi say 'Anna?' before it slides shut again behind her.

The old voices from the garden grow louder as he continues down the corridor. They hit him like a wall when he steps outside.

He puts the urns down on the table in front of Nina and hesitates. 'Do you have a minute?'

'That depends on what it's about. I'm at work,' she says without looking at him.

'Right, I get it. I just wanted to tell you I'm sorry about how things turned out the other day.'

'Okay,' she says. 'Sure.'

'I'm not saying we have to be best friends again. I just don't want to leave it like this.'

She heaves a sigh, but at least she's looking him in the eye now. 'You know what, we're good.'

'Are you sure?'

'Yes, I'm sure. You seem to be the one who has a problem.' Her eyes are cold. 'I've grown up and moved on. Maybe you should consider trying that, too?'

Then she gets up and leaves him at the table.

Rage roars through his veins like petrol, making his heart rate shoot from zero to a hundred. At least he tried. He apologised. But she's never going to say sorry for the things she's done. Not the other day, not twenty years ago.

You ruined everything, he thinks. *I hope it was worth it, that you're fucking happy now.*

Wiborg bursts into tears. She's still staring at what's left of the cake and shaking her head.

'I'm that old?' she says. 'I'm ninety-five?'

The bloke with the guitar sits down next to her, carefully drying her cheeks with a napkin. 'You are,' he says. 'Imagine, that old and still so healthy.'

'But then . . . then my parents must be really old. How could they be that old? And my husband, how can he . . .'

Her voice trails off as she's overcome with sobs. Her grief is unbearable to watch. But none of the other residents seem to react.

Joel tries to catch his mother's eye, but she's staring at something with great interest. He follows her gaze. Nina is standing at the entry to D corridor. Sucdi is speaking quietly to her; they look like something's happened.

Nina

Nina opened the window in Anna's suite to let in some fresh air. Then she carefully washed the body and put on an extra thick nappy, combed her thin hair and dressed her in a navy dress with white palm fronds that she knows made Anna feel pretty.

From the street beyond the carpark, she can already hear intoxicated voices. It's just gone three in the afternoon. Nina has been awake for over twenty-four hours, but she wants to sit here with Anna until the doctor has been by to pronounce her and the body has been taken away. She shouldn't have to be alone. If Anna's awareness is somehow still in the room, she should know someone cares about her.

Nina has lit a candle on the bedside table and removed all the schedules from the walls, anything associated with illness, in the unlikely case a relative decides to visit.

Before she started working at Pineshade, she'd never seen a dead body. Death was something scary and strange. But here, it quickly became familiar. Nina has seen hundreds of people pass away. Many of them in this very room. She has watched over them, moistening their lips with wet cotton wool. She has seen death come relatively suddenly, like now, and she has seen it creep in slowly, inexorably. A few times, she has been unable to hold back her tears and been comforted by the dying person. *Don't cry for me, lass.* Other times, she has tried to comfort the dying, held their hands as they've crossed to the other side, terrified of what might be waiting for them there.

For her part, Nina hasn't been scared of death since she sat at the deathbed of a man called Benkt. She was working in C Ward back then. It was the middle of the night and she was alone on the ward. His breathing had grown weaker and weaker, the pauses between his breaths longer and longer. And then, he stopped breathing altogether. She tried to find a pulse, but it was gone. She was just about to close his eyes when he started awake and looked at her. *It's so lovely over there*, he'd said in wonder. *That's why we're not allowed to know. If we knew, we wouldn't wait around here on Earth.*

Nina strokes Anna's cheek and hopes Benkt was right, that she's in that lovely place now.

'I'm going to miss you,' she says softly. 'I liked you so very much. We all did.'

A car turns into the carpark; she recognises the sound of the engine. They've come to pick Anna up.

The suite will be cleaned out. The bed disinfected. Elisabeth's going to call the next person on the waitlist. But for a little while longer, this is Anna's home.

Nina takes her cold hand and stays seated until there's a knock on the door. She gets up to lean over and kiss Anna lightly on the forehead. When she straightens, she feels a droplet land on her cheek, and raises her hand to touch it as she looks up.

A shiny spot on the ceiling above Anna's bed. A bit larger than a head.

Has it been there all along?

Nina rubs her fingers together. The liquid has no smell, no colour; it feels slick against her skin.

Like the stain on the wall in Monika's room. But this is . . . fresh.

She rubs the back of her hand hard against her cheek to get rid of the greasy sensation.

The ventilation. The fluorescent lights. And now this. It feels like Pineshade is falling apart. As though the cracks that let the chaos in are appearing here, too.

Joel

It's almost midnight. Midsummer. He's lying motionless on the living room sofa, listening to the dry wings of moths fluttering against the bug screens. The hum of the refrigerator.

He can't take it anymore.

Ever since he got here, it's been nothing but illness and decay. Everything has reminded him of broken relationships, old dreams that never came true, the long series of mistakes that has brought him to this dead end.

He needs something else. Just one hit. Breathing space. A break. He's going to make another mistake. He knows it and doesn't care.

Joel sits up on the sofa and reaches for his phone. Fires off a text. The reply is almost instantaneous.

I WAS JUST WONDERING WHEN I'D HEAR FROM YOU / K

Pineshade

Bodil looks at the men outside her window. Her hand is moving fast under the duvet. She drives them wild. It's almost more than they can bear. They're strong, grown men and yet completely helpless. They would do anything to be in here with her. To touch her with their big, warm hands. Cover her with their skin, pushing up on her from every direction. They worship her. One of them presses his naked, aroused body against the glass. *Come on in, then*, Bodil chuckles. The gratitude in his eyes makes her laugh out loud. He's standing next to her bed now. The others press themselves hungrily against the window behind him. Her hand moves faster and faster. Her bedside lamp flickers.

In D5, Lillemor has her ear to the wall. Listening, incensed, to the moaning coming from next door. *That filthy woman is going to make the angels turn away from us.* She cups her hands around her ear to hear better.

Monika is lying in bed in D6 with a crossword puzzle open on her knees. She's writing feverishly, pushing down so hard the paper tears. She's in a hurry. He's never far from her. And he's growing stronger. It's her fault somehow, but she doesn't understand why.

D7 is empty. The window's closed. Anna's last breath was aired out hours ago. Most residents of D corridor have already forgotten they ever knew her.

But Gorana remembers. She's sitting in the staffroom thinking about her first day here at Pineshade. It was a year and a half ago, in the middle of winter. She had no education, no experience, and she didn't know if she could handle the job. Anna was the one who made her believe it would work out. Anna, who just laughed when Gorana failed to insert the applicator with her anti-fungal medication into her vagina. *'You're all whoopsie-daisy.'*

This is the first time Gorana has worked a night shift and had no hope Anna will wake up for a bit of a chat.

The fluorescents outside D6 flicker.

Monika throws the magazine aside; it lands near the door with a soft rustle. The motion sensor is set off and the alarm starts to beep in the corridor. Monika struggles to breathe. Her whole body tenses up, straining for one more breath, making muffled noises in her throat. Seconds pass.

In D8, Vera's knitting needles click against each other. From time to time, she looks up at the bathroom door. She's hung a towel over the mirror in there, but tonight, she's less afraid than usual. She's crawled into bed with Dagmar. Dagmar soothes her with her even breathing.

Gorana opens the door to D6 and hears a metallic rattling from inside. She hurries in and almost slips on the magazine. Monika's sitting on the floor next to her bed, her head drooping on her chest. She's breathing heavily through gritted teeth, and her left hand is clutching the guard rail, making it shake.

Monika looks up. Her eyes flash.

'Get out,' she says, her voice deep and rough.

For a moment, Gorana is paralysed with fear.

'I'm here to help,' she says.

Monika's chapped lips draw back, baring her teeth. She slams her right hand into the undercarriage of the bed. A lump on her forearm tells Gorana the bone inside is broken. She finally manages to move and squats down, grabbing Monika's shoulders, but the old woman is surprisingly strong. She wrests free and strikes the underside of the bed again. This time, Gorana can hear bone scrape against bone inside her flesh.

Nina

'Cheers, everybody. Hey, this is the turning point. Winter is coming,' Håkan says for the third time this evening.

The others laugh and raise their schnapps glasses, but Nina's too tired to do more than smile politely. Exhaustion has filled her head with a dull, static whirring. She takes a sip of cranberry juice and realises her fingers still smell faintly of shellfish from dinner. Soon, it'll be late enough for her to go to bed without being rude. She has already prepared her apologies, her contrite smile.

While the others have worked on getting drunker, she has sat quietly. No one comments. She explained at the start of the evening that she had to work a double shift on account of a crisis at the home. They asked no questions. No one wants to know what goes on at a place like Pineshade.

It goes without saying there was no time to nap when she got back. Markus hadn't even started to clean the house and the guests were expected to arrive in just a couple of hours. But at least the lawn had been mowed. Nina has kicked off her shoes and is dragging her toes through the cool blades of dense, even grass.

Håkan and Lena's dog has finally gone to sleep. Ingo is an American bulldog that runs around incessantly, panting and begging for treats and affection. He's impossible to build a relationship with, since every second is spent fending him off.

'I met Joel Edlund,' Lena announces suddenly and lights a cigarette. 'I'm selling his mother's house. I take it she's been admitted to Pineshade?'

Nina looks up. Lena sucks on her cigarette without inhaling and looks at her expectantly.

'Who's he?' Håkan asks.

'He was Nina's best friend when we were teenagers,' Lena replies. 'They were in a band together.'

Markus looks grim.

'You were in a band?' Håkan says with a chuckle. 'What do you know. I had no idea.'

'Oh yes, they were proper local celebs,' Lena says. 'Or at least they fancied themselves famous.'

She snickers. Håkan continues to peer at Nina, clearly astounded and struggling to picture her in a band. 'Did you play an instrument, or . . . ?'

'Guitar.' Nina does her best to sound breezy. 'Acoustic.'

'What do you know,' Håkan says again.

'And she wrote songs, too,' Markus puts in. 'Though she's never let me hear them.' He swats at a mosquito. His face is still carefully neutral.

'You're not missing much,' Nina says.

'So what kind of music did you play?' Håkan wants to know.

Nina shrugs – she just wants them to move on now. Talk about anything else, so long as it has nothing to do with her.

'They played a gig up in Stockholm and got in the evening papers and everything,' Lena says. 'Didn't you land a record deal, too, before you got pregnant?'

'Yes.'

'It's probably for the best that nothing came of it,' Lena says.

'Why?' Håkan exclaims. 'Wouldn't it have been pretty cool to be friends with a bona fide popstar?'

'Joel was on the skids,' Markus says. 'He did quite a lot of drugs. Still does.'

Nina shoots him a pleading look, but he either doesn't catch it or he doesn't care.

'Yeah, he's not exactly the picture of health,' Lena agrees and empties her glass with a jerk of her head.

For the first time in a long time, Nina remembers how she and Joel used to make fun of her. Lena Jonsson who wanted to be a supermodel and always carried around a plastic carrier bag from Harrod's that she'd bought when she was on a language exchange trip. They would make their eyes vacant, their faces expressionless, their voices high-pitched and nasal.

Nina realises she's about to start giggling. She's dangerously tired now. Can't trust herself.

'He was thin as a rake,' Lena remarks, pouring herself another glass of wine. 'And he sounds like a Stockholmer.'

'Well, he must be on drugs, then,' Nina hears herself say. 'If he sounds like a Stockholmer.'

The others stare at her. She manages to smile as if she didn't mean what she said.

'Have you talked to him yet?' Lena wants to know.

Nina nods.

'What was it like?'

'He was high when he brought his mum in,' Markus says.

Nina looks at him again. Now she knows he's doing it deliberately. Punishing her because Joel's back.

'That's fucking tragic,' Lena says.

'I can't talk about it. Confidentiality.'

'Of course,' Lena says. 'But if you already told Markus, surely you can tell us, too?'

Nina shakes her head.

'I still can't believe you were in a band,' Håkan says.

'Would anyone like more coffee? Or whiskey?'

They all shake their heads, assuring her they're good.

'I hope he's not sick,' Lena says. 'I mean, there were rumours before. He's so bloody skinny.'

Nina doesn't look at her. She knows exactly what gossip Lena's referring to. Back then, being gay meant only one thing.

But there were other rumours about Joel, too. Like that he was Daniel's real father. She has no idea if Markus still thinks about those rumours, if he ever has doubts.

Nina can't go to bed now, not so soon after this conversation. Lena and Markus are going to think she's sulking. And worse, they're going to keep discussing Joel without her.

She thinks about how she sold out after Joel moved away. Nodded along when people gossiped about him. It was her penance for having been friends with him, for having had conceited dreams.

And now, here she is.

Joel

Multi-coloured fairy lights have been strung along the red wooden wall, the veranda gutter and among the branches of the apple tree. Speakers balance precariously on a windowsill. On the ground below, a record spins on a gramophone.

Joel is stretched out in a hammock, rocking himself with one foot in the grass. A breeze caresses his bare arms, making him shudder with pleasure.

The wine tasted bitter, almost like metal, after Katja chopped up the white MDMA crystals and let them fall like snowflakes into his glass. She wrote the time on his wrist to help him remember when it's time for another hit. It's been almost three hours since the world became beautiful.

It was so easy.

He recognises the feeling from ecstasy but it's not exactly the same. He doesn't need to move. Doesn't need anything. Even the air tastes good. This is what he has tried to achieve through drinking, but with this, there's none of the murkiness that comes with alcohol. All his thoughts are clear. He understands how they fit together. How *everything* fits together. The grass under his foot is as cool as the night air. It's the same grass Katja is dancing on with her old junkie friends. They're singing along to the same Pink Floyd songs Joel has heard here a million times before.

Katja sniffed the banknotes he handed her. *They don't smell like chlorine anymore*, she said with a grin. During high school, he'd worked extra at the snack bar at the communal pool. A lot of the notes, worn soft by wet children's hands, had ended up in his own pocket. And then in Katja's.

His mum never seemed to suspect anything. It was only when he moved to Stockholm that she suddenly got worried about him doing drugs. She'd read about all the dangers lurking in the capital in the evening papers. Little did she know there were massive amounts of drugs flowing through the forests around her.

He watches a couple of girls breathing in and out of yellow balloons filled with nitrous oxide. They grow and shrink like tiny suns. The girls' lips are blue from oxygen deprivation. They're so young and beautiful. Waves of warmth break over him when he looks at them. He gently runs his fingertips up and down his arm and shudders all over. It seems like a miracle that he can make himself feel this good. He's going to regret it tomorrow, he knows that, but the thought can't get to him here. His problems are so trivial under the vast starry sky. There's an inherent freedom in being so insignificant. He's going to remember that tomorrow; that will make the comedown easier to endure.

Someone changes the record to 'Love Will Tear Us Apart'. One of the first songs he taught Nina to play. His mum had come into his room, washing basket in her arms. *No wonder you're so gloomy, marinating in that kind of thing. Can't you listen to the kind of music Björn likes?* She never comprehended that it was the other way around, that it was the inane eurotechno that made him depressed, because it was about a simple, carefree world he had no access to. Joel laughs. Björn who always commented on his black clothes. *Are you going to a funeral?* Of course they didn't understand him. How could they have? He wasn't like them.

He'd thought he was so special when he moved to Stockholm. He tried to live his and Nina's dreams on his own, but Stockholm was full of people like him, who'd come with their dreams and talent and almost-signed record deals. He'd seen himself in their desperate eyes at Hanna's Basement, Gino, The Studio. And he'd missed Nina every day. Couldn't understand why she'd abandoned him. Not that he spent much time trying to figure it out – he just wanted to forget.

Now, he finally understands. Nina hadn't been able to come with him. He's fucked everything up. He would have fucked her up, too. Markus did save her from him, just like she said. She'd done the right thing by staying, he has to remember to tell Nina that. Suddenly, he misses her. It's an amazing thing to be able to miss someone. To like someone so much you long to see them. He's going to tell her what happened then doesn't matter anymore. At least they had the time before that.

'Mind if I sit down?'

Joel pulls his legs up to make room for the bloke standing at the foot of the hammock. It sways when he plops himself down.

'You can put your legs on top of mine,' he says, and Joel does.

The physical contact sends a jolt through his system. His body is a starry sky of its own, where points of light twinkle on and off and on again.

The guy seems to notice, because he grins and pushes one of Joel's trouser legs halfway up his calf, then starts caressing his skin. Every hair stands on end in the wake of his fingertips. It's completely asexual and at the same time better than any orgasm.

'So, you like this?' the guy says.

Only now does Joel take a closer look at him. He has thin lips, big eyes and a neatly combed rockabilly hairdo. He might look too plastic, too perfect, but it doesn't matter. Joel can see his *soul.*

'Katja tells me it's your first time,' he says.

His hand comes to a rest. It feels good in a different way. Heat pulsates from his hand into Joel, filling him with an energy that sends lightning crackling through his limbs.

Joel wants more, and yet he's in no hurry, has no fear of not getting it. It's perfect the way it is. Immaculate.

'I needed this,' Joel says.

'I can tell. You look like you're having a good time.'

He introduces himself as Diego and when Joel shakes his hand, he never wants to let go. Diego laughs, looks at the time written on Joel's wrist and nods.

'Are you sure you don't want to be left alone?' he asks.

Joel shakes his head and caresses the unfamiliar palm of Diego's hand with his fingers.

'I've been alone enough,' he replies. 'I'm sick of being alone. That's why I came here.'

Diego nods. He understands. They are two people who understand each other. It's really not so complicated. Everyone's the same deep down inside, where it matters. No one's ever alone, actually. Everything fits together.

'You know,' Joel says. 'I never saved any of my mum's Christmas cards. She sent me one every year. Isn't that sad? But also beautiful?'

'Yeah,' Diego says. 'Why didn't you save them?'

'It never even occurred to me. But I can picture her cursive. It was very . . . neat. And now it's gone. She can't write anymore.'

Diego strokes his leg again. Leans closer. Studies him with interest. 'Tell me more,' he says. 'I want to hear.'

'I don't have any of the Christmas presents she sent, either,' Joel says. 'Or birthday presents. I always dreaded picking them up from the post office, because it was always the same – they were always just dead wrong.'

'What was so wrong about them?'

Joel ponders that for a minute. And suddenly, it all becomes clear. It's as though he can see from the perspective of the stars in the sky.

'It was clothes and ornaments and practical things she imagined I needed. Like a pasta maker. I don't even cook. It always made me think she didn't know me. I thought she didn't care. But deep down inside, I knew she *had* in fact picked those things with care. Get it? She'd found them in a shop, or ordered them from a catalogue, thinking that *this maybe, this might be something for Joel.* Maybe she hesitated at first and then told herself that *yes, that's good.* She was hopeful as she wrapped the things. And if I had admitted that to myself, I would have had to admit that it was my responsibility, too. I never gave her a chance to get to know me. And to be honest, I never thought she was particularly interested, but then I found all these things she saved, and I realised she cared all along. She just didn't know how to talk to me about it. Because I wouldn't let her in. But she preserved my teenage bedroom like some fucking shrine, that has to mean something, right? She never said she loved me, but she showed me all the time. And I thought it was too late for me to meet her halfway, now that she's ill, but maybe she can still tell. Somehow. Either way, I have to try.'

He has no idea how long he goes on for. Diego listens, riveted.

The world around them disappears. Their touch and all the words and this joy fill him, so unfamiliar, even though it must have been here all along, because this is the natural state.

'Want more?' Diego says. 'Or a bit of K, maybe?'

He pulls out a miniscule silver spoon that's been dangling off a chain inside his shirt.

'I don't know,' Joel replies. 'Do I?'

'You've never tried that, either?' Diego says, lighting up. 'You're going to love it. What you're exploring now is going to become even clearer. It's brief, but it's *intense*.'

Joel hesitates. He doesn't want to be completely out of it tomorrow. He needs to remember all the amazing things he's experiencing right now. Carry them with him.

'Think of it as a new plateau,' Diego says, scooping powder out of a small plastic bag. 'The view's incredible.'

He holds out the spoon, which is still on the chain round his neck. Joel sits up in the hammock and leans forwards. He can feel heat radiating from Diego, from himself, can feel it colliding in the air. He snorts, then wipes his nose while Diego scoops some up for himself.

'It's going to take a while,' he says. 'Move over.'

They lie down next to each other. Two bodies blending together, weightless in the hammock. The waves of heat grow stronger. Time and space bend, embracing them.

Nina

Monday morning is bright white light and pouring rain. The windshield wipers work furiously but are overwhelmed by a deluge that obscures her vision and covers the roadway with water. Nina parks as close to Pineshade as she can and dashes towards the entrance, the wind tearing at her umbrella.

She changes in the basement and runs into Adrian on her way back upstairs. He tells her about a party he went to in the old mill behind Lycke Church. Apparently one of the actors from the theatre group lives in it. There was night swimming and sunrise; barbecuing and making out.

'And you?' he says.

'It was quiet. We had a couple of friends over for dinner.'

Adrian seems to be waiting for more, but there's nothing to add. She doesn't want to think about the dinner. The awkward mood has lingered between her and Markus all weekend.

'We did drink quite a bit of wine, of course,' she says.

'Goes without saying.' Adrian grins. 'Speaking of Midsummer, I saw you talking to that guy during the lunch. The one whose mother just moved into your ward. You used to know him, right?'

'Joel?' Nina says, feeling her smile growing stiff. 'Yes?'

'What's your story? Did the two of you used to be an item, or what?'

Her shrill little laughter bounces back at her from the lobby walls. 'What makes you think that?'

Adrian shrugs. 'You seemed so pissed at him I figured you must have dated.'

'We . . . no. Hardly.'

She shakes her head, says something about being in a hurry. While she swipes her card through the reader, she offers up a silent prayer that Joel left town over the weekend.

Gorana lies slumped across the table in the staffroom. She doesn't even lift up her head, which is resting on her crossed arms, when she spots Nina.

'Good morning,' she says with a yawn. 'Good Midsummer?'

'Not bad,' Nina replies. 'How were things here?'

Gorana rolls her eyes as though she's trying to look at her own eyebrows.

'It's been lively. Monika in D6 broke her arm, so I spent the night in A&E. I just *loved* being there on Midsummer's Eve. One bloke walked around all bloody with a knife sticking out of his shoulder, yelling about needing to smoke and another—'

'How did it happen?' Nina cuts in. 'How did she break her arm?'

'She'd climbed out of bed. When I came in, she was sitting on the floor, punching the bottom of the bed. Completely off her rocker. Faisal had to come help me so we could call an ambulance. They pumped her full of sedatives.'

'How is she now?'

'She's been asleep for the most part since we got back. I've lowered her bed as far as it'll go in case the crazy old bat decides to climb over the guard rail again.'

Gorana seems to sense that Nina is shaken, because her face softens. 'I'm sorry. I forgot that you used to know each other.'

'It's not okay to talk like that regardless. Has someone let Joel know?'

'He hasn't been answering his phone all weekend,' Gorana says.

Nina knew it. He's probably still high. He might even have gone to Katja's.

'Try again,' she says, and walks out into the hallway.

Monika is sitting up in bed, staring out the window when Nina enters D6. Her right forearm is in a cast to the fingertips. The white light rests on her face, making her grey eyes look even paler. She seems to have lost more weight over the weekend, so her head looks too heavy for her thin neck. Her nightgown has come down a little and her collarbones are stark and clearly visible.

It's as though something's eating her from the inside.

'Monika?' she says.

No reaction. The only sounds are Nina's breathing and the rain hammering against the window. The vinyl floor makes a faint sucking noise when she takes a step towards the bed.

'Can I sit with you for a bit?'

Monika heaves a deep sigh but doesn't answer. Nina hesitates before pulling up a chair and sitting down. Waiting.

At length, Monika turns to her. Her grey eyes stare vacantly.

'What happened?' Nina says. 'When you broke your arm?'

No answer.

'I'm sorry. I hope you're not in pain.'

Monika cocks her head. Looks at the cast, as though seeing it for the first time. Then she looks back up at Nina.

Something has shifted in her eyes. The dementia look is gone. But she's not herself, either.

It's not her, she's not Monika.

Nina doesn't know where the thought comes from, but she realises she's afraid.

It's Monika, of course it's Monika.

'What happened?' Nina says again.

'Monika's a little bitch,' Monika says hoarsely. 'But now she knows her place.'

Joel

His chest contracts as soon as he takes his first waking breath. He opens his eyes and sees a mural: an excessively green landscape under an excessively blue sky; stone columns in the foreground; a babbling fountain and dramatic clouds.

He has no idea where he is, but the anxiety is familiar. A chemical process that makes every synapse in his brain scream out a single thought, a single word.

No no no no no.

Joel gingerly sits up in the strange bed. Notes that he's naked. There's a pressure behind his eyes, a thudding, pounding pain in his head.

Someone's lying next to him in the rumpled sheets. The rockabilly man from last night.

Diego? Was that his name?

Joel puts one foot on the floor and feels carpet.

Breathe, breathe, just breathe.

He spots his jeans on the floor, his underwear still inside. When he folds the duvet aside to get out of bed, he finds his tank top. It stinks of old smoke. When he bends down to pick up his jeans, his head feels like it's coming apart at the seams. For a split second, he's afraid he might have hit it during the night. He raises his hand to feel his skull and concludes it's in one piece after all.

The blinds are closed, but there are city noises coming from outside – a car blowing its horn; high heels against pavement. They must have left Katja's house in the woods sometime during the night. He tries to remember but can find nothing after the hammock and the tiny spoonful of ketamine.

Joel looks at the body in the bed again. It's motionless. Too motionless. A new wave of anxiety makes Joel's chest contract as though he's imploding. He walks around the bed and gently shakes a freckled shoulder. Holds his breath.

Diego mumbles something in his sleep and rolls over. Joel exhales. He pulls his phone out of his jeans pocket and stares at the screen.

It's Monday morning.

He's lost two and a half days. And he has eleven missed calls from Pineshade. Three voicemails.

He staggers out of the room and finds himself in a sitting room with gold walls and a black grand piano. People are piled on a gigantic sofa. Katja's one of them, rolled up against one of the arm rests. Some people have fallen asleep on the floor next to the sofa. The air reeks of booze and stale smoke. There are ashtrays and bottles everywhere, empty plastic bags with white residue in the corners. How much of it did he take? He spots needles and almost throws up. He touches the crooks of his arms, inspecting them carefully in the gloom.

Look, Mum, no holes!

Joel tiptoes over to the table, stepping over a sleeping woman. He picks up an unopened bag, guessing it's a quarter of speed – he needs something to get through this day.

He finds a bathroom and leans over a fancy marble sink to drink from the tap, meeting his own wildly staring eyes in the mirror when he wipes his chin. He quickly looks away and pours the white powder onto a sheet of loo roll, then squeezes it into a tiny ball and swallows it whole.

He walks through rooms with stuccoed ceilings, full of ostentatious furniture, tacky paintings and glass art that looks like intestines and corals. Eventually, he spots his Converses in a hallway, lined up surprisingly neatly in the middle of the mess.

Joel keeps one hand on the banister as he walks down the stairs. When he pulls open the front door, the sunlight stabs at his eyes like knives. Squinting, he can just about make out Järntorget Square at the end of the street. He's in Gothenburg. He pats his pockets, relieved to feel the outline of both his wallet and keys. Stringing together coherent thoughts is a challenge, but at least he's able to come up with a bullet-point plan of sorts. Buy painkillers. Head up to Nordstan. Take the Marstrand Express from there. Call Pineshade from the bus. And then home.

Home.

Monday.

Joel frantically pulls his phone out. It's half past seven. The photographer from the real estate agency is going to be at the house in just a couple of hours.

He's still staring at the phone when it rings again. Pineshade's number appears on the screen.

Nina

Staff meeting in the common room. Elisabeth informs everybody of what happened in D6 on Midsummer's Eve. Nina has read the full report, but she still instinctively cradles her own forearm as if to protect it. Monika has suffered a radial fracture, the most common injury sustained by old people who fall out of bed. But the fracture had also been dislocated when she banged her arm against the undercarriage of the bed, so they'd had to realign it.

'She was given sedatives and local anaesthesia,' Elisabeth says. 'Luckily, she doesn't seem to have any memory of the incident.'

Monika's a little bitch. But now she knows her place.

'She remembers,' Nina says.

Elisabeth shoots her a glance.

'She's going to have a full recovery, so long as there are no unexpected developments,' she continues. 'I've put her on an Oxazepam schedule. Fingers crossed it can keep her calm until her arm heals.'

'Let's just hope her son isn't the type to start talking about neglect,' Rita puts in.

'Yes,' Elisabeth says. 'Gorana managed to get hold of him this morning; he will be here later today. Be careful how you talk about the incident. It's important to remember that no one here has done anything wrong.'

Nina stares at them incredulously. Not a word about how Monika feels.

'She's managed to climb over the guard rail before,' she says. 'I asked you to check with rehab if the risks don't outweigh the benefits in this case. Have you?'

Elisabeth smiles stiffly. 'Getting an answer from them takes time, as you are well aware. We have lowered the bed for now.' She looks down at her papers, ready to move on.

'We should have them run some tests on Monika,' Nina says. 'She's losing weight too fast. And she's . . . She's not herself.'

Elisabeth looks up again. This time she doesn't bother hiding her displeasure. 'This is a care facility for people with dementia. What did you think she was here for?'

'She's never been aggressive before. It could be something medical, or—'

'You knew her, before,' Elisabeth interrupts.

'Yes?'

'That makes it difficult for you to be objective. These things happen, you know that.'

'What about her weight? She could have a digestive issue we don't know about, or some kind of deficiency, there could be worms—'

'We would have noticed,' Elisabeth says.

'Not necessarily.'

'I think running some tests might be a good idea. It's something to tell the son, if nothing else,' Adrian puts in. 'If he's concerned, it might reassure him.'

Elisabeth heaves a deep sigh. She rarely listens to anyone except Adrian; Nina wonders if it's because he's a man or because he's good-looking. Maybe it's both. Either way, she's grateful for the help. Adrian winks at her when Elisabeth looks back down at her papers.

'I promise I'll think about it,' Elisabeth says. 'And now, if you don't mind, I'd like to move on.'

Rita nods agreement.

'Apparently, I'm the only one who cares that we have to start making lunch soon,' she says with a catty look at Nina.

Adrian and one of the girls from the C Ward exchange a pointed look. They hate Rita in a way Nina can't allow herself to do. She wouldn't be able to work with her if she did.

Someone enters the common room; Nina turns to look along with everyone else. It's a woman her own age. She's wearing glasses and has a thin ring of plaited gold through her septum. Her hair is pulled back into a messy bun.

'I'm sorry I'm late,' she says.

'That's right!' Elisabeth exclaims and claps her hands together. 'I almost forgot!'

She has changed to her most effusive tone – the one she uses with new relatives and staff, before they start asking awkward questions and making difficult demands.

'This is Nahal, our new casual employee in D. She's starting tonight, but I asked her to stop by the meeting to say hi. She just moved here from Uddevalla.'

'That's a proper metropolis compared to Skredsby,' Adrian says. 'How did you end up here?'

Nahal laughs and blushes in that way so many women do when they first meet Adrian. 'I met a guy online,' she says, waving her phone around. 'Thank God for technology, eh?'

'Nahal has a lot of experience working at a care home in Uddevalla,' Elisabeth says.

'It was a factory compared to this,' Nahal says. 'Five floors, three wards on each. I had to quit – it was so depressing. We never had time to do anything properly. This place is quaint.'

'And speaking of quaint,' Elisabeth says. 'I believe you'll be bringing a four-legged friend sometimes as well, isn't that right?'

'Yes, I'm training my dog to be a therapy dog. He's almost certified and I figured he could do his internship here.'

Elisabeth laughs a little too loudly. 'It sounds wonderful,' she says. 'As you know, contact with animals has been proven to have a very positive effect on people with dementia. Rita, would you mind giving Nahal a tour?'

'Sure,' Rita says. 'If we ever get out of this meeting.'

Joel

The amphetamine had given him the energy to clean the whole house in a couple of hours. Determined, organised, efficient. He has no idea when he last ate, but he's not hungry. After the photographer left, he got in the shower and scrubbed every part of his body, staying in until he ran out of hot water. His skin is still tingling and he feels dehydrated inside and out. He's on the verge of crashing and wishes he'd brought one of the tiny plastic bags home. Just to get through the rest of this day.

He parks outside Pineshade. The moment the car falls silent, a fluttering of panic returns. The inside of his skull crackles. Things seem to be boiling in there.

Just a bit more, eh, Joel?

He sneers at himself and climbs out of the car. He should call his sponsor and confess about his relapse, but they haven't spoken in years. And he doesn't want to admit he's drinking again. He steps into D Ward and is greeted by the familiar smells of vinyl, cleaning products, urine and cooking. They seem to seep into him; become part of him.

Lillemor is sitting in front of the TV in the lounge, watching a black and white film. When she spots him, she heaves herself out of her armchair.

'Are you here to see Monika?' she hollers after him. 'Would you say hi to her from me?'

'I will,' he says, and walks on.

But Lillemor has come out into the hallway and is following him with heavy steps. 'Don't you think it's wonderful a guardian angel has come to us?' she shouts.

Joel turns around. 'I'm not sure I think it's doing its job,' he replies. 'Seeing as how my mum broke her arm.'

Lillemor smiles at him patiently, as though he were a slow-witted child. 'That was for her own good,' she says. 'You see that, don't you?'

'No, I don't, actually.'

'She tried to resist one of the Lord's messengers.'

He almost envies Lillemor. Her existence must be so uncomplicated. Devoid of doubt. She has no need for drugs. She has her angels instead, helping her to endure this world.

Joel walks away.

'The Lord always finds a way to enter our hearts!' Lillemor calls out after him.

Joel passes the common room but quickly looks away when he spots Nina clearing up after the midday meal. He's not sure he'd be able to hide the fact that he's high from her and he doesn't want to add fuel to the fire of her self-righteousness. Continuing down the corridor, he picks up a faint '*. . . name is Edit . . .*' as he passes an open suite door.

When he stops outside D6, Lillemor is still standing in the hallway, watching him as he takes a deep breath and enters.

His mum's sitting up in bed, staring out the window. She's even skinnier than a few days ago. Looking at her cast, he wants to cry. She's so frail.

Lillemor's guardian angel can go to hell.

The perspectives of the room feel warped until he realises the bed has been lowered so far the undercarriage is almost touching the floor.

'Mum?'

He sits down and studies her profile. Her jaw is clearly visible, a razor-sharp line.

'Mum? How are you feeling?'

She turns towards him. Her eyes have sunk deeper into her skull. Her gaze pierces him. Turns him inside out. He takes a step back.

Stop being paranoid, Joel.

He tries to look away, but his eyes are caught. Prickles run along his scalp and his skin crawls. One corner of his mother's mouth twitches up into a crooked smile.

She hasn't blinked. Not once.

'Would you like me to open the window?' he continues. 'It's a bit stuffy in here.'

She chuckles. A low, hacking sound from deep inside her chest. 'I know what you've been doing,' she says. 'You don't even remember, but I can see everything from here.'

The voice is so cracked it seems to split apart, making it sound like two overlapping voices, double sets of vocal cords, vibrating against each other.

The prickling spreads down his neck, fanning out across his back. 'What do you mean?' he asks.

'You're never going to be able to quit. You're so *weak*.'

Can she tell he's high? She never could before. Or did she see it and pretend she didn't?

He wants to get up, wants to walk away, but his legs wouldn't carry him.

And she still hasn't blinked.

'Mum . . .'

'*Muuum*,' she heckles. 'I'm not your mum. Not anymore. Thank God. You've disgusted me since the day you came out of this body. Haven't you figured that out yet? Surely I wasn't *that* good at hiding it?' She's speaking faster and faster. Bubbles of saliva swell and burst on her lips.

'Stop it,' Joel says, but she doesn't react.

'I knew who you were from the very beginning. I saw the way you looked at other men. Do you have any idea how ashamed I was?'

He gets to his feet. Grabs hold of the guard rail of her bed to make sure he stays upright.

'Stop it,' he says again.

'I can smell his filth on your breath.'

Joel shakes his head and backs up a few steps. He knocks over a chair; the crash sounds unnaturally loud in the small room. When he turns around, he can feel her eyes boring into the back of his neck. Her unblinking eyes.

'You had to check he was alive, didn't you?' she says, and this time he could have sworn it was more than one voice.

Something sinks inside him. Faster and faster. Free fall.

He walks towards the door. Hears his mother's wheezing breaths behind him, closer and closer, as though she's right behind him, reaching out to grab his T-shirt. Panic explodes inside him when he pushes down the handle and shoves the door open.

The corridor is shockingly unremarkable. When he glances back over his shoulder, there's no one behind him. Of course not. Just the coat and jackets hanging limply on their hooks. He can't see the bed from here, but he can still hear his mother breathing. Joel shuts the door.

Nina

Snip. Giggle. Snip. Giggle. Snip. Giggle.

'Careful, I might cut you,' Nina says, pinning the pale, veiny foot against the mattress.

'It tickles!' Vera retorts.

But she presses her lips together and nods bravely. Her foot stops moving.

Snip.

The small sliver of nail, hard and yellow, shoots across the sheet. Vera's foot jerks and she giggles again, then looks guilty when Nina glances up at her.

'Halfway done,' Nina says, and picks up the clipping before gently grabbing the other foot.

But she no more than grazes the big toe before Vera whimpers and kicks out.

'I can't take it!' she chortles.

Nina laughs. Dagmar grunts over in her bed; when Nina looks over, she's met by a toothless grin.

'I might need your help to pin your sister down,' she says.

Dagmar's smile broadens and Nina turns back to Vera.

'Ready?' she asks.

Vera nods.

Nina opens the nail scissors and wedges the nail of Vera's big toe into the gaping steel beak. She's just about to cut when she hears a shriek out in the corridor. Wordless, pained, barely human. Vera looks at her worriedly.

'I'll be right back,' Nina says, getting up.

Dagmar grunts in her bed, watching her with amusement. And for a moment, Nina's sure Dagmar *knows* what just happened.

The scream stops momentarily before resuming with renewed force. It sounds like two people now. Nina follows the voices to D6.

Monika.

The lights are out in the suite, but hazy afternoon light is pouring in through the window.

'Hello? What's going on?' she says, and enters the room.

Monika's on all fours in her bed, with her back arched. Her head is burrowing into her pillow, and her lilac nightgown only covers half her thighs, revealing her loose and shrivelled skin.

Nina quickly glances over at the open bathroom door. No one's in there.

She could have sworn she heard two voices.

Monika looks up. Her face has contracted into a rictus around her wide-open mouth. When she meets Nina's eyes, she bursts out crying. All the strength seems to drain from her and she collapses onto her side, hiding her face behind the arm that's not in a cast.

'How are you feeling?' Nina says, as gently as she can.

She carefully takes Monika's arm and lowers it. Her face is red and wet with tears.

'I don't want to do this anymore,' Monika says quietly. 'I can't.'

'What do you mean?' Nina asks. 'Are you in pain?'

Monika shakes her head.

'Tell me. What is it you can't do anymore?'

'I want him to leave me alone,' Monika says. 'But he won't let me be.'

Goose bumps spread up and down Nina's arms. The voices. There had been at least two voices in here. Hadn't there?

'Who?' she says, looking around the room, even though she knows full well there's nowhere a person could hide.

Monika glances up. Her slate-grey eyes are so pale, as though her tears have washed away their colour. Nina reaches out to touch her cheek. Monika slaps it away.

Nina feels childishly hurt. But Monika looks unhappy, too.

'Go,' she says. 'Go away.'

Nina shakes her head; Monika heaves a frustrated sigh.

'You have to,' she says. 'Before . . .' Her brow furrows. She snaps her mouth shut.

'Before what?'

Monika lowers her eyes and strokes her cast. 'Before he comes back.'

It reminds Nina of Anna's fear at the end. She swallows. She can't let herself be drawn in or she'll start imagining things, but she has to know what Monika's experiencing if she wants to help her.

'Who is he?' she says.

'Please leave me alone. Please, Nina.'

'Tell me.'

Nina doesn't know why she's insisting. She's forcing Monika deeper into her paranoid delusions.

They're just delusions.

When Monika looks up again, her eyes are ablaze with impatience. 'Get out,' she says. 'Get out!'

Nina realises that if she were to stay, it would be for her own selfish reasons. She may not understand why, but her presence is upsetting to Monika.

'If you're sure . . .' she says tentatively.

'Get out of here!' Monika screams. 'Go be a good girl somewhere else, I never want to see you again!'

Nina hurries out into the corridor, heart pounding and spots Sucdi coming through the front doors. Her shift is starting. Nina's is almost over.

They meet outside the staffroom.

'Did something happen?' Sucdi says, studying her searchingly.

Nina shakes her head. 'Monika's having a rough time. Would you mind checking in on her a few extra times tonight?'

She looks into the staffroom. Rita's sitting at the table, drinking coffee and reading a gossip rag, waiting for handover. Gorana, who has to cover the evening shift with Sucdi, is nowhere to be seen.

'Can I just ask you something, speaking of Monika?' Sucdi says quietly, nodding for Nina to come away from the doorway.

She looks uncomfortable, and Nina doesn't want to know. No more unsettling news about Monika, not after what just happened.

'Of course,' she says.

Like a good girl.

'It's so silly,' Sucdi says. 'But there's just this thing I don't understand. I've never told you about my dad, have I?'

Nina looks at her uncomprehendingly. 'Your dad? No. I don't think so.'

She doesn't need to search her memory. Sucdi's the only person at Pineshade who is as private as herself. The only person who's not constantly airing every last detail about her spouse, adulterous affairs, annoying parents, ungrateful children.

'He's moving back to Somalia this autumn. Before he's too old,' Sucdi says, and a shadow of grief passes across her face. 'He doesn't want to depend on Sweden's elderly care when he can no longer get by on his own.'

'Do you still have family there?'

'He's moving in with his cousin's children,' Sucdi says. 'They've only met a few times, but it's different there. They look after their old people.'

'But . . . but is it safe down there now?' Nina says, ashamed that she has no idea.

'He says it is. I've never been. I don't know.'

Sucdi tries to hide her concern, but is not entirely successful. And Nina realises Sucdi has been carrying this around for a long time, without her noticing.

'Dad says he feels safer there than in Sweden,' she continues. 'Things have changed so much in the past few years.'

Nina can only nod. It seems incomprehensible. She obviously hears about all kinds of terrible things, but they never seem to happen to people who exist in the real world. At least not in *her* world. That being said, three refugee facilities have burnt down in recent months.

And she remembers what it was like in the nineties. What people in school used to say. Back then, it was the Yugoslavians who should be sent home or they would keep waging war on Swedish soil. And she knows what people said about Joel. That people like him were going to make humanity extinct with their AIDS.

'Anyway,' Sucdi says. 'Monika knew about it, and I don't get how she could. I figured maybe I'd mentioned something to you and forgot about it.'

'No,' Nina says. 'Couldn't it be Faisal? That night he was here covering for Johanna?'

'He says he didn't say anything. And I don't know what reason he could have had to talk to Monika about my dad.'

Sucdi's voice falters. A smile, clearly forced, on her lips. 'It doesn't matter,' she says. 'Never mind, okay?' There's a determined glint in her eyes. It's not a question.

They head into the staffroom together.

'I'm not going to wait around until Gorana decides to show up,' Rita announces, aggressively turning the pages of her magazine. 'I have better things to do, even though some people clearly don't care.'

Sucdi rolls her eyes behind Rita's back and pours two cups of coffee. She hands one to Nina, who accepts it and sits down at the table.

Everything's normal. Or at least it looks normal. She tries to hold onto that.

But when she opens the binder to start the handover, she can tell Sucdi's mind is elsewhere.

If Monika knows things she shouldn't about Sucdi's dad . . . could what she said about Nina's mother be true, too?

She's not happy with you, let me tell you.

Joel

He stays in the carpark and watches his mother's window. He glimpsed Nina in there a while ago.

What did they talk about? Has Mum told her, too?

How could she know?

Stop thinking about it, Joel. You're crashing. You're unlikely to reach any useful conclusions. You're just making the anxiety worse.

Of course she doesn't know. You're just imagining things.

Joel closes his eyes and rubs them hard, then studies the resulting clusters of bright dots flashing against a black background. They come at him in waves, changing shape, approaching and retreating by turns.

He stays in his seat and fights the urge to text Katja.

A hard rap on the window makes him jump. One of the girls who works at Pineshade is looking in at him gravely, bending down with one arm resting on the roof of the car. The dots continue to dance across his field of vision, translucent in the white light from outside.

He rolls down the window. Thoughts race through his overheated brain, now in a different direction.

Something's happened, something about Mum.

'I'm sorry to bother you,' she says. 'I was wondering if I could bum a smoke off you? I left mine at home and I don't have time to run out for new ones before my shift.'

'Sure,' he says.

He climbs out of the car, pulls a packet out of his pocket and fishes out two crumpled-looking cigarettes. She smiles at him and straightens out the one he hands her. It's a smile that transforms her entire face. Her hard features suddenly soften. She reminds him of a young Nina, a dark-haired little doppelganger.

'So, why are you sitting here?' she asks after taking a drag.

He shakes his head but can't think of anything good to say, so he opts for the truth. 'I'm having a pretty bad day.'

'Plenty of those to be had around here,' she says, leaning back against the car.

Joel chuckles and lights his own cigarette. 'I suppose so,' he says.

They smoke in silence. She's definitely not the ingratiating type, but he likes her.

'My mum broke her arm on Midsummer's Eve,' he says. 'And they couldn't reach me all weekend.'

'I know. I was the one who brought her to A&E. You and I spoke on the phone this morning.'

He glances furtively at her. Wonders if he was even able to form complete sentences when he picked up.

'Thanks for calling.'

'No worries, it's what they pay me for. But I'm sorry I had to give you such bad news. It sounded like you were having a rough go of it already.'

He looks away. 'It's just so fucking typical you couldn't get hold of me all weekend.'

'Don't get worked up about it,' she says. 'You stop by almost every day. Do you know how many of the old gits never have a single visitor?'

'I don't have much else on.'

'Still. People don't give a shit about their elderly. Did you know they had to change the laws about burials a few years ago?'

He shakes his head.

'Now, you have to be buried within a month. Before, people would leave their relatives in the freezer for ages because a funeral didn't fit into their fucking schedules.'

Joel doesn't know how to respond to that, but she's not waiting for a reaction.

'We see things like that all the time. I mean, people don't give a toss about their relatives even before they die. It's hard coming here, I get it. I try not to judge. But they should be able to bring themselves to do it *every once in a while*. It means a lot to the old people. My point is, you're here.'

'I have some catching up to do. I should have spent time with her before she got sick.'

She shrugs. 'Not a lot you can do about that now. Don't be so hard on yourself.'

She stubs her cigarette out against the sole of her shoe and says goodbye, leaving him standing by the car.

'I don't even know your name,' he calls after her.

'Gorana.'

'Joel.'

'I know. Thanks for the cigarette.'

She stuffs the butt into the wall-mounted ashtray and disappears through the front doors.

Pineshade

On Monday evening, roses are delivered to Monika. The card reads *'Feel better soon Mum/Mother-in-law/Grandma, love Björn and family'*.

The greasy stain on the ceiling of D7 has been removed. On Tuesday, the new client moves in. Olof is only sixty-nine and has Alzheimer's. His hair is thin and white, sitting like a wreath around a bald pate spattered with age spots. It's his daughter who brings him to Pineshade. She looks around while Elisabeth gives them the tour and tries to say hi to Dagmar, who stares mutely back at her with her runny eyes. Monika is screaming in the room next to Olof's.

His daughter is terrified she has inherited her dad's illness, so terrified, in fact, that she refuses to let his doctor run the tests he has offered her. She has seen the X-rays of Olof's brain. The dead nerve cells, millions and millions of them, like a dark butterfly spreading its wings. Gradually, bit by bit, plunging everything that was once him into darkness. He has gone downhill fast, despite the drugs. And yet, not fast enough. Olof still has lucid moments when he's aware of his own decline. It will be easier on him when he no longer understands. At least that's what his daughter's telling herself. But right now, Olof is crying, and Elisabeth tilts her head to the side and pats his shoulder.

'This is going to be great, you'll see,' she says, but she's not looking at him, she's looking at his daughter.

* * *

On Wednesday, Petrus discovers that there's another man on the ward, and it makes him so angry he refuses to eat.

* * *

On Friday night, Nahal finds Lillemor on her knees in her suite. Her folded hands are raised towards the ceiling. She's speaking tearfully to her angel, asking him to reveal himself again, show her he hasn't forsaken her.

* * *

June turns into July over a series of dreary days, each of which seems identical to the next. The roses in Monika's suite wilt and are thrown out. The staff binder fills with reports of violent episodes. She's spitting, scratching, biting. One afternoon, she manages to get her cast off and rams her arm into the windowsill in D6. The bone, which had started to heal, is broken again, and this time Rita's the one who takes her to A&E. *She's not even ten years older than me*, Rita thinks to herself while she waits for the car to pick them up. *I hope someone shoots me if I end up like her.*

Joel

Joel is sitting completely still in the armchair in his mother's room and doing his best not to listen to the voice that no longer sounds like hers.

Elisabeth has informed him about more 'episodes'. It's so hard to accept that she's talking about his mum.

He misses her. That old woman in the bed isn't her.

'Just wait and see,' she hisses. 'You're going to end up in a place like this yourself. You don't have a lot of time left.'

She grins at him. Her teeth look yellow against her ashen face, her chapped lips.

'You know that. Don't you? You long for the day.'

Mum. Mum, come back.

She plays with the new cast around her arm. Her tongue is grey and spongy when she opens her mouth. An ancient muscle writhing in its cave.

'Your mum's not here. The cow gave up eventually. Just like you should.'

The voice begins to hum quietly and Joel gazes out the window. The light makes his eyes water. Out there, life goes on as though nothing has happened. Since Midsummer, more cars have been rumbling past on the motorway. Tourist season has begun. Lucky people who are on their way somewhere, who never have to think about places like Pineshade.

'Why don't you just leave?' his mum says. 'You never cared about her.'

She laughs hoarsely. Mirthlessly.

'Poor Monika. All alone in that big house, with nothing but her memories. No wonder she let me in.'

A moan rises from her ribcage. Joel turns back towards the bed. She has stiffened under her duvet. Her eyes are staring fixedly at the ceiling.

'Mum?' he says. 'Mum? Are you okay?'

She is panting heavily through her nose. Her front teeth slide across her flaking bottom lip, drawing blood.

Joel jumps up. 'I'm going to get someone,' he says.

His mum opens her mouth as though she wants to speak. Her eyes widen.

What should I do, Mum? What do you want?

There's crackling under the duvet as her legs and joints move. Her head bends back until the top of her skull is resting against her mattress, her throat's exposed, the tendons of her neck stretched to breaking point. Her mouth opens in a silent scream when her body arcs up and starts shaking. The metal parts of the bed rattle.

Panic surges through him as though his heart's pumping out ice water.

His mum's fingers contract into claws, fumbling across the duvet and throwing it aside. Her heels dig into the mattress, and her body arcs higher, and her hipbones are clearly visible through her nightgown.

Joel runs out into the corridor.

Wiborg is standing outside his mum's door as though she's been waiting for him. She's clutching her dementia cat to her chest. Joel ignores her and looks down the hallway, but sees only Edit, bent over her rollator.

'Hello?' he calls out. 'Hello, we need help in here!'

Wiborg presses a dry, bony finger to her lips and shakes her head. For a moment, Joel is convinced that she knows something, understands what's happening. But then he looks at the cat's light-blue glass eyes and realises he's the one going crazy.

Sucdi comes running from the common room with Nahal hard on her heels.

'There's something wrong with Mum!' he shouts. 'She's having a fit.'

They follow him into the suite. His mum is on her side on the bed with her back to them. She's breathing heavily. The duvet is still on the floor. Her legs are so thin there is a wide gap between her thighs.

'Monika?' Sucdi says. 'Are you okay?'

Joel watches the body on the bed.

'Monika?' Sucdi says again.

His mum mutters something and slowly turns around. Looks at them drowsily.

'I'm sleeping,' she grumbles. 'Leave me alone.'

'She was awake a second ago,' Joel says. 'She was doing a full bloody backbend. Her whole body was shaking.'

'What's this nonsense you're spouting?' says his mother.

Nahal gives him a brief glance before bending down to pick up the duvet. He wonders what they're thinking. What he's claiming sounds insane – doesn't it?

It feels like vertigo when he suddenly has to ask himself if he imagined the whole thing. Could he have dozed off and dreamed it?

'What are we going to do about your lips, Monika?' Sucdi says.

She picks up a jar of Vaseline from the bedside table and gently dabs them with a cotton wad. His mother's bottom lip glistens wet and red where a flake was ripped off just before the seizure.

It wasn't a dream. He saw it happen.

'Is it lunchtime?' his mum asks, pushing herself up into a sitting position.

'Almost,' Sucdi replies, putting a hand on her forehead. 'At least you don't seem to have a temperature.'

'Of course I don't have a temperature,' his mum says. 'Can't a person have a nap in this place without everyone making a fuss?'

'Of course you can,' Nahal assures her.

'There's always someone poking and prodding at me. I might as well get up.' She yanks the guard rail. It rattles, but doesn't move.

'Hang on a minute,' Sucdi tells her, nodding silently for Joel to step into the corridor.

They leave the room. He turns around one last time and sees his mum bare her teeth in something that might be a smile, but might also be something else entirely.

'I get if you don't believe me,' he says quietly in the corridor. 'But it was like she was having an epileptic fit or something.'

'We believe you,' Sucdi says.

'You do?'

'Of course,' she says, eyeing him. 'Why wouldn't we?'

'I don't know,' Joel says, running a hand through his hair. 'It's all just so bloody strange.'

Nahal's eyes are sympathetic behind her glasses. 'I need to talk to Elisabeth,' he says. 'Is she here?'

'She is,' Sucdi says. 'I'll come with you. Nahal will keep an eye on Monika.'

Joel nods gratefully. The fluorescent lights tinkle above their heads as he follows Sucdi down the corridor and around the corner, where she knocks on the door to the ward director's office and enters without waiting for a response.

'It's about Monika in D6,' she says.

'She had some kind of attack just now,' Joel says as he steps inside.

The glow of the fluorescents is steady in here.

'An attack?' Elisabeth says, tilting her head to the side.

'It looked like epilepsy or something. I was there with her.'

'When did this happen?'

'Just now. I obviously wouldn't put off informing you about something like that.'

'Of course.'

Her voice sounds calm, but red splotches spread across her chest while he describes his mother's arced body, the shaking, the crackling joints.

'How is she now?' Elisabeth asks.

'She's normal again.'

'Then it wasn't an epileptic fit,' Elisabeth says. 'If that was what it was, she would have been completely exhausted. It's like running a marathon, physically speaking.'

'She needs to go to the hospital.'

'I don't think that's necessary,' Elisabeth says. 'I understand that this is difficult for you, but it's nothing we haven't seen before. Isn't that right, Sucdi? These things sometimes happen with people with dementia. A sudden drop in a person's blood pressure can trigger it, for example. Did she get up suddenly?'

'No. She was lying down.'

'If she seems all right now, I'm sure there's nothing to worry about.'

Joel has to force himself to remain calm. 'I want to take her in. It's not just this attack. She's changed . . . and, yes, I know, she has dementia, but her personality is completely altered. Like how she deliberately broke her arm and has been acting out . . . and she's talking about herself in the third person and saying she's not my mother and it's . . . it can't be normal.'

Elisabeth nods, but he knows she's not really listening, just waiting for him to finish. Maybe it's no wonder. He doesn't even know what he's saying himself. He can't explain what he doesn't understand.

'Maybe she has a brain tumour,' he hears himself conclude.

It's only as he says it that he realises that thought has been there a while, he has just not wanted to acknowledge it.

Elisabeth frowns. 'I don't think that's something you need to worry about. As I said, I understand that this is difficult for you. It's always difficult for the loved ones.'

'But it's not about that! I don't know how to explain it, but she . . . She's not like herself at all. She's completely spaced out but she's still . . . needling people.' He regrets his words the second they leave his lips.

'What do you mean, needling?'

If that cool, patient tone had been able to deceive him, the red splotches on her neck would still have given her away. Elisabeth just wants to get rid of him now – she isn't taking him seriously. If she only knew what he's *not* telling her.

She knows things. It's as though she can see right through me. Read my mind.

Elisabeth might call the men in the white coats, but they would be coming for him, not his mother.

He looks helplessly at Sucdi. 'You don't see it?' he says.

Sucdi seems to hesitate. 'We have doctors on call,' she says. 'Maybe it would be a good idea to have one of them come over. Just to be safe.'

Elisabeth stares at her coldly. 'Fine,' she says. 'I'll make the call right now.'

Joel looks at the ward director with surprise. He can't help but wonder what happens to all the old people at Pineshade who don't have relatives to advocate for them, to make trouble on their account. Who's going to stand up for Edit Andersson, or Lillemor, or the odd sisters at the end of the D corridor who no one ever seems to visit?

'Good,' he says.

'We'll call you when the doctor has seen her,' Elisabeth says.

'There will be no need. I'd like to be present to ask questions, so I'll stick around.'

Elisabeth nods grimly. Joel struggles to hide his smug smile when she picks up the phone.

It's a small victory, but he needed it. He looks at Sucdi, nodding a thank you.

Nina

The fluorescent lights in the basement of Pineshade hum faintly when Nina exits the changing room. She's painfully aware they're about to switch off any moment and has to force herself not to run.

She doesn't know what's wrong with her. Last night, she dreamed about a sea full of mareel; she was looking for something in the dark among the thousands of dots of light eddying around her. It wasn't a nightmare, and yet she was afraid when she woke up. She's still afraid. A part of her is still bobbing in the cold water, searching for something that might be gone forever.

The lights go out. The switch glows like a red eye at the end of the hallway.

Something is down here with her.

Don't turn around. If you turn around, you lose.

She turns around. The corridor behind her is deserted. And yet, it feels like something's staring back at her. Watching her silently, safe in the knowledge that she can't see it.

The door to the changing room is wide open.

Didn't I close it?

Nina picks up the pace and pushes the light switch as she passes, just so she doesn't have to feel the shadows behind her back as she steps out into the stairwell. The fluorescent lights turn on with a faint tinkling and she realises she's been holding her breath.

Her heart rate slows as she crosses the lobby. When she enters D Ward, her fear has already morphed into vague shame at the memory of it.

Vera and Dagmar are sitting close together in the common room. As usual, it's as though there's an invisible wall around them. Vera's knitting needles click rapidly against each other; a cascade of red wool growing longer, stitch by stitch, in her lap.

Olof from D7 is sitting in an armchair. He looks unhappy. Bodil is perched on one of the armrests. She has crossed her legs and is bobbing her foot up and down but she's failing to catch his attention.

Bodil eyes Nina crossly when she enters. She clearly doesn't want any competition.

'Hi, Olof,' Nina says, squatting down next to him. 'How are you today?'

Bodil's bobbing foot stops moving.

'Are you here to pick me up?' Olof says.

'Are you expecting someone?'

He sighs. 'I don't know, but I have to get out of here. I'm supposed to drive the ferry out to Instö Island. The tourists are already going crazy – you know what they're like.'

Nina has read the letter Olof's daughter wrote. He captained the Instö Ferry for over twenty years, before they built the bridge that made it obsolete in the early nineties. Joel and she took the ferry to Marstrand lots of times. They probably saw Olof on it. He must have gone back and forth more times than he could count. The route must be etched into his deepest memories, the ones that are the last to fade.

'Look,' Nina says. 'Don't worry. It's your day off. You don't have to work.'

'Day off!' he exclaims. 'It's peak season. And there are bags everywhere.'

'They're going to have to wait.'

'Tell that to the woman in the red dress yelling at me.'

Nina glances over at Vera's knitting and wonders if the wool is what's making Olof imagine a woman in a red dress.

'Never mind her,' Nina says.

'I could lose my job.'

'Someone else is going to take care of them. It's already been arranged.' She pats his hand. 'Bodil, maybe you would like to come with me for a while?'

'No, thank you,' Bodil replies curtly, her foot bobbing once more.

'Nina? Don't you have handover with the morning staff to get on with?'

Elisabeth is standing in the doorway. Her neck and chest are blotchy with stress. Nina braces herself.

'I'm sure they're keen to go home, so you'd better get to work,' Elisabeth goes on.

She's never going to understand that talking to the old people *is* her job.

'Don't worry,' Nina tells Olof as she stands up. 'The tourists are fine.'

'Your old classmate's on the warpath, by the way,' Elisabeth tells Nina in the corridor. 'I had to call a doctor over to calm him down.'

'Joel? Did something happen with Monika?'

Elisabeth snorts derisively. 'Well, *he* certainly seems to think so. To be completely honest, I'm not really sure what he was rambling on about, but given everything that's happened, I figured I'd better placate him. Adrian was right about that, actually.'

Nina can tell from Elisabeth's conspiratorial glances that she's expecting agreement. And it disgusts Nina to realise how often she has played along when Elisabeth is in this mood. No wonder she's expecting the usual response. But Nina can't deliver. Not now. Not when it's Monika.

'Is the doctor there now?' she asks. Elisabeth nods.

Nina hurries towards D6, ignoring Elisabeth calling after her about the handover.

When she steps into the suite, Joel's standing in the middle of the room. His arms are crossed and he's shifting from one foot to the other, staring at Monika, who's sitting on the edge of her bed. It has been raised so her feet don't touch the floor. Her thin, pale legs look lifeless. She's watching the doctor, who's sitting on a chair in front of her, with a kind of lazy curiosity. Nina recognises Ulf Hansson even before he turns around to greet her.

'What happened?' she says.

Joel suddenly seems to become aware of her presence. 'She had an attack,' he says.

'So far, I haven't found any sign of neurological problems,' Hansson reports. 'Her pupils react normally and her reflexes are in order.'

Joel looks helplessly at Nina. 'Mum was bent back in a rictus and shaking ... I don't understand why everyone's telling me there's nothing wrong with her.'

Nina nods mutely.

'All I'm saying is that there are no neurological problems,' Hansson replies calmly. 'I've spoken to Elisabeth and ordered blood and stool samples.'

Hansson's a good doctor. Always kind and patient, even with Dagmar and Petrus.

'You should have seen her,' Joel says. 'They might not be able to find it by tapping her knees, but if you'd seen her . . .'

His voice trails off. Out of the corner of her eye, Nina sees Hansson run the reflex hammer along the soles of Monika's feet. He gives a satisfied nod when her toes curl.

'She's not herself,' Joel says, without taking his eyes off Nina. 'It's like she's literally someone else.'

Nina has heard countless relatives say exactly that. The same words, the same tone of voice.

'Can't you tell?' Joel says. 'It's not just dementia, is it?'

Hansson's looking at her now, too. What is she supposed to say? It's just a gut feeling, and how can she trust her gut in a case like this? Elisabeth must be right. It's different when you've known the old person before they came to Pineshade.

'I don't know,' she says. Joel looks away, disappointed.

Hansson stands up.

'Thank you,' he says to Monika before turning to Joel. 'I don't think there's any need to worry. These things happen sometimes, I'm afraid. The human body is a mystery, and dementia makes everything even more complicated. Monika can't tell us anything, since she doesn't remember.'

Nina shoots Monika a furtive glance. She seems unaware they're talking about her.

'I'm going to write a prescription for Stesolid,' Hansson says.

'More sedatives?' Joel asks.

Monika chuckles, an eerily out of place sound. 'Go fish.'

Nina and Joel stare at her. She blinks and gnaws her bottom lip.

'If she has another attack, I promise I'll write a referral for a CT scan,' Hansson says. 'One step at a time.'

'Can't you do that now?' Joel says. When Hansson doesn't reply immediately, he smiles bitterly. 'No, of course. Too expensive, I'm guessing?' He turns to Nina. 'Thanks for fucking nothing.'

Joel

His mother's old bike hasn't been used in years. The handlebars shake in his hands as he zooms down the steep slopes towards Tjuvkil. He stands up on the pedals to struggle up the equally steep inclines. The chain skips from time to time but doesn't stick.

The physical exertion drains his mind of energy, keeping it from racing. From circling back to the same place again and again. Katja's house.

I'm going to quit again the moment this is over, as soon as I'm back in Stockholm. Right now, I need whatever help I can get. I've quit before, I can do it again, it's no big deal.

But when is this going to be over? How is he supposed to go back to Stockholm and just forget what it's like for his mum at Pineshade?

The clouds disperse as the sun begins to set and the wind greeting him as he pedals harder up the final incline is warm. He can smell smoked shrimp from the hostel, which has its own smokery. The road to the Instö Island Bridge forks off to the left, but he continues straight ahead towards the Tjuvkil promontory. The road finally becomes flat and he sits down and studies the beautiful houses lining the road as he slowly pedals the last stretch.

The bike has no kickstand, so he leans it against the concrete lip around the carpark at the end of the road. The wooden deck by the water's edge is crowded by what seems to be several generations of the same family. He doesn't recognise anyone, thankfully. Maybe they came in one of the boats moored in the little harbour. A lady in a navy bathing costume is pouring coffee from a thermos. Cling-filmed sandwiches are being passed out. A front tooth glints golden when she laughs at something one of the children shows her on their phone. She's older than his mum, yet so much younger.

Joel feels like an intruder when he steps onto the wooden deck. He pulls off his sweaty tank top and hangs it over the railing, then puts his phone and keys on top and kicks off his shoes. His legs tremble from the ride as he walks down the steps to the sea. The wood of the banister is velvety smooth. He looks out over clear blue waves, at distant cliffs that seem to glow in the light of the setting sun. The water envelops his feet, so cold it draws a gasp, but he presses on and dives from the bottom step before he can have second thoughts.

The cold is a shock. He forces himself to stay in until his body gets used to it. Treading water. Tasting the salt on his lips. The voices of the family up on the deck blend together. The grown-ups have broad west-coast accents, but the children are nattering away in a southern dialect. He turns onto his back and water fills his ears, muffling every sound from the air.

He stays submerged until he begins to shiver, then dips his head one last time and swims back. He feels around for the bottom step among slick stones – his body feels heavy after the weightlessness of the water.

'Your phone's been ringing off the hook,' the old lady says, smiling at him as he emerges.

Worry explodes in his chest. He mumbles a thank you and

wipes his hands on his tank top so he can use the screen. But the missed calls are not from Pineshade. They're from Björn.

Joel sits down on the concrete lip some way away from the deck, closes his eyes and lets the wind caress him dry.

'Are you back?' he says when Björn picks up.

'Yes, we got back this morning. We were supposed to be back yesterday, but the flights were delayed and no one could bloody tell us why.'

Joel only half-listens while Björn goes on and on about his family's travails.

'My God, it's fucking windy,' he says eventually. 'Are you at sea or something?'

'I've gone for a swim at Tjuvkil.'

'Fuck me, must be freezing. I don't know if I could handle it, having just come back from the Mediterranean.'

'Sure,' Joel replies. 'But then, I haven't.'

There's a moment's silence.

'The kids always want to swim no matter how cold it is,' Björn says. 'I guess we were like that, too, at that age.'

Joel's taken aback. It's unusual for Björn to talk about the two of them as a *we*. He's not used to thinking along those lines himself. It's so easy to forget they actually used to like each other, once upon a time.

'I just checked out the real estate photographs online,' Björn says. 'Bloody hell, would it have killed you to make a bit of an effort? They look terrible.'

And everything's back to normal.

Joel tries to explain in a calm manner that the real estate agent told him there's no point. Björn doesn't seem to have much of a reaction when he's told the house might be knocked down.

'I hope you'll give it a once-over before the viewing tomorrow,' he says.

'If you're so concerned, why don't you come down here and help?'

'I have some stuff to get on with at work, but give me another week at most and I'll—'

'Are you kidding me?' Joel breaks in.

'I didn't have time to get to everything I wanted to have done before the holiday.'

Joel resists a clichéd urge to hurl his phone into the sea.

'Mum thinks I'm keeping you from coming to visit.'

Björn bursts out laughing, as though there were something funny about that. Maybe there is, with enough emotional distance.

He can almost taste the bitterness in his mouth, like bile. 'Shouldn't you ask me how she is?'

'I just talked to her on the phone. She sounded the same as ever.'

Of course she did.

Joel gets to his feet. He has a childish feeling his mum is putting on an act for Björn just to bother him.

He's stayed here too long. He's losing all perspective.

He walks up and down the length of the carpark, trying to describe their mother's attack. It suddenly occurs to him that Björn might be angry. He should have called and told him straight away.

'Well, if everyone agrees it's fine, then I'm sure it is,' Björn says. 'They know what they're doing. It's probably nothing to worry about. I mean, poor her, obviously. But—'

'You don't get it!' Joel says, much too loudly. He notices the family over on the deck staring at him and lowers his voice again.

'She shouldn't have been able to do what she did. *I* wouldn't be able to. Especially not with a broken arm.'

'You always hear about unexpected feats of strength, though, don't you?' Björn says. 'You know, mothers lifting up cars to save their kid or whatever.'

Joel stops. The will to keep protesting is seeping out of him. There's no point.

'Sure,' he says. 'Great. I'll let you know if there's a bid on the house, but you promise to come out here soon, right?'

'Of course,' Björn says, and he has the temerity to sound offended. 'It's not like I don't give a shit, you know.'

Nina

Monika's screams carry all the way to D2, three suites away. Even after they stop, Nina feels an echo resonate within her. It reminds her of when she was a child, listening to her mum and her friends being drunk and rowdy. Intoxicated voices that sounded like *someone else*, as though demons had taken over their bodies.

It's only half past six; Nina doesn't know how she's going to make it through the rest of the evening shift.

'Someone needs to shut that bitch up,' Petrus says. 'Maybe a bit of cock is what she needs. That might calm her down. I can ram mine down her throat.'

'And how do we shut you up?' Nina retorts.

Petrus laughs delightedly.

She empties his catheter bag into a plastic bottle, walks over to the sink by the door and pours out the dark yellow urine. She rinses the bottle carefully, then pulls off her gloves and goes back in to Petrus.

'Do you need anything?' she says, straightening the duvet across his chest.

A new scream erupts in D6. Reverberates through the walls and floor.

'Is that woman from the telly working tonight?' Petrus asks.

'Who? No.'

Monika's screaming makes it hard to focus.

'Shame. She's my favourite.'

'Go to sleep. Maybe you'll get lucky and dream about her.'

Petrus grins. A split second later, his hand has shot out and grabbed Nina's forearm. She yelps when his fingers dig in, hitting a nerve.

'Let go of me!'

'Why don't you join me?'

Nina pulls and tugs at her arm. Tries to pry Petrus' fingers off without hurting him.

'Aren't you a feisty kitten?'

She manages to wrench free and quickly backs out of his reach, panting slightly. Petrus grins smugly but his smile fades when Monika screams again.

'That bitch needs to pipe down!' he bellows.

Nina turns out his light and closes his blinds before leaving the suite.

She finds Nahal in the staffroom. She's spreading a thick layer of butter on a teacake.

'Bodil's hungry,' she informs Nina.

More screaming from D6.

'I just checked on her,' Nahal says. 'There's nothing wrong. I think she's just looking for attention.'

Nina nods. 'I'll go check,' she says.

Nahal puts the bread down on a plate and gives her a searching look.

'Are you sure? If we give her what she wants, she might never stop.'

Nina knows Nahal's right, but it makes no difference. She can't not go. She thinks about the ragers her mum threw in their small flat in Ytterby again. The terror she felt as she crept out of bed to find out what was happening. It was scary, but staying under her covers, imagining it, was even scarier.

She walks down to D6. The screaming from inside stops abruptly when she pushes the handle down.

You see. She just wants attention. You don't have to go in.

Nina enters. The suite is dark. Only a diffuse, golden light trickling in through the blinds. She can hear Monika's snuffling breathing.

'Monika?' she calls out. 'Are you okay?'

No reply.

Nina steps into the room and sees a figure sitting up in bed, pressed against the wall. A shadow among shadows.

She walks over and turns on the bedside light. Monika shields her eyes with one hand. The sleeve of her big T-shirt slides back, revealing a hairy armpit, a web of blue veins over the pale skin on the inside of her arm.

'I'm sorry,' Nina says. 'I just wanted to make sure you're all right.'

More snuffling, but this time, Monika's giggling.

'You're such a good girl,' Monika says. 'Neat as a pin.'

Her voice is hoarse from all the screaming. She lowers her hand. Her eyes sparkle in their sockets.

'It doesn't matter how well you stock your fridge or how much you clean and wash and scrub. You're always going to be the filthy little child of an alcoholic.'

The room beyond the pool of light from the lamp on Monika's bedside table, seems to shrink. The shadows press in from every direction.

'Your mum told me,' Monika says. 'You killed her.'

The blood drains out of Nina's face turning it cold and numb.

'Stop it,' she says quietly. 'Please, stop.'

'How could you kill your own mother?'

'I didn't.'

'Tell her that, if you have the guts. She's standing right behind you.'

The muscles around Nina's tailbone contract.

Don't turn around. Don't turn around.

'Who told you this?' Nina asks.

Monika smiles. 'I already said. She's sitting on the sofa, rambling on and on; I can barely keep up.'

Who planted this in Monika's head? Joel? No. He doesn't know what happened. Not even Markus knows.

No one knows. Monika's making things up.

'You don't want to talk to her?'

'No.'

Nina backs away from the bed and keeps her eyes averted from the sofa as she turns and runs towards the door. But even so, she thinks she can smell a faint puff of exhalation, the sickly sweetness of stale alcohol.

Mum.

She steps out into the corridor and slams the door shut behind her. Nahal pops her head out of Bodil's suite and gives her a strange look.

'Did something happen?'

Nina can't get a sound out. Only manages to shake her head.

On the other side of the door, the screaming starts again.

Joel

He has left Lena Jonsson at the house. The viewing starts in a few hours. Strangers are going to be walking around his mum's things, opening doors and peeking into every nook and cranny, judging what for fifty years was her entire world. And she has no idea.

He stops at the supermarket to buy a large chocolate bar. Orange crisp, his mum's favourite.

When the front doors to Pineshade slide open, Joel feels like a giant maw is opening up to devour him. Suddenly, he wants to turn and run. Doesn't want to know which mother is waiting for him in there or what she's going to say this time. But he enters.

She's sitting with Lillemor and Wiborg on the sofa in the lounge, watching a rerun of *The Good Old Days.* The volume is turned up so high it makes the speakers rattle. Both Lillemor and Wiborg are swaying along with the audience on the screen. Joel's mum's sitting stock still, pressed against one of the armrests, but she seems fascinated by the programme.

'Hi, Mum,' Joel says, loudly, to make himself heard over the music.

She takes the chocolate when he gives it to her but immediately puts it down on her lap without so much as a second glance.

'Do you need help opening it?' Joel asks, nodding at her cast.

'No, thank you,' she replies politely.

Lillemor has stopped moving and is throwing greedy glances at the chocolate.

Joel pulls up a chair and sits down next to the sofa. He leans forwards, folds his hands and watches the TV for a while. Bright evening sun, lush trees. He doesn't recognise the two little girls on stage. Maybe they're from *Idol* or *Eurovision*. He doesn't keep up anymore.

The credits start to roll. His mum continues to stare intently at the screen, but Lillemor's tired of waiting. She snatches the chocolate bar from his mother's lap, tears open the wrapper and breaks off two rows, then shoves them into her mouth and sucks vigorously. A documentary about farmers organising a tractor competition comes on the TV.

'Look who's here!' someone calls out from the hallway.

Joel's the only one who turns around. Sucdi enters the room with Fredrika, who's pushing a light-blue pram. She gives Joel a happy smile. He smiles back and reaches for the remote on the table to turn the TV off. The black screen crackles. His mum mutters something under her breath.

'Wiborg,' Sucdi says. 'Someone wants to say hi to you.'

Suddenly, there's crying coming from the pram. Joel catches a glimpse of a dark-red, scrunched-up little face when Fredrika picks the baby up.

'Oh, you're awake now, are you? Maybe you could tell it was finally time to meet your great-grandma.'

'Come over here, Wiborg, you'll want to see this,' Sucdi coaxes.

Wiborg gets up and shuffles over to Fredrika with tiny, tentative steps.

Lillemor stands up, too. She coos and makes a fuss over the baby.

'Oh my,' she says. 'So teeny tiny.'

Wiborg's considerably more reserved.

'His name's Sigge,' Fredrika says. 'Like Grandpa.'

Wiborg nods but doesn't seem to understand.

'And you and Sigge have the same birthday,' Fredrika continues. 'Remember? That's why I couldn't come on Midsummer, even though it was your birthday. I was in the hospital.'

Wiborg gives her an uncertain smile and backs away.

Joel goes over to join them. Studies the baby, who has stopped screaming. His eyes stare out into the room, unseeing. An inconceivably small hand flails across the little face.

'Congratulations,' he says. 'He's adorable.'

He gently strokes the baby's bald head and shudders when he feels the edges of the fontanelle, thinking about the unprotected brain inside.

'Thank you,' Fredrika says warmly. But her gaze returns to Wiborg. 'Nana? Don't you want to come over and say hi?'

Wiborg shakes her head. 'It can't be mine,' she says. 'I'm not even married.'

Joel sees Fredrika's smile stiffen. Suddenly, the moment feels far too private. They should leave them alone. But now his mum is pushing in, too. She leans over the baby in Fredrika's arms.

Sigge's whole body flinches at the new presence. His hands begin to flail wildly.

'Can I hold him?' his mum says. 'It's been so long since I held a little one. And they smell so good.'

She inhales deeply with her nose pressed against the baby's head. Fredrika glances at Joel.

'You can't, Mum, you've hurt your arm,' he puts in quickly.

She replies with a derisive snort.

'Mum,' Joel says. 'Why don't we go back to your room for a bit?'

'Be quiet, you!' she hisses and her eyes burn with hatred when she looks at him.

The baby starts to wail again. Joel's mum smiles pleadingly at Fredrika in a way that makes Joel's skin crawl.

She's acting. Just a little old lady who loves babies. She knows exactly what she's doing.

'Won't you let me hold him, just for a minute?' his mum says.

'I don't think so,' Fredrika replies. 'I think I'd better feed him.'

His mum's eyes narrow. But then she nods. 'Of course,' she says. 'Of course you have to eat when you're so tiny and hungry.'

Nina

'Sweetheart?' Pause. 'Sweetheart?'

She opens her eyes. Focuses until she sees a close-up of Markus' face. Stubble like black stippling on tanned skin. A few dry flakes of skin around his nostrils.

'You have to go to work soon,' he says, and kisses her on the mouth. 'Did you sleep poorly?'

She nods. Stretches. She was slipping in and out of dreams all night. At some point, she noticed the TV was on in the living room, heard Markus walk to the fridge and back. The familiar sounds seemed to belong to a completely different world.

She dreamed about that day at the hospital in Kungälv. Her brain was exhausted from sleep deprivation. It wasn't just Daniel keeping her up nights; it was the thoughts his very existence stirred up, as well. Becoming a mother was like stepping through a mirror to see her own childhood. See what she had never had.

In her dreams, Nina's mother was with them in the GP's office. Yellow eyes, yellow skin, her face prematurely aged. Old booze on her breath. *How could you do this to me?* she'd said. *How could you kill your own mother?* Her voice so rough it was obvious she was an alcoholic even though she was sober.

Nina sits up in bed and looks out the window. The sky is blue with fluffy tufts of cloud, like something out of a child's drawing.

Everything looks normal out there. The water's glittering in the bay. The cows are tirelessly chewing grass.

Monika's wrong. I didn't kill Mum. She killed herself with booze, slowly but surely. I didn't know what I was doing. I was too young. It wasn't my fault. She did it to herself.

'What time is it?' she mumbles.

'Almost half eleven,' Markus replies. 'Come down to the kitchen, I have good news.'

Nina manages to smile at him before going into the bathroom, where she sits down heavily on the toilet and pees. Her eyes linger on a pubic hair on the edge of the tub. She leans forwards and picks it up, dropping it into the toilet bowl.

After flushing and washing her hands, she walks downstairs and sits down at the kitchen table with a glass of water she drops a multivitamin into.

'You're not coming down with something, are you?' asks Markus, who has joined her in the kitchen.

She shakes her head and looks up when he sits down across from her.

What would you say if you knew what I did? If you knew I've been keeping it from you all these years?

Nina's fingers intertwine until she realises that's an overtly nervous gesture and deliberately pulls her hands apart.

'What were you going to tell me?' she says, raising the glass in which the multivitamin is still frothing on the surface.

The smell of synthetic pineapple fills her nostrils. She drinks slowly and carefully.

'Lena called the other day,' he says. 'She's set up an interview for me at her dad's car dealership. I'm going over there the day after tomorrow.'

What's left of the multivitamin ends up in Nina's mouth. She lets it sit on her tongue.

'That's great,' she says. 'Very decent of her.'

'I do know him a little, so I should get the job,' Markus says, and takes her hand. 'I know it hasn't been easy for you, either, but this is a turning point, you'll see.'

She nods and knocks back the last of her water. The bubbles continue to froth and sizzle at the back of her throat.

Pineshade

The residents of D Ward are gathered in the lounge when Nahal enters. Dogglas, a golden retriever, is walking obediently at her side, whisking the air with his tail and looking up at her for her next command.

Lillemor lets out a shriek of joy when she sees him.

Nahal is nervous. Especially so because Elisabeth is present. And Rita and Gorana. But Dogglas is doing well. He's panting with excitement but doesn't take his eyes off her. He resists the impulse to rush towards the old hands reaching out for him, the strong smells of their bodies.

Bodil calls him. Vera laughs. Even Petrus is smiling. Wiborg is bouncing impatiently up and down in her chair, so excited she's crying. She wants to pet the dog. Feel its fur.

Only Monika's unmoved. She's sitting apart from the others staring mutely at the dog.

Nahal squats down next to Dogglas.

'There now, good boy,' she says softly. 'Go say hello.'

He lumbers over to the old people and patiently lets them pet and hug him. A light is switched on in several old eyes – memories of dogs they once owned; a love of animals; being close to another living creature. Petrus and Olof chuckle when Dogglas licks Petrus' stumps. But happiest of all is Wiborg. She calls him

Iago and buries her face in his thick fur when he finally goes over to her.

Nahal begins to relax and Elisabeth gives her a pleased nod. Several of the old people are talking excitedly to one another. Dogglas walks over to Vera and Dagmar, wagging his tail and putting his head on Dagmar's knees so she can pet him. His brown eyes look up at her calmly.

'I want to give him treats!' Wiborg shouts. 'I want to give him treats so he'll like me the most!'

Dogglas' tail stops moving. He has discovered a new smell in the room. He sniffs the air and walks towards Monika but stops when their eyes meet. Hesitates. Licks his lips. He's curious about this new smell, which he has never noticed on a human before. Monika's lips draw back when Dogglas moves in closer and a low rumbling rises from her chest.

'Iago!' Wiborg calls. 'Iago, come here instead!'

Nahal watches in horror as Dogglas puts his front paws on Monika's knees and barks loudly in her face. Nahal dashes over and grabs him by the collar, tries to pull him off. Monika's barking back now. Saliva sprays from her lips. Dogglas' paws skid across the vinyl as Nahal drags him away. He's barking louder and louder and Nahal's cheeks burn with shame. She's afraid to look at Elisabeth and her new colleagues.

'Bad Iago,' Wiborg chides. 'Bad doggie. Bad Iago.'

In the chaos, no one notices that Lillemor is staring at Monika, terrified. She can see the angel now. He's standing right behind Monika. Almost melting into her. It's hard to see where he ends and Monika begins. But Lillemor can see one thing clearly, and that's that he's not a messenger of the Lord. *How could I have been so stupid? And I sang hymns of praise and everything.*

Monika falls silent once Nahal has dragged Dogglas out of sight. His claws click against the floor of the hallway and he whimpers unhappily, looking up at Nahal with his tail between his legs.

Nina

The smell of faeces is heavy and sweet in D7. Nina has just changed Olof's nappy. She pulls off her gloves and washes her hands meticulously in the sink.

It's a relatively calm evening on the ward. So far, she's been able to avoid Monika. Nahal served her dinner in bed and took care of her bedtime routine without asking why Nina begged off.

Nahal's unusually quiet. Nina knows the visit by her emotional support dog earlier in the day was a disaster, but she hasn't wanted to ask about it.

She sanitises her hands and goes back into Olof's room. He's crying silently.

'What's the matter?' she asks.

He turns away, doesn't want to look her in the eyes.

'Growing old is hard,' he says. 'I have so much left to give, but no one wants it.'

His daughter hasn't come back since the day Olof moved in. Nina can't help but wonder who would visit her if she ended up here. And if they did, would it be because they wanted to or out of obligation? Hopefully, she'd be too far gone to know the difference.

She tries to console Olof, but he doesn't respond and clearly wants to be alone. She heads over to the staffroom where she makes nutrition drinks with extra cream and prunes for Sucdi to distribute during the night. When she turns off the tap after washing the hand blender, she thinks she hears someone whining.

Nina straightens up, unsure if she really heard it. She turns around and catches a movement on the other side of the glass.

She steps out into the corridor and walks over to the dark common room. The sky above the glass ceiling is covered in thick cloud, making the evening unusually dark for this time of year. Nina can make out the outline of a plump figure on one of the sofas.

A sniffle. Mumbling sounds from wet lips. Something that sounds like a prayer.

'Lillemor?' Nina says, stepping in among the shadows.

The mumbling ceases.

'Yes,' says a surprisingly small voice.

'You're still up? Are you having trouble sleeping?'

'I can't be in my room.'

'What do you mean?'

Nina's eyes are adjusting to the gloom and she sits down on the long coffee table. Spots Adrian trotting down B hallway behind Lillemor.

'Do you want me to walk you back?' she says.

Lillemor shakes her head.

'He's with Monika now, but he can come back any time.'

'Who?'

Lillemor looks around. The light from B Ward flashes in her glasses, which are covered in greasy fingerprints.

'Tell me,' Nina says.

'He's no guardian angel,' Lillemor whispers. 'I was wrong this whole time. I think he's from the other place.'

'The other place doesn't exist,' Nina says. 'You don't believe in that.'

But she's not sure of that. She has watched Lillemor fussing with her angels all these years. Talking to them. Singing to them. It all seemed so innocent. Childish, even. But was Lillemor in fact trying to fend something off?

'The Devil himself was a fallen angel,' Lillemor says. 'How could I have been so blind?'

'Lillemor. The Devil doesn't exist.'

'You do know that's his biggest deceit, don't you? Making us believe he doesn't exist?'

Nina shakes her head. She has no idea what to say.

Whatever's the matter with Monika, the Devil's not to blame. But for Lillemor, that's apparently an irrefutable truth. It must be awful to live in a world where the Devil and his minions can appear at will when you least expect.

'If you don't believe me, you can go to Monika's room,' Lillemor says, and starts rocking back and forth again. 'They talk to each other. I hear them through the wall.'

The plastic around the cushions creaks faintly under Lillemor's heft.

'Come on, let's get you to bed,' Nina says. 'I'll give you a pill to help you sleep.'

'I don't want to sleep.' Lillemor shakes her head. 'I might never wake up again.'

'You have to sleep some time.'

'Not until they're quiet in there.'

'Okay,' Nina says, and stands up. 'I'll go have a look. If you promise you'll go back to bed afterwards.'

She leaves Lillemor in the common room and steps out into the brightly lit D corridor, looking down it towards D6.

She doesn't want to go into Monika's suite. The reluctance is physical.

I could ask Nahal to check on her.

That thought is what finally gets Nina moving. This is crazy.

There's nothing to be afraid of. It's Monika. And Monika needs my help.

Nina stops outside the door. Does, in fact, hear voices from inside. She can't make out what they're saying, but they sound excited.

Monika's standing in the middle of the room, as though she were expecting Nina.

'I almost thought you'd be storming in here brandishing a cross,' she says.

There's no mistaking the taunting tone. Nina looks around the suite while fear weaves a freezing web inside her. Monika's alone.

Nina tries to look unperturbed as she peeks into the bathroom. No one there either. The web tightens.

'Why would I want a cross?' Nina says.

'I don't know. Lillemor's the expert, no?'

How does she know? Was she listening to us?

'I thought I heard voices in here,' Nina says.

Monika spread her hands. 'It's just me.' She grins. 'Who else would be in here? Your mother, perhaps?'

Nina swallows. 'No,' she replies. 'My mother's dead. But I'm worried about you, Monika. You're not well.'

'What do you care? You never have before.'

Monika's voice falls another octave, wobbles.

'You killed me,' she slurs.

Mum's voice.

'No.'

Nina's heart is beating so hard it must be about to break free of its moorings.

'Yeees,' Monika says mockingly. Her voice is clear again. 'If you hadn't told the doctors she was drinking again, they would have given her a new liver.'

'Who told you that?'

'You know who,' Monika replies. 'Your mum told me.'

Nina shakes her head.

Does everyone know? Have they known all along? Do they talk about it around town?

'I didn't know that was why the doctors asked me if she drank,' she hears herself say.

'You knew exactly what you were doing,' Monika retorts.

She takes a step closer and now Nina can smell the nauseating reek of alcohol steaming from Monika's mouth, seeping out of her pores.

'It's all your fault,' she slurs. 'Why would I stop drinking when you just up and left me? I had nothing. You wouldn't even let me see my grandchild.'

Nina backs away towards the dark hallway, fervently wishing she'd turned on the light when she entered.

Monika follows and stumbles. She reaches out to the wall for support.

Just like her.

'You think you're so fucking amazing!' Monika shouts.

Mummy.

'You think you're so fucking high and mighty, with your big house and your fridge full of food. But you're not alive. You might as well be dead!'

In the gloom of the hallway, Nina thinks she can glimpse her mum's face, pudgy and swollen. She reaches out for Nina. Her fingers reek of nicotine and they're trembling, just like they always did before she could down the first bottle of wine of the day.

'You can't even fuck your poor husband without him scrubbing himself first,' Monika hisses. 'You're so afraid the slightest smell of piss might remind you of Petrus and the nappies and the filth here.'

'Stop,' Nina says. 'You don't know what you're talking about.'

She can feel the door against her back—

Did I close it?

—and fumbles for the handle.

'I'll be waiting for you, you'll see!' Monika screams—

Mummy

—into Nina's face.

Monika inhales. Nina's sweaty hands slip on the door handle. Suddenly, she's sure she's never getting out of this room, that she'll be trapped in here forever.

The door opens and she tumbles backwards out of the room. Monika doesn't follow. A strangled sound escapes her and a gurgle rises from the back of her throat.

Nina stops. Monika's thin fingers clutch the doorjamb. Her chest heaves so violently her ribs are clearly visible through her nightgown.

And then she collapses. Her knees thud hard against the floor. A puppet with its strings severed. Her whole body begins to shake. Her back arcs and her bones creak.

Nina shouts for Nahal.

Joel

A big red cross glows at him in the dark: he has finally found his way to the A&E in Kungälv. He parks the car diagonally across a parking bay, doesn't give a toss, sprints towards the entrance. The automatic doors open slowly, so slowly. He bounces up and down until he can slip in between them. The woman at the reception counter has warm eyes and a drawling voice. Joel can hear himself speaking faster to compensate. He's out of synch with the rest of the world. She promises a doctor will come by to speak to him soon.

'Perhaps you could take a seat in the meantime,' she suggests.

But he can't sit. He paces up and down the hallway. There are people on gurneys everywhere. A couple of police officers are standing in one corner, talking to two girls who can't be older than fifteen. They're holding hands and their eyes are glazed.

Joel realises he's lucky he didn't have any wine tonight. He wouldn't have been able to drive here if he had. Or he would have driven anyway, and that would have been even worse.

Nina comes towards him from an examination room. For a moment, it feels like they're going to hug, but his arms stay at his sides.

'What happened?'

'She had another attack. We gave her drugs, but they didn't help, so we called an ambulance. I came with her.'

'Is she okay?'

Nina smiles to reassure him, but can't hide that something's amiss. She's too tired to keep up appearances.

'She's fit as a fiddle.'

There are dark circles under her eyes and she smells faintly of sweat.

'They ran a lot of tests and everything looks good,' Nina continues. 'She has just come back from a CT scan, so they'll know more soon.'

He has only the vaguest idea of what a CT scan is. Pictures people on gurneys sliding into cylindrical machines. But at least they seem to have taken his mother's attack seriously this time.

'She's awake,' Nina says. 'You can go in if you want.'

Joel realises his legs are shaking. Adrenaline has kept him going, and the slightest hint of relaxation almost makes him collapse.

'I'm glad you're the one who was with her,' he says.

Nina nods, but there's something strange in her eyes. He wonders what she's thinking.

'I'm going home now,' she says.

They say an awkward goodbye and Joel enters the examination room.

A bunch of tubes are attached to his mother's head, like the tentacles of a jellyfish. There are IV stands and screens next to the bed, cannulas in her hands. Yet another cord runs from a clamp on one of her index fingers.

What if there's a physical explanation for all of this? Maybe they'll find something that can be fixed with drugs or surgery and then she'll be herself again. Maybe I can have her back.

'You really gave everyone a fright,' he says.

His mum looks at him, surprised. 'I did?'

'How are you feeling?'

She frowns and seems to ponder the question. 'I don't know why I'm here,' she says.

'You don't remember?'

'Only that I woke up and there were a lot of people staring at me.' She adjusts her nightgown and looks truly offended. 'And I don't have any proper clothes to wear.'

Joel can't help smiling.

'I want to go home,' she says. He wonders if she means the house or Pineshade.

There's a knock on the door and a blonde doctor enters. She holds her hand out and introduces herself as Emma.

'Your mum seems to be a tough old broad,' she says, smiling warmly.

'What happened?' he says.

The doctor glances at his mother. 'We're not sure yet. We're going to run more tests, but I thought I'd come tell you what we've already done first.'

'Okay.'

'When she came in, she'd been convulsing for almost twenty-five minutes.'

Twenty-five minutes of what he witnessed in her room the last time she had an attack?

The doctor nods as though she knows what he's thinking. 'It's a long time. Especially since she'd been given a muscle relaxant at the care home and the seizure still didn't subside. We administered oxygen and more intravenous Stesolid. Eventually, that did alleviate the seizure.'

'And . . . and what kind of attacks are they?'

'I can't say for sure yet. If it were epilepsy, she should have been postictal after the fit. Which is to say sleepy, disoriented, physically exhausted. But she was alert and clear-headed and able to answer questions.'

He has to laugh. It's just too absurd. His mother has apparently retained the ability to come across as the picture of health whenever she's talking to a doctor.

'I've just had a look at her CT scan. Neither it nor the blood samples show any new pathologies. We've checked her respiratory rate, oxygen levels, temperature, EKG . . .' The doctor lists things off on her fingers. 'There are no signs of stroke, traumatic head injury or a brain tumour, so you don't have to worry about that. And no infection, hypoxaemia or metabolic problems. In fact, we can't find anything wrong with her.'

She gives Joel an encouraging look, but the relief refuses to come. Joel would have preferred real information about what's happening to his mother. A disease with a name and a cure.

'So, what happens now?' he says.

'I'm going to admit her to neurology for more testing. I think we should do an EEG and a lumbar puncture to rule out a CNS infection. Then we'll take it from there.'

He opens his mouth to ask what that means, but his head's too full to take anything else in right now. 'How long is that going to take?'

'We could have results as early as tomorrow afternoon,' she says. 'If I were you, I'd go home and get some sleep. You look like you need it.'

He shakes his head. 'No,' he says. 'I'm staying right here.'

Pineshade

Lillemor is lying in her bed with her hands folded on her chest. It's quiet on the other side of the wall, but that doesn't make her feel a jot calmer. *Our Father who art in heaven. Hallowed be Thy name.* She looks at the faces of her angels and tries to draw strength from them. *Thy kingdom come. Thy will be done on earth as it is in heaven. In heaven . . . be Thy name.* She's breathing heavier and heavier. The angels watch her coldly. She let herself be fooled. She doesn't deserve them. Lillemor squeezes her eyes shut and searches inwardly for the words, but the Lord's own prayer has forsaken her. *Our Father who art in heaven. As on earth. Deliver us from evil and those who trespass against us, give us this day our daily bread. Help me.* There's no answer. The angels are silent.

The motion sensor goes off in D4 when Bodil shuffles out into the corridor. She's looking for her secret lover. She's hollow inside. It's an aching emptiness. When he's inside her, she feels young again. She can feel what he feels – his wonder at the flavours and smells of this world. Bodil caresses the wall with her fingertips, knowing he would enjoy it. She stops outside D6 and presses her ear against the door, touches the wood with her lips. She tugs at the handle, but the door's locked. She puts her nose in the gap between the door and the doorpost and sniffs. *They're not in there. No one's in there.* Bodil understands. Monika has moved and taken her lover with her. He likes her better. Always goes back to her; Bodil never manages to make him stay. That thought hollows her out further, makes the emptiness vaster.

The alarm has made Sucdi sprint up from the basement with a basket of freshly laundered sheets. She sighs when she spots Bodil.

'Shouldn't you be asleep?' she says. 'It's the middle of the night.'

But Bodil doesn't seem to hear. Sucdi puts the basket down outside the linen closet and walks over to her.

'Why does he like her better? I do everything he asks,' Bodil says, her eyes wet with tears.

'I don't know,' Sucdi replies.

She's feeling uneasy. Relieved, in her heart of hearts, that Monika isn't here tonight.

'She's always trying to get rid of him,' Bodil says, pointing accusingly at the door to D6. 'It's so unfair. That's always the type the menfolk chase after. The type that doesn't deserve them.'

Vera's knitting in her bed in D8. From time to time, she scratches her bare leg with a needle to stay awake. She's watching over Dagmar. But it's hard not to nod off. And besides, she doesn't think he's here tonight. She closes her eyes. Is just going to rest her eyes for a minute.

In D7, Olof is sleeping soundly for the first time since he came to Pineshade. He has done a good day's work. Someone else can captain the ferry tonight.

Darkness blankets the furniture in D6 like velvet. A greasy stain under the bed has dried up. The surface is cracking and flaking like egg white.

Sucdi has just tucked Bodil into her bed when she hears a racket from Lillemor's suite. She runs over and stares at the mayhem.

Can't quite take it in. The shelves are empty, except for a thin layer of dust around the spots where angels used to sit. Their porcelain faces have been smashed. Yarn has been unravelled and stuffing is peeking out of holes in crocheted angel bodies. The floor is littered with plastic arms, legs and wings. The framed sayings and cherubs have been comprehensively destroyed. Lillemor herself is standing in the middle of the destruction, crying, her fingers bleeding.

Joel

Another hospital bed in another department. Another doctor and another nurse.

His mother's sitting on the edge of her bed, leaning forwards. Her hospital gown is open at the back. Joel is holding her hand. The nurse takes out a cotton swab dipped in alcohol.

'This is going to feel a bit cold,' she says, and starts swabbing his mother's skin with circular motions.

Then she drapes a blue paper sheet with a hole in the middle over her spine. Joel's glad he didn't ask until early this morning what a lumbar puncture is – he's feeling nauseous already.

'And now you're going to feel a slight pinch,' the doctor says. 'This is the anaesthesia going in.'

His mum's grip on his hand tightens. Then it's over. The doctor puts the syringe down and pats his mother on the shoulder.

'Are you doing okay, Monika?'

'Yes,' she says. 'I'm okay. I've had worse.' But her voice is shaking.

There's the sound of footsteps outside in the hallway and someone screaming in pain. The smells are different, but it's still a lot like Pineshade.

This is Mum's life now. Shuttling back and forth between these places. Poked and prodded by strangers wearing protective gloves.

The doctor picks up another syringe from his tray. There's a flash of gleaming metal before it disappears out of sight behind his mother's back. The needle's four inches long. As wide as a thin straw.

Joel's nausea is augmented by light-headedness. He feels carsick.

'Have you started yet?' his mother says.

'Just about to,' the doctor says, and turns to the nurse. 'Look, here, behind the vertebrae . . .'

She nods and then his mother lets out a shriek. 'No! I don't want to!'

Something wet lands on Joel's hand. Saliva or tears.

'I'm sorry,' the doctor says. 'I think the needle hit bone.'

'Be careful,' Joel says.

'We're doing our best. I'm afraid older backs can be tricky. It can take a while to find the right spot, unfortunately.'

The doctor inserts the needle again; his mother sobs.

'Try to keep still, Monika,' the nurse says.

'We have a drip now,' the doctor says, and the nurse nods, studying his mother's back, fascinated.

'Why are you doing this to me?' his mum whimpers.

'She needs more anaesthesia,' Joel says.

'It doesn't help,' the nurse replies, looking up at him. 'We can only the numb the skin.'

Joel has no doubt the sympathy in her eyes is genuine. But it does nothing for his mother, who's breathing erratically through gritted teeth.

'This is like the fucking Middle Ages,' he says.

His mother moans loudly. 'I don't want to do this, I don't want to do this, I don't want to do this . . .'

Joel hears a plop and the nurse sets a test tube full of transparent fluid down on the tray.

'Is it almost done?' his mother says pleadingly, looking up at Joel.

He tries to nod encouragingly, promising that it'll be over soon, even though he can plainly see there are five more tubes to fill.

'Try to sit still now, Monika. You're doing great, but you have to keep bending over properly,' the doctor says.

His mother's head falls forwards and Joel studies her scalp. The roots that still haven't been dyed.

New droplets on his hand. From time to time, his mum's moans swell into screams. It feels like it's never going to end.

He has no idea how much time has elapsed when the nurse finally pulls out compresses. His mother gasps, then the big needle clatters against the tray.

'There we are,' the nurse says, removing the blue sheet and buttoning his mother's hospital gown back up. 'All done.'

His mother slowly straightens back up and grimaces. New tears trickle out from under her closed eyelids.

Her face is so close to Joel's. The light from the window makes each little downy hair on her cheeks glow like gold. Her breath smells fusty.

'You can lie back down now, Monika,' the nurse says as she removes her gloves. 'Here, I'll help you.'

His mother pulls her legs up and lets the nurse tuck her in.

'What happens if you don't find anything?' Joel asks.

'Then we schedule an MRI and a sleep EEG. There's a bit of a wait involved, especially in the summer, and—'

'But she gets to stay here, right?'

The doctor shakes his head. 'We don't have the beds.'

'But . . . what if she has another attack?'

'Then she'll have to come back in.'

As though he's talking about some cosy fucking social call and not an attack requiring an ambulance.

Joel looks at his mother, who's gasping for air in her bed, eyes closed. A ticking time bomb, with no timer for anyone to see. Impossible to know when she'll go off next.

The nurse pulls the curtain back around the bed. The doctor says something else, but Joel's not listening.

He's going to have a cigarette and call Björn. Surely now he'll get that this is serious.

'Mum?' Joel says when they're alone in the room. 'Are you asleep?'

No answer.

'I'm going to go call Björn, but I'll be right back. Can I get you anything before I go? Would you like some water?'

He looks at the beaker and the plastic jug. Wonders if he should try to force some fluids down her. But she has been forced enough already.

'I'll be right back,' he says again.

He's almost at the door when he hears a deep exhalation.

'It was weeks before they found him,' she mumbles.

Joel's heart starts beating double time. As though his body has processed the words before his brain has even had a chance.

She can't mean . . . That's impossible.

He turns around. His mum's eyes are still closed but she's smacking her lips tentatively.

'Who?' he says.

'His parents still haven't forgiven themselves. They thought he was a drug addict, and they didn't see the signs . . .' She shifts, grimacing in pain.

'Mum,' Joel says. 'What are you talking about?'

Panic is washing over him in growing waves. Threatening to pull him down into the abyss.

'It was only the second time he tried anything.' His mum's eyelashes flutter. 'He wanted to act tough in front of you, he didn't know you could handle a lot more than him . . .'

Joel shakes his head.

'Imagine that, being so young and no one to miss you . . . And you left him there to rot. You only cared about yourself. You always did.'

His pulse is roaring in his ears and yet he can hear every word clearly.

'It was his sister who talked the police into breaking into the flat. She could smell the body. She had to see him like that . . .'

Who knows?

'Can't you see him?' his mum says, and opens her eyes. 'He looks so horrible. His face all blue and swollen.'

'Is he here?'

The fact that he's asking must mean he's lost his mind. The thought is almost comforting.

He's never going to have to worry about it happening again. It already did.

'He's standing right behind you, silly,' his mum says wearily, looking out at the room.

Joel turns around; he senses a shadow in the corner of his field of vision, but it disappears in the blink of an eye. All he sees behind the half-drawn curtain is the other bed, empty.

And yet, he's sure. Something is standing there. Something he can't see, that can see him.

The lights in the hallway outside flicker as if in confirmation.

Nina

'Remember what we talked about yesterday?'

Lillemor looks at her sadly and shakes her head.

Nina contemplates what to say next. She looks around D5 – the room is hardly recognisable with the empty shelves, the bare walls.

'You said Monika's guardian angel wasn't an angel,' she says tentatively.

Lillemor looks away. 'I don't want to think about that,' she says.

'So you do remember?' Nina's voice echoes in the room. 'Please. I know you're scared, but maybe we could help each other if you told me—'

'No,' Lillemor cuts her off. 'There's no point. He's going to do as he pleases.'

Nina had considered calling in sick. She couldn't bear the thought of being here. But she couldn't bear the thought of staying home, either. Knocking about the house with Markus and wondering whether everyone knows what happened to her mother, if people have been gossiping about it, if that's why Monika knows. There's no other explanation. No other *sane* explanation.

She looks at the wall D5 shares with D6. It would be insane to believe her mother was in there the other night. She shouldn't even be thinking things like that.

So why is she sitting here with Lillemor? And tormenting her, to boot?

'Do you know who he is?'

Lillemor squeezes her lips shut.

'Lillemor. Is there nothing you can say to help me?'

'Forget it. He's going to go away sooner or later.'

'How do you know?'

Lillemor looks around as though to make sure no one's listening. 'He's obviously not going to hang around here forever,' she whispers. 'Surely you see why he wouldn't want to?'

'No, I don't!' Nina says. 'You have to help me.'

Lillemor wraps her arms around herself. 'He's back now. Don't say anything else.'

Nina can tell there's no point pushing her. And she has to get a grip now. Give some serious thought to what she's being dragged into.

She has always prided herself on her ability to talk to the old people. She never questions what they tell her. Instead, she tries to follow their trains of thought and understand them.

Maybe she has become too good at it. Maybe she has been doing it for too long.

Nina steps out into the corridor and spots Joel and Monika coming in from the lobby. Monika shuffles forwards slowly, looking like she has aged a decade in the past twenty-four hours. Joel looks shaken, too.

Nina goes to meet them. He looks up and raises his hand in a weary wave. Monika doesn't notice.

Broken. We're all broken.

'How did it go?' she says.

'They didn't find anything,' Joel replies.

They look at each other. The alarm goes off in the hallway. Nahal calls out for Nina from one of the suites. She whips around. The red light is flashing above the door to D2.

Petrus.

Nina jogs over. She hears Nahal yelp but can't tell if it's in pain or anger.

Petrus is sitting up in bed with all ten fingers buried deep in Nahal's hair. The duvet has slipped off him. His stumps are spread wide.

'Let go of her!'

Petrus turns to Nina and grins. 'You want in on this?'

Nina tries to loosen his grip. Long strands of hair are wrapped around his curled fingers. There are angry red marks on Nahal's pale scalp from Petrus' fingernails.

'Has he ripped any of it out?' Nahal says with a sob, while Nina coaxes. 'I feel like some has come out.'

'You're okay,' Nina says. 'Just stand completely still.'

'For God's sake, I was just giving him his insulin, I thought I was being careful . . .'

Nahal's crying. Nina shushes her. Doesn't want her to give Petrus the satisfaction.

'This whore has been sucking me off all day,' Petrus says. 'She can't get enough; she even does it for free.'

He laughs. Nina wants to punch him. Hard. She would never do it, but the mere thought of it fills her with deep satisfaction.

'I'll let go if you crawl in here with me,' Petrus leers.

His grip tightens and he squeezes the strands of hair. But his arms have begun to tremble. He won't be able to hold them up much longer.

In the end, Nina manages to pry his hands off. Nahal backs

away. Her eyes are red and swollen. She picks her glasses up from the floor and smooths the front of her smock; Nina wonders if Petrus managed to get at her breasts, too, if she's trying to get rid of the memory of his touch.

'There's enough here for two.' Petrus grins, tugging on his flaccid penis.

Nina is suddenly heartily fed up. With Petrus. With everything.

'Fine,' she says. 'Let's go then.'

Nahal stares at her. Petrus' eyes widen.

'Show me what you've got,' Nina says, sitting down on the edge of his bed. 'I can't resist you any longer.'

'What are you doing?' Nahal whispers.

Nina stares challengingly into Petrus' eyes. Sees a glint of fear. She leans over the mattress as though she's about to climb on top of him. Her face moves closer to his.

'Come on, then. Let's see what you can do.'

Petrus turns his face away from her.

'Fuck me,' Nina says. 'Go on.'

'Leave me alone,' Petrus says, closing his eyes. 'I don't want to.'

'That's what I thought,' Nina says, and stands up.

She picks up the duvet from the floor and spreads it over him. Feels Nahal's eyes on her.

The forbidden triumph is intoxicating. She almost laughs out loud. She can already feel the guilt that is about to supersede it, but right now, she doesn't care.

'I guess you're all talk and no action,' she says.

'That's because you're so fucking hideous!' Petrus yells after them as they leave his suite. 'Revolting cow cunts!'

Nina shuts the door. He continues to rage in there, but she can no longer make out the words.

Joel

Black spots dance around his field of vision. Melting together, sliding apart.

Breathe. He has to remember to breathe all the way down his lungs. He needs air, but there doesn't seem to be any oxygen in the suite.

His mother fell asleep the moment her head hit the pillow. Her eyes are moving rapidly under her thin eyelids and he wonders what she sees in her dreams. Who she is in them.

He stands up and steps into the bathroom where he splashes cold water on his face.

Who told her?

That was the morning he quit drugs.

Six years and two months. Almost three now.

Is she going to tell anyone?

But who would believe her?

He goes back into the main room and studies his mother's peaceful face. Gets the feeling she only just closed her eyes.

Playing possum. That's what she used to call it when I was little.

Nothing's right. Nothing fits together.

But he knows one thing. The realisation comes to him, pure and simple: he can't stay here. He has to get away. Away from Pineshade. Away from the house. Away from this town.

The staff will look after his mum. The real estate agent has a set of keys. Björn has promised to stop by tomorrow.

He doesn't have to stay. If he leaves tonight, he can be back in Stockholm before morning.

Björn's going to have to take over. Joel has met his obligations.

A few days from now, he's going to think he imagined his mother being visited by the dead.

Or, more accurately, he's going to *realise* that he imagined it. It has to be his imagination. He just can't see clearly from where he is; it's like he's a co-dependent participant in her delusion.

He can feel his relief grow with each step as he walks out of the suite, leaving his mother behind. He doesn't turn around.

Pineshade

Nina carries Wiborg's dinner into D1 and sets the tray down on the nightstand. Wiborg's sitting up in bed with the phone pressed to her ear. Tears are streaming down her cheeks, tracing the lines of her wrinkles, but Nina barely notices. Thoughts of Monika fill her mind. She pats Wiborg on the shoulder and leaves the suite.

Wiborg waits until she's sure she's alone again.

'I promise,' she says. 'I will.'

At the other end of the D corridor, Dagmar is staring intently at Vera from her bed. Dagmar's voice is little more than a whisper. She hasn't used her vocal cords to speak in so long.

'You have to tell him yes. If you do, I can come back to you like I used to be.'

Vera shakes her head. Dagmar's eyebrows contract above her nose.

'You have to. Don't you see? Why don't you want to help me?'

Joel

He knows he's dreaming, but it makes no difference. It doesn't make it any less scary to be back, to know what's going to happen next and still be unable to stop it.

His feet are entangled in the sheets and soon it's going to feel like the bed's trying to trap him.

The body he's hugging is warm. Just like it was in real life.

In his dream, very little exists outside the confines of the bed, just momentary, disjointed impressions: a wave of dirty laundry spilling out of a closet, dusty potted plants, a wide-wale corduroy sofa, sooty flakes surrounding an overflowing ashtray on a coffee table.

He's two Joels. The one who knows, and the one who has no idea what's coming.

The one who doesn't know sits up in bed and looks at the person lying on his side next to him. Dark hair covers the top half of his face. His mouth is open. White teeth can be glimpsed inside a pair of full lips.

The Joel who knows what's coming wants to wake up. But the dream is a runaway train. He can't get off before it crashes.

He lies back down on his side. The stranger next to him feels cooler now. Dream-Joel puts an arm around him, snuggles in closer and puts a hand on his chest. His fingers play with soft, curly hairs.

This is the moment when he realises his chest isn't moving.

The terror that fills him is familiar, but to Dream-Joel, it's brand new. He pulls away and gingerly shakes the cool shoulder. No reaction.

His feet are entangled in the sheets. Joel kicks desperately to free them. He pulls the duvet along when he rolls out of bed and turns around.

The naked body is exposed like an artefact in a museum. There are a handful of stains on the sheet from whatever oozed out of it during the night.

Joel walks around the bed and looks at the face with its half-open mouth; gently pushes the hair back and is met by a pair of vacantly staring eyes. This is where the dream ends. It always ends here. Joel feels like he's falling, faster and faster, and then lands in his own body and wakes up again, for real this time.

He fell asleep in his clothes after coming back from Pineshade. He sits up and presses his hands to his head as if to keep his skull from bursting. All the memories of what happened are flooding in, spilling over.

Six years and almost three months ago, he'd run into the bathroom and thrown up until he thought he was literally going to turn inside out. Then he'd sat down in the tiny kitchen where the sink was full of dirty plates and glasses. He'd tried to collect himself, but all he'd been able to think about was the dead body in the next room. The eyes that would never see again. The blood that had stopped pumping. The blood that was full of drugs. Drugs Joel had supplied. He'd tried to piece together the fragments of the night before: the staff and some of the regulars had stayed after hours at the bar where he worked. There'd been shots and coke. Lots of coke. On to the club in Gula Gången. Afterparty in a dark flat on the ground floor on Östermalm. Small, crowded rooms everywhere, strange passageways. The party had spilled out into the courtyard. Late April and the first warm spring night. That guy no one had seemed to know. Making out in the taxi. Making out on the corduroy sofa while they shared everything Joel had brought from the party. Sitting on the wooden chair in the strange kitchen, Joel had started to wonder who might have seen them leave the party together. He couldn't think of anyone.

He'd gathered up all his things. Wiped down any surface he might have touched, even though his fingerprints weren't in any database. He'd fished the used condom out of the bin and flushed it down the toilet. He'd refused to think about the fact there would be traces of his DNA in the bed and on the body. As far as he knows, no one saw him leave the flat; the sunny pavement outside the building had been deserted. It was a suburb he'd never been to before.

The police were never going to open a criminal investigation into the fatal overdose of some junkie. Even if they did, how would they ever connect him with Joel? And, if they did that too, he was going to say the guy was alive when he left. He had nothing to worry about.

That's what he'd told himself all those sleepless nights, all those days when it was all he could think about. He'd replayed the scene on the corduroy sofa over and over in his mind, as though he would somehow be able to rewrite history. Change the course of events. *Are you sure you want more? Nah, fuck this, let's just go to bed.* But back then, Joel never stopped taking drugs until he ran out.

The police never came calling. No one he knew ever brought that bloke up. It was as though he'd never existed.

It was weeks before they found him. His parents still haven't forgiven themselves. They thought he was a drug addict, and they didn't see the signs . . .

Six years and almost three months ago. He's always known what happened would come back to haunt him. But he could never have imagined *how.*

Joel longingly eyes the packed suitcase on the floor.

He can't run again. Not from this, too.

His phone's on the bedside table. He brings it out into the garden. It's almost eight in the evening.

Nina picks up at Pineshade.

'Would you like me to check if Monika's awake?' she asks dully.

'No. I wanted to talk to you.'

Silence. Only the trees rustling up on the mountain. He frets about what to say next. She might think he has lost his mind. But on the other hand, she might already be of that opinion. And she'd probably be right.

'There's something wrong with Mum,' he says. 'I don't know what, but it's not something the doctors are going to find with their tests.'

'I know,' she replies.

Those short words don't just take a weight off his shoulders. His entire being feels lighter.

'I get off at ten. Do you want me to come over?'

'Yes,' he says. 'Yes, please do.'

They hang up. When Joel turns to go back inside, he thinks he sees a shadow in the window of his room.

Nina

The sound of the car door slamming shut is unnaturally loud in the silence. There's a for-sale sign on the lawn and the barn door is ajar. The darkness inside is dense, like a painted black line. Nina waves away a swarm of mosquitoes from her neck and turns towards the house. There are lights on in every window, on both floors.

She walks up the front steps and rings the doorbell. Hears footsteps and sees Joel's silhouette, warped by the textured glass in the door. The lock clicks.

Joel's eyes are swollen and he smells of booze. It's only a faint hint, but having been permanently on the lookout for that smell growing up, Nina never misses it.

She follows him into the kitchen. An old R.E.M. song is playing softly in the background. Everything looks the same. The same vinyl floor that was old even back when they were teenagers. The same kitchen table and chairs. She glances into the living room. The furniture is sparser in there now. The music is coming from a small speaker connected to a laptop on the coffee table.

'What would you like to drink?' he says. 'Coffee? Or wine, perhaps?'

'Do you have whiskey?'

Joel shoots her a surprised look. She thinks she glimpses the shadow of a smile before he turns to get them each a glass from the cabinet above the sink.

She sits down at the kitchen table and runs her index finger over the pine, tracing the veins, circling the darker knotholes. Just like she used to. She pulls her hand away. Joel sits down across from her and slides her one of the glasses. Nina looks at the amber liquid. She was never a big drinker, and in the past few years she has been virtually abstemious, but if ever there was an excuse to calm her nerves with a drink, this is it.

'Cheers,' Joel says. 'Or whatever.'

'Or whatever,' she says, and takes a small sip.

The whiskey is mellower than she'd thought it'd be. It makes her breath feel hot, but it doesn't burn. She takes another sip.

'How does Markus feel about you coming here?' Joel asks.

'I texted him to say I have to work late.'

Joel nods.

'I don't usually lie to him,' she says, slightly too quickly. 'We're not like that with each other.'

'I get it. You don't have to explain.'

Michael Stipe is singing about nightswimming.

'You still listen to the same music?' she says.

'I'm only just getting back into it.'

She takes another sip and suddenly her glass is empty. He tops it up.

Just one more. She has to be able to drive home later.

'Thanks for coming,' Joel says. 'I didn't know if you . . . if you'd believe me.'

'I don't know what I believe.'

'Sure. Of course. Me neither. But you know there's *something*.'

She watches him quietly. Now he's the one looking down at the tabletop.

'I know she has dementia and that it can make people act weird,' Joel says. 'But sometimes . . . sometimes, Mum doesn't seem confused in the slightest. Quite the opposite.'

'What do you mean by *the opposite*?' She has to be sure they're talking about the same thing.

Joel sighs. 'She knows things she shouldn't,' he says.

Nina raises her glass and downs her drink in one. 'Yes,' she says.

A new song starts. She recognises Suede immediately, Brett singing about being so young. She's becoming increasingly aware of the living room behind her, and of Monika's bedroom beyond that.

'What has she told you?' Joel says.

Nina reluctantly decides she has to tell him. Not everything, but enough to give them a chance of figuring out what's going on.

'It was about my mother. She even acted like her. Fairly convincingly. And I don't think they ever even met.'

It feels like Monika's in the house. Like she can hear them.

'She knew things about Sucdi's dad, too,' Nina presses on quickly, to pre-empt any questions about exactly what Monika said to her.

'She mentioned that,' Joel said. 'But he's still alive, right?'

'Yes,' she says. 'Why do you ask?'

'With me, she spoke about my dad . . . and about this guy I used to know. Both are dead, like your mum.'

He rubs his forehead. Chuckles. 'This is pretty twisted. I'm trying to be logical about something that . . . isn't.'

'She knew things about me and Markus, too,' Nina says. 'Things I haven't told anyone.'

Joel watches her silently. She's glad he's not asking for details about this either.

'Sometimes she talks about herself in the third person, as well,' Nina continues. 'She says heinous things about "Monika".'

'Yes,' Joel says. 'I've heard that, too.'

Nina focuses on him. It's a struggle not to look over her shoulder to see if Monika's standing in the doorway. Summoned by their talking about her.

'Her voice changes,' Joel says. 'As though there's someone else inside her.'

Nina's eyes water. It's hard to breathe. She fiddles with her empty glass. 'Lillemor's afraid of Monika,' Nina says. 'She told me the guardian angel is no guardian angel but rather comes from the other place.'

'So what is it, then?' Joel says. 'Like, a demon? Maybe we should call a Catholic priest?'

His attempt to lighten the mood has the opposite effect – Nina just wants to cry. Monika and this house were safe havens. Some of the brightest memories of her life took place in this kitchen. And now, Monika's something scary.

'I was *kidding*,' Joel says, and Nina realises he has misinterpreted her silence.

'I know,' she says. 'But I'm wondering if there's someone out there who can help with this kind of thing. Like a medium or something.'

'I don't want anyone else involved. If it's the wrong person, they could just as easily make it worse.'

She nods. The silence between them grows and she casts about for something to say.

'If the Catholic priests have been right all along, I'm definitely destined for hell,' Joel says.

'Me too,' Nina replies.

He chuckles. 'Surely if anyone's a saint, it's you?'

She makes no reply.

You knew exactly what you were doing. It's all your fault.

'Could it be a ghost? Did something happen at Pineshade?' Joel asks. 'Did someone die?'

'People die there all the time.'

'But no one special?'

She shakes her head. They're all special, but no one's special in that way. Whatever *that way* is.

Joel holds out the bottle to her. She shakes her head.

'I've already had too much.'

'You can stay over if you want.'

'I don't think so,' she says.

'You could have Björn's room.'

There's desperation in his voice and it suddenly occurs to her that it has to do with the fact that all the lights in the house are on.

'No,' she says. 'I have to go home.'

But does she really have to?

She doesn't want to go back to her house, where she's alone with her thoughts, even if Markus is there. She would never, ever be able to tell him about this. The thought of his reaction makes her stifle a hysterical giggle.

Joel doesn't seem to notice. He's turning his whiskey glass in his hands.

'I get it,' he says. 'I just don't want to be alone. I'm . . . I'm scared.'

Hearing him admit it confirms her own fear. Amplifies it.

It's so easy to imagine the sounds of bare feet behind her. That rough voice dropping low, splitting into two.

Nina looks up at the ceiling lamp. Its light is steady.

'I've noticed it, too,' he says. 'That the lights go funny sometimes.'

Tears are burning behind her eyelids again.

'These greasy stains have appeared in more suites at Pineshade,' she says.

He looks over her shoulder towards the bedroom. The muscles in her back contract.

Don't turn around, she might be there.

'There was a stain in her bedroom,' Joel says. 'But it hasn't come back since she moved.'

'So what's happening at Pineshade . . . came with Monika,' she says.

There's a long pause.

Nina doesn't know how to deal with this. She has no fucking idea.

'I was high when I dropped Mum off at the home,' Joel says suddenly. 'But it wasn't what you think. I was so anxious I took one of her sedatives. It was Haloperidol and . . . it didn't work out great. I just want you to know that I've been clean for over six years. Or, well, I was, until I relapsed over Midsummer.' Joel raises his glass in an ironic toast. 'As you can see, I'm teetotal now.'

She doesn't raise her glass in response. Joel looks back down at the table. Seems to be working up to something. She waits.

'Nina,' he says. 'I'm sorry about what I said when you came

here before. I . . . I wouldn't have gone to Stockholm with me, either, if I were you. It's probably a good thing you didn't. And I get it now.'

She shakes her head. 'It doesn't matter anymore.'

'It matters to me. I blamed all kinds of shit on you for so many years, thinking my life would've been different if you'd come with me. But my mistakes were my own. They try to teach us about this stuff in DAA, but apparently I'm a slow learner.'

She wonders if the dead bloke Monika talked to Joel about was one of the mistakes. But she says nothing. He spared her any follow-up questions and she returns the favour.

'Is Monika's bike still around?' she says instead. 'Because if it is, I can ride that home later.'

He nods, and she pushes her whiskey glass towards him.

Pineshade

It's almost midnight and Rita has just started a round. She pulls off her gloves, logging a capital S on the stool record in Wiborg's room. Wiborg is unusually calm tonight. No tears, no desperate phone calls. She just mutely watches Rita work.

Petrus says nothing when she checks his nappy. Shakes his head when she asks if he needs anything.

'Good day. My name is Edit Andersson and I am Director Palm's secretary,' Edit tells her sleepily.

Rita grits her teeth and nods. Methodically handles the old body and tries not to lose her mind.

'Good day. My name is Edit Andersson and I am Director Palm's secretary. Good day. My name is Edit Andersson and I am Director Palm's secretary.'

Bodil wakes up when Rita enters. She doesn't like Rita. But it doesn't matter right now. She's happy again. Her secret lover has promised to come back. He has explained that he can't live without Bodil. She just has to be patient for a while longer. Soon, he'll be able to come and go as he pleases. Bodil relishes the thought and allows Rita to handle her without complaint.

Lillemor lies still, too, staring at Rita, who's beginning to feel uneasy. She hurriedly gets done what needs doing and is just about to enter D6 when loud voices make her jump. She turns towards the lounge and notices a flickering blueish light inside.

Rita resolutely walks over. The TV is on. Police officers are squatting next to a naked woman's body; the lights from their cars make the shadows in the lounge dance. Rita turns on the overhead lights. *No one here.* She checks behind the sofas, but there's nowhere else to hide. She finds the remote on the coffee table. The TV turns off with a crackling when she angrily pushes the power button. *It has to be a jokester from one of the other units. It can't have been one of the residents. They're too slow for a successful getaway.* She turns the lights off again and walks away. She's careful to look calm and in control, in case they're watching. She only has time to take a few steps down the corridor before the loud voices start to rumble out from the lounge once more.

Olof has pulled his duvet up to his chin in D7. He trembles in his sleep as though he were cold.

In D8, Vera has clapped her hands over her ears. But the voice she hears isn't coming from outside.

'You have to be ready,' it says. 'Not too early and not too late. Soon.'

'That's enough,' Rita says loudly and puts the remote back down on the coffee table. She's sure the people pranking her are hiding around the corner in the A corridor, but she's not going to go looking for them. *They probably have another remote*, she muses. *It's the same TV sets everywhere, after all. That's how they're doing it.* She unplugs the TV. *Let them try it now.*

Rita steps back out into D corridor with her head held high. She can feel that she's being watched in every part of her body. *It's probably Adrian and one of the other brats.* She goes back to D6 and listens down the hallway one last time before pushing the handle down. As soon as the door opens, she hears a faint jangling sound from inside. But when she enters, Monika's in bed, asleep. The guard rail trembles slightly and a loose screw rattles in its hole.

Rita puts a hand on the cold metal of the guard rail and the vibrations cease. Monika opens her eyes. They're completely white, like hardboiled eggs pushed into her skull. Rita lets out a shriek.

'Don't you know it's just a hallucination?' Monika says softly. She blinks and her eyes are normal again. 'You're imagining things. You're becoming one of us. I can smell it. Your brain's rotten.'

Out in the lounge, the TV turns back on. The air is thick with electricity.

The microwave dings again and again in the staffroom.

'You're going to end up here with us,' Monika says, and laughs, a hoarse cackling that makes Rita's stomach turn. 'Sucdi will be changing your nappies. And all your colleagues are going to know that no one loves you, because no one will come to visit. You'll have only me and Petrus and Wiborg and the others, and then you'll die.'

Joel

'I can't believe we're even talking about this,' he says.

Nina nods. She seems a bit tipsy already. Probably isn't used to drinking. He, on the other hand, can't get drunk, no matter how much he tries.

'It's, like . . . Monika,' Nina says. 'She never had a mean word for anybody. And now . . .'

She breaks off.

'Maybe that's why,' Joel says, topping himself up. 'Maybe she's kept so many things inside all these years, it's finally coming out now.'

'That's not how dementia works.'

'But this isn't dementia,' Joel says. 'Or not just dementia. Right?'

She shrugs. Tries to act unruffled and fails.

Joel's careful to keep his eyes squarely on her. Doesn't want to see the living room behind her back. The door to his mum's bedroom is ajar in there.

He thought he heard noises coming from it earlier in the evening.

'I'm sorry you got mixed up in this,' he says. 'I mean, I might deserve her going after me . . . But you have nothing to do with it.'

Joel's completely unprepared for the anger that flashes in Nina's eyes.

'You really don't get it, do you?' she says. 'I just disappeared after you left. I abandoned her, after everything she'd done for me.'

He stares at her mutely.

'Monika was like a mother to me,' Nina says. 'I have her to thank for so much. But I never did. And now, she's getting her revenge.'

He can see teenage Nina underneath the grown-up. It's like two overlapping layers.

'You've felt this guilty?' he asks.

'Yes,' Nina says. 'Of course I have.'

'I'm sorry. I didn't know.'

'No, you didn't know. You didn't get it then and you're never going to. You always took her for granted.'

'Nina—'

'If things had gone tits up in Stockholm, you could always have gone back home to Monika,' she says. 'I had nothing to go back to.'

She doesn't sound angry anymore. Contemplative, rather. As though she's realising this as she's saying it.

But now *he's* angry.

'There was no way I could come home,' he says. 'Things did go tits up, in case you haven't noticed, and I've barely been back here because I didn't want people to think of me as a fucking loser . . .'

'But I *was* a loser. For real. You never understood that that was the difference between you and me.' Nina falters again, shooting him a frustrated look. 'I get that it sucked for you here – people are fucking narrow-minded – but at the same time I feel a bit . . . stop being such a cry baby, already. You had a safety net, even if you didn't want it. You never had to end up on the street, you could have gone home. I didn't have that luxury.'

He opens his mouth to respond, but since he has no idea what to say, he shuts it again.

They stare at each other.

'Did you really just call me a cry baby?'

Nina giggles. 'Apparently. I'm sorry. I don't even know what I'm talking about. It came out wrong.'

'You don't have to feel guilty about Mum.'

She averts her eyes. 'Never mind,' she says. 'It doesn't matter anymore.'

Nina seems to think a lot of things don't matter anymore. She is good at shutting down. Just like him. Just by different means.

In the silence that falls, Joel glances over at the door to his mum's bedroom. Nothing there. And the light is steady.

He realises he has always thought about it as his mum's bedroom, but once upon a time, it belonged to her and his dad.

His dad.

Joel takes a sip of whiskey to chase away the cold spreading through his body.

Nils was waiting for me.

The memories shift inside him, forming a new pattern.

Nils came back with me but it's so hard for him to stay here on Earth. He's not supposed to be here.

And then the second time he visited her at Pineshade.

Nils has found his way here.

She'd been so sure. And she'd seemed happy. Hadn't she?

He's sleeping. He's still weak. He needs to build up his strength.

That had been the third day.

The dad Joel had never known. Only from photographs and his mum's stories.

His mum, who never wants to admit when something's wrong, never wants to remember the bad times.

You always hear about unexpected feats of strength, though, don't you? You know, mothers lifting up cars to save their kid or whatever.

Maybe Björn was more right than he could have imagined. Joel pictures the attack, his mum's body arching backwards. Had that been his mother resisting?

'Dad has been with her since the heart attack,' he says. 'She told me he'd come back with her from the other side.'

Nina stares at him. 'You think it's Nils? But she loves him. It was all she ever talked about.'

'I don't know,' he says, glancing over at the bedroom again. 'I don't know anything. But it was only when she moved to Pineshade that he grew strong enough to be with her all the time.'

Nina makes no reply and he raises his glass again.

'They didn't happen to build the home on an ancient Indian burial ground, did they?' he asks. 'Native American, I mean. You know, like in the movies?'

A sudden snort of laughter into his glass and the smell of alcohol fills his nostrils. Nina looks at him inquiringly. Maybe he is pretty drunk, after all.

He puts the glass down. Stands up and turns on the kettle. 'Coffee?'

Nina shakes her head. He spoons instant coffee into a cup and tries to focus on the normality of the task.

'Has anyone other than Lillemor said anything about Mum?' he says.

'Only Sucdi. And Gorana said Monika was completely unhinged that time she broke her arm . . . but you have to understand that the things we've talked about tonight happen all the time at Pineshade.'

'Yeah, thanks, that much is clear to me,' Joel says, raising his voice slightly to make himself heard over the kettle.

'I can't exactly up and ask people if they think she might be possessed,' Nina says.

Then she suddenly sits up straighter. 'Or actually,' she says. 'Maybe there is one person.'

'Who?'

'She used to work with us. I just don't know how to ask. How the fuck do I put it?'

Joel finishes making the coffee and sits back down. Nina looks at him and shakes her head.

'Bloody hell, Joel, what if this is all in our minds?' she says. 'This is nuts. But if it's true, do you get what that means? Not just in relation to Monika but . . . *everything*. Do you get what we're talking about here?'

He feels dizzy when her words sink in. So far, he hasn't allowed himself to consider the magnitude of the questions implicated in the mystery of his mother.

Life. Death. Everything in between. Everything beyond.

He lights a cigarette, noting that his hands are trembling.

Nina's crying silently. He considers getting up and hugging her, but he has no idea how she would react. They were never particularly physical even back when they were best friends, except when they slept in the same bed. The darkness and feigned sleep made it easier.

'So, what do we do now?' he says, and pulls hard on his cigarette.

She knocks back her drink and stands up. Wobbles slightly when she pushes her chair in.

'I'm going home now,' she replies.

'Are you sure? The roads are dark and there's no light on the bike.'

Nina nods. He gives up on trying to persuade her.

'I'll walk you to the barn.'

They move into the hallway. Nina grabs the shoehorn hanging on the hat rack and slips into her trainers.

'If it's your dad . . .' she says. 'Maybe we can talk to him.'

When she opens the front door, the night seems to push its way inside.

Joel already knows he's not going to sleep tonight.

'You think he'd answer us?' he says.

As if Nina has any way of knowing.

'If it's Nils, he's already talking to us,' she says. 'Maybe we can find out what he wants.'

Nina

Her head hurts so badly she has to hold onto the banister when she walks down the stairs. She shuffles into the kitchen and downs two glasses of water in quick succession. Her stomach lurches, threatening to throw it all back up. She waits for it to pass then fills the glass one more time and dumps in both painkillers and a multivitamin.

'Markus?'

She walks around the house, calling him, glass in hand. Slips her feet into a pair of sandals and steps out into the garden.

'Markus?'

He's slumped in a sun lounger out back. Reading a crime novel in his underwear. When she walks up to him, he slowly lowers the book.

'You've put on suntan lotion, haven't you?' she says. 'It's the middle of the day.'

'I know. I've been up for hours.'

He lifts up his book again. Turns the page. A poor actor pretending to be engrossed in the plot.

'I had a late night last night,' she says.

'I noticed.'

She sips her frothy drink. It occurs to her that the judgemental gaze, the one she thought Joel was going to aim at her life, might in fact be her own.

The sun's too hot. It's searing her shoulders, making her hair feel like it's on fire.

'What's got you so surly?' she says.

Markus closes the book with his finger as a bookmark. Pulls the back of his chair into the upright position.

'I called Pineshade around midnight,' he says. 'You weren't there.'

'I was at Joel's.'

Markus sneers. 'Great,' he says. 'And why did you lie?'

'It was about Monika, so it *was* work.'

He clenches his jaw so hard his temples bulge. 'Fucking bullshit.'

'I knew you would react this way,' she says. 'Which is why I didn't tell you.'

'Come off it. Don't blame me.'

Nina doesn't argue. He's right. 'I'm sorry. I just didn't want to discuss it last night. It was a last-minute thing. Monika's sick and he's worried. We both are.'

'Yes, you must be incredibly bloody concerned. Our bedroom reeks like a fucking brewery.' He looks at her glass with a mocking grin. 'Are the two of you going to be BFFs again? Isn't that just lovely. You can plait each other's hair and talk about boys.'

Markus leans his chair back and hides his face behind his book.

Fucking martyr.

She doesn't have it in her. Not now, not with this sun, with this hangover.

Nina walks back towards the house. She's going to try to force down some breakfast and then she has to get going if she wants to have time to swing by the flats in Skredsby before the evening shift.

She suddenly realises her car's still at Joel's. She has to bike back and get it.

'I got the job!' Markus shouts after her. 'Thanks for fucking asking!'

She turns around. The interview was today?

'I start Monday,' he says.

'Congratulations,' she says, and she can hear how sarcastic she sounds.

She should have known. Lena Jonsson and Markus' parents are from the same world. They always help each other. Markus was right all along. There was never any need to worry. She has been anxious for no reason all spring and summer.

Joel

His mother's asleep when he arrives at Pineshade. He stands by her bed for a moment, studying her haggard face, then walks over to look at the wedding photo on the wall.

She's so young, her smile so hopeful. Joel knows how things turned out, but she has no idea what life has in store. She doesn't know yet that death will indeed part them, far too soon. That she's going to be so very lonely. His dad looks proud. Safe. His warm eyes gaze back at Joel. Joel searches the black and white face for answers. Suddenly, he wonders if he can't see a faint hint of determination in his father's smile. Isn't there something grim about the tiny frown line between his eyes?

Last night's conversation with Nina was terrifying, but also brought a measure of relief. There might be answers. They might be able to find them. Together.

But what if the only answer is that they've both fallen prey to delusion? He hadn't realised how guilty Nina felt about his mum. Wouldn't it be more believable, infinitely more *likely*, that they've both been imagining things? Maybe the reason everything had seemed to fit yesterday was that they'd merged their fantasies into a *folie à deux*, each confirming the other's psychosis.

A light tap on the door makes him jump.

'And how are we doing in here?' Elisabeth says, tilting her head to the side when she spots his mother. 'Aw, she's dozed off. Don't they just look so peaceful? Like children.'

Joel makes no reply.

'I heard your brother's coming today,' Elisabeth continues. 'Won't that be lovely for Monika? And I have more good news.' She holds out two sheets of paper. 'We've had the results of the tests Doctor Hansson ordered, and everything looks great. Nothing to worry about at all, other than that she's a bit anaemic.'

Joel skims the tiny print but doesn't understand much of it.

'Isn't that fantastic?' Elisabeth says, so enthusiastically it feels like a demand.

'Is it?' he replies. 'We still don't know what's wrong with her.'

Elisabeth's smile doesn't falter. But it also doesn't reach her eyes. 'It's good news,' she insists. 'And Monika will be getting an MRI soon as well, so I think we should take things one step at a time.'

He just wants her to leave him alone. 'Sure,' he says, returning her smile with an equally disingenuous one. 'Thank you so much.'

After she leaves, he starts to tap his thighs. His mum seems as soundly asleep as before. He glances at his phone. No texts from Björn. It's almost two. They agreed to meet here at one.

Restlessness makes his body itch. He pulls one of his mum's magazines from the cloth bedside caddy. The cover is rumpled, almost coming off the staples. He finds a pen and sits down in the armchair. Braces himself before flipping to the crossword section. Doesn't want to see any more jumbled letters.

But in this magazine, the letters are scrawled in the margins and across the grid pattern and the Botox-smooth forehead of an actress. The uneven lines are etched so hard there's holes in the paper. The words are desperate.

HELP ME IT'S NOT ME IT'S HIM HE CAME WITH ME
I CAN'T LIVE LIKE THIS I JUST WANT TO DIE IT'S
NOT ME DOING THESE THINGS AND SAYING SUCH
TERRIBLE
YOU HAVE TO BELIEVE

Joel closes the magazine. Looks at the cover again. It's one of the last ones he bought her before she broke her arm.

Lillemor said it was for her own good. Because Mum was trying to resist the damn angel.

He swallows cold saliva as he looks at the cast covering his mother's right forearm. Tries to fend off the insight, but it's too late.

It was her punishment for asking for help. She can't write with a broken arm.

The room has gone dead-still. He looks up and meets his mother's eyes. She's smiling at him from her bed.

'Is he finally on his way now?' she says.

'Who?'

His voice sounds strange, as though he's being strangled.

'Björn, silly,' his mother says, pushing herself into a sitting position.

He hasn't told her Björn's coming today. Didn't want to disappoint her in case Björn cancelled again.

She overheard me talking to Elisabeth.

Finding a natural explanation has become a reflex, but it's pointless now.

'Yes,' Joel says, and clears his throat. 'He should be here any minute.'

His mother nods.

'We have to have the coffee ready. He has travelled a long way.'

'I'll sort it out when he gets here.'

His mum runs the fingers of her left hand through her hair and pushes a strand of it behind her ear.

'Do I look awful?' she says nervously.

He shakes his head. 'You look lovely,' he says.

His mum looks happy.

Who are you? he thinks. *Who are you right now?*

She blinks quickly a few times and coughs.

'Are you okay?' he asks.

She studies him silently, her face expressionless. Seconds tick by and seem to stretch out into an eternity.

That other gaze is back. Someone else peering out through her eyes.

'I heard you talking about me last night,' she says.

Joel doesn't move, but the magazine slips from his lap.

'You seem surprised. I was sure you could tell I was there,' she says.

The noises from the bedroom. The shadow in my window when I was calling Nina.

His mum giggles like a little girl. A child who has learnt a new trick, and he's the adult who's supposed to pretend to be impressed.

'Dad?' Joel says. 'Is that you?'

There's another knock on the door, and when Joel looks over, he sees Björn standing in the hallway with a paper bag from a bakery.

His slicked-back hair's thinner, but he looks healthy. Out of place in here with his few extra pounds and tan, wearing a polo shirt and khaki shorts with an insane number of pockets.

'What are you two gabbing about, then?' he says in a deliberately over the top west coast accent.

But Joel can tell he's nervous as he enters the room.

'Hi, sweetheart!' his mum exclaims. 'I'm so happy to see you. What did you bring? Is it for me?'

'Well, I don't see any other beautiful ladies around here.'

Björn shoots Joel a look as he leans down and hugs her. He's clearly shocked by how skinny she is. How much she's aged since moving here.

When the hug's over, their mum opens the bag and peers into it.

'Custard hearts,' she says. 'My favourite. You remembered.'

Nina

The stairwell smells of cooking and sour mopping water. Nina's panting slightly by the time she reaches the third and topmost landing. There are two doors, but only one has a name on it. RÖNNBERG DAHLIN. The doorbell button feels greasy to the touch. The intro to 'Für Elise' tinkles loudly inside.

Footsteps thump towards her. A pause, during which Nina assumes she's being studied through the peephole. Each passing second is proof of hesitation.

A chain rattles, then the lock clicks and the door opens.

Without make-up, Johanna looks about twelve. She's wearing a white terry dressing gown; her toenails are painted neon pink.

'Hi. Thanks for letting me stop by.'

Nina's voice echoes in the stairwell. Johanna yawns and leans against the doorpost.

'You were proper cryptic on the phone,' she says.

'Can I come in? It won't take long, I promise.'

'I don't know,' Johanna says. 'The place is a bit of a mess . . .'

'I don't care about things like that.'

Johanna cocks one eyebrow. 'Yeah, right.'

'People can do whatever they want in their own homes,' Nina says. 'It's only at work it's important to keep everything neat.'

Oh my god, she sounds like an old schoolmarm. Johanna nods in a way that comes across as infinitely reluctant.

Nina follows her into the flat. There are clumps of dust along the walls, piles of clothes on the sofa, dirty dishes on the coffee table. On the other side of a door standing ajar, Nina glimpses more piles of clothes on the floor and a hairy leg sticking out of a bed.

Johanna steps out onto the balcony and lights a cigarette. Nina goes out to join her, putting her hands on the round, white-painted metal railing. They gaze out across a carpark and the rest of the estate. Between the other three-storey blocks of flats, Nina can see a corner of the football field. Beyond it, out of sight, is Pineshade. Johanna lived so close to work it's almost impressive she managed to be late as often as she was.

'So,' Johanna says, slipping her lighter back into the pocket of her dressing gown. 'You need someone to cover some shifts or what?'

'No,' Nina says. 'I wanted to ask about the night you quit.'

Johanna turns to her. 'What about it?'

'What happened?'

Johanna flicks ash over the railing. Her eyes narrow as she studies Nina. 'Why?' she says. 'I didn't do anything wrong.'

Aside from just taking off, Nina thinks reflexively.

But now she knows Johanna might have had good reason.

'No, don't worry,' Nina says. 'No one thinks you did. But Faisal said you seemed scared. I just want to know what happened.'

Johanna resumes her contemplation of the carpark. Leans forwards with her elbows on the railing. Puffs on her cigarette.

'I don't want to talk about it,' she says. 'You wouldn't understand anyway.'

'I might.'

Johanna shakes her head.

'Did it have something to do with Monika?' Nina says.

Johanna glances furtively at her. Nina catches a flash of fear before the mask of indifference slides back into place.

'Why would it?'

'Because . . . strange things have been happening with her recently. She's been saying things.'

Johanna wraps her dressing gown tighter around her and takes another drag. 'Things?' she says. 'What kind of things?'

'Things she should have no way of knowing,' Nina replies. 'But we might all be imagining it.'

'What did she tell you? Did she say something about me?'

'No,' Nina hurries to assure her. 'Nothing like that. This is just a shot in the dark on my part.'

Johanna seems to be trying to judge whether or not she's lying. And it occurs to Nina that what she's doing might be wrong. What's the point of making Johanna afraid all over again?

'She said things I've never told anyone,' Johanna says quietly, looking over her shoulder at the flat behind her. 'Not even my boyfriend. *No one*. I guarantee you, you're not imagining it.'

'Did she say anything about being someone else?' Nina said. 'Or about there being someone else in the room? Someone you couldn't see?'

Johanna stares at her. 'What? No! Why would you ask that?'

Nina looks away. 'We're just trying to understand what's happening so we can help her.'

'Shoot the old cow,' Johanna says, and flicks her cigarette over the railing.

'I don't think we're going to do that,' Nina replies.

'I hate her. I'm going to have to fucking move, just because I keep thinking about how she's right over there,' Johanna says, jabbing her thumb in the direction of the football field.

Joel

'These pastries are just the ticket,' their mum says, picking up another custard heart.

'I don't suppose the coffee breaks are much to write home about here,' Björn says.

'Oh, I shouldn't complain. It's not too bad. But I do miss baking for myself sometimes.'

'I'm sure they'd let you bake sometimes if you asked them.'

'Yes, I'm sure they would,' their mum replies. 'But I reckon I'm a bit lazy, to tell the truth.'

They laugh. Björn sips his coffee. She gazes at him dotingly, and Joel's constantly aware of the wedding photo on the wall.

'It's so good to see you, Mum,' Björn says. 'I've been so worried about you.'

'Whatever for?'

She smiles mildly at him. Leans forwards and puts her hand on his cheek. Björn stops chewing and looks tearful.

'Don't you worry about me,' she says. 'I'm just fine.'

'I would have come sooner if I could have. You know that, right?'

'Of course I do. But you have your own family to think about. They come first. You can't go running off to visit your old mother all the time.' She strokes his cheeks a couple of times. 'The important thing is that you're here now. And now you have to tell me how you're all doing. How are the children?'

Björn clears his throat and starts telling her about school events and football games and boat excursions in Spain.

Their mum listens, enthralled. Nods in all the right places.

Once, though, she turns to Joel and shoots him a tiny grin.

See? it seems to say. *See how well I can play your mother when I want to?*

Nina

As she pulls her smock on over her head, Nina catches a whiff of ingrained sweat from her armpits, despite having showered earlier. She wets a towel and rubs vigorously under her arms. Puts on fresh deodorant and closes the locker door.

Her steps sound too loud in the basement corridor. She strains her ears and stares at the light switch, ready for the fluorescent lights to go out at any moment. Waiting is the worst part.

She breaks into a run, then shoves the door to the stairwell open. Almost falls on her way up to the lobby, certain someone's following her.

This time, the familiar smells and sounds of D corridor do nothing to dispel her fear. Lillemor looks up from a sofa in the lounge and anxiously watches her pass. Edit is bent over her rollator, repeating her endless chant. Nina hurries on towards D6, knocks on the door and enters without waiting for an answer.

They're sitting around the table and turn to her in unison.

Joel's brother has aged. Grown heavier. His tan brings out the blue in his eyes. He looks even less like Joel now.

'Well now, would you look at this, all of us, together again,' Monika says with a tinkling laugh. 'Björn, you remember Nina, don't you? She was practically part of the family.'

'Of course,' he says, and gets halfway out of the chair, extending a hand. 'How are you?'

'Fine, just fine.'

His hand envelops hers. The hairs on his knuckles shimmer like gold.

'So, you work here now?' he asks, sitting back down.

'Yes.'

'That's great for you, Mum,' he says. 'Having a familiar face around.'

'Oh yes, we've been having such lovely conversations about all kinds of things,' she replies.

A twitch at the corner of her mouth makes Nina shudder.

'Remember the way the two of them used to dress?' Monika continues. 'And always changing their hair colour. I thought for sure they'd end up bald.'

'Yes,' Björn says. 'And Joel always wore black. It was like he was going to a funeral every single day.'

Nina looks at Joel. She can tell something has happened.

'I was actually looking for you, Joel,' Nina says, managing with effort to match their cheerful tone. 'Do you have a minute? We could just pop outside?'

Monika chuckles again. 'You see? Just like the olden days. The two of them always sneaking off to talk secrets. They stayed up until the wee hours last night.'

She shoots Nina a significant look. Joel gets up from his chair and picks up a rumpled magazine from Monika's bedside table before leaving the suite ahead of Nina.

'Good to see you again,' Björn says. 'Take care.'

'You too.'

Nina makes sure the door shuts behind her after stepping out into the hallway. She looks around, then quietly tells him what Johanna had to say. Joel nods and nods as though he wants her to speed up. When she's done, he opens the magazine and holds it up to her without a word.

Nina looks at the holes where the pen has gone through the paper, staring at the large upper-case letters.

'She wants help,' Joel says. 'And that *thing* broke her arm to stop her from writing more.'

The corridor lurches. Nina leans against the door, intensely aware that Monika, or whatever is pretending to be Monika, is on the other side of it.

'She ate paper in the common room,' she says. 'Did you know that?'

Joel nods. And she can tell he understands. Is thinking the same thing she is.

Had Monika written a message then, too? Tried to ask for help? *Was the message for us?*

Nina wants to run away, but it's too late.

They stayed up until the wee hours last night.

There's nowhere to run to.

'We can't wait any longer,' Nina says. 'We have to confront whatever's in there.'

Joel swallows so hard she can see his Adam's apple move, like an animal scurrying back and forth under a blanket of skin.

'Björn's going home tomorrow.'

'I'll check with Gorana. She's working the night shift tomorrow. I can probably persuade her to trade with me.'

They look at each other in silence. Monika is audibly laughing in the suite.

'It's calmer here at night,' Nina says. 'We'll have her to ourselves.'

It's the last thing Nina wants. But they have no choice.

Joel

'I suppose it's getting to be that time,' Björn says, and stands up the moment Joel comes back in.

Joel nods. Looks at their mum's warm smile and the cast on her arm. If it isn't her, then who is it?

Is she aware of what's happening?

He hates the thing sitting there, wearing a disguise made of his mum's flesh and blood, hates it like he's never hated anything before.

Give her back.

Björn says something about hitting the loo before leaving. He pushes past Joel in the small room, so close he can smell his cheap body spray.

Joel stays standing until he hears the bathroom door close. Then he sits down next to his mother and forces himself to look at the familiar face that now belongs to someone or something else.

'You don't fool me,' he says quietly.

She—

it

—slowly turns to him. Considers him calmly.

'No. There's no need for that anymore.'

His mother's throat clicks and hisses.

'Let her go,' Joel says.

'I can't.'

Her face is a parody of pity.

There's a flush in the bathroom. The toilet lid closes with a bang.

'I've grown strong,' says his mum, who's not his mum. 'And it's thanks to you.'

The air around them seems thicker. It looks like it's shimmering at the edge of his vision. Reality is falling apart.

'What's that supposed to mean?' he says.

Water rushes out of the tap on the other side of the bathroom door. Björn's humming something in there.

His mum's lips stretch into a smile. Her teeth are grey, sticky with custard.

'Why is it thanks to me?' Joel demands.

'You're the one who brought me here.'

The bathroom door opens and she turns towards it, smiling happily at Björn. A perfect imitation of the mother she once was.

'It's so good to have both my boys with me again,' she exclaims.

Nina

Dagmar stares intently at Nina and spits out half-chewed pieces of boiled potato, dissolved in factory-made tartar sauce. It's a struggle for Nina to stay seated next to her bed, calm and in control. She has to keep reminding herself that it's not Dagmar's fault. She's deteriorating. Nina has seen fear and frustration make old people act out before. And Dagmar can't even speak. Spitting and making a mess is all she has left. She tries to feel sorry for her.

But it's not doing the trick today. Something's building inside Nina. Her body won't be able to contain her own fear much longer. Her head's throbbing. Any moment now, something's going to snap. A fuse is going to blow.

'I'll do it,' Vera says, putting her knitting down.

She gets out of her own bed and comes up next to Nina, who hands her the spoon.

'There, there,' Vera coos and sits down on the edge of the bed. 'There, there, there. You know what to do.'

She touches her sister's lips with the spoon and Dagmar's mouth opens. She sticks her food-smeared tongue out. Vera nods encouragingly and puts the food in, gently touching the underside of Dagmar's chin with her knuckle to make her close her mouth again.

When Dagmar seems to want to spit the food back out, Vera shakes her head.

'Try,' she says.

And Dagmar tilts her head back. The tendons of her neck strain. The corners of her mouth pull down with the effort. But she does swallow.

'Lovely,' Vera says. 'Good girl.'

She continues to speak gently to Dagmar. So much love in her voice, endless patience.

'You see, we don't need him,' Vera says.

She quickly glances over at Nina. Looks caught out.

'What did you say?'

'Nothing,' Vera replies quickly.

Dagmar smacks her lips. Wants more.

'Who don't you need?' Nina says.

'I don't know what you're talking about,' Vera says. 'Now leave us alone so I can give my sister some more dinner.'

Nina puts a hand on her arm. Strokes it. The old skin wrinkles under her fingers.

'Tell me,' she says. 'You have to tell me what's happening so I can help all of you.'

Vera stubbornly refuses to look at her. The spoon taps against the plate when she fastidiously pushes little bits of breaded fish and sauce onto it.

'Vera,' Nina says. 'I'm scared.'

But Vera doesn't reply. She holds the spoon out to Dagmar, who opens her mouth eagerly.

'Please.'

Vera starts. Drops the spoon onto the duvet.

'You're hurting me,' she whimpers.

Nina looks at her hand. It's squeezing Vera's forearm hard. Too hard. She immediately lets go. Her fingers have left four distinct marks that are going to turn into bruises. Old people's skin is so sensitive.

'I'm sorry,' Nina says. 'I'm so sorry, I really didn't mean to. I just want you to help me.'

'I can't. Now go away.'

Vera turns to Dagmar, picks up the spoon and resumes painstakingly dragging it across the plate again.

Nina leaves them, walks two doors down to D6 and pulls the door open quickly, before she can change her mind. But Monika's not in her suite.

She walks down to the common room and spots Monika sitting across from Olof, eating greedily. He's just picking at his food.

'Was Dagmar okay?' Sucdi says when Nina passes her.

'Absolutely,' she says, and continues towards Monika's table.

Monika raises her glass of milk and drinks calmly and deeply. Pretends not to notice Nina standing next to her.

'Why are you doing this?' Nina says quietly. 'What is it you want?'

Monika sets her empty glass down on the table and looks at Olof, who shifts uneasily. At length, she turns to Nina. Her breath smells like milk gone bad.

'Someone wants to talk to you,' she says.

'Who?' Nina asks. 'What do you mean? Who wants to talk to me?'

But she already knows the answer. The impossible answer.

Mum.

Nina wants to shake Monika, wants to hit her. If they'd been alone, she may not have been able to control herself. She can imagine the headlines: *Care Home Employee Assaults Seventy-two-year-old with Dementia.*

She looks at the old people in the room and wonders how many of them have been in contact with whatever Monika brought here. How much they know about what's going on.

Sucdi clears a stack of plates. Soon, it will be time to help the old ones get into bed and to start writing reports.

Reports.

The binder.

Every day Monika has been here is documented.

Nina realises Wiborg is walking towards her, her eyes eager. She's slow but determined as she raises one of her birdlike little hands and waves her over.

'You have to come,' Wiborg says, and grabs the sleeve of Nina's smock, dragging her towards D corridor with surprising strength.

'Hurry, before they disappear,' she says.

'I'm coming, Wiborg, calm down.'

The door to D1 is wide open and Nina's suddenly scared.

'Wiborg,' she says. 'Is there someone in there?'

Wiborg shakes her head. 'But I was right, you'll see,' she says.

They enter the suite. Wiborg's duvet is on the floor, as though she threw it off in a hurry. The phone receiver is lying on its side on the nightstand. Wiborg picks it up gingerly, holds it out to Nina.

She stares at the grey plastic and shakes her head, but Wiborg coaxes until she reluctantly takes the receiver.

It's warm from Wiborg's hand. Almost feels alive.

She puts it to her ear. Hears only static. Distant waves. Wind through trees.

Someone wants to talk to you.

'Hello?' she says.

The line crackles a few times, dead echoes of who knows how many miles of wires.

'There's no one there,' she says with relief, handing the receiver back.

But Wiborg presses it back to her ear.

'There is,' she says. 'You have to *really* listen. They're so far away, you see.'

Nina listens to the static. Hears it ebb and flow. Hypnotic.

Whispering. Almost imperceptible. But it's there.

Wiborg nods eagerly.

'. . . I'm coming, Nina . . .'

Mum.

'. . . thought you could just ditch me . . .'

'It's not you,' Nina says.

She thinks she hears a laugh on the other end, but it could be the crackling of the static. She slams the receiver down. Stares at it. The phone remains silent.

'Why did you say my parents are dead?' Wiborg says triumphantly. 'Of course they're alive. They'll be here to pick me up before you know it.'

Joel

They're eating pizza straight out of the box on the terrace. Drinking beer from bottles Björn brought. Waving away flies and early-evening mosquitoes.

'Well, she seemed fine to me,' Björn says. 'Makes you wonder if she even belongs at Pineshade.'

She's messing with both of us, but you don't see it. Of course you don't.

And I can't tell you without sounding completely mad. That's the ingenious part of it.

'She has ups and downs,' Joel says.

'She's lost a lot of weight, though,' Björn goes on as though he didn't hear him and tears off a slice of his Skredsby Special with sirloin steak and shoves it in his mouth. 'Are they not being fed properly or what?'

'They say they keep track on everything going in and coming out.'

'Pardon?'

'Didn't you see the stool record on the bathroom door?'

'Bloody hell,' Björn says, wiping Béarnaise sauce from his chin. 'I'm eating, okay?'

'You asked.'

Björn rinses out his mouth with a swig of beer and makes a

revolted face. He picks his cutlery up, but leaves it hovering in mid-air.

'Sorry,' Joel says.

'It's fine,' Björn says, and cuts a piece from the middle of his pizza with intense concentration. 'It was just hard to see her like that. You must have thought so at first, too, right?'

Joel nods. It's barely been a month since their mother moved to Pineshade, but it feels like a lot longer.

'Of course,' he says.

How quickly he has forgotten what it was like to bring her there that first day. The uncertainty of whether it was the right thing to do. And back then, she was very clearly confused. Not like today.

'The other people are full-on nutbags,' Björn says. 'Did you see the one with the stuffed animal?'

'Wiborg? Yes.'

'And that old geezer with no legs, sitting in front of the TV with a pee bag strapped to his wheelchair. How much would it suck to end up like that?'

Björn heaves a sigh. Puts his cutlery back down in the gloopy mix of sauce and half-dissolved dough in his pizza box.

Joel hasn't been able to even touch his pizza. He takes another sip of beer.

A wind blows through the garden. Before he came back, Joel had forgotten how much he loves the air here, on nights like this. Fresh and salty, sifted through foliage and the needles of the evergreens.

'Hey,' he says. 'How much do you remember of Dad?'

Björn looks at him inquiringly.

'We've never really talked about him,' Joel says. 'What was he like?'

'What do you want to know?'

If he's the type to come back from the other side and possess Mum.

'Anything.'

Björn sighs again and seems annoyed by the question; Joel wonders if he should have waited until they'd had a few more beers.

'I wasn't much older than you,' Björn says slowly, and Joel realises his brother isn't annoyed. He's just searching for the right words.

This is our first ever grown-up conversation.

'All I have is fragments,' Björn continues. 'We went fishing at some point when we were on holiday up north. In a river. Mum was pregnant with you, I think. I remember parts of the drive up there, too. We spent the night somewhere along the way and I thought the hotel was so exciting.'

Joel nods. He's seen the pictures, faded in shades of yellow. Their mum had long hair and a centre parting. Seems to have laughed a lot. Her belly was only just beginning to show, but not enough for a casual observer to be sure she was pregnant. Björn had whitish-blond curls and was running around in dungarees. Their dad looked straight into the camera with a cigarette between his teeth, his fingers sticky with fish blood.

It's a family Joel was never a part of. And there are barely any pictures from after their dad's death.

'But what was he like?' Joel says, and pulls a cigarette out of the packet in his pocket.

He lights it. Slowly blows out his first drag. Waits.

'I don't really remember, that's what fucking sucks,' Björn replies. 'But I must have . . . He must have been a pretty fun dad before, because I remember being really angry when he never wanted to play anymore. He stopped working and just spent all his time in bed. And I had to help out with you when he napped. We would be out here, so we couldn't disturb him.'

Joel turns around in his chair, looks out across the garden. Tries to summon some kind of memory but fails.

It must have been a confusing time for Björn. A little brother stealing all the attention. A dad who was changing. And a mum who must have been exhausted, with both a sick husband and two children to look after.

'Poor Mum,' Björn says. 'Good thing they were so in love.'

'They were?'

'Yes. How can you not know that?'

'I know Mum says they were, but she never wants to admit that anything was ever bad.'

'True, she's not like you that way.'

'What's that supposed to mean?'

'Nothing. I'm just saying you usually focus on the bad things.'

Joel opens his mouth to argue but stops himself. Puffs on his cigarette. Ponders if Björn's right.

'I know what you mean about Mum,' Björn says. 'But they were good together. Even I could see that, little as I was. They were always kissing and stuff like that. Hell, maybe sometimes that's why they sent us outside, so they could be alone . . .'

Björn shoots him an embarrassed grin. There's a glugging sound as he empties his bottle.

Joel thinks hard. If their parents really were happy together, despite illness and other strains, why would their dad want to hurt their mum now? Would he have changed that much, just because he's dead?

Björn gives him a look when he chuckles out loud.

'What?'

'Nothing,' Joel says, putting his cigarette out in the glass jar. It's just . . . everything's so fucking weird right now.'

'You can say that again.'

They sit in silence for a while. Joel studies the bushes, which need trimming, the flowerbeds full of purple coneflowers and Mexican asters, which could do with some weeding. He remembers all the endless summer holiday days he spent lying in the grass, reading or listening to music, always alone before he met Nina. He'd felt ashamed about it in front of Björn, who was surrounded by friends, or had a worshipful girlfriend trailing in his wake, laughing at his jokes, eyeing Joel with thinly veiled pity or contempt.

Nina saved him.

'Did you know he was a good singer?' Björn says suddenly.

'Who was?'

'Dad.'

'No. I had no idea.'

'I guess you get it from him.'

Joel is surprised by how much that moves him.

'At least I have one thing in common with the man, then,' he says. 'I thought we were as different as two people can be.'

'You look alike too, don't you?' Björn says. 'I got his colouring, but you're the same build and stuff.'

He drains his beer. Stifles a belch as he gets to his feet.

'I guess I should get on with packing some things up,' he says. 'Do you want to see what I find up there, or . . .'

'No. Take whatever you want.'

Björn seems to hesitate. Maybe he thinks it's a tactic. That Joel wants to make him feel guilty so he doesn't filch everything that might be worth something.

After Björn goes inside, Joel stays in his chair for a long time before heading over to the bin to discard the pizza boxes. He looks up at the house that may not exist for much longer. But they haven't had any bids yet, and he can't help but wonder why, in this moment, that makes him feel so relieved.

Nina

Her shift ended an hour ago, but Nina's still at Pineshade. Flipping through the binder one last time, looking for things she might have missed. It's hard when she has no idea what to look for.

The staff like to make *The Exorcist* jokes in the staffroom whenever they're subjected to unusually abrupt mood swings or personality changes, the sudden appearance of an imaginary friend, projectile vomiting. So how is she supposed to know what things are dementia and what things might be something else?

At first glance, there's nothing unusual in the summer's reports. But that obviously depends on how you read them. She has searched her recollection for additional things. Tried to make a timeline. She's aware the notes she has made look like the ravings of a madwoman.

But there are patterns.

Some of the residents were scared when Monika moved in. Vera hung towels over the bathroom mirror and talked about someone trying to kidnap Dagmar. Anna stopped going for walks and wanted her lights on so the new ghost couldn't come for her.

The new ghost. He's trying to scare me.

Others were overjoyed at the new presence. Lillemor got her angel. Bodil her men. Wiborg's parents finally picked up the phone.

And then the angel and the men disappeared. Nina has no

doubt Wiborg's phone is going to fall silent, too. Nothing makes you unhappier than having all your dreams come true, only to have them taken away again in an instant.

Whatever it is that has come to Pineshade, it has been systematically terrorising the old people.

She finds no corresponding pattern among the reports from the other wards. And they didn't have ventilation problems early in the summer. No flickering lights. No greasy stains.

Nina goes back to the reports from Monika's first days at the home and looks at her own handwriting, remembering how happy she was the first time Monika recognised her.

I'm so happy to see you.

You've done more than enough for us. You were always so kind and capable.

Monika had told her exactly, word for word, what she wanted to hear.

You have nothing to apologise for. You did what you had to do.

Then Monika had turned on her. Worse than Nina could ever have imagined.

Cuckoo.

Had started to scare her.

She'd scared Joel, too. And Johanna. And Sucdi, to some extent. Maybe more people here at Pineshade. They've been shaken so badly they've begun to doubt themselves and the reality around them.

Monika has achieved it by holding their secrets up for them to see. As though she can read their minds. Knows their pressure points.

It all started with Monika. But according to Joel, her companion only grew strong when she arrived at the home.

Monika fits neatly into the pattern, as well. She was overjoyed that her beloved Nils had come back to her. And then she grew scared of him.

The desperate doodles in the crossword puzzle magazine show Monika has been trying to warn them. She has been trying to resist – they just haven't seen it.

You shouldn't be here. Monika scratching her own cheek. *Get out. Get out, get out, get out! Leave!* She wasn't talking to Nina. She was talking to whatever's inside her. She was trying to stop it.

Another instance. *Go away.* She'd looked down at her cast. *You have to. Before . . . Before he comes back.* She'd known something was coming. That it was going to make her say things she didn't want to say.

Nina writes and writes. When she's done, she leans back in her chair. Her head's spinning, and yet the pattern feels almost complete.

But that's a form of madness, too, isn't it? Thinking you can see patterns and signs in random events? She doesn't trust herself. How can she, when she hears ghosts whispering through Wiborg's phone?

Footsteps approach in the corridor and Nina rips the page out of the notepad, shoving it into her pocket. Gorana yelps when she enters the staffroom and spots Nina.

'I thought you'd left,' she says. 'I just weed myself a bit.'

She bends down to pick up some crumpled pieces of paper she dropped on the floor.

'I had some things to sort out first, but I'm off now,' Nina replies and stands up. 'I wanted to ask you a favour, actually.'

Gorana looks up at Nina and pushes her fringe out of her eyes.

'Would it be okay if I took your night shift tomorrow?' Nina continues. 'We need some extra money. Car trouble.'

'I need the money, too,' Gorana replies, straightening up. 'Though that being said, I wouldn't mind skipping a night shift in this place.'

'Why, is something the matter?'

'Isn't the usual bad enough?' Gorana says with a carefree laugh. 'But Elisabeth's not going to like it, given as how you cost more than I do.'

'You could always get food poisoning at the last minute and I could just happen to be the one to answer the phone when you call in sick in the evening,' Nina says. 'I'll deal with Elisabeth the next day, when it's too late to change. I'm the one she'll be angry with.'

'Sly. I'm almost starting to wonder what's happened to the prim and proper Nina we all know and love.'

'I wish I were as prim and proper as everyone seems to think.'

'Well, I like this Nina better. Nahal told me what you did to Petrus.'

Nina shakes her head.

'I shouldn't have—'

'Yes, you should,' Gorana breaks in. 'Do you know how many times I've wanted to give him all his insulin shots at once so we can be rid of him?'

'Don't joke about things like that.'

Gorana rolls her eyes. Holds the crumpled scraps of paper out to Nina.

'I found these when I tidied the lounge. Someone had shoved them behind the paintings and on top of the cabinet. Do you know who it might be?'

Nina takes the notes from her and instantly recognises the handwriting. She nods, her heart pounding in her chest, making her cheeks flush.

'Monika wrote these,' she says.

I CAN'T HELP IT I'M SORRY

Monika when the doctor visited. *Go fish.*

The Marcus Larson paintings in the lounge. Ships on stormy seas.

'What do you reckon, should I make a note in her report?' Gorana says while Nina continues to read.

IT WASN'T NILS WAITING FOR ME. HE WAS JUST PRETENDING

IT'S SO DARK AND I CAN'T TAKE IT ANYMORE I WAS SO STUPID TO BELIEVE NOW HE WON'T STOP

HE SEES EVERYTHING I SEE WHEN HE'S HERE I HAVE TO HIDE THIS PLEASE FIND THIS

IT'S NOT NILS IT'S NOT NILS

The words were clearly scribbled in great haste. The notes are so crumpled the pencilled capitals are smudged in places. She must have been hiding the notes in the lounge the night Nina found her in there.

Monika had been terrified.

'So, do they go in the report or not?' Gorana says.

'I don't know. Sure, maybe. I have to go now.'

Gorana gives her a weird look. Nina manages to put on a smile.

'Thanks for helping me out tomorrow,' she says. 'Just call about an hour before and I'll make sure I'm the one who picks up.'

She exits into the hallway. Looks over at D6. Monika's alone in there with whatever's holding her captive.

Even in the grip of fear, Nina feels relieved. It's not Nils. And it's not her mother, either. Her mother has nothing to do with this. That thing in D6 has been lying this whole time about who and what it is. And tomorrow, she and Joel are going to find out more. They're going to finish this, one way or another.

Joel

He wakes up on the living room sofa. Björn's sitting on the coffee table, leaning forwards slightly, looking amused.

'You weren't entirely easy to wake,' he says. 'But I figured you might prefer your bed. I'm turning in now.'

Joel blinks at the gloom, then sits up and pulls off the blanket. Goose bumps immediately spread up and down his arms.

'Okay,' he says, rubbing his face. 'Thanks.'

He shudders and glances out the window. It looks like another balmy summer's night. But dusk comes earlier now.

'It's cold,' he says.

'You think?' Björn replies. 'You must have a temperature or something. I'm sweating like a whore in church.'

'Wow,' Joel says, resting his forehead in his hands. 'I haven't heard that expression in a while.'

He picks up his phone to check the time.

A text from Nina.

It's not Nils. Call me if you can.

Joel quickly swipes through pictures of crumpled, handwritten notes. The bright glare of the screen makes the room around him retreat into a compact darkness.

It's not his dad. Something has been masquerading as him.

That must be the worst form of torture. To believe you're being tormented by the person you love.

Poor Mum.

'Anyway,' Björn says. 'Goodnight, then.'

'I'm coming.'

Joel manages to muster enough strength to stand up, but exhaustion fills every part of his body, making his blood stand still.

There's a cold draught from the kitchen, but Björn doesn't notice.

'Thanks for tonight,' Björn says. 'It was nice, circumstances notwithstanding. We don't exactly get together much, do we?'

'No,' Joel agrees. 'I guess we don't.'

He pulls up short at the threshold.

A shadow is moving along the kitchen counter. When he tries to look directly at it, it dissolves.

'You know you're always welcome to visit us, right?' Björn says.

But Joel can't reply. He's trying to catch a glimpse of the shadow, looking away and then quickly back again.

It's moving closer. Creeping slowly along the wall towards the doorway. Out of the corner of his eye, he can see it flow into a solid shape.

'Are you all right?' Björn asks. 'Maybe you *are* sick?'

'You don't see it?'

Joel instantly regrets saying anything. He already knows the answer. Yet even so, he points at the shape.

'What?' Björn asks.

The kitchen window's open. The air wafting through it is warm and humid. But Joel shivers.

'Bloody hell, Joel, are you on something? Did you start that shit again?'

He shakes his head. The shadow's gone. It just wanted to show itself. Show him what it can do.

I've grown strong. And it's thanks to you.

'It was a spider,' he says. 'Never mind, it's gone now.'

Björn shoots him a sceptical look. 'That's hardly a reason to go all psycho, is it?'

Pineshade

Nina has left Pineshade. Gorana's standing out back, outside the open door to D Ward. She's smoking a cigarette and playing a game on her phone. The constantly changing colours on her screen illuminate her face. From time to time, she looks up to make sure the corridor's empty.

Lillemor's lying in bed with her ear pressed to the wall. She's trying to hear if there are any sounds coming from D6, but the thing on the other side is silent tonight. Lillemor knows it's gathering its strength. She can feel it in the air. *Dear Lord if you exist help us now deliver us from evil if the Beast exists you have to as well I'm never going to doubt again if you make your face shine upon us deliver us from evil and lead us not into temptation amen dear sweet Lord.*

Thinking she saw something out of the corner of her eye, Gorana looks up from her screen. But it's just the fluorescent lights flickering, making big patches of shadow flit up and down the corridor. They seem to change shape, grow and shrink. Gorana stares at them for so long her cigarette burns down to the filter, singeing her fingers. She lets out a curse and shoves the butt into the wall-mounted ashtray. Blows on her fingertips.

Lillemor has come to a decision. She's going to save Monika. She's going to bring her back to the Lord. Everything started with

Monika. It has to end with her, too. It's clear now, so clear the angels must have told her. The real angels. Lillemor struggles out of bed, setting off the motion sensor. She grabs her pillow and remonstrates with herself when she feels doubt bubble up inside her. *Lord let your angels give me strength let Monika be asleep don't let her notice what's happening receive her with open arms let the lamb come back to the flock forgive us both Thy kingdom come for thine is the kingdom and the power and the glory for ever and ever.* Lillemor's prayers are cut off abruptly when her bedside light goes out, plunging the room into darkness. She hugs her pillow more tightly and makes her way to the door as quickly as she is able.

Gorana sees her step out into the corridor.

'Lillemor?' she calls out. 'Where are you going?'

Vera's sitting up in bed, knitting. She can't stop. The red wool is so beautiful. The needles are a size three, thin, but not delicate; the stitches come out tiny and neat. Dagmar's sitting on the edge of her bed.

'Now do you see what's going to happen if we don't do as he says?' she hisses. 'You said you'd do anything for me.'

Vera carries on knitting. Doesn't want to listen.

Lillemor has collapsed on the floor in front of D6. She can't breathe. Black spots fill the corridor, dancing in front of her like a swarm of angry bugs, merging into a darkness only she can see. She hears Gorana's footsteps approaching and tries to scream, but the darkness won't let her. It fills her mouth and nose.

Monika's lying dead-still in her bed. Her eyes have rolled back into her skull. Her fingers clutch at the guard rail.

Nina

She opens her eyes. The bedroom is pale and washed out by the early morning light. A shadow is sitting at the foot of the bed. It has no face, but she knows it's watching her.

Markus is snoring softly next to her; she tries to open her mouth. Can't. Can only move her eyes. When she looks straight at the shadow, her gaze seems to dissolve it. As soon as she looks away, it solidifies, contracts into a shape.

Her body's heavy against the mattress. As though she were dead.

Am I dead?

She needs to wake Markus up so he can help her. Has to scream so she can wake herself up.

Before I get stuck in this state.

She fights to squeeze out a sound. Manages only a faint whimper. Something about the angle of the shadow's head suggests it is amused. It's sitting perfectly still. A greasy stain on the world.

Nina fights to make her body move. Manages to rock back and forth a couple of times. At least she thinks she does. She's not sure. But Markus has stopped snoring.

She inhales through clenched teeth. Manages another whimper. Finally, Markus turns over next to her. He looks at her. The shadow watches them both but Markus doesn't notice.

'Nina?' he says. 'Nina, are you all right?'

He touches her shoulder and she snaps back into her body. It becomes her own again. She opens her eyes, which have been closed the whole time, and looks around frantically.

The same pale early morning light, but the shadow's gone.

It was real. It was here, in bed with us.

'Come here,' Markus says, pulling her close and wrapping his arms around her.

He smells like warm, sleepy man. Only now does she realise she's crying.

'Was it a nightmare?' he murmurs.

She nods. Closes her eyes and lets him hold her.

There's nowhere to run.

Nina doesn't know how long they lie there. She's the one who eventually pulls away. She dries her eyes and looks at him.

'I'm going to get up and make coffee,' she says.

'It's barely morning.'

'I know. You go back to sleep.'

She kisses him lightly on the mouth and gets out of the bed they share.

'Why were you late coming home last night?' he asks.

Nina looks at him. 'I told you. I had to work.'

Markus' eyes narrow suspiciously as he studies her. 'Were you with Joel again? Is that why you're so bloody weird?'

She leaves the bedroom without a word. Walks through their beautiful house, which is full of things she has picked out with the utmost care. So lovely, so broken.

Everything has fallen apart. Just like she always knew it would.

Pineshade

By lunchtime, Lillemor's suite has been emptied. The body has been taken away. Nahal was the one who put her last possessions in a cardboard box that's now sitting on the disinfected bed. A hymnal and a Bible. Face powder and a dried-up lipstick. Reading glasses. Photographs from her life before Pineshade. Nahal didn't know Lillemor very well, and she was busy thinking about Dogglas while she cleaned out the suite. The dog's still not himself after his visit to the home. He barely eats. Jumps at every sound. Whimpers all night long. Nahal's new boyfriend wants them to give him away.

When Nina gets to work that afternoon and finds out Lillemor is dead, she goes into D5. She sees the nails where the angel paintings used to hang and thinks about how scared Lillemor was of what she could hear through the wall. About how she died outside Monika's door with a pillow in her arms.

'We're going to sort this out for you, Lillemor,' she says out loud, hoping Lillemor has turned into one of her beloved angels.

Fredrika has brought the baby into Wiborg's room. Sigge stares at the ceiling while his mother and her grandmother sip coffee.

'They've stopped answering the phone,' Wiborg says. 'They're angry with me again.'

Fredrika nods. Feels a forbidden desire to be rid of her nana. To not have to come back here anymore and listen to the same nonsense over and over. But she pushes the urge back down; she can't bear the guilt that comes with it. *After everything Nana has done for me, this is the least I can do.* She lifts the baby out of his pram and tries to get Wiborg interested in him. But Wiborg just cries. Her eyes are remote.

'Now it's just that horrible woman every time I call. She doesn't listen to me. No one wants to help me.'

Dagmar slowly makes her way over to Vera's bed as dusk falls. Vera watches her shuffling progress and remembers that Dagmar used to be faster than her when they were young. Always on her feet, always restless. Unable to sit still for even a minute. Dagmar grunts and raises her arm, pointing at Vera's knitting basket.

Wiborg glares angrily at Nina when she enters with Sucdi for the evening rounds. She strokes her cat. Now she knows Nina's the mean woman who pokes fun at her on the phone. Her mum and dad told her.

Petrus stares at Nina in terror while she brushes his teeth. He meekly spits the toothpaste into the plastic container she holds under his chin. Doesn't dare not to. The siren's face is distorted by the water billowing around her. Dripping everywhere. *You should have died at sea*, she tells him without opening her mouth.

Olof seems afraid of Nina, too. Even Edit is silent while they change her nappy and take out her dentures.

'What's with everyone tonight?' Sucdi exclaims.

Nina shakes her head. They pop their heads into D6 and note that Monika's already asleep. Nina has slipped her a few extra Oxazepams without telling Sucdi or logging it on her medication list. She's going to keep Monika as sedated as possible until Joel arrives. She checks her watch. Gorana will be calling soon. To say she's sick, so Nina can cover the night shift.

Joel

He drives through the Skredsby roundabout. The petrol station is a brightly lit island in a sea of darkness. He continues past the town square and the deserted football field. A sulphurous glare fills the car, ebbing and flowing as he passes each streetlight. It fades away one last time and disappears when he turns into the Pineshade carpark.

He hasn't slept since Björn woke him the night before. He should be exhausted, but he has never felt more awake. Every fibre in his body is poised and ready.

He spent the whole night in bed with his warm laptop on his thighs Googling exorcisms and possession and near-death experiences. He found Latin quotes, contradictory advice, instructions about salt and sage. None of it was persuasive enough to induce him to raid the spice rack for weapons.

Joel pulls the key out of the ignition and the car falls as silent as the world around it. It's the first time he's seen the home at night. The faint glow of his mother's bedside table lamp illuminates the closed blinds in her window.

He swallows a wave of nausea and thinks about what Nina told him on the phone. If she's right, and that thing in his mum's body can read their minds, his secrets must have been virtual neon signs. What happened that morning more than six years ago is always with him.

He can't believe what's happening. It's like a bad joke, and he's waiting for a punchline that never comes.

Nina's waiting for him right inside the glass front doors.

Pineshade itself seems to have been waiting for him, holding its breath.

Nina unlocks the doors when he climbs the front steps. They say nothing. Just exchange nods. The lobby's dark – the only light is coming from the A and D corridors and a single sconce on the landing halfway down the stairs to the basement. He wonders what they keep down there. While he looks at it, the light from the sconce seems to waver, but he's not sure. Nina swipes her card and they step into D Ward together.

It's eerily calm and quiet. Very different from what it's like during the day. He looks up at the fluorescent lights. They're steady.

'Why don't we talk for a bit, first,' Nina says, leading him into the staffroom.

They sit down and she hands him a cup of coffee without asking. He accepts it, even though he hardly needs the caffeine.

'Look at this,' Nina says, and pulls a folded piece of paper from her pocket. 'This is what I was talking about.'

When she unfolds it, he realises it's a page ripped from a notepad. Nina has meticulously picked off the fringed edge where it was stuck to the spiral back. The page is full of scribbled notes. Dates, and in some cases times, are underlined in the left margin. Seeing it makes it more real, even though it's still unfathomable.

His mum has tainted Pineshade. Both Lillemor and Anna were afraid of the thing that had come to the home. To *their home.*

'It's my fault they're dead,' he says. 'I brought her here.'

'How were you supposed to know? And they may have died of natural causes. They were old, and—'

'But you don't think so, do you? Because I don't.'

Nina looks at him for a long time.

'No,' she says at length. 'Anna and Lillemor were on to it.'

'It already knows we are, too,' Joel says.

His own words sink in. He feels like he needs to throw up.

'We can still walk away from this,' Nina says. 'I mean, we don't even know if there's anything we can do to help.'

Joel studies the dark circles under her eyes. She probably hasn't slept much either.

'Is that what you want?' he says.

Nina looks down. 'No. I can't abandon the old people. Especially not Monika. We have to find out what it wants. It has to be something.'

'Does it, though? Maybe this is just how it gets its kicks.'

She tries to smile. 'It's too late for me to back out anyway,' Nina says. 'I wasn't going to tell you, but it . . . it was at my house this morning. I saw a shadow.'

Joel gags and shakes himself. He puts his coffee cup down.

'It was at my house last night,' he says.

They look at each other.

'If it's trying to scare us, it means it's scared of us, too,' Nina says. 'It wants to make us weak.'

Joel nods and wishes he could believe that. He stands up. His legs are shaking and his fingertips tingle.

'If it can pick the thoughts out of our heads, there's no point discussing this any further,' he points out. 'The more we try to prepare, the more information we give it. Right?'

Nina stands up, too. Puts a warm hand on his shoulder. 'Are you ready?' she asks.

He makes no reply. There's no need.

Neither one of them is ready, but then again, they never will be.

They step into the corridor. The fluorescent lights tinkle above their heads; when Joel looks up, the light flickers.

'Go to hell,' he says.

But his words echo hollowly inside him. He knows the thing following them towards suite D6 can hear it, too.

A door opens a crack as they pass. Something moves in the darkness inside. White strands of hair and milky eyes. A tiny hand clutching the door handle on the inside.

'Good day.' The door slides open further. 'My name is Edit Andersson and I am Director Palm's secretary.'

'Hi, Edit,' Nina says. 'It's the middle of the night, you should be in bed.'

Joel studies her. She sounds so calm. Professional. Maybe that stuff runs on autopilot after so many years at Pineshade.

Edit Andersson takes a tottering step into the hallway, holding herself up with the help of the door handle. Her curved back peeks out between the buttons of her nightgown. Pale skin and age spots.

'Good day. My name is Edit Andersson and I am Director Palm's secretary.'

Nina bends down and takes her arm, kindly but firmly.

'Let's go back to bed,' she says.

Edit shakes her head.

'Good day,' she says, staring at Joel. 'My name is Edit Andersson and I am Director Palm's secretary and *you have to stop right now or he will have his way.*'

Nina gasps. Stops dead. Joel barely dares to breathe.

'What did you say, Edit?'

Edit blinks. Looks up at the fluorescent lights. Looks at Joel.

'Good day. My name is Edit Andersson and I am Director Palm's secretary.'

'Edit,' Nina says. 'Edit, do you know something about—'

'Good day. My name is Edit Andersson and I am Director Palm's secretary.'

Joel hangs back in the hallway while Nina leads Edit back into D3. He stares down at the vinyl floor while the lights flicker around him. Tries not to wonder whether those are shadows he can see out of the corner of his eye. He doesn't look up again until Nina comes back out.

They press on towards D6 and stop outside the door. He listens to the sound of Nina's breathing next to him. His blood singing in his ears, a rushing noise rising and falling much too fast.

In the end, Nina's the one who opens the door.

The suite is freezing. Only the bedside light is on, casting harsh shadows across his mum's face. Her eyes are so sunken he can barely see them.

'Finally,' she says. 'Is it time?'

Nina

It's so cold she should be able to see her breath. But maybe it's not the room that's cold. Maybe it's her. The fear is like frost spreading underneath her skin.

Nina looks at the emaciated figure in the bed. The chapped lips. The lank, lifeless hair. Whatever has taken over Monika is a parasite sucking all her strength; eating away at her flesh until all that remains is a skeleton in an over-sized skin suit.

'We want to talk to Monika,' Nina says.

Joel sits down heavily in the armchair. He's pale, keeping his hands in his pockets to hide that they're shaking.

'Mum,' he says. 'If you can hear us—'

An affected, cackling laughter from the thing in the bed.

'She's not here anymore. I finally got rid of her.'

'I don't believe you,' Joel says. 'She's been trying to get help.'

'That was before I grew stronger. The sow gave up in the end. There's only me and Nina's mum in here now.'

'My mum has nothing to do with this.'

Nina stares intently into the eyes she no longer knows and something shifts in the face on the pillow.

'No, I suppose you've puzzled that out by now. But does it really matter, Nina? She still haunts you, doesn't she? You know what you did. What do you think Joel would say if he knew?'

The voice drops lower, like a tape being played too slowly.

Nina leans over the bed and smells the sour, ingrained reek of the body lying there.

'Monika,' she says, forcing her voice to stay steady. 'We know you're in there. We're going to help you.'

Another cackling laugh. It sounds eerily familiar from hundreds of horror films and nightmares and fairy tales. Not at all real. And Nina has a sudden epiphany. The thing in the bed is just pretending. Showing them what they expect to see. *This isn't its natural behaviour.*

'Good girl,' the creature in the bed says, and nods. 'But you can't blame me for putting on a bit of a show. You're incapable of understanding what I really am.'

It slowly pushes itself up into a sitting position and looks genuinely amused this time. It doesn't take its eyes off her.

Nina backs away.

'I think you want to tell us, though,' Joel says. 'You want to scare us, so go ahead.'

He's trying to sound strong, unafraid. But it's not even remotely convincing. Nina doesn't have to be a mind reader to know Joel's about to crack.

No reply. The creature continues to study Nina. What little courage she has been able to muster is deserting her. She would give anything not to have those eyes staring at her.

'Are you a demon?' Joel presses. 'The Devil?'

'Oh, Joel. I never would have thought you'd be so traditional.'

What was once Monika finally looks away from Nina. Its gaze bores into Joel instead.

'You will never understand. I can only show you. Would you like me to show you, Joel?'

Nina's looking at him, too. He's shaking. It's a matter of seconds before he breaks.

She has to be the strong one.

'I don't give a shit what you are,' she says. 'I want to know why you're doing this to Monika.'

The thing in the bed whips its head around so quickly Monika's neck creaks.

'You really think this has anything to do with Monika? It was pure happenstance it ended up being her.'

Its eyes glitter in their hollows. It's enjoying this. Joel's right. It wants to tell them its secret.

'I'm just a hitchhiker catching a ride from the other side,' it says.

The frost under Nina's skin spreads all the way into her marrow. Turns her to solid ice.

'Just a hitchhiker,' the cracked voice hums. 'A wanderer, seizing an opportunity.'

Nina doesn't know why, but she's sure it's telling the truth this time. There's a terrifying logic to it. This thing is afflicting Monika like any other kind of disease.

Monika was never chosen, never special, there is no grand scheme. She was just in the wrong place at the wrong time. She was available. That's all.

'And the other old people?' Nina says. 'What have you done to them?'

'I've borrowed them when Monika needed respite from me. They let me in. Their minds are wide open.'

'Because they're ill,' Nina says. 'They have no defences.'

'They're healthier than the rest of you. They can see the things you learn to ignore before you're old enough to walk.'

Monika's eyes narrow. Nina suddenly gets the feeling she's about to walk into a trap.

Why is it telling us this? Doesn't that weaken it?

'Look around,' says the hitchhiker. 'What you call reality is only a small part of what's moving in here. The old people know it.'

Nina's eyes start scanning the room before she can stop herself. The shadows seem to bleed into one another beyond the pool of light from the bedside lamp.

Her stomach flips. The bedside table. The metal of the guard rail. The structure of the walls. The everyday things, the normal things. They're nothing but a thin veneer. A layer, hiding other layers, infinite depths.

Monika's neck crunches and creaks when the hitchhiker nods.

'But you're ready to see it now, too. I made you seek out the answers for yourselves. It was the only way to convince you of what you've learnt not to believe in.'

Its mouth widens into a smile and its bottom lip cracks.

Nina looks away. Looks at Joel, who's rocking back and forth in the armchair.

And she understands what the hitchhiker means. They would never have believed this if they'd been told. They had to go hunting for clues themselves. Question their own sanity and still continue to look for signs, for patterns. They've been playing into the hitchhiker's hands all along.

And now, they're ready. The hitchhiker has broken them down. Made them receptive.

There's a next step in that train of thought. A realisation she has to ignore for as long as she can.

'Get out of here,' she says.

'I will. I'm heading out into the world. You're the only one who stays here, Nina. Even the old people make sure to die so they can leave.'

The hitchhiker licks Monika's dry lips. Its tongue is spongy and grey, as though it's dissolving in its mouth.

'You should give up, Nina. No one loves you. Not even your own family. And you know what's even worse? You don't love them either. And you're too much of a coward to admit it.'

'That's not true,' Joel says, looking up at Nina. 'Don't forget: it's just trying to psych you out.'

She nods.

The hitchhiker smiles and says nothing. It knows.

She doesn't love Markus anymore. Maybe she never did. She just settled. For security. For *knowing what you have*. And Daniel . . . What if the hitchhiker's right? What if Daniel's constant rejection has eroded her love?

A mother is supposed to love her child unconditionally.

'You see,' the hitchhiker says. 'It was all in vain.'

But Nina's barely listening.

There's something wrong with her. There has to be. She's letting down all the people who trust her.

She's broken.

A shadow moves at the edge of her vision. It's Joel, who has stood up. He grabs Monika's shoulders and shakes her violently. Her head wobbles back and forth on her thin neck.

'Shut up!' he shouts. 'Mum, I know you're in there! Come out! You have to tell me what to do!'

He sounds like a child.

'Joel,' Nina says, her voice barely more than a whisper. 'Be careful, you're hurting her.'

'Mum, please! Come back!'

He's snapped. And Nina has to face her realisation.

It's through the cracks the chaos seeps in.

We're the endgame. It wants to get inside one of us. That's why it put us through this. It was about us all along.

The creature begins to laugh. Something cracks in Monika's neck. Joel lets go abruptly.

'Nina gets it now. What do I need your old mother for? Why would I want to lie around here until this body dies of old age and I'm sent back to where I came from?'

Nina stares at it. Tries to keep her face expressionless. Tries to not even think about what she has just realised.

It slipped up.

It can be sent back. But we have to kill Monika.

The thought makes her stomach lurch. That's not an option.

'Isn't it?' the hitchhiker says. 'You're already a murderer. You murdered your mother.'

Nina can tell Joel's looking at her, but she can't bring herself to meet his eyes.

Suddenly, she glimpses the hitchhiker's face behind Monika's and knows that if she ever saw its true self, she would never be whole again. Everything holding her together would fall apart forever.

She forces herself to shut down.

It's Monika's face again. And it's frowning.

'Joel, she wants to murder me, too,' Monika's voice says. 'You have to save me.'

Nina glances over at Joel and sees the doubt in his eyes.

'No,' she says. 'I would never.'

But suddenly, suddenly, she wonders. If killing Monika is the only way of stopping the hitchhiker, isn't that the right thing to do? Shouldn't they do it for the old people's sake? For her and Joel's? Even for Monika herself, because who knows what she's going through right now?

An alarm goes off in the corridor. Then another one, and another.

'You stay with Monika,' she says.

Pineshade

Bodil starts screaming the moment she sees Nina step out into the hallway and she runs at her as fast as her old legs allow.

Alarm lights are flashing outside almost every suite.

Wiborg hangs up the phone and slides out of bed. The floor is cold. Winter morning and Dad hasn't lit the stove yet. Frosty apples still cling to the branches outside the windows; there is a thick layer of blueish-white snow on the window ledge. The cat rubs itself against her legs and meows; she picks it up and its fur warms her chest. She opens the front door and peers out. Sees flashing lights. *There she is.* The mean woman who won't let her talk to Mum and Dad.

Petrus climbs out of bed aided only by his powerful arms. He unhooks his catheter bag from the bedframe and it drags after him as he crawls over to the door, where he heaves himself up onto his stumps to reach the handle. He continues out into the corridor.

Olof stays in bed in D7. The woman in the red dress is angry with him because he's not helping. The ferry's about to leave. But he doesn't want to get on it. Something's wrong. It's too cold for summer tourists. They shouldn't be here.

Edit covers her ears in her room. She knows Director Palm is outside looking for her. She has to stay very quiet.

Dagmar holds Vera's knitting basket out to her then bends down and kisses her on the mouth. So many memories in that simple gesture. Long, lazy summer days in their house in the woods. Reality couldn't get to them there, get between them. Everything was simple in their sun-drenched vacuum, where Vera's husband and his hands were far away. They didn't have to pretend to be sisters. Didn't have to hide anything. But here, they never get to be alone; they're always watched, told when to eat and sleep. Vera doesn't even remember how they ended up here. Sometimes it feels like they've always been here and all the other things were just a dream.

'I can't,' Vera says quietly.

But it's so hard to say no to Dagmar. And Vera knows she has to be the one to do it, her body's stronger than Dagmar's now.

Dagmar whispers softly that 'if those two can't get it done, we have to help him.'

She pulls one needle out of the knitting and hands it to Vera.

'Things can be like before.'

Bodil has wrestled Nina down onto the shiny floor of the corridor. She's clawing and scratching; her eyes burn with hatred. Nina's the one who's trying to hurt her lover.

Wiborg is crying hysterically. She falls to her knees and tugs at Nina's clothes with strong little hands.

Petrus' elbows race towards them.

Nina catches a glimpse of Vera and Dagmar at the end of the hallway. *Dagmar. She can walk.*

The alarms beep and beep.

Bodil's fingers close around Nina's throat.

Joel

Joel sits motionless in the armchair. If he doesn't move, doesn't give in to the shaking, he can't feel the cold as much.

He can hear a racket out in the corridor, but doesn't take his eyes off the creature in the bed.

'It's your fault Monika's gone,' the hitchhiker says.

Joel shakes his head.

'You're the one who came back with her,' he says. 'I didn't ask for that.'

'But you're the reason I *could* follow her. The heart attack was your fault. She was worried sick about you.'

Joel shakes his head again. His teeth are chattering now.

It's a lie. It's just trying to psych me out.

'I think it's working,' the hitchhiker says. 'Monika's not the only one who has suffered for you. You're a murderer, too. You killed someone and ruined the lives of everyone around him.'

'Sure,' he says. 'But I want to talk to my mum now.'

She's in there somewhere. He knows it. And she shouldn't have to think for even a second that he has given up on her.

'This could all be over,' the creature says. 'You just have to let me in.'

An elderly voice roars something he doesn't catch out in the corridor.

He studies his mum's hands resting on the duvet. Blue veins under pale skin.

'Wouldn't it be nice to let go?' the hitchhiker says. 'Be rid of yourself? Isn't that what you've longed for all these years?'

Joel doesn't realise he's crying until tears burn against his cold cheeks.

'There's no need to fight it anymore.'

The duvet rustles when his mum's body moves closer to the foot of the bed. He pulls away in his armchair.

The bedside lamp crackles and the light grows stronger, blinding him.

There is pressure against his skull. His ears pop. The light crackles louder and louder, then goes out with a hollow little crackle.

The darkness is compact. The sounds from the corridor fade and disappear. The world outside his mum's room ceases to exist. He can't feel the cold anymore.

Hallucinations flutter, black on black, right in front of his face, taunting him. The room seems to shrink and expand like something breathing. He can no longer tell up from down, or if it even matters.

This is the darkness at the bottom of the abyss.

'Joel?' the hitchhiker whispers softly right next to him. 'Let me in. You can see Monika again. You can tell her all the things you want her to know.'

'No.'

'You're already halfway there. You just have to give in.'

And he can feel how easy it would be to let the darkness in. Let it fill him.

But he doesn't want to. He's surprised at how strongly and clearly he knows that, how easy the choice is. He wants to live.

The bedside lamp crackles back to life. A flash of light. He glimpses his mother looking at him from the bed, a shadowy shape crawling across the wall behind her. Then it goes dark again.

'It's not going to hurt. You won't ever feel pain again. You're just going to . . . disappear.'

The voice is still gentle, but there's an edge of impatience to it.

The filament in the lightbulb is etched into his cornea. It dances through the darkness when he moves his unseeing eyes.

'You know you want to,' the voice says, so close he can smell its rank breath.

'No.'

The light turns back on. His mum is staring at him, terrified. Perspiration covers her face and glistens on her neck.

Joel's hand goes to his mouth.

'Let go,' the hitchhiker coaxes. 'Go back to the darkness.'

Joel's lips were moving under his fingertips. The hitchhiker was speaking through him. It was inside him.

Cold seizes him again. His mum wraps her arms around herself. She looks around the room, breathing heavily through her nose.

'Joel?' she says.

'Mum?'

Is it you? Is it really you?

She opens her mouth and screams.

Nina

The scream from D6 cuts straight through her. It's a scream that has torn free from its body and become a creature in its own right.

Just like Daniel when he had night terrors.

Bodil's grip on her throat goes limp. Nina takes a greedy breath that sears her throat.

She pushes up into a sitting position. Petrus is lying prone by her feet. He's looking at her, bewildered. Dagmar has collapsed further down the corridor. Whatever kept her upright has left her. Vera is crouched down next to her sister. Sobbing unintelligibly.

The scream from D6 stops. The adrenaline continues to pump through Nina. Her face stings; when she touches the skin where Bodil scratched her, her fingers come away bloody.

Nina swallows; it feels like a punch in the throat. She gets to her feet. The old people make no objection. The hatred in their eyes is gone.

This is all just a distraction.

And now Joel's alone with Monika.

She runs back into D6 and instantly realises the suite's no longer cold.

Monika's eyes are wide-open but unseeing. Her arms flail wildly. Her hair is sweaty at the temples and her breathing is ragged.

Just like Daniel when he had night terrors.

Joel's sitting on the bed next to Monika. He looks up at Nina with tears in his eyes.

'I think it's her,' he says. 'I mean, really her.'

Nina runs over to the phone and calls B Ward.

'Things have got out of hand over here,' she says, when Adrian picks up. 'I have to take care of Monika in D6. Would you mind seeing to the others while I do?'

She hangs up as soon as Adrian promises to hurry. He's bound to wonder why so many of the residents are out of their rooms, but he won't waste too much time pondering it. At first blush, it's no stranger than many of the other things that happen at Pineshade.

Nina walks over to the bed. She exchanges a look with Joel, sits down on the other side of Monika and puts her arms around her. Monika writhes just like Daniel used to, trying to break free. Nina tightens her grip and murmurs softly in Monika's ear. She smells rank, revolting even, but Nina kisses her damp temple anyway.

And eventually, Monika stops struggling and starts to cry. She tries to say something, but it's hard to make out between the sobs. Her voice is tight, as though something in her throat is blocking it, trying to keep it from getting out.

But eventually, Nina manages to catch the words.

'You have to kill me. Please.'

Joel

He's vaguely aware that Nina's watching him, but his mum's terrified eyes make everything else fade away.

'You have to let me die,' she whispers. 'You have to let me get away. I can't do this anymore.'

Joel takes her hand. His tears make it hard to breathe.

'I can't,' he says. 'You have to understand that I can't.'

'He still needs me. Without me, he can't be here.'

'It's over now,' Joel says. 'He's gone.'

But that's wishful thinking. He knows that. They don't have long. And there are so many things he wants to tell her. So much he wants to know.

'He'll be back any second,' his mum says. 'I can't keep him out . . .'

She looks at him desperately and Joel can clearly see it's her now. Just her.

It's Mum.

'He almost broke you. I could *feel* it,' she croaks. 'You mustn't believe him. You don't know what it's like being trapped inside your body with him . . . You don't know what it's like. To say those horrible things and . . . and do things that . . .'

She trips over her words until she runs out of breath.

'He tricked me too, he made me believe he was Nils,' she

continues. 'But he's not Nils . . . He's not even human. He never was.'

His mum sobs. Shakes her head.

'Mum,' Joel says. 'We're going to fix this. It has to be possible somehow.'

His words are empty and pathetic. His mum turns to Nina and gives her a pleading look.

'Your mum . . . she was never here . . . He was just making it up.'

Nina pulls her closer.

'I know,' she says.

'Please,' his mum begs. 'You have to help me. I'm not afraid to die.'

Joel wants to scream at Nina not to listen. But Nina nods quietly.

'He wants the two of you,' his mum says, turning back to him. 'He'll take the first person who lets him in.'

She bends over in bed. Coughs.

'I'm not going to survive this anyway, don't you see?'

Nina strokes her back and looks at Joel.

'No,' he says, and gets up, dragging Nina with him towards the door.

'Joel . . .'

'Have you lost your mind?'

'What if it's the only way?' Nina whispers.

He stares at her in disbelief. His mum coughs again in her bed. The light from her bedside lamp falls across one side of Nina's face.

'I can't,' he says.

'I know. But I can.'

She's crying now, too. A door opens and closes in the corridor. The alarms continue to beep.

'Joel, listen to me. We have insulin shots here on the ward. If I give her enough . . .'

'Are you hearing yourself?'

'She's not going to feel it. She's going to go to sleep. And no one will ever know.'

'That we *murdered* her?'

'She's asking us to. If she could have, she would have done it herself already.'

He shakes his head.

'It's the only way,' she presses. 'The hitchhiker said so. It will disappear with her.'

'I just got Mum back,' he says. 'I just got her back and it can't . . . it can't . . .'

It can't be too late. She has to stay with me. I need her.

'Joel,' Nina says with a sob. 'Shouldn't it be up to her? She's suffering.'

His mum has gone quiet in the bedroom. He wonders if she's listening.

'It's for the others as well,' Nina says. 'And for us. I don't want that thing inside me.'

'I'm done talking about this.'

Joel puts his face in his hands. Tries to breathe normally. When he lowers his hands, he notices that his mum has got out of bed.

She's standing in the middle of the room, watching them with big, frightened eyes. And Joel suddenly shudders.

'He's back,' his mum says. 'God help us, he's back.'

Nina

The cold is spreading through the suite again. The frigid waves rippling through the air are even more frightening now that Nina has a word for them. *The hitchhiker.*

'I have to get out of here,' Monika says.

Joel takes a step towards her. She roars at him wordlessly and hits him in the face.

'Monika . . .' Nina says, stepping back into the room.

When Monika turns around and shoves her, it's with a strength that takes Nina utterly by surprise. She stumbles backwards, losing her balance. A hard blow across the back of her neck. She's on the floor looking up at the sharp edge of the bedside table. The pain crashes through her like a black wave.

She hears Monika scream again. A chair toppling over. The temperature seems to drop another couple of degrees, but Nina can't tell if it's inside her body or outside it.

The darkness is trying to pull Nina down. Undertows want to suck her into the depths.

She forces herself up on her elbows. The room re-emerges from behind the darkness. She sees Monika wrest free of Joel's grasp and run towards the door, sees him chase after her. Nina struggles to her feet, leaning on the bed. She trips over the toppled chair and staggers out into the hallway as the door slams shut.

The air resounds with the crash. She follows. Reaches for the handle and is just about to touch it when the cold caresses her back.

There's something behind her. She can feel it swelling, reaching out to her as if for an embrace. Her hands are slick with sweat as she fumbles with the handle.

She gets the door open and falls out into the corridor.

The fluorescent lights are flickering, turning the world into a silent film. A darkness that erupts between each frame, beating as one with Nina's heart.

Joel has caught up to Monika, who is kicking and screaming to break free.

Vera is standing further down the hall, watching them with terrified eyes. Dagmar's still on the floor, grunting excitedly.

Everything moves in slow motion. The air is thick like in a dream.

Strong arms close around Nina's ankles. Petrus is holding her back.

One of Vera's knitting needles slides out of the sleeve of her nightgown and lands on the vinyl with a dull rattle.

Joel

Bones and tendons and adrenaline are writhing in his arms. Nails, short but sharp, scratch at him, break his skin, draw blood.

'Let go of me!'

His mum headbutts him and his eyebrow splits open; hot blood trickles into his eye. And suddenly, she has managed to get free of him.

He reaches for her in the flickering light. Grazes the fabric of her nightgown, then she's gone. She has thrown herself to the floor and is crawling down the corridor, toes bracing against the vinyl. Joel wipes the blood from his eyes and watches her pick something up from the floor next to the two sisters. She pushes up onto her knees.

'Mum? What are you doing?'

'I'm sorry,' she says.

She turns around. Looks at him pleadingly.

'Nils is going to be there. The real Nils.'

Her left hand is clutching a black knitting needle with a metal point.

no

Joel runs the few steps that separate them. The metal tip glints in the air as she stabs herself in the neck. Her eyes widen and bulge out of their deep holes.

He screams. But it's too late.

The needle slips out of her throat. A red plume of blood follows.

Nina shouts something. There's the sound of running feet. His mum collapses in his arms. Wet sounds against the walls and floor. Vera whispers *I'm sorry*, over and over again.

'Mum?' he hears himself yelling. 'Mum!'

Her grey eyes, so like his own, blink at the fluorescent lights.

Someone comes out of one of the suites and falls onto his knees next to them. The young man who plays the guitar. He presses his hands against his mum's throat. Blood gushes through his fingers, far too tanned and healthy against her skin, which is turning whiter with each beat of her heart.

Her blood is no longer contained in a closed system, hidden in the dark inside her body. It glistens red in the flickering corridor. Spatters Joel's T-shirt, mixing with his own blood from his eyebrow.

Nina has brought compresses, she's saying something about calling an ambulance, but it's no use. It's too late. He cradles his mum's head in the crook of his arm, as though she were a child. Blood trickles out of the corners of her mouth, down her cheeks, painting a Joker smile.

Joel manages to catch her eye. She blinks to stay awake. Stay with him.

Sterile packaging is being ripped open, white compresses are being pressed to her throat, but she never takes her eyes off him.

'I love you,' he says. 'I love you.'

She opens her eyes even wider. Nods once. And then she's gone.

Pineshade

If you were to visit Pineshade today, you'd never suspect that the green walls of D corridor were recently covered in blood. That there were pools of it on the vinyl floor.

The memory of last week's events has faded for almost all the residents of D Ward. But the carers whisper about it in the staff-room when Elisabeth's not around; they discuss it quietly in the changing room. Some of them tell their friends and families. Adrian discovers that it's a great story for picking up girls. Gorana entertains herself by using it to frighten a new employee before his first night shift on B Ward.

Sometimes, she can still be seen wandering the D corridor at night.

Monika's death will soon turn into a ghost story everyone in Skredsby has heard.

If you see flashing lights in one of the windows overlooking the carpark that means someone's going to die.

In another version, Monika wanders the woods on the mountain with a knitting needle in her hand. Trying to find her way home.

If you run into her, she'll stab you to death. She wants company.

But the story hasn't spread very far yet. The furniture has just been collected from D6. The sofa, made by Monika's father many years ago, is on its way to a charity shop, along with the table and chairs, the cornflower-blue armchair, the dresser and Monika's coat. The rest of her clothes have been binned. The framed pictures have been taken down and put in a cardboard box. Tomorrow, a new client is moving in. Maybe it's someone you love. Maybe you yourself.

The bedsore on Petrus' hip has become necrotic. Gorana opens the window a crack to air out the stench while she shaves him.

'No one wants to fuck your pig cunt,' Petrus tells her. 'Disgusting fucking pig cunt.'

Bodil is sitting right next to Olof in the lounge. He's staring intently at the football match on the TV. Pretends not to notice Bodil's breasts grazing him from time to time, as though by accident. But he shudders with pleasure when her fingers toy with the white, downy hairs on his forearm.

Wiborg is slumped in an armchair next to them. Glaring. She knows her mum and dad would never forgive her if she put on such a vulgar display. Wiborg strokes the fur of her dementia cat. Suddenly remembers when Iago came to visit. *Someone scared him. A really mean person.* She's so deep in thought about the dog she gives a start when her mum taps her on the shoulder. Happiness swells inside Wiborg. Makes her glow. *They've finally come to pick me up.* Wiborg's mummy is carrying Wiborg's infant brother in her arms.

'Hi, Nana,' she says. 'It's me, Fredrika.'

Wiborg laughs at her mum who's always trying to pull her leg. She looks at her little brother. Gives another start.

'That's not my brother,' she says. 'It's not him anymore.'

And her mum looks at her with disappointment in her eyes.

Joel's sitting in one of the visitor's chairs in the ward director's office, signing the papers terminating Monika's tenancy. Elisabeth looks at him nervously when he hands her the papers. Still doesn't dare to believe that Joel won't press charges and give the newspapers something to write about. He looks sober right now, but she hasn't forgotten the time when he first brought Monika. *Junkies and alcoholics can't be trusted.* She pictures the headlines, words like CARE HOME SCANDAL. Elisabeth tells herself she can defend herself in good conscience. She did everything right. She offered Adrian and Nina counselling, but they both declined. Nina has taken a few weeks' sick leave, and Elisabeth is far from sure she's coming back.

Maybe it's for the best. If anyone did something wrong, it's actually Nina. She should have known better than to let a relative visit so late at night.

Of course, bending the rules for visitation is hardly an example of serious professional misconduct. The strange thing is that Nina shouldn't even have been working that night. Elisabeth has tried to talk to Nina about what really happened but has received only evasive answers. She has decided not to dig too deep. The less she knows, the less she's obligated to report. And it was indisputably suicide. Adrian saw the whole thing and the police investigation confirmed it. Everyone's in agreement. Elisabeth feels reassured, at least for the moment. She looks at Joel.

'We're going to miss Monika,' she says. 'We thought she liked it here, but I guess you never know.'

Maybe that made her sound like she doesn't know her clients. But he barely seems to have heard her. Still looks like he's in shock.

'Let me know if there is anything we can do for you,' she says.

Joel just nods, then gets up and shakes her hand. Walks towards D corridor to collect his mother's things.

Joel

He looks up at the fluorescent lights when he enters D Ward and walks towards D6 for the last time.

The TV is on in the lounge. Some kind of sporting event. A frantic commentator, the sounds of a crowd.

The real estate agent has had a bid. The buyers do, in fact, want to tear the house down. They offered barely half the asking price, but she advised him to accept. He told her to talk to Björn. He doesn't give a toss about the money. Doesn't want to make any more decisions.

Next week, he's taking the train back to Stockholm the day after the funeral. There are still a lot of things that need doing before that. He has no idea what he's going to do once it's over. He doesn't know what awaits him back home in Stockholm, if it even is his home anymore. All he knows is that it's time to get a life. Whatever that means.

'Joel?'

He turns around. Fredrika has come out of the lounge with her baby in her arms. A thin cloth covers one of her breasts. Sucking sounds and contented grunts are coming from underneath.

'I heard about your mum,' Fredrika says, smiling uncertainly. 'I'm so sorry.'

Joel looks at the tiny human in her arms. A hand opening and closing, opening and closing. Bare feet with impossibly smooth soles that have yet to take a single step.

Was he ever that tiny? Completely unafraid of the world outside his mother's arms?

He doesn't realise he's crying until Fredrika puts an arm around him.

He's always on the verge of tears these days.

Fredrika gives him an awkward hug.

'How are you holding up?' she says.

'I don't know,' Joel says. 'I don't think it's really sunk in yet.'

She nods.

'How's your grandmother?' he says, and they both turn to look into the lounge.

Wiborg is sitting quietly in her armchair, stroking that pathetic stuffed animal.

'She's sad,' Fredrika says. 'Her parents have stopped answering their phone again.'

A shiver runs down Joel's spine. He glances up at the fluorescent lights.

'I'm hoping she'll get more curious about this little guy,' Fredrika says, and adjusts her breast before folding the cloth aside.

The baby blinks at the light with his big eyes. His toothless mouth is open and Joel catches a whiff of milky sweetness. He tickles his round belly. The baby hiccoughs and kicks his legs.

'I suppose this is the last time I'll see you, then,' Fredrika says.

'I guess so,' he agrees. 'I'm picking up her things now.'

'This place is going to be empty without you.'

They smile at each other, and in that smile is an acknowledgement of the strangeness of having shared such intensely private moments without really knowing one another. Joel's relieved the moment isn't ruined by empty promises to get together sometime, outside Pineshade.

'At least no one's trying to touch my belly anymore,' Fredrika says, and he laughs.

They hug briefly again before he continues down the hallway. He studies the green walls, the banister, the shiny vinyl. Hears angry shouting from D2. The door is open a crack; Joel glances that way as he passes. Petrus' wife is standing just inside the door, removing her shoes. A strange smell is coming from the suite, as though there's something wrong with the plumbing inside.

Joel continues down to D6 and looks at the spot on the floor where his mother died in his arms. It feels like the soles of his shoes are sticking to the floor but he knows it's just his imagination.

He opens the door and enters. The room's virtually empty – looks almost exactly like the first time he was here. The only difference is the cardboard box on the stripped mattress.

Joel stands stock still waiting for something. A sign. An echo. A sense that his mum's still around.

Nothing. He can't tell if he's relieved or disappointed.

The things you learn to ignore before you're old enough to walk.

He mustn't think about it too much. He's never going to find any answers; he would be insane to try. He has to try to focus on this reality. The one he can see and hear and touch.

Joel picks up the box and leaves D6 without looking back.

He starts walking towards the lobby but changes his mind – turns around and walks further down the corridor.

Stopping outside the closed door to D8, he gives the sign on it a good look for the first time. Vera and Dagmar it says, in a shaky but surprisingly beautiful hand. A frame of flowers around the edge of the paper.

Sucdi opens the door with her elbow after he knocks. She's wearing gloves, and there is a faint but unmistakeable smell of faeces in the air.

'I'm sorry, I was hoping to talk to Vera,' he says.

'One minute,' she says with a stressed smile. 'Would you mind waiting here?'

'Of course.'

He helps Sucdi to close the door. Then he just stands there with his box, shifting from one foot to the other.

Sunlight is pouring in through the glass in the door leading out to the backyard. Gorana is walking back and forth out there. Talking on her phone and smoking. She waves happily when she spots him. He nods back.

The door to D8 opens and Sucdi comes out. The gloves are gone.

'Hi,' she says. 'How are you doing?'

'I'm fine,' he says automatically. 'I'm . . . I'm okay. Considering.'

She looks at the box in his arms.

'I'm so sorry for your loss,' she says.

'Thank you,' he says. 'For everything. Especially for that first day when Mum moved in. You made it easier for her and me.'

'Don't mention it,' Sucdi says with a smile.

He wonders if he should add anything, maybe apologise for his mum making Sucdi uncomfortable. But Sucdi beats him to it.

'Monika seems to have been a wonderful person,' she says.

He smiles back.

'Yes,' he says. 'She was.'

'You can go in now, if you want. And take care of yourself, in case I don't see you before you leave.'

'You too.'

He enters the suite. The air is fresher in here now. One of the windows is open a crack.

'Hello?' an old voice calls out.

The room is a little bigger than his mum's. Two beds, one at either end of it. A small table and two chairs. A crocheted doily. A knitting basket full of red wool.

Joel looks away and sets the box down on the table. He says hello to both the old ladies before going over to Vera's bed.

'I don't know if you remember me, but my name's Joel. Monika, who used to live here, was my mother.'

The old woman eyes him anxiously.

'Yes?' she says.

'I was just wondering . . . How come you were in the corridor that night? It was almost like you were waiting for Mum with that knitting needle.'

Vera glances over at the other bed from which her sister is watching them in silence.

'It's okay,' Joel says. 'I just want to know what happened.'

She presses her lips closed.

He can sense Dagmar shaking her head behind his back. But when he looks over, she's sitting dead-still. Smacking her mouth, as toothless as Fredrika's baby's.

The wall next to Dagmar's bed is covered with watercolours and pencil sketches of a beautiful young woman. He gets the feeling the artist was in love with her. Every brush and pen stroke seems sensual. He walks over for a closer look and is shocked to realise it's Dagmar in the pictures. The same woman who's now sitting in bed, glaring at him with hostile, runny eyes.

'These pictures are lovely,' he says.

Dagmar is naked in one of the sketches, leaning back in a sea of flowers.

They're drawn by the same hand that drew the flowers on the sign on the door. And he suddenly gets it.

He turns back to Vera.

'I wish someone had loved me enough to draw me like this,' he says.

If Vera realises he's figured it out, she doesn't show it.

'You don't have to tell me what happened,' he says. 'It makes no difference now.'

He picks up the box and is just about to say bye when Vera opens her mouth.

'It was supposed to make Dagmar well again.'

Joel keeps his face expressionless. Waits without speaking, afraid of interrupting, of causing her to change her mind.

Vera's bottom lip trembles.

'It wasn't Dagmar. He made her say those things.'

'He tricked me, too,' Joel says.

Vera heaves a heavy sigh and looks at him bravely.

'At least we're rid of him now,' she says. 'He got what he wanted.'

Joel suddenly feels cold fingers along his spine. He looks over at the window. The curtain flutters.

Just the wind.

'What do you mean?' he asks.

'He tricked your mother, too,' Vera says.

'How?'

'She had to die to set him free.'

'Free?'

Vera nods.

Mum. Did she sacrifice herself for him and Nina for no reason?

Joel swallows. 'Where did he go?'

'I don't know,' Vera replies. 'He comes back here sometimes, but he leaves us alone. And he always goes away again.'

Joel looks at her. Has to summon all his courage to ask the question.

'Is he in me now?' he says. 'Is it me?'

But Vera shakes her head firmly. 'No,' she says. 'You were too strong.'

Dagmar smacks her lips in her bed. Sucks her gums.

Nina.

Is it in Nina?

Was that why she was so quick to jump at the idea of killing Mum?

Nina

Something has woken her up. Daylight outside the closed blinds. Birdsong. But the house is quiet. She looks at the lamp she always keeps turned on these days and makes sure it's not flickering. She sits up in bed and checks the walls for greasy stains.

Nina puts her head down again. Closes her eyes and tries to slip back into the oblivion of sleep, but the images have already penetrated her conscience. Monika in the hallway. The blood. The pale eyes staring up at the fluorescent lights.

They will haunt her forever.

Markus asks how she's doing, what it was like, what really happened. Nina has no answers to give. She declined Elisabeth's offer of counselling. What's the point? She can't tell the truth.

The doorbell rings downstairs. She opens her eyes and realises that was the sound that woke her up. She reluctantly gets out of bed, pulls on a pair of sweatpants and walks downstairs.

When she passes the kitchen window, she spots Monika's old Nissan in the driveway. Nina considers going back up to bed. Hiding from the world.

The doorbell rings again. She continues out into the hallway and opens the door.

Joel's pale eyes—

Monika's eyes

—looking at her searchingly.

'Did something happen?' she says.

'I don't know. Can we talk?'

Nina can see a box full of Monika's belongings in the passenger seat of the car, so he must have come straight from Pineshade.

An iron band tightens around her chest.

'Do you mind if we do it outside?' she asks. 'I need some fresh air.'

'Sure,' he replies. 'Is Markus home?'

'No. He's at work.'

They walk into the garden together. The grass under her bare feet is healthy and lush. It will need mowing again soon. Regardless of what she has been through, it continues to grow like before. It feels tangible. Real.

'This place is idyllic,' Joel says after they sit down on the terrace.

Nina nods. Looks out across the glittering water of the bay.

Maybe it's just a backdrop. It might not even be real.

The thought makes her stomach lurch. She catches herself clutching the armrests of her chair, as though she might fall off the face of the Earth if she lets go.

She's never going to forget the glimpse she caught in D6 of all that hides beneath the veneer of so-called reality.

'How are you doing?' Joel asks.

The sunlight is making him squint, but even so, he continues to study her as though he's analysing her every movement and facial expression.

Or maybe she's imagining it. Maybe she has already forgotten how to interact with other people. Markus is the only person she's seen since that night at Pineshade, and she has been doing her best to avoid him, too.

'I don't know how to live with this,' she admits. 'I feel like I'm losing my mind.'

'Me too. Though for what it's worth, I'm used to feeling that way.'

Nina smiles wanly.

A cow lows down by the water's edge. A handful of gulls screech.

Or do they? Are they real?

'Have you been back to Pineshade since . . . since we were there?' Joel says.

Nina shakes her head.

'But you have, right?' she says. 'What's going on?'

He finally looks away. Down at his hands.

'I talked to Vera. She said the hitchhiker's still around. That Mum had to die to set it free.'

The words sink into her and push the remaining air out of her lungs. Her hands squeeze the chair's armrests again.

'So the hitchhiker *wanted* Monika to die? That was its plan all along?'

'It seems that way.'

How could she have believed she'd outwitted the creature in that bed?

The perspective shifts again. Everything's turned upside down once more. There's nothing to hold onto.

'But that was Monika in the end, wasn't it?' she says. 'In the hallway? I could tell the difference.'

Couldn't I?

It has to have been Monika. That she was able to find peace in the end is the only consolation Nina has.

'Yes,' Joel replies. 'That was Mum.'

The relief is so overwhelming her eyes well up with tears.

'The hitchhiker has found a new body,' Joel continues. 'Someone who only visits Pineshade occasionally.'

And Nina suddenly understands why he was studying her so intently before. The iron band tightens again.

'I asked her if it was me,' Joel presses on. 'But Vera said it was someone else.'

He picks a blade of grass, spins it between his fingers.

'So that's why you came here?' Nina asks. 'To check if it's me?'

Joel shakes his head. 'It's not the only reason. I wanted to make sure you were okay, too.'

'And what's your conclusion? Is it me, sitting here, or is that thing inside me now?'

Joel looks up at her. She digs her toes into the lawn.

'No,' he says. 'The hitchhiker isn't here.'

'How do you know?'

Joel shakes his head again. 'I just do.'

'That's not good enough,' she says. 'Joel . . . I don't recognise myself anymore.'

'It can't be you,' he says. 'You haven't been back to Pineshade since it happened. And Vera said the hitchhiker has.'

She swallows hard. Knows she has to accept that it's the best proof she's likely to get.

They sit in silence for a while. Joel lights a cigarette. The sound of the lighter, the first drag, brings back a flood of memories. He smokes just like he used to.

Nina has missed him. And she needs him. Without Joel, she's alone with what happened.

Joel needs her, too.

She did the right thing not going with him to Stockholm half a lifetime ago. Their friendship was burned too brightly, too intensely. It would have consumed her, in the end.

But they're both so different now.

'What are you going to do?' he says.

'I don't know if I can go back to Pineshade.'

'I get that.'

'But I might have to. What happened to Monika is happening to someone else now. If I knew who it was and could warn . . .'

She breaks off. Joel looks at her queryingly.

'Adrian,' she says. 'It might be Adrian. He was in the hallway.'

She pictures him in the changing room. A young, strong body. He must be exactly what the hitchhiker wants.

'But Adrian doesn't work in D Ward,' she adds. 'Things didn't happen anywhere else. At least I don't think so. And the hitch-hiker had to wear us down to—'

'It could be anyone,' Joel cuts her off. 'And I have the distinct feeling the hitchhiker will make sure we can't find it. It got what it wanted.'

He seems to have given this careful thought on the way over. She's struggling to catch up.

The hitchhiker's still in this world. It's out there, somewhere.

'And besides, even if we did figure out who it is,' Joel says, 'what would we do about it?'

Nina shakes her head.

'I don't know. I don't know anything anymore. I don't even

know what the hell I'm going to do with my life. Maybe it's time for something drastic.'

'What kind of drastic?'

'I have no idea,' Nina says, and surprises herself by laughing.

She has fought all her life to hold everything together. She was always so sure things would fall apart if she took her eye off the ball for even a second. Her own fears of losing control have worn her down for so long. Since way before the hitchhiker showed up. She had wanted to feel safe at any cost; had clung desperately to things that no longer seem to matter.

Nina closes her eyes. The sun is warm on her face, but she can tell summer is coming to an end.

'When are you going back?' she asks, and opens her eyes again.

'I don't know. Björn called when I was in the car. He wants to keep the house. He said I could live in it if I want, so long as they can use it for vacations sometimes.'

'Do you want to?'

'I have no idea what I'd do around here. But then again, I don't know what I'm going to do in Stockholm either.'

'We're quite the pair,' Nina says.

He grins.

'Either way, I do have to swing by Stockholm. I have some things to sort out and . . . Some people I have to talk to.'

Nina nods. Knows it relates to the secrets the hitchhiker used against him. If Joel ever wants to tell her, he can.

Maybe one day she'll tell him her own secret. Tell him about how her mother died.

I knew what I was doing when I talked to the doctor. I just haven't been able to admit it to myself. Until now.

'I'm going to hold off on making plans until after the funeral,' Joel says. 'Speaking of which, are you coming?'

She hasn't given it any thought. But now, she suddenly feels a strong desire to say goodbye to Monika. The real Monika. To remember her properly. Wash away the memories of the other thing.

'Yes,' she replies. 'Let me know if I can help with anything.'

He sucks on his cigarette.

'I'm happy so long as you turn up.'

Pineshade

'Bye, Nana,' Fredrika says. 'See you soon.'

But Wiborg has already drifted off in her bed. Fredrika strokes her cheek. It's cool. So cool Fredrika feels compelled to check she's still breathing. Her chest is rising and falling under her duvet. *That's good, Nana*, she thinks to herself. *Stay with us just a little longer.* Fredrika releases the foot brake on the pram and quietly pushes it out of D1. Sigge moves restlessly when she walks past the lounge where the TV is on. A solemn news reporter is talking about yet another catastrophe, hundreds of dead in a part of the world Fredrika knows very little about. She punches in the door code at the end of the hallway and steps into the lobby. Continues out onto the front steps and pushes the pram down the ramp. She realises that she hasn't taken her grandmother on an outing since before she got pregnant. *We should go over to Hålta Church and have cheesecake. That always cheers her up.*

Sigge's pulling faces in his sleep when they reach the asphalt of the carpark. Fredrika smiles and straightens his hat. When she reaches the car, she pulls the car keys out of her handbag. It's still early afternoon. Her husband has taken their five-year-old to the Lökeberg beach for a swimming lesson. She decides to head over there to join them. She opens the front passenger door, gently transfers Sigge to the car seat and buckles him in. He opens his beautiful eyes and looks at her, flailing his arms and legs. Her heart overflows with love. His eyes have really started to focus in the past few days and she can't help feeling proud that he's so advanced. She's hoping he'll give her a first smile soon. Fredrika bends down. Sniffs his neck, breathing in the smell that's like a drug to her.

'Hi, baby boy,' she says. 'Did you have a good nap? Want to give Mummy a smile? Hmm?'

He looks at her with interest. His tongue pops out of his mouth.

'No, not today? I see. Is someone playing hard to get?' She walks around the car, folds up the pram and heaves it into the boot. She's just about to close it when she notices a grimy stain at the head of the bassinet. She drags her index finger across the greasy spot and sniffs it suspiciously, but it's odourless. She has seen a greasy stain in Sigge's crib, as well.

Maybe there's something wrong with his ears? Fredrika closes the boot and wipes her finger on her shorts. Sigge watches her as she climbs in behind the wheel. She strokes his soft, round cheeks. Quickly checks his ears but can't see anything unusual.

'There's not going to be anything wrong with you, baby boy. Okay?'

His blue eyes study her evenly. Blink when she turns the key in the ignition and the engine starts.

'Want to go say hi to Daddy and your big brother now? Yes, you do. Yes, you do.'

She turns out of the carpark and watches Pineshade recede in the rear-view mirror.

ACKNOWLEDGEMENTS

Thank you to my dad, the best pensioner I know.

Thank you to my publisher, Susanna Romanus, and editor, Fredrik Andersson, and the whole team at Norstedts.

Thank you to Lena Stjernström and everyone at Grand Agency.

Thank you to all my readers.

Thank you to Pär Åhlander, Mårten Sandén and Stina Wirsén, who have endured my snoring on the sofa in our studio.

Thank you to everyone who has shared their knowledge about prolapse and property titles, drugs both illegal and prescription, fanzines and lumbar punctures, knitting needles and bed rails, demo tapes and dementia: Elvira Barsotti, Martina Bergsjö, Ylva Blomqvist, Rickard Folke, Susanna Helldén, Jenny Jägerfeldt, Nelli Karlsson, Ulf Karlsson, Maria Martinsson, Bahar Nabavi, Sudi Osman, Tina Norman, Göran Parkrud, Karl Romanus, Julia Skott, Johan and Linda Skugge and Elisabeth Östnäs. A special thank you to Emma Hanfot.

Thank you to everyone who read and made astute comments. I'm eternally grateful to: Levan Akin, Anna Andersson, Åsa Avdic, Maria Ernestam, Nahal Ghanbari, Karl Johnsson, Åsa Larsson, Alexander Rännberg, Mattias Skoglund, Erika Stark, Johan Theorinand, Anna Thunman Sköld. A special thank you to Sara Bergmark Elfgren. I also want to thank Margareta Elfgren for allowing me to come back even though I keep putting my feet through your floors.

This book is dedicated to Johan Ehn, with whom I hope to grow old.

Also Available from

Jo Fletcher Books

BLOOD CRUISE

MATS STRANDBERG

Welcome aboard the *Baltic Charisma*.

Tonight, twelve hundred expectant passengers have joined the booze-cruise between Sweden and Finland. The creaking old ship travels this same route, back and forth, every day of the year.

But this trip is going to be different.

In the middle of the night the ferry is cut off from the outside world. There is nowhere to escape. There is no way to contact the mainland. And no one knows who to trust . . .

On the Baltic Sea, no one can hear you scream.

Help us make the next generation of readers

We – both author and publisher – hope you enjoyed this book. We believe that you can become a reader at any time in your life, but we'd love your help to give the next generation a head start.

Did you know that 9% of children don't have a book of their own in their home, rising to 13% in disadvantaged families*? We'd like to try to change that by asking you to consider the role you could play in helping to build readers of the future.

We'd love you to think of sharing, borrowing, reading, buying or talking about a book with a child in your life and spreading the love of reading. We want to make sure the next generation continue to have access to books, wherever they come from.

And if you would like to consider donating to charities that help fund literacy projects, find out more at www.literacytrust.org.uk and www.booktrust.org.uk.

Thank you.

*As reported by the National Literacy Trust